VINEGAR & WINE

VINEGAR
&
WINE

COLIN HILL

Copyright © 2023 Colin Hill

The moral right of the author has been asserted.

Front cover by Tim Jarvis

Apart from any fair dealing for the purposes of research or private study, or criticism or review, as permitted under the Copyright, Designs and Patents Act 1988, this publication may only be reproduced, stored or transmitted, in any form or by any means, with the prior permission in writing of the publishers, or in the case of reprographic reproduction in accordance with the terms of licences issued by the Copyright Licensing Agency. Enquiries concerning reproduction outside those terms should be sent to the publishers.

This is a work of fiction. Names, characters, businesses, places, events and incidents are either the products of the author's imagination or used in a fictitious manner. Any resemblance to actual persons, living or dead, or actual events is purely coincidental.

Matador
Unit E2 Airfield Business Park,
Harrison Road, Market Harborough,
Leicestershire. LE16 7UL
Tel: 0116 2792299
Email: books@troubador.co.uk
Web: www.troubador.co.uk/matador
Twitter: @matadorbooks

ISBN 978 1803136 530

British Library Cataloguing in Publication Data.
A catalogue record for this book is available from the British Library.

Printed and bound in Great Britain by CMP UK
Typeset in 12pt Adobe Jenson Pro by Troubador Publishing Ltd, Leicester, UK

Matador is an imprint of Troubador Publishing Ltd

To Henry:
My life and muse.
What larks we've had!

CONTENTS

A Trilogy: I The Hermit's Tale	1
A Trilogy: II Dr Socrates Speaks	12
A Trilogy: III The Band of Brothers	21
Reprise	31
The Magic Money Tree	38
Obsession	44
University Challenge	54
Elizabeth's Condition	62
Brief Encounter 1: Black Country Dogging	75
Eulogy for Ridley Tulk	79
The Disgruntled Mr Speight	87
Separation	99
Heaven Sent	107
Love Is All You Need	116
The Dudbridge Project	142
The Sisters	152
Brief Encounter 2: Morning in Normandy…	170
Slices of Sam	176
Ten Tips for a Longer Life	186
The Girl and the Guy	192
Olga Smiles Again	204

The Deal	224
Retirement Rankles	230
God Willing	237
Old Man Knocking	241
Tom and Harry Discuss the Facts of Life	249
Muddy Waters	254
Brief Encounter 3:	
Brittany – Harry's French Lesson	267
The Chip Shop Caper	272
A Trilogy: I Betrayal	277
A Triology: II Rose Tinted	287
A Trilogy: III Gold Rush	297
To Hull and Back	312
An Embarrassment of Riches	316
A Curious Cancellation	338
Brief Encounter 4: Sunshine's Short Story	343
Coming up Roses	349
Through Etta's Eyes	360
Art for Art's Sake	364

A Trilogy: I
THE HERMIT'S TALE

In a cave high on the bare, rocky slopes of Mount Parnassus, in Greece's Peloponnese, lived a hermit. In ancient times the cave, now known as the 'Corycian' Cave, had been a sacred place for the worship of the God, Pan – the God of Nature and wild things. The hermit knew this – it was what had lured him to this desolate, almost secret, space. He had lived in the cave for around a year, now. Local peasants and farmers knew, barely, of his existence; but no-one knew from where he came, or why he had chosen a different, isolated way of life. And no-one knew his name.

In fact, Yannis was his name. Yannis was not the typical image of a hermit – an old, morose man with straggly grey beard, and covered in sackcloth. Indeed, quite the contrary: for Yannis was a young man, with a mane of fine, rich black hair. He was also handsome – and fit and strong, as was necessary, since his daily life was arduous and demanding. Yannis dressed modestly in black robes, and spent his days meditating – and foraging for food. He would find edible leaves, fruits and berries among the scrub of the parched limestone scree, whilst olives, oranges – even wild honey – might be found upon the mountain's fertile foundations.

The young man was a hermit by choice and temperament, rather than through religious vocation or spiritual conviction. He wished to live a life of a free spirit; of communion with wild nature, with the birds, trees, and stars; he needed to feel, to find, his connection with the Earth.

Yannis viewed his human counterparts, though not with disdain, with an innate wariness, and a desire to keep his own counsel. He was aware that local people were different from him, with different beliefs and values; local farmers and 'peasants' might pose or present a risk if their paths came too close. The farmers, too, were naturally suspicious of loners and strangers. So the young hermit kept his distance from the villagers, and from the scattering of farms and homesteads that pock-marked the lower slopes and valleys that spread down from the mountainside.

Yet, as time wore on, his neighbours came to acknowledge the hermit's existence, and even appreciate his charm and simple dignity; and would leave him occasional gifts of bread, butter, feta cheese and retsina wine close to the path that led to his cave. Even so, the entrance to his cave was cloaked with thornbushes, and disguised from sight. For many months, Yannis lived undisturbed by a single soul.

Such was the hermit's lonely and secretive habits that there was surprise amounting to consternation that, a year or so after first arriving on the mountain, whispers began to spread, at first faintly and discreetly, and then in a more open, astonished way; rumours suggesting the young hermit's ministrations could help women conceive a child. The astonishment merely related to the hermit's lifestyle, since he appeared to shun, and studiously avoid, all society. However, a community brought up on the mysticism of religions old and new, imbibed along with their mothers' milk, seldom questioned the dabblings of the supernatural in their daily lives.

Quite how Yannis performed such miracles remained a mystery, but that was in the nature of mysteries; beyond human calculation or concern. It was simply the case that any 'barren' woman desiring a child would take the long, dusty path that wound up the mountain-side, to find the hermit's cave. Whether the matter at hand involved the husband's inability to perform his duties, or indeed his unwillingness, or was due to a medical condition affecting husband or wife, Yannis's counselling appeared unfailingly efficacious. For, invariably, within weeks, the fruit of being, the gently swelling belly, was joyously revealed. Husbands and wives alike were delighted; and sent celebratory gifts of wine, brandy, chicken and goats meat to the reclusive young hermit.

Just as no-one knew how the hermit achieved such miracles, no-one really cared. These were God-fearing people, vaguely conscious of the mysteries of life; lives still overlaid by the echoes and instincts imbued from more ancient deities, of a myriad gods and magical rites. The iconic temple of Delphi still stood proudly, nearby, and was clearly visible from the summit of Mount Parnassus. Perhaps the gods of ancient Greece still roamed the countryside, still interfering, for pleasure or mischief, in the lives of peasants and village people. The richness of life was all; embrace and celebrate this richness, and the plenty ordained by the gods.

*

Georgio Papandreu's family had farmed in this place since time immemorial. Georgio was desperate for a son, to continue the family line. But, after ten years of marriage, there had been no issue; not even a pregnancy. His wife, Anya, was now 33 years old; there seemed to be no hope of children. Of course, this failure was blamed by her husband on Anya's moral or physical corruption. Increasingly, the couple's love making, if so it could be called, was sporadic, brutish, and fuelled by drink. Anya now dreaded her husband's approaches, and loathed his animal smell, the closeness of his body, the anticipation of his touch. Every fibre of her being rejected her husband's moronic fumbling, with intense physical disgust.

But now, clearly, Anya was unyieldingly barren. Georgio bitterly regretted his choice of wife, even while he sensed – knew – that she recoiled from his still-searching hands. And the admiring glances of other men who passed their farm, and saw Anya working in the fields, or who chanced to brush against her in the crowded taverna, caused a cold fury to course through her husband's veins. His own mother had proudly borne seven strapping children; and all Georgio's brothers and sisters had their own burgeoning families. Nothing could ease or calm the husband's resentment or hard anger at this perverse stain on the family. Georgio's very manhood seemed to be under suspicion. And there would be no son to inherit his farm. Why had this happened to him? Of what crime was he guilty? And why had his wife been cursed by God?

Under this cloud of anger and bitterness, Georgio's drinking became increasingly heavy, and his work around the farm, in consequence, desultory, slack and slovenly. Under the weight of worry and overwork in a parched, arid climate, Anya's face became lined and drawn, and her looks began to fade; and with them, Georgio's attentions. Though Anya felt nauseated by her husband's love-making – such a bitter phrase! – and by his angry, drunken groping, she yet feared that she was losing him; losing his affection and, worse, losing his respect. A mere four weeks following a desperate flight to Yannis's cave – which had involved a steep and dangerous climb in unrelenting heat through scrub and scree – Anya discovered that she was pregnant.

The villagers were careless of the good news brought from the hermit: that is, they celebrated the news; why question Providence, or the workings of God? But, alone in the village, one man did care. Georgio cared. He cared, and he suspected, and he burned inside. Georgio was a hard, brittle man, with a violent and jealous disposition. All those years ago, Georgio had been irresistibly attracted to Anya's large, sparkling eyes, comely face and generous curves. But she was independent, and spirited, and had refused him at first. Imagine! The daughter of a shopkeeper refusing him, Georgio! And he, the eldest son, who had just inherited the family farm from his elderly parents! He recalled with grim satisfaction that he had pledged his life's mission to subdue that proud spirit. He, Georgio, had broken in many an obdurate mare. And, over time, his wife had suffered, and surrendered her spirit; had wilted into almost abject submission to her husband's will.

Anya had not told Georgio about her visit to the cave. She knew her husband, and she knew that the knowledge would make her very existence unendurable. But Georgio did not need to hear the truth from his wife. Instinctively, he already knew. He knew about himself; knew that the life-force had drained from him. And Georgio knew about the hermit. And he knew also that the hermit was a young man; a secretive man; a vital man.

Despite his taunts to his wife that she must be incurably barren, Georgio nurtured dark suspicions that Anya had been unfaithful with the reclusive hermit. While, for some time, now, his relations with his wife had been perfunctory and unsatisfying, in recent times, and quite unusually, *she* had been bold and insistent. The most sinister explanation presented itself as the only truth. His wife had betrayed him; made a fool of him; had shamed him for all time. The 'mad monk' was an impostor, who prayed on other men's wives. When, late one evening, through an alcoholic haze, Georgio forcefully put these claims to his wife, Anya was compelled to confess that she had visited the hermit, but only for counselling; only to receive his words of wisdom; only because she was desperate for a family, for her and her husband's sake. She vehemently denied any immodest contact, any hint of impropriety, any taint of unfaithfulness. Anya desperately, furiously, defended her honour; she knew that her marriage, her very existence, lay on the cusp of disaster. Though every day was an agony of self-doubt and self-recrimination, most of all she feared the daily torture she knew would be inflicted upon her by her husband's constant, cloying suspicion, and by his insane jealousy.

The black seed of anger continued to fester in the husband's heart. He could not eat or sleep; he only drank. The blackness in him mushroomed into a vast, engulfing canker of rage and hatred. One evening, deep in drink, Georgio drilled further into his wife's account of her conduct. Anya proudly, furiously, defended herself – and the hermit – with every ounce of her courage and spirit: 'He's a good, kind man. The hermit just talked to me, and offered me counsel.' She added, defiantly: 'He only gave me a herbal potion to drink! After that, I fell asleep and remember nothing! Nothing else happened, I swear it!' Georgio leered, his face contorted in violent disbelief. His cunning, crab-like mind dissected his wife's every twitch, spasm and inflection of speech extracted under duress; he strongly suspected her of Delphic dissembling. Then he sneered: 'I bet he gave you something, you shameless slut!'

Georgio was grimly determined, if such be needed, to beat a confession from his wife; she was his, and must obey him. He closed upon her, denying her space, so she could hardly breathe. Fearful of her husband's temper and terrified for her child, Anya broke down and confessed as much as, so long as she had breath, she could: yes, the hermit's potion had relaxed her, and made her sleepy; she had felt a power upon her as she fell into a deep reverie. That was all; she could not account for the night, but had woken, alone, at first light.

Hearing these further, hesitant words that denied him the unvarnished truth that he sought – words that still resisted explanation and confession – only infuriated the husband still further. He knew now that he had not broken the spirit in her;

it was still there, hidden, lying secretly, cunningly, in wait for its moment of joyous release. Despite her weasel words, he now *knew* that his wife had sacrificed her honour to the accursed hermit; he could penetrate through the mists, could sense the smell, the hot touch, of another man upon her. It was more, much more, than flesh and blood – his flesh and blood – could bear. Wild with loathing and rage, with bulging eyes and foaming mouth, and snarling like a beast that has been speared, Georgio lashed out at Anya; she shrieked, and fell heavily to the ground. She lay, prostrate and sobbing hysterically, at his feet. Exploding with a lust that had been building for weeks, the man slowly unbuttoned his fustian trousers, and stood over the convulsing body of his wife.

There could be no going back.

*

As dawn was breaking, Georgio hurriedly left his farm and set off on the winding path towards the mountain. His eyes were blood-shot, brought on by a night of furious drinking, as he struggled to subdue images that curdled in his mind. But he had left prepared: an ancient leather belt was slung around his waist, bearing a sheath that barely disguised a murderous hunting knife. Fuelled by anger and adrenalin, and a desire to settle scores, Georgio made steady progress. Two hours into his task, the vast, whale-backed colossus of Mount Parnassus lay before him, protruding from the morning mists that girdled its heights. While energized and emboldened by his torment, Georgio was light-headed with the impact of drink and trauma, and there was no shade or shelter from the scorching sun. Without water, and finding the steep uneven trail dizzying and laborious, the farmer fell heavily on the devilish scree, bloodying his face, and gashing his knee and elbow.

It was mid-afternoon, under a broiling, merciless sun, before the panting, limping Georgio, dripping with sweat and covered in dust, attained his goal – the mouth of the hermit's cave. He had found the spot – secluded, and disguised by gorse – with some difficulty; but now felt like a hunter, elated at cornering his unsuspecting prey. Straining to control his heavy breathing, Georgio ventured cautiously into the darkness. Faint human sounds could just be heard – murmurings, and the intimate tones of two distinct voices – within the dark recesses of the cave. Georgio lumbered clumsily across the uneven stone floor, and dimly discerned two figures in embrace – the man's broad back naked and mobile. Without challenge or warning, Georgio shuffled towards the now silent, barely moving figures, and raised his blade. In an instant, the calm was shattered by the tumult of violent struggle: by terrible cries, and groans, followed swiftly by the shudder of sudden death.

The blood-caked, discoloured and bloated body lay sprawled outside the cave for two days in merciless heat, before police finally arrived, by train from Patras, to examine Georgio's corpse. After interviewing the hermit and, later, the still-traumatised witness, the wiry, and wily – and world-weary – Inspector Pantazis quickly concluded that this was an open-and-shut case of self-defence. Georgio, only, had been armed, and seeking to commit murder. However, it was the alert, stronger Yannis who had prevailed, turning his own knife upon the attacker, following a brief but desperate struggle. His courage and self-awareness had prevented a worse tragedy, that might easily have resulted in two innocent deaths – those of both Yannis and his companion. It was quickly decided that no charges would be brought. The scales were weighted heavily against the deceased: Georgio was a deeply unpopular man, a well-known violent drunkard, and suspected wife-beater. The world would be a better place without him.

Even so, the kindly Inspector advised the hermit to leave the area immediately. News – and particularly rumours purporting to be news – spread very quickly, and local men might jump to some rather unpalatable conclusions concerning the conduct of their wives, and the progeny of their offspring, when the full picture emerged. Yannis nodded sagely, collected his few possessions, and departed the same day, never to be seen in those parts again.

Anya's thoughts on the news of her husband's death, and by the hand of the hermit, can only be surmised. Inspector Pantazis was less circumspect. 'He was a bad man, your husband, Anya; you are well rid of him. As for the hermit, well, people are fickle. Ignorance is bliss but, when the facts become public knowledge – or at least the perceived facts – the mood music will quickly change. The man will have to leave the area. I've told him that. And maybe give up hermiting, if that's what they call it…' The Inspector laughed at his own little joke. He continued, solicitously: 'The main thing, my dear, is your child. Legally, he or she will belong to you and Georgio. Always remember that. And none of the women I've interviewed want to press any charges against the hermit. Any embarrassment they may feel is submerged beneath the cries of a bouncing baby boy or girl. Perhaps they feel they've had enough of charges!' He laughed again, then corrected himself. 'Mrs Papandreu, a hundred apologies. My attempts at humour sometimes get the better of me. This is a serious and sensitive matter, and I wish you well. Good-day.'

*

Anya spent several months enjoying the feel of her rich, taffeta, widow's weeds close to her skin. She quickly blossomed again, and regained her fine looks, quickness and spirit. With almost indecent haste she was besieged with offers from a wide variety of suitors, all anxious for her hand, and all eagerly bearing gifts. She laughed them off, and waved them all away. What need had she for another useless husband? Eight months later, Anya gave birth to a strapping young boy, with a crop of tousled black hair.

Anya had inherited a farm that was mean, miserable and thoroughly neglected. The farm had been run into the ground, and the family were heavily in debt. But now she was free to use her energies and initiative, and quickly transformed the property into a thriving business. Within a couple of years, Anya found herself in possession of a valuable and, under her careful husbandry, increasingly prosperous farm. Nurturing the property, and bringing up her handsome young son, Yannis, became her whole life's work. Anya's life was complete: there was no desire, and certainly no need, for another man.

Young Yannis grew up a strikingly handsome, thoughtful and studious lad. In fact, a model young man, who was also somewhat detached at school – useful in avoiding the smiles and attractions of his admiring female counterparts. Although he never knew a father, his mother ensured that Yannis lacked for nothing; she was fiercely ambitious for her only son. In time, the young man would attend university in far-away Athens, and then become a teacher and, finally, Professor of Ancient History at the University itself. As his mother grew older, Yannis would also help her to manage the prosperous farm that, one day, would become his.

As he grew to manhood, Yannis matured into a strong, confident man with an easy grace and comely smile; he was never short of admirers. Each time he visited his mother, Anya smiled winningly. Yannis, like his mother, knew the truth; and, like her, was glad in it.

At the age of 23, Yannis married his sweetheart, Olympia, and they soon had two fine children of their own. His was a rich life, lived mainly in the mind, in the imagination, and in the retelling of his country's glorious history. There would be no more hermit's tales.

A Trilogy: II
DR SOCRATES SPEAKS

Mr Toby Bright was the main man, or so he liked to think. And his judgement was invariably correct; or so he wished the world and his wife to believe.

Toby was, or so that world believed, a happily married man, wedded to the beautiful blonde, Scarlett; a successful businessman, with an established, if eclectic, travel agent business, in partnership with his long-term friend, Dick; the owner of a spanking, six-bedroom detached house, shared only with his lovely wife; and a shrewd investor, with investments showered like confetti across the world's stockmarkets. A leading light in both the local Rotary Club and Chamber of Commerce, Toby was viewed and reflected in the light of his own self-worth: a supremely successful, supremely fortunate, lucky sod.

But although armed with supreme self-confidence, Toby always sought advice before undertaking a new venture, or making a major decision. And he had long sought, and received, this advice from one Dr Socrates. Dr Socrates had advised Toby concerning his choice of wife; his choice of business partner; and his choice of investments, amongst many other critical, even life-changing, turning-points.

Naturally, all such advice had been ignored. Toby loved to view a problem from every perspective, every conceivable angle, every viewpoint. He would chew over every aspect of the case, poke into every crevice, examine every remote nook and cranny. No man stretched more intellectual sinew in pursuit of the ideal solution to every situation. Toby viewed this process as a sort of personal due diligence; an intellectual exercise, a challenge, even as a form of entertainment. Dr Socrates may be his trusted adviser, sparking further nuances of thought, even reflection. But, in this game called 'life', he was no match for Mr Toby Bright.

Take his marriage to Scarlett, for instance. She was young; beautiful; a trophy on his arm, a testament to his power. And she was phenomenal in… Well, Toby had pursued her, wooed her, won her. This, he told himself, had been a complete no-brainer. Dr Socrates had gently suggested that this was indeed a no-brainer, since the decision was made by a part of Toby's brain that lay entirely outside his head. As for that shifty, slime-ball Dick… .Toby had listened – or at least heard – and shrugged his shoulders.

Dr Socrates knew exactly what that shrug indicated.

But now – and his admission of the truth to himself was not without difficulty – Toby Bright was a worried man. His business was, unaccountably, sinking. His marriage – to the sexiest woman on the planet – was failing. And the value of his investments seemed to shrink by the day. Since there was no other conceivable explanation, Toby put all this down to the most damnable bad luck. Too much negative energy. We must do some creative thinking, he reasoned to himself, and get life back on an upward trajectory.

One fine day, unable any longer to bear the burden of ever-increasing, indeed, excruciating, anxiety, Toby tripped up the stairs to Dr Socrates' consulting room – more surely described as a garret – on the top floor of a down-at-heel office block in Reading. For once, he was not regretting the £100 consultation fee charged by Dr S to his clients. But, this time, perhaps he should listen more carefully; extract more value for his hard-earned cash; get more bang for his bucks. He reflected, ruefully, what a pretty pass he had come to. That Dr Socrates had better start earning his fee!

*

Let us leave Toby for a moment, while he is making introductory small talk to Dr Socrates; and let us enjoy a quick look under the bonnet of Mr Bright's shiny new Ferrari, as it were, since it is now parked and idle on the office forecourt, where it continues to depreciate at a rate of knots.

Toby's marriage to Scarlett was floundering, because all that one saw – and that *that* was quite something – was all that you got. Scarlett appeared vacant, selfish and extravagant. Scarlett did not *do*; she just was. Was, that is, a high-maintenance, high-performance, young woman. She had won the coveted Miss England title in 2016; Toby had sought her out, and swept her off her feet. The Miss England Competition had catapulted Scarlett into a whole new social milieu. Toby was handsome, charming and a millionaire (she read this as 'billionaire'). Soon after meeting Toby, Scarlett dumped her shopfitter fiancé of two years; she wanted to go places, in every sense of the phrase.

For Toby, too, there was (as it were) no contest. Scarlett was simply stunning; with Scarlett on his arm, Toby knew he would be the envy of every man he knew. Toby had promised the world to Scarlett: she could have everything – anything – she wanted. She took him at his word, and spent money – on dining out, on *haute couture*, on jewellery, on holidays – as though such 'necessities' were about to be abolished by government decree. Coming from a deprived, permanently hard-up family, Scarlett was like an exotic plant, that is suddenly pitched into the light, and given permission to flower. Her true, native instinct flourished. The outflow of funds was so gi-normous that the couple were now arguing constantly over Scarlett's endless expectations. The happy duo now occupied separate bedrooms. Sex was an angry, distant memory.

Meanwhile, Toby's business was failing, owing to friend Dick's siphoning off company revenues, illicitly. Toby and Dick had been best friends since school days. They had similar, pleasure-seeking temperaments, appreciated the finer things in life, and delighted in their pursuit. A travel agency business had seemed the ideal business vehicle, whereby they could combine travel and glamour with a high-value experience to their local, well-heeled, community. Toby trusted the handsome, charming Dick implicitly, even though his brow furrowed when he saw a new Aston Martin parked outside the office window.

And Toby's investments – which were supposed to support and underpin his lifestyle – had sunk to levels not seen since Gladstone was an awkward youth. Frustratingly, these losses had occurred quite contrary to the strong 'bull' market that had propelled most shares, and markets, to vertiginous new heights over the last five years. This had all been counter to Toby's early experience, a spectacular run of success, of winner takes all; of who dares wins. His decision making had been inspired; phenomenal. What had happened? What had caused such a run of bad luck? The wheel of fortune must, surely, turn soon?

Dr Socrates was tall, lean, swarthy and, for all his fifty-and-some years, remarkably well-preserved. The good doctor had retained a head of rich, black hair that, despite half a lifetime of absorbing other people's troubles, had stubbornly resisted tones of grey. Dr S was in fact a Greek national, who had arrived in the UK thirty or so years ago, following a little local difficulty with the Greek authorities. He had eked out a living in a variety of menial roles before qualifying as a counsellor; a role in which he excelled.

The name 'Dr Y. Socrates' was proudly displayed on a

brass plate on his office door; the 'Doctor' an honorary title. Dr Socrates was not a specialist adviser – the ones with posh offices, letters after their names, and eye-watering fees. Dr S was a generalist, and called upon to provide a basic, honest and confidential counselling service – sign-posting clients to more specialist advisers (for example for marriage guidance or financial planning) as necessary. Dr S used to joke to clients, in that perfect English spoken only by those for whom the English language is an acquired taste, that he had been educated in the university of life, and the school of hard knocks. The claim was always made with a smile, and delivered with humour; but it was also largely true. So Dr S gave advice on any and every subject raised by his client: for £50 quid an hour, nothing was off limits. It was for the client to decide whether or not to take that advice. If they did not, Dr S knew from experience that the client would return for more. Such a client was Toby Bright.

'Good of you to drop by, Toby. So, what can I do for you, today?'

Toby had considered his opening gambit carefully. He wanted to discomfort the good Doctor. We needed blue sky thinking. We needed to think outside the effing box. But, at the last minute, Toby's nerve failed him. He simply could not admit to the tsunami of calamity that had engulfed his once perfect, faultless life.

'Well, Doctor, I'm considering renouncing clothes.'

The good Doctor coughed. 'Indeed? Renounce clothes? Well', he laughed, 'you can't really renounce clothes. It's not like religion or a club – clothes are a practical, useful thing – like food, and wine. So what's the problem, exactly?' Dr S suspected that there was a major, unspoken carbuncle lurking beneath, as it were, the clothes chimera.

'Look, I'm quite serious. If you can give me six good reasons why I *should* wear clothes, then I'll do it!'

'Tell you what, Toby. I'll give you *seven* sound reasons why we – you – need clothes. OK?'

'OK, fine – let's hear 'em!' responded Toby.

'And then you'll tell me what's *really* troubling you?'

'OK; deal!' Toby replied, with some uncertainty.

'Toby, how long have we known each other?'

'Around seven years, I think.'

'There's no 'around' about it. You know that the one thing I insist upon is total honesty between us. So when I've given you seven sound reasons not to relinquish clothes, can we get to the real nitty gritty?'

Toby shifted uneasily in his seat. 'OK, Doc', he replied with a forced grin. 'As I said, I'm beginning to find clothes a bit of a bore. My suits are expensive and uncomfortable. Much of my business can be conducted by 'phone, internet and Zoom. And Scarlett spends a bloody fortune on new outfits every month. The smaller the garment, the more expensive it seems to get. And, I might tell you, she looks even better *sans* lingerie…'

'OK, then let's begin. Modesty. We don't normally go around, as it were, tackle out!'

'Well, Scarlett has nothing to be modest about. She's gorgeous. God knows why she buys all those clothes; looks a million dollars without them. No-one's going to complain about *that*, I can assure you. And I think I'm pretty passable, to be honest. All that time in the gym hasn't entirely gone to waste!'

'I'm sure you're both terrific human specimens. But do you want the world to see your dangly bits when you visit Waitrose? And do you want your lovely wife to be gawped at, leered over and brushed against by old men who protest: 'sorry love, mistook you for the wife!' You must know that there's a pandemic of inappropriate touching on trains, buses and supermarkets at the moment? It's really quite deplorable!'

'Surely,' Toby protested, 'not all men are sex *mad*?'

'Well,' Dr S replied, following a slight but deliberate cough, 'that's a bit rich, if I might be so bold. You may know that all the major religions advocate keeping one's kit firmly on, and for that very reason.

By the way, do you have a picture of Scarlett with you?'

Toby reached into his wallet. 'Here's one of her in Barbados, on the beach.'

Dr S adjusted his spectacles, and peered closely at the photograph. And emits a small sigh. 'Ah, yes. I see. Just what is it about blondes and red bikinis…? OK, let's move on, swiftly. Comfort. Both genders have dangly bits that need support. Unless you want to be king of the swingers, or start a cabaret act, I'd suggest that supporting your meat and two veg might be a sensible thing to do. Comfort isn't mandatory, but might be sensible. And you mustn't think only of yourself: there may be long term consequences, particularly for the well-endowed figure…'

'Well, we get away with playing tennis on our naturist trips… but over the long haul, Doc, you may have a point…'

'Third, climate. We live in the UK. That's three months Spring, and nine months Winter. It's wet, windy, cold, and then very cold. A jumper and a good coat are therefore most welcome.'

'OK, but skin dries more quickly on it's own; clothes get wet, dirty, and have to be cleaned, and so on. It's a real chore. And it's all so costly!'

'Wet clothes may be preferable to frostbite. And clothes don't *need* to be expensive. Ever heard of charity shops? Still, Toby, I can see you're not yet convinced. Sometimes, one strand of argument may not be sufficient. But I'd like you to consider the weight of arguments in total; in the round, as it were. Let's move on.

So, fourth: protection. Boxers wear headgear. Footballers war shin-pads. Cricketers wear boxes. And for very good reasons.

Pray, what will you wear when you next start the strimmer, or the chainsaw?'

'Point taken. I'll get the gear' – slight laugh – 'headgear, pads and of course the box. Or maybe employ a gardener!'

'Very droll. Fifth – there's vanity. Good clothes enhance our appearance. Even Scarlett – *particularly* Scarlett – is aware of the magic of dress. The most beautiful women know that, in attending a cocktail party, or going to the opera, or putting in an appearance at Royal Ascot, they must dress for the occasion; make an effort, put on their finest dress and jewellery; wow the audience. An appearance *au naturel* just won't do, I'm afraid. Certainly not in the Royal Box.'

'Again, you have a point,' Toby conceded. 'But how many handbags does a woman need? But maybe for social events, or if we're trying to impress…'

'Then there's power, and social status. Clothes can define us; help make us who we are. Provide status, and elan. Your sharp suit, Gucci shoes, Rolex watch. It's the uniform of power and class. Helps to influence, make deals, get things done; overawes the plebs. All the world's a stage, and all that.'

'Again, that's pretty persuasive. As a businessman, I do have some idea how the world works; how deals are done. Maybe I haven't entirely thought this thing through…'

'Which brings me to point seven: legality. Now, while wandering around in the all-together may not be strictly illegal, it's still pretty borderline. The police would be bound to investigate complaints, and therein lies loads of hassle. If the aim is to achieve a simple, carefree life then, well, forget it. If you ended up in jail, just think of that rough, itchy stuff you'd be compelled to wear. Not to mention the rough stuff in the shower, when you're told to pick up the soap!'

'Blimey, Dr S, I do believe I'm convinced. Whatever was I thinking of? What the hell's happened to my life…to my thinking?' Toby burst into tears, and hid his head in his hands. 'The truth,' Dr Socrates, 'is that my life is in the most godawful mess. I think I'm ready to talk about it!'

'I'm afraid our time is up for today, Toby. We'll arrange another session; come back this time next week. I suspect I know what's wrong. A case of multiple failures; a real car crash. I'm afraid that the treatment may be painful, at least in the beginning. But I'm pretty sure that, over time, we can begin to put things right.

And – oh – Toby, old man, just a thought: any more pictures of Scarlett?'

A Trilogy: III
THE BAND OF BROTHERS

Toby Bright bounded up the stairwell, towards the consulting room of Dr Y Socrates. It was exactly a week, to the minute, since his last, infamous, visit. Toby was dressed in a smart check shirt, with cravat, and tailored fawn trousers. But, despite his hopeful burst of energy, Toby looked drawn, red-eyed, and his usual *bouffant* of fair hair was disheveled. Toby was mightily relieved that this hour had come; bringing with it a fresh dawn of promise – of the hope of recovery and renewal.

'Morning, Toby. Still wearing clothes, eh?' smiled Socrates. Toby looked confused. 'Oh, yes, of course!' There was a slight blush, before he remembered, and tossed a USB stick on to the Doctor's desk. 'What's this?' asked the Doctor, raising his dark eye-brows with an enquiring glance.

'Photos.' Socrates gave another quizzical look. 'Of Scarlett.'

'Of course; cheers!'

'Some of them are a bit…'

'Revealing, do you mean? Toby, I may be a single man, but I'm sure there's nothing I've not seen before. Anyway,' he smiled, 'it's a purely professional interest, you understand. I need to *know* my clients.'

'So, how have you been?' This was Toby's entreè to 'hit' the Doctor on the traumas of the week just gone. His discovery that his business partner, Dick, had been swindling him blind. His discovery that his financial adviser was an incompetent jackass. And his realisation that his marriage, far from hitting a bump in the road, was a full-on car crash. Every aspect of Toby's world had come tumbling down. And, although there was no-one else to blame, he hadn't a clue how to begin to put things right. It wasn't just one – life-critical – issue. It was everything at once; his life on the edge of a precipice. Did he have a pit to climb out of? Or a mountain to climb? He felt like a naked rambler in a snowstorm. Bereft; cut off; alone; deserted; desperate. What in hell was he to do? Where even to begin?

Socrates listened, absorbed. This was not a matter of life and death; but it was pretty damned close.

'I see,' said the Doctor, at length, calmly, but with knitted brows. 'Well, this just won't do. We'll need a plan. It will take time. There will be pain, both emotional, and financial. But, together, we'll get through it. I promise you Toby, you'll emerge stronger from this ordeal. But there's no time to lose. So let's make a start...'

After two hours of intense discussion, designed to bottom-out every conceivable element of Toby's life – there could be no room for any more, nasty, sudden surprises – the Doctor rose from his chair, to stretch his legs. 'Toby, that's really all for today. Next week, please do bring Scarlett with you, if she'd be so good. We need to sort this out together.' 'But...' Toby ventured, in consternation. 'No buts!' replied Socrates, with some firmness, and closed the door.

The Doctor's last gesture had been to waive – wave away – his normal fee. Such generosity gave Toby a relief beyond the mere immediate and financial. Toby had emptied himself of all his acute concerns. His problems had not gone away, but he felt he now had a friend and ally; he was already feeling lighter, relieved of a mighty, unsupportable burden.

Dr Socrates, with his acute knowledge of the world – that world composed of volatile and unpredictable – but so predictable – human beings – felt that he had a sacred mission to perform; a mission to rescue Toby from himself. But more than that: to help Toby to *grow*, to develop, so that he could not only surmount his sea of troubles, but begin to make sound, *good* decisions; and go on to lead a successful and fulfilling life.

Socrates remained deeply troubled – and inspired – by his own past. Alone in his office, for the first time that day, the Doctor felt along the deep scar on his lower left arm – the wound that had saved his life, as he had moved swiftly to deflect Georgio's lunging blade. He did not regret killing Georgio: there had been no time; no choice. A moment's hesitation would have seen his own life lost. The very recollection of that deadly embrace sent shivers down his spine. The trauma – of desperate struggle, of death, and near death – had been the cause of recurring, visceral nightmares: he wished things had been otherwise; that there had been a different way.

But while, ultimately, he did not regret Georgio, he did regret Anya. It was now thirty years since he had met, in the strangest of circumstances, this beautiful but desperate woman; and offered her the human sympathy and comfort that she craved. He had known Anya for only one night, but had fallen utterly under the spell of her beauty and vulnerability. Anya had opened up her heart to him. Though Anya, in her modesty and loyalty, had given only a lightly drawn picture of her husband's character, Socrates had quickly surmised that Georgio was a worthless, violent drunk, who had cruelly abused his wife.

Socrates had never seen Anya since the fateful day they first met; but he had felt the tenderness of her love. Even now, her image, her voice, burned within him. He had, of course, met many women since; but not anyone with those dark, flashing eyes, and that unquenchable spirit; and he had never married. In the years since this climactic event in his life he had strived, he had struggled, in his own small way, to give something back to the world; to be a force for some *good*. He believed in the power of love, of personal commitment, of *giving*, through human impulse and positive energy. Bringing Toby through this godawful mess would be his way of reconciling himself to the world, of making amends, of finding some resolution, closure, even, for the events, the questionable decisions of his youth…

Exactly a week after the new-era interview with Toby, there was a soft tap on Socrates' already open door. An apparition stood smiling before him. 'Good afternoon, Mrs Bright! How delightful to meet you!' The apparition strode in, followed by her pensive husband. 'Please!' she soothed: 'Scarlett will be fine, Doctor.' 'And please, do call me Yannis!' he responded, with a small laugh, somewhat to Toby's dismay. 'It is after all my name.'

'I wonder…' – she avoided calling Socrates by his first name – 'if you could tell me a little about yourself. Of course I've heard a few bits and pieces from Toby, but I am a little intrigued about your past…'

'Well,' he averred, 'it's usually me who asks the questions, but of course I understand. It's absolutely necessary to set your mind at rest. These sessions will be vital for both of your futures, and it's critically important that you have total confidence in me.'

Socrates looked intently into Scarlett's extraordinary blue eyes. 'More than thirty years ago now – please don't laugh – I lived as a hermit, in central Greece. I wished – and tried – to distance myself from human society, and to live my life on a spiritual plane, in meditation, in the midst of nature.'

'Didn't you feel lonely?' enquired Scarlett. 'Never!' replied Yannis. 'How can anyone feel lonely, in the midst of nature; and in their own company? Your English poet, Andrew Marvell, writes that *'Two Paradises 'twere in one, To live in Paradise alone.'* I've only ever felt lonely in a city – such as Athens, or of course London.'

Scarlett was captivated by the Doctor's insights, his power of speech. She felt sufficient confidence to venture: 'I've heard of Marvel films, Marvel comics; is there any connection?'

Socrates answered gently, with a confiding smile, 'Remarkably, no.'

'But Marvell – he's still around?'

'He's still around, in the sense that he's still inspiring new generations. But, no, he died in 1678, in the reign of Charles II.'

'Gosh…Yannis, that's pretty cool. So tell me: what happened…I mean to the hermit thing?' Scarlett asked, beneath her breath, and with a look that sought to plunge into Socrates' soul.

Socrates sighed. 'Well, it worked for a while, and I was happy. And then society kind of intruded on me, and life became complicated again. In truth, someone died, in tragic circumstances. It was my good fortune to make my way to England, and to find my true niche. But perhaps it's better to leave the details to another time; we have a great deal to get through!'

Socrates took a deep breath. 'Mrs Bright…Scarlett…I know we've only just met, but I ask with all my heart that you place your trust in me. We need to undertake this journey together. That other poet, Sinatra, used to joke that a problem shared was a problem doubled. It's a funny thing – joking apart – that, in my early years here, when I was struggling with the language, listening to Sinatra really helped to improve my English diction.'

'Sin…at..ra?' enquired Scarlett: 'That's a name to conjure with. Sounds like a made-up name, like Elton John, or Lady Gaga.' Socrates laughed, showing his regular white teeth, beneath a curling black moustache. 'No, indeed', he replied. 'Sinatra was the family name. He was second generation Italian–American, whose parents had emigrated to America for a better life. He was an only child, and a loner, growing up in an alien, hostile culture.

I felt that Mr S and I had a lot in common.' He added, laughing again – 'apart from the talent, that is!'

He looked at Scarlett earnestly: 'But, seriously, Scarlett: permit me to share your burden. Only believe, my dear lady, that my own experience is now at your service; and that I will always have your best interests at heart.'

Scarlett nodded, in gratitude for the Doctor's honesty, indeed his intimacy, to someone he had known for only a matter of minutes. She, too, had been frightened, conscious that her life stood on the edge of an abyss. Now, she felt a strange relief, a comfort, as though a cosmic support was wrapped around her shoulders. Toby, surprised into silence, looked at the Doctor, and then at his wife, in a kind of silent disbelief. The session continued…the first of many, many more…

It would be more than a year – to be precise, fifteen months – before Toby Bright had overcome the mental breakdown that the implosion of his life had brought on. Fifteen months in which both he and Scarlett – with the Doctor's daily support – had turned around a life – read *'lives'* – that had seemed to be spiralling towards a deep abyss. Now, once again, if only fitfully, the sunny uplands appeared again on the near horizon.

Scarlett had proved to be a revelation to the Doctor; and not just for reasons of personal allure. Remarkably, her pictures did not do her full justice; did not fully reveal the woman behind the facade of beauty; the personality who brought that beauty to life. Over the last year or two Scarlett had matured, forced to grow up through the daily ordeals involving pain and argument, heartbreak and disillusion. She, too, had entered a furnace burning at white heat; if her character had not transformed into diamond, she had at least developed greater depths, and more facets, than the superficial character she had displayed hitherto. She was a woman, now; stronger, and developing an acute sense of what was really important: what she *needed* from life, rather than just what she craved. She began to feel a new sympathy for Toby, whilst realising that the marriage was a mistake based on false values.

Almost despite herself, Scarlett was drawn instantly to the good Doctor. She recognised his sincerity in respecting and protecting her interests; but was fascinated by hidden depths, and the sense of mystery – even danger – that he projected. But she did not feel afraid; she felt comforted and borne up by his presence; by the accumulated wisdom behind his words. It was as though he had lived several lives…and she wanted to explore them all.

The view from these sunny uplands was remarkable indeed. The partnership with Dick had been dissolved, with the agreement of all parties. Dick knew that he was on a very sticky wicket. He agreed to take 100% of the business, with Toby giving up his share in exchange for modest compensation. But Toby escaped a situation where further losses, and possibly bankruptcy, beckoned.

Toby's beloved Ferrari was swapped for a second hand Ford Focus. Who knows – another Ferrari might come along some day. It was only money. And vanity. And that share portfolio was completely overhauled, by an adviser who the Doctor trusted implicitly: himself. Though a half-million quids worth of assets had, under previous stewardship, shrivelled to little more than a hundred grand, that was sufficient for Toby to meet his short-term living expenses; and enough to begin building a new portfolio that could weather every storm.

With both sadness and relief on both sides, Toby and Scarlett divorced, by mutual consent. The marriage had been too superficial, too star-struck, too one-dimensional, to last the course. There had been unrealistic expectations from both parties. And now there was too much baggage – emotional baggage. Too much had been said; harsh, angry words, that could not easily be forgotten. It was time to make a clean, fresh start. And, since there was no longer the pressure-cooker expectations of husband and wife, a new sympathy and respect would emerge, over time, from the carnage of marriage; a sympathy that would ultimately mature into friendship. Although Scarlett was gifted the house – no ifs, no buts – Toby continued to live there, rent free, for the time being. Scarlett had resumed the modelling career that she had given up on meeting Toby. As beautiful and charismatic as ever, she was in popular demand, and had recently featured in a TV advert for a popular brand of shampoo. And, thinking of the longer term, Scarlett was also training to become a beautician, starting her own business – a role for which her personality and interests made her eminently qualified.

Toby had given up his upwardly-mobile social pretensions – at least for the present. He was helped to re-build his life by training to become…yes, a counsellor, with the delighted encouragement of the Doctor. Toby would, of course, require intense professional mentoring from Dr Socrates. However, with a surfeit of Tobys and Scarletts in the world, there was little danger of a shortage of clients…

By now, Yannis and Toby had become firm friends; there was no longer any need for 'counselling'; just a cool chat over a beer. They met often for drinks, for meals, for nights at the theatre – and the bouzouki bar.

But Socrates was also seeing Scarlett. From hesitant, uncertain beginnings, their relationship had become deep and passionate. Even so, the relationship was far too important for Yannis to wish to rush things along. Time and nature would take their course; he was laying the foundations for the rest of his life, and was determined to make the best, and most lasting, impression. Socrates therefore played the gentleman that he wished to be with all the experience and wisdom that he possessed. These days, with an almost perpetual smile on his face, Yannis could often be found – in the shower, or when waiting for Scarlett to appear – humming one of his favourite Sinatra tunes: *'Nice and easy....'.*

It was towards the end of a long Summer evening, with the setting sun glancing on the beatific River Thames, that Socrates found the courage to ask Scarlett to marry him. She had been half expecting his proposal, but teased: 'Only if you quote me some more of that dead white guy – Marvell!'

Without hesitation, and grinning from ear to ear, Socrates duly obliged:

'Now, therefore, while the youthful hue
Sits on thy skin like morning dew,
And while thy willing soul transpires
At every pore with instant fires,
Now let us sport us while we may...'

Scarlett laughed with pleasure. 'So you *do* fancy me, after all? How could a girl say 'no'?' Playfully, she took hold of his tie and, thrilled, turned her power on her man. Searching, silkily, she invited: 'Doctor, I think it's high time you gave me a proper consultation...'

The friendship between Yannis, Socrates and Toby Bright proved strong enough to survive the evening when the good Doctor confided to Toby, with choking voice, that he had fallen in love with Scarlett. Scarlett was not Anya. In part, that was the attraction: she was a kind of beautiful, sympathetic antidote to Anya. Socrates could never forget; but, at long last, he could move on.

To Yannis Socrates' infinite delight, Toby insisted on being best man at the wedding. An exciting new chapter had begun. Toby, too, had moved on. They had *all* moved on. The ghosts of the past had, finally, been laid to rest. Bonds linking past, present and future bound them together. They had become – Yannis, Scarlett, and Toby – a band of brothers. With their lives now built on firm foundations, all three could look forward to the promise of a calmer, and more serene, future life. At long last, they had arrived at those balmy, sunlit uplands.

REPRISE

He awoke drowsily, his head slumped on his chest, his brain still soaked from last night's binge. His eyes struggled to focus on the rough ridges of the concrete floor. A fierce hand grabbed his hair, and jerked his head sharply upwards. The young man cried out, his pain aggravated by the surprise of the moment. The man's bloodshot eyes met his assailant's naked breasts, as her body arched over his, her outstretched hand still clutching his hair.

The sudden, unexpected pain cleared his head; he was instantly, powerfully awake. The man's eyes moved upwards, to the face that was almost bending over his. The man, Chris, recognised the girl: she was Miriam. They had had a few dates. Nothing much had happened. So what the fuck was this all about?

Chris tried to move, but his limbs were stiff, and taut against the solid frame of the chair. He looked down: he was encased in a heavy wooden chair – as solid as a throne – but pinioned at the wrists and elbows, and again at the ankles and knees. Chris let out a gasp: he was sitting in his underpants. Only his underpants! Was this some sort of sick joke? Or a stag-do stunt that had gone too far?

Only his head could – would – move, and the man named Chris swivelled his head to glean as much intelligence as his position allowed. Good God! There were three of them! And all semi-naked. Chris recognised all three: over the months, he had dated all three women. They were: Miriam – the hair yanker; Claire, and Summer.

Though each young woman looked gorgeous – soft, luminous and lovely – Chris had no sensual musings. This was no time for delicious contemplation of what might be, in different circumstances, a young man's dream. Chris looked around, urgently, for any small scraps of information that might help: he appeared to be in a double garage, or maybe a small warehouse. The walls were brick-lined, but the whole space empty, and cool; he could see his own breath on the air. The frame on which Chris was pinioned was placed, bleakly, in the epicentre of the rough concrete floor.

The three women began to move around him – before him, beside him, behind him – but never taking their eyes from his face, and his almost naked body. Chris felt acutely exposed, and vulnerable. Despite the cool air, beads of perspiration formed on his brow, and began to trickle down his face. Any embarrassment he might have felt had been submerged beneath a growing, gnawing fear: he was utterly at the mercy of these women, in god-knows-where. Chris had no idea where he was, or why. Worse, no-one else knew his whereabouts; his mobile was nowhere to be seen.

'OK girls, what's going on? I can take a joke, but this is a bit much. I promise, if you let me go now, I'll forget the whole thing. I mean, you've had your fun. Let's put this silliness behind us!'

"Silliness' you call it!' exploded Miriam, her dark eyes flashing, her mouth an angry gash, inches from his face. Chris's mouth felt dry, as though he'd been chewing sandpaper. He managed to splutter a few words of bravado: 'Yes, Miriam. We had a date or two. It was fun. No harm done, eh?' Same with you, Claire, and Summer. You're all great girls. We had some fun, then went our separate ways. Way of the world, and all that. What's the problem, exactly? I really don't get any of this! As I said, no harm done...'

'No harm done!' echoed Summer, screeching. 'No fucking harm done! Except, Chris, that you told the whole world – I mean the whole world – that I was a six and a half!'

Chris forced out a chuckle, intended to pacify. He was proud of his social media profile, his website, and his 'reach'. Anyway, it hadn't been 'six and a half'. His score had been precisely 6.5 – though, perhaps, on reflection, and appraising Summer again, he'd been a bit mean...

'So which was the half – these?' – pointing accusingly at her breasts. 'You think it's OK to objectify me to everyone on the *planet* – providing a detailed description of my anatomy!'

'It was only my opinion' shrugged Chris. 'A kind of appreciation. I got the idea from Blake Edwards' film, '10'. Remember that?'

'I don't care if you think I'm a bloody eleven – I'm not going to be defined by your eyes, your brain or your dick! Your opinion, your 'mark', isn't wanted, and just isn't right. In fact, offensive – intrusive. It objectifies me; *limits* me – and I'm not being limited by a scum-bag like you!'

'Nor me!' added Claire, with some venom. Then a small smile: 'Though I'm apparently a 7.5. 'My thighs are too big, and my nose could be shorter. No mention of the boobs. For this relief, much thanks! But, then no mention of my successful business, or the fact that I'm the county tennis champion, either!'

'And,' fumed Miriam, 'you had the effrontery – though I'm an '8' – to criticise *my* boobs. Go on – take a good look. Any better, now?'

'Miriam, I don't think it would help... But if you insist, of course they're very nice...boobs.'

'Yes, they are. In fact, they're fucking *great!* But they're mine, and nothing to do with *you*. And they're part of me, not something separate, made for your gratification, or your stupid comments. It's a bloody good job I didn't let you sleep with me… you'd be rating me out of ten in bed!' Chris attempted a weak smile; but felt nauseous, and seriously vulnerable. 'Look, it was all supposed to be light-hearted – and complimentary: can't you see that?'

'O, light-hearted, was it?' Summer interjected. 'Well, I'm more than a face and a fanny. I'm a living, breathing, thinking, feeling, paid-up member of the human race. Did you mention my history degree? Or my Grade 5 piano? No – just the tits!'

'Summer, that's not the end of your story?' enquired Claire, gently.

'No. Sadly, no' replied Summer, indignantly. 'On our second date, he asked to take some pictures, of me in my bra and knickers. I really wasn't sure, but I thought that we might become an 'item'. I never heard from the bastard again; he never replied to my calls or texts. Then, weeks later, pictures started to appear in my friends in-boxes. I felt like I wanted to die. I felt so embarrassed, so humiliated. I didn't want to go out, see anyone, face anyone, explain to anyone. The very friends to whom I'd normally turn to for help were now party to my degradation. Everyone whose shoulder I wanted to cry on was already embarrassed by my sense of shame. Though I'd done nothing wrong – just made a mistake – the mistake of trusting someone who'd flattered me into believing he cared about me…'

'And you Claire?' asked Summer. 'What's your story?'

'As you know,' Claire said, 'it's remarkably similar to your own. Sadly, I went on three dates with this nerd,' she said, bitterly, looking angrily at the still, bound man. On the third date, he persuaded me to get my boobs out for a few pics. He was quite the charmer – said he was a semi-pro, and I had the potential to be a model. And I thought it might be getting serious, so what's the problem? I never heard from him again. And then – my image all over the bloody Internet. I could have died. I mean – they'll be there for ever – when I'm a granny – for strangers to drool over – or worse. I just don't have any control over my own body, or how it's used. Who gave him the right to do that? What had I done to him, except snogged him? The piece of shit! So that's me. How about you, Miriam?'

'You guys were dead lucky!' spat Miriam, sarcastically. 'We dated four times – it seemed like he might actually be the *one*. How wrong can you get! But he was handsome, charming – and quite the flatterer. We hadn't quite 'done it', but I felt we were pretty close. So when he asked to take some nude pictures, in my bedroom, I felt up for it. Why not? I can't quite remember being so rash – I'd had a few Bacardis by then – but, as I now know only too well, I gave him the full money shot. After that, complete silence. And then – there I was, displayed, in all my knickerbocker glory, plastered all over the Net. I couldn't go out for weeks. Couldn't face my friends. I contacted the social media company – complaining of hate mail, sexual abuse and exploitation, or revenge porn. Surely, they had to take the pics down? But they just shrugged – I was a consenting adult. The shame will haunt me forever. What will my new boy-friend think, if he finds out? The whole bloody world's been there before him. What a complete bastard!'

'Well,' hissed Summer: 'Mr Fucking Perfect, how'd you rate yourself? 'Cos we're going to rate you! Every bit of you! Miriam! Time for the scissors!'

Chris sighed: 'at last, you've come to your senses!' 'Oh, yes, we've come to our senses all right!' cackled Claire.

Miriam approached, brandishing a very large pair of scissors. The approach was slow and menacing, not relaxed and reassuring. Any trace of a brave smile that had flitted briefly across Chris's face disappeared in a terrified grimace, as the reality of his predicament dawned. Leaning over the shaking young man, rather than cutting through the ropes that bound him, Miriam began – carefully, deliberately, skillfully – snipping at the fabric of his underpants. Chris squirmed, swore, and protested for all he was worth; but to no avail.

'Be still, you fucking idiot! I don't want to cause you actual injury!' Chris groaned; his head slumped on his chest in despair and resignation. He was powerless and defeated; his manhood embarrassed and ashamed.

'There, now!' beamed Miriam. 'Wasn't so bad, was it?'

'You can't do this! It's immoral! It's – illegal! It's an abuse of my human rights!' yelled Chris, in his impotent anger.

'And what about *our* human rights?' returned Miriam, coolly.

Summer interposed: 'What a big fuss about such a little thing! Still,' she sniggered, "it is a little cold in here. I'll just take a few before-and-after pics, just for old times' sake. Smile for the birdie!'

Chris did his best to look away, and spat out 'you fucking bitch!' as the flash bounced off his naked, straining form.

'And now, you ungrateful boy, this is your lucky day!' beamed Miriam. At her signal, all three of the women deftly removed their pants, in an act of exaggerated, theatrical choreography. They stood proudly, splendidly, naked before the unclothed young man whose own nakedness represented abject humiliation. What might have been Paradise was in fact Hell. A Hell of their making: a Hell of *his* making.

Despite his humiliation, Chris fixed his eyes on the women, *willing* that anger, hatred and loathing would subdue any other thoughts, any other feelings. Any other instincts…

Music began to pulse. It was *'Fever'* that blared out, from speakers everywhere. The girls began to dance, slowly at first, then gaining pace and rhythm, gyrating round, and round, the grim, straining, sweating figure of Chris.

'Oh, no!' he cried. 'Christ, no!' "Look, girls!' said a faux-startled

Miriam: 'It seems we're being appreciated at last! Summer, is it right that he gave you a six-and-a-half? Looks at least a seven, from where I'm standing!' Summer laughed: 'Young man: I think you may be enjoying this too much! Have we scored a ten? Just a couple more close ups, then: smile for the birdie…'

Chris let out a horrible groan, a groan born of shame and disgust, then burst into tears; the hot tears of abject humiliation. 'There, there…let's just wipe your… runny… nose…'

Miriam mused: 'What do you think, Claire, Summer? What's your score?' They conferred. 'Chris, don't worry. We're giving you a five and a quarter – I mean a 5.25.' The girls whooped in laughter. 'Guess what the .25's for!'

The spectacle concluded, the women hurriedly dressed, in a business-like fashion. Chris shrank in his chair. He wished he could disappear into thin air. The shame; the endless shame…

'We're off, now!' said Summer. 'We'll leave you with the scissors. See you soon… Miriam, don't forget the camera!'

Miriam, on the brink of elated departure, turned to the man, smiling, and brandishing the camera in the air: 'Yes, see you soon…in fact, every Internet clickety click!'

Sobbing, but left alone in his misery, the man – Chris – quickly cut through the bonds that had restrained him. And then curled up on the hard floor; and wept. Uncontrollably.

THE MAGIC MONEY TREE

One fine day, Joseph Wood made an astonishing discovery. More incredible, even, than the sudden, fabulous riches unearthed at Klondike, or the Comstock Lode. For 50-year old spinster Wood had found what all the world desired – a Magic Money Tree.

At first, Wood's family had merely laughed at his apparently preposterous claim. How absolutely ridiculous! How absurd! Wood's brothers, sister, and even their offspring had humoured him; even patronised him. Joseph had felt rebuffed. Snubbed; belittled. He would show the sneering bastards! Now, a mere handful of years later, Wood's family were bitter; angry, jealous, resentful. It might have been so different...

The source of Wood's almost surreal good fortune was a magnificent, 400 year-old English oak tree that resided deep in his spacious but rather unkempt back garden. On several occasions Wood had thought about seeking permission to have the ancient giant felled. True, it was handsome, as well as ancient; but, particularly in the Summer, it did block out an awful lot of light; and in Winter's gails the tree seemed to roar in distress. If the damned thing keeled over it would bring the house down with it...

Joseph Wood lived in a quiet way, with a modest, unadventurous life-style. Wood worked in the warehouse of his local supermarket. He had learned to be frugal, and parsimonious, taking full advantage of the staff discount on his weekly shopping. Joseph's diet, too, was unadventurous; he drank a little, and smoked even less. Very occasionally, he might indulge himself with a flutter on the horses – the Grand National, maybe, or the Derby. But, since these occasional bets rarely resulted in any success, such activity remained confined to the margins of Wood's daily life.

The Spring of 2018 had proved unusually warm, and Wood began to enjoy sunny mornings in a rocking chair, seated beneath the spreading arms of the giant oak. The tree, Wood grudgingly agreed, *did* provide a comforting presence, and welcome shade. On one particular morning, musing over the sports pages of his daily newspaper, a strong, persistent thought lodged in Joseph's brain. The thought suggested: '*Beta Boy*' – Kempton. Wood's face registered a frown. Where had *that* come from? Looking down, Wood saw the name '*Beta Boy*', a 7-1 shot, in the 3.30 at Kempton Park. He laughed; a laugh that signified 'don't be a clown!' Surely not? But then his mind persisted: how curious! Maybe a strange coincidence – he had never heard of '*Beta Boy*' before…but worth a fiver? Wood popped into a bookie's on his way to work; then thought no more about it.

It was not until masticating his evening meal – a pork chop, with mashed potatoes and greens – that Joseph remembered his bet. Blow me! The damn thing had won! Next morning Joseph collected his winnings – a very handy 35 quid, minus tax. Not a king's ransom, but welcome all the same. And the sense of satisfaction was almost palpable.

Days later, gently rocking in his chair, Joseph became aware of a stimulating charge surging through his brain. It seared '*Minoan Maid*' across his consciousness. Quickly checking, he found that this horse was running at Wolverhampton that very evening. But, in an eight-horse race, '*Maid*' was a ten to one outsider. He shrugged. Why ever not? This time, a ten pound bet was laid and, later that evening, Wood took a keen interest in discovering the result. Blimey! She'd won! That was a 100 smackeroons to the good!

What on Earth was going on? Was this purely coincidence, good luck, or something more? A secret power...? He really must find out; get to the bottom of it, for good or ill. A further 'chill' in his favourite chair quickly resulted in words appearing, as if by magic, in Joseph's mind. They said: '*Lucky Lana*', Ascot. The horse was quoted at 5/1. Not great – but worth a twenty quid punt. Such was Joseph Wood's nervous excitement that he couldn't bear to watch the race on TV, but quickly checked the result on the Internet. Success! He had discovered Alchemy! He could turn lead into gold! But how? What was the secret of his power? Surely not the bloody chair? And, no, not some sort of innate genius, or God-given inspiration. And then the truth dawned…it must be the tree!

Joseph tested his theory. He sat beneath the tree. Seconds later, '*Sweet Dreams*' entered his mind. Sure enough, '*Sweet Dreams*' was an entry in the 4 o'clock at Worcester. The horse was second favourite at 3/1, but what the heck? Maybe worth 50 quid? '*Sweet Dreams*' romped home by seven lengths. Joseph gave the giant tree a great, smiling hug.

This was getting to be fun. Maybe a little scary; certainly exciting. It was at this point that, unable to keep his own counsel any longer, Wood blurted his good news to his family. News that was met with disbelief – even derision. A bloody magic money tree? Just what had he been smoking? Or maybe early-onset dementia? Silly old fool! A chastened Joseph vowed never to mention the tree, or his new-found enthusiasm for gambling – for *winning* – to anyone, ever again.

The pattern of events continued. But the outline expanded, and diversified. Bigger bets. And not just on racing – but football, cricket, even greyhound racing. And using a range of different gambling platforms – since Joseph risked being outlawed by outraged betting firms – becoming a victim of his own success. And the money just kept rolling in; cascading down: predictably, remorselessly; endlessly.

Joseph gave up his job. They were sad to see him go: he had been loyal, and dependable, for more than twenty years. But what the heck? He was quickly forgotten. Joseph was now a free man. He swapped the Ford Focus for a Ferrari. He bought luxury houses, on the beach-front in Majorca, and the Caribbean. In fact, Joseph spent more and more freely – but always on his own luxuries, his own enjoyment: his own pleasures.

Joseph began to grow immensely rich on the back of his tree's genius for, as quickly as he spent his winnings, they were replenished with yet more. Soon, however, Joseph Wood became insatiable; he never had enough wealth. And irascible. For Joseph could not afford to be away from home for too long...he needed the bloody tree's invaluable, infallible advice. For the tree had never failed.

Then, three years in, the tree stopped co-operating. Words and phrases stopped – refused to enter Joseph's eagerly receptive mind. At first Joseph was puzzled; confused. Then he became furious. How dare the tree! It was *his* tree! In his garden! 'Serve me!' he commanded. 'Or die!' One day, Wood bought a huge axe, and smote the bark-fissured torso with a mighty blow. A chunk of bark flew off the tree, leaving an angry gash on its ancient trunk. Wood threatened the tree: 'if you let me down again I promise I'll kill you – it'll be a chain saw next time!'

The very next day, the veteran oak again provided a pulse into Wood's eager, inviting mind. West Bromwich Albion, 3/1 against Leicester, away. Sounded bloody improbable. Was this a trick? Was he being conned? Overcoming his reservations, Wood placed a £1,000 bet at 20/1. 3/1 was indeed the final score – West Brom scoring twice in extra time. Wood received his winnings with a quiet satisfaction. All was well again with the world.

Wood continued his extravagant, spendthrift lifestyle. Money multiplied, made more money. It all stuck to Joseph, and his extravagance; his extraordinary, spendthrift lifestyle. Fabulous apartments, luxury holidays, limited edition watches – even a yacht. The relatives – at first scornful, then dismissive, then bemused – were no longer laughing. They were furious; they were seething. Why had this selfish monster not shared his good fortune with his down-at-heel brothers, his sister, or even his nephews and nieces? How much money did the old sod need? Worse, Joseph simply binned the plethora of begging letters received from those who had watched his wealth burgeon, even while they were bemused at its source. Eventually, and to his dismay, the secretive tycoon was listed in *The Sunday Times Rich List* – the source of his wealth described as 'sophisticated financial engineering.' Meanwhile, scores of appeals by charities – in the realms of research into disease, poverty relief and child welfare – even environmental protection – were scornfully burned in a specially designed incinerator.

One fine day, Joseph, glass of fine claret in hand, sat gloomily beneath the magic tree. He had everything he could ever need, if he lived to eternity. So why was he not happy? Another car, perhaps? Another luxury cruise? No – he could never go too far, for too long, because he needed the thrill of winning ever more money; of seeking help from that bloody tree. He hated it. Perhaps he should kill the bugger off. Serve it right. It was only a tree, after all. Really, thought Wood, it was *he* who was the genius. How could such wisdom come from a frigging tree? In a flash of seething anger, the multi-millionaire took up the giant axe, and smashed its blade deep into the bark of the trunk. The tree groaned, and a surge of electricity, with the power of a hundred headaches, pulsed through his head. The raw, red lettering that burned into Wood's skull spelt: 'SELFISH BASTARD!' Joseph cried out, in torment, and helpless fury.

Then, to his horror, he heard the tree groan, and lurch violently. There was a great roar, as the whole, huge organism lurched ground-wards with an almighty crack, like a thunderclap; the earth itself shuddered. Joseph's house was crushed beneath the falling monster. Joseph himself was trapped beneath the immense trunk, screaming and cursing. Joseph Wood died alone and in agony, before help could be summoned.

Wood died intestate. He had had no intention of dying. A grateful nation accepted his immense estate, in aid of servicing the national debt. As for the tree, it was dismembered by a team of tree surgeons, and transported to a sawmill. The timber sold for a few hundred pounds: as firewood – heating a few homes, fitfully, for a few days. Giving a little cheer, briefly, to a few, grateful souls. The tree's magic disappeared with the wood-smoke. But the legend of a magic money tree refused to die…

OBSESSION

George Flanders was not a happy man.

On the face of it, there was no reason for his wretched state of mind. Although George had recently celebrated his 80th birthday, he owned a handsome house in the scenic Cotswolds, drove an Aston Martin, and was very comfortably off. To cap it all, George remained in robust good health. A member of golf club and tennis club, George seemed to epitomise the good life, and oozed relaxed good humour, *bonhomie,* and middle-class charm.

However, a closer examination of George's life would have quickly revealed the cracks beneath the surface. His wife of some 50 years, Wendy, had passed away five years ago, now. George and Wendy had had no children. Although there were a scattering of relatives and friends, none were what might be termed 'close'. Although there were many, many 'acquaintances', of varying degrees of reliability and depth, in reality there were no longer any true, long-term friendships. One by one, George's life-time friends had fallen aside, victims to life's inevitable vicissitudes: heart disease, cancer, dementia; alcoholism. There would be no-one with whom to share old age, or to comfort and share in whatever time might still be forthcoming.

George's 80th had been celebrated at his local, *The Green Lion,* with twenty or so 'friends' from his sports clubs, a few relatives on his late wife's side of the family, and a neighbour or two. Though an enjoyable evening – with a rousing speech given by Dave, his main tennis-partner, good food and wine, and plenty of good-natured, but inevitably optimistic banter about the future – George returned home feeling lonely and depressed. It was late May, with Spring foliage at its most prolific and luxurious, and the evenings drawing out invitingly. Should he decamp to the chalet in North Wales for a few days sea air at Barmouth, or just relax in the (manicured) garden here, at Chipping Sodbury? Choices, always choices.

Though George's diary was pretty full, there was nothing that could not be changed, in an instant. There were no permanent fixtures, or obligations. George's time – that is, whatever he had left – was his own.

The problem was – women. George missed their company; their closeness. Their intimacy. In fact, this need burned fiercely within him. George kept telling himself that he was now 80 years of age. He had known, experienced, and appreciated the companionship of a loving, caring, woman all of his adult life. Was there really time to open a new chapter? Even if there was – time – dare he embrace that time? Should he, rather, suppress these awkward and untimely yearnings? But George's latent desires stirred deep within him, gnawed at his being: they would not be suppressed; would not go away.

George thought to himself – with a wry smile – that he was regarded as a 'catch'. A catch, that is, for any 65 or 70 year-old widow or divorcée, who desired a comfortable life-style, and the prospect of an impressive inheritance. And who did not? And there was always a Jonathan, and Miriam – the deserving, insufferably entitled, but inevitably hard-up, 40 year-old children – waiting in the wings. George, as he assured himself daily, was no mug, even if some of his neighbours – and 'friends' – seemed keen to take advantage of his advancing years. No: gaga he was not. But, quite aside from these financial considerations, George simply did not fancy another tour of the track. His marriage to Wendy, despite the inevitable ups and downs, had been a lifetime's mission. Done that, seen that, experienced all that marriage had to offer. No need – no point – in a repeat performance.

It was true that George had dabbled – if 'dabbled' is the right term – with a number of women in the last few years. Lunch dates and dinner dates, with different women at various times – all very pleasant, very convivial – but the motivations – and expectations – all too apparent. Sex would have been easy – but, again, with expectations attached. George remembered a story about white, middle class America from the '50s: that an evening with a girl decorating the Christmas tree was tantamount to an engagement.

George's problem – and the secret behind his unhappiness – was that there were beautiful women everywhere. But they were not *his* women. Staring down from billboards. Gazing from magazine covers. Appearing every evening on television, in dramas, or even on 'soaps'. And then there was the Internet, where veritable multitudes of young women seemed eager to reveal everything to the impatient camera.

But George knew that these women were not 'real'. They were glossy paper; they were lit screens; they were an amalgamation of pixels. Yet the women who he passed in the street while walking, or driving his car, were real women: women with real bodies, with real lives, who were out shopping, commuting to work, jogging, or on some other secret mission whose purpose mystified but thoroughly absorbed him. It was one of these delectable creatures that George desired to meet – to know; to – yes, *love*.

George was an 80 year-old in a thirty year-old – OK – grudgingly – fifty year-old, body. Rather vainly, when looking in the mirror, George fancied that he could pass for maybe 70. True, there was grey hair, and a few wrinkles, but he looked distinguished and, he said to himself with a wry smile, everything still functioned. But, clearly, he could not pass for bloody *thirty*. What he really wanted, yearned for, was beauty; freshness; youth. But how, exactly? Who in his preferred age group could *possibly* fancy him? James Bond in a bath chair didn't have the same cachè. George knew plenty of 70 year-old women; a bevy of 60 year-olds, even. And a sprinkling of 50 year-olds. But certainly no thirty year-olds – and twenty year-olds were an extinct species within George's personal orbit.

He needed to meet someone; to get to know someone. But again, how? There were several routes available, of varying degrees of attractiveness and suitability, that George might consider. He might join a dating agency. He might 'research' the Internet for a suitable 'model', and contact her via any one of a number of social media platforms. He might discreetly ask former business contacts for telephone or online contacts for suitable, er, women, who might welcome him, either by virtue of their situation, or indeed their profession. He could book a trip to an exotic location, and enjoy a freedom denied him in his home village – so impersonal, but so interconnected. For many months, George fretted within himself, waiting and wondering. But none of these options appealed; in fact, they appalled. In desperation, George confided to some of his sporting buddies – in his best 'throw-away' manner – that he was seeking additional domestic help: maybe a student; maybe an 'Intern'…

Then, suddenly, miraculously, George's labyrinthine thought processes and stratagems were overtaken by events, rather like Alexander the Great's solution to the Gordian Knot. One boringly overcast Tuesday morning, there was a polite rap on George's front door. His first thought was double glazing, or maybe an irresistible offer of a new gas boiler, or loft insulation. No: almost miraculously, there stood the most exquisite young woman, her eyes and mouth smiling in his direction.

George smiled, too. 'Yes?' he said. 'Can I help you?'

A picture of perfection beamed back at him. 'Hi, sorry to bother you, but someone in the village said you might have some odd jobs that need doing?'

The gorgeous vision standing before him was wearing a white T-shirt and black slacks. They hid everything; yet they hid nothing. George looked again for a moment, and suppressed a sigh.

He smiled again. 'You'd better come in!' George added, quietly, while his eyes swept the drive. 'I'll put the kettle on.' When they were settled, George asked a few pertinent questions. 'My name is Georgia' – 'What a coincidence!' 'I've recently graduated from Worcester Uni.'

'In what, exactly?' George probed. 'Paleontology', she replied. 'But it's hard to find a job, messing about with old bones.' George laughed, despite himself. 'On the contrary, you've come to exactly the right place!' It transpired that Georgia had done some waitressing, and a bit of modelling – nothing beyond lingerie – 'of course,' George affirmed, in an avuncular tone – to supplement her student income. But now she needed work – work that would pay her way, and give her some satisfaction.

Hardly believing his luck, but wisely raining in his premature hopes of dreams fulfilled, George tersely explained his own position. He was a widower, living on his own. He had a woman come in twice a week to help with cleaning, and to see to the laundry. And a gardener chap who came once a week to mow the lawns and generally keep things tidy. But, yes, he did need some sort of housekeeper – to generally help him maintain his home, and 'keep on top of things.'

Georgia responded with alacrity. 'I'm your girl!' The details were quickly settled. Georgia would be paid £1500 per month, for a 30 hour week. She would, of course, continue to live with her parents, in the village. George – not entirely throwing caution to the wind – asked for references. If these were quickly forthcoming, and satisfactory, Georgia could start the following week. All things settled, Georgia thanked George profusely, climbed into her battered Ford Focus, and scuttled down the drive.

George allowed himself a moment of quiet reflection. Perhaps he was being rash, foolhardy, even. And, of course, there was no mention – how could there be? – of romance, or sexual favours. No; these matters, pressing though they were to George, must remain firmly on the back-burner. Softly, softly, catchee monkey, he heard himself whisper. No: it would be a constant delight just to have Georgia around. To talk with her. To observe her in different outfits. To admire her face and figure. To watch her move…

The references received were glowing. Georgia seemed, in every respect, the model young woman: intelligent, honest, and reliable. As though to underline these credentials, she arrived promptly on the following Monday morning to begin her new role. Georgia quickly familiarised herself with the five-bedroomed house, and with George's particular needs and preferences. Almost inevitably, following Wendy's death, domestic arrangements had been left to 'slip' a little.

Georgia quickly proved herself to be efficient, diligent, and caring. When all the tasks were completed, Georgia might make a coffee, or fix a sandwich, and she and George would talk: about his life and career, about his views on any number of subjects; even about his marriage. Georgia was a sympathetic listener, and seemed to enjoy George's long tales about his career and rise to local prominence (he had owned a car-dealership, and been a local Councillor for ten years). In both practical and emotional terms, Georgia soon made herself invaluable. And, as if that were not enough, there was the added frisson of speaking to, and looking at, a young woman whose beauty almost hurt her eyes.

So indispensable did Georgia prove, and so great was George's reliance upon her, that George became jealous and irritable when Georgia left the house, as she did at 3.00 o'clock every afternoon. 'Do you have a boyfriend, Georgia? He'll be a lucky chap!' Georgia would always laugh away such questioning. 'I know loads of guys. But none of them' – an elegant finger touching George's waistcoat – 'as splendid as you!' Such reassurances delighted George, though he knew that Georgia was humouring him, in a delightfully feminine way.

From time to time George would press expensive presents upon Georgia: a sapphire necklace; a finely wrought gold bracelet; a Hermes handbag. Georgia would always thank him profusely, but always politely decline his generosity. What would people think? That she was a kept woman? George's mistress? No: let's not spoil things: let's keep it simple, and professional. Whatever happened between them was Georgia's gift. Georgia did not wish to consider herself a 'bought' woman; still less did she wish to appear as a trophy on George's arm at some pathetic civic bash. George respected Georgia's disinterestedness, even while his feelings for her, his passion to claim her, grew almost unbearable.

On a certain, memorable day, Georgia gazed directly at George, and sighed. 'Is everything OK?' he asked, solicitously. 'I've been thinking.' 'Yes?' George responded. 'Sometimes, I'm aware that you're looking at me…In a certain way. Are you sure there's nothing else I could do for you?' She looked at George, intently, seeming to widen her eyes; questioning. He stared back, hesitating to declare the truth. 'You already do so much for me…' In that moment, if she had not known before, Georgia knew *now*. George was her man. She placed delicate, warm hands on George's shoulders, and kissed him on the mouth. 'George. I won't be a kept woman. I need my independence. I'm not a trophy. I'm not going to be paraded about. And I don't want your money. But I give you myself, freely. I will be your woman.'

George was delirious with pleasure and, hugging Georgia tightly, shed warm tears on her face and neck.

Later that week, after moving a few essentials from her parents *petite*, cluttered, semi, Georgia moved into George's spacious home; albeit occupying a separate bedroom, complete with *en suite*. Georgia's mum and dad were happy, indeed delighted, with the new arrangements. Parents George and Georgia, (strangely enough), were satisfied that their daughter was responsibly and respectably situated – in supporting a frail old gent who, apparently, could hardly dress himself, or boil an egg. And Georgia would, they preened, have her very own bedroom, and her very own bathroom. And, in the fullness of time, they reasoned, Georgia would have enough money saved to be able to participate in one of those exciting digs – maybe on the Jurassic Coast, or even Arizona.

Appearances did indeed need to be maintained – to parents, friends, and the ever-suspecting world – even if the reality was that George was now experiencing the height of human bliss. Georgia would still leave the house around 3.00 o'clock most days, either to go shopping, or to visit friends. But she would always return, after darkness fell. George now became pretty sanguine about this arrangement; they gave him time to relax, recuperate, and reflect delightfully on his great good fortune. And to anticipate the pleasures soon to come. For months, for years, even, George was blessed, and his mind and body responded with joy and exhilaration to a generous and freely-given partnership – a partnership apparently made in heaven.

A full three years later, George and Georgia indulged in a particularly energetic and intense session of love-making. Georgia had promised something special a day or two earlier, and George made sure he was absolutely prepared, and 'up for it'. For George the experience was sensational or, as today's kids might say, 'awesome'. He had never experienced such utterly perfect, seismic pleasure. Shortly afterwards, Georgia rose, showered, dressed and left the house, to go clubbing in Birmingham, with friends. It was 11.00pm; the night was still young.

Georgia returned at 9.00am the following morning. It was a bright, sunny day in early June. Yet the house seemed silent, still; cold. And there was no sign of George. 'George, are you there? I'm back!' she called out. There was no reply. Georgia raced up to his bedroom, to find George, apparently asleep, but stone cold. Georgia called an emergency ambulance, but nothing could be done. George had suffered a massive heart attack shortly after her departure.

With commendable, typical, efficiency, Georgia made all the funeral arrangements, and George was buried, with due solemnity, two weeks later. Such was Georgia's efficiency – and economy – that the undertakers, Dunn & Dusted, presented her with a bouquet, and a 10% discount. Georgia herself penned the glowing 'tribute', although it was delivered by a celebrant. More than 200 mourners crammed into the small church, to give George a splendid 'send off', along with Frank Sinatra belting out 'My Way'. To a man, the male mourners, churning out 'All things bright and beautiful' were crowing, in their hearts, 'George you lucky, ba-a-stard…'

Although he left some small bequests to charity, and to his sporting chums, the bulk of George's Estate passed to Georgia – the main beneficiary of his Will. It was Georgia, after all, who had brought comfort, and joy, to his old age. But the wheel turned full circle when, a few weeks following the funeral, Georgia married Jamie (Jamie?), and they moved into George's house. A few changes of decor and furnishings maybe – Georgia had never liked the curtains, or the wall-paper in the master-bedroom – but otherwise perfect.

And Jamie was bowled over with the Aston – he'd only ever driven Georgia's battered old Ford Focus.

George Flanders' ancient life had ended in a climax, as he would have wished; and his remains were buried, wrapped in pomp and circumstance. Now Georgia's young adult life could begin in earnest. That big, paleontological dig, awaited. All was well; and so ends well.

UNIVERSITY CHALLENGE

It's late September, and Freshers' Week, at Donfield University. Professor James Morrison is about to welcome half a dozen new undergraduates into his cosy den on the fringe of the Philosophy Department. Prof. Morrison's door, complete with brass plate, is ajar in silent readiness.

At the dot of 2.00pm six young people, smiling appreciatively, edge shyly into the Professor's office. 'Welcome all!' beams the Professor. 'Please make yourself comfortable!' The Professor introduces himself; 'but please call me Jim...'

One by one the students introduce themselves as: Hannah, Noah, Sunita, Thomas, Barclay and Imogen.

'Well,' said the Professor, 'I'll be one of your tutors for the new academic year. I very much look forward to working with you. I hope you'll find Philosophy the most fascinating subject of study. And I hope you find the learning environment, and the syllabus, stimulating and enjoyable. Of course, there will be a lot of hard work. But, if you're enjoying your time here, you'll find the work will be that much easier...'

'The point of this first, rather informal, session is to get to know each other a little better. And to do this we have a – hopefully fun – mind-stretching exercise, that I hope you'll enjoy. Now, I'm pretty sure you're all ambitious – because, after all, you're here: you have keen plans for a bright future. You want to make a difference. Right? So, though you're young – believe me, a good place to be – you will already have dreams for the future.'

'So, we're going to discuss: 'Our best time – ever!' I'll join in with my own – but, you'll understand,' said the Professor, stroking his streaked goatee beard, 'my best ever days may be behind me! However, I'm sure that yours lie straight ahead. I don't want to pick on anyone who may still be thinking about this, so do please let me know when you're ready…'

Hannah cleared her throat. 'Yes, Hannah?' smiled the Professor. 'I'm Hanna Shepherd. I'm from Nottingham, and I'm a huge fan of Formula 1 Racing.'

'Really? How interesting,' smiled the Prof. 'I wonder which driver, which team, you follow? But please do carry on, er, Hannah.'

Hannah's eyes moistened. 'That'll be Lewis, of course; best ever,' she said firmly. And Mercedes. 'As for my favourite time… Well, I've never actually attended a Formula One race. The tickets are so expensive. And then there's the travel and accommodation costs, if I'm travelling abroad, with my family. So, to be honest, we simply can't afford to go. I always watch on TV. I've thought long and hard about this since I was a schoolgirl: my dream is to attend the Monaco Grand Prix. I'd watch the race – whizzing along the sun-drenched streets of Monte Carlo – from the balcony of the Hotel Mirabeau. And I'd have a glass of champagne in my hand to toast the start, and to celebrate the finish.' Hanna's voice began to crack, and her eyes moisten again, as she neared the end of her story. 'But it doesn't end there. My plan would be to attend every F1 event, in every scheduled country – including Italy and Brazil.'

Jim Morrison quickly jumped in, to stifle any wayward comments. 'Thank you so much, Hannah. Absolutely fascinating. Let me assure you that your dream is perfectly achievable. It can happen – and I'm sure that it will. Any positive thoughts, anyone?'

All but Noah shook their heads; they were contemplating the telling of their own stories, with some apprehension. But Noah, taking the Professor's hint, simply said: 'sounds awesome!'

'Well,' said the Professor with a knowing smile, 'we're in Monaco at the moment. Or possibly Rio. So where are we going, what are we doing, next?'

'May I go next, please?' enquired Sunita, gently. 'But of course,' returned the Professor, with unfeigned enthusiasm. 'I'm delighted that you all have such finely worked-through ambitions. Sunita?'

'I'm Sunita, from Wolverhampton. Although I've never been there, my grandparents came to the UK from Sri Lanka. Until 1960, Sri Lanka was called Ceylon. I'd like to return to the country for an extended visit – we still have family there. But, in the course of my life, I'd like to visit every country on the planet that begins with a 'C'.'

'Wow,' said the Professor. 'How many countries would that be?'

'Twenty,' replied Sunita. 'They include Canada, Cambodia, Columbia, Costa Rica, and Congo. All so different, so diverse – so culturally amazing.'

'I see,' said Prof Morrison, 'that sounds quite wonderful. Challenging, of course – but that's the point. Perfectly do-able, in the modern age, with ambition and drive. And I'm sure, Sunita, you have those qualities in abundance. Any questions?' Hannah looked up, still appearing a little fazed. 'That sounds really great, Sunita. But why countries beginning with C?'

'Well, Hannah, when I was studying geography for my GCSEs, there were certain countries I felt drawn to, for all sorts of different reasons. Maybe it was the topography. Maybe it was the culture. Or maybe it was the wildlife. And it just so happened that most of them began with 'C'. So I thought to myself, could I possibly visit them all?'

The Professor jumped in: 'And your conclusion was?' 'I concluded that, if I made the right life-choices that, yes, it might be possible...'

'Well, thank you so much, Sunita. Quintessential point, that – making the right life-choices. We'll come back to that crucial issue, again and again, during our studies. This is becoming rather fascinating...'

Thomas raised his hand. 'No need for formalities, Thomas,' said the Prof. 'Please do share your dreams – or your proposals – with us.'

'My family are from Sussex. But every year we holiday in the Scottish Highlands, and roam around some of the most beautiful, remote countryside on the planet. My aspiration is to climb every Munro in Scotland, preferably before I'm thirty.'

'Munro?' quizzed the Professor.

'That's a mountain over 3,000 feet, in old money,' laughed Thomas. 'There's 282 of them, to be precise, scattered across the Scottish Highlands. A Reverend Robertson first 'bagged' them all in 1901.'

'Blimey,' puffed the Prof, 'I've done some climbing in my time – including Ben Nevis. But that's something else! Again, though, provided you have the time, energy and fitness, eminently doable. Yes, Imogen?'

'*Why?*' said Imogen, with a shrug of her shoulders. 'I mean, why isn't the scenery enough? Why all the climbing?'

Thomas's sunny features became darkened by a frown. 'I suppose it's a fusion of factors,' he replied, carefully. 'There's the excitement of the challenge – and of actually reaching each summit. There's the physical exhilaration of stretching body – and mind – beyond where they've gone before. And, yes, there's the scenery – I'll be documenting every trip, every view, including all the fauna and flora that we encounter.'

'We?' enquired the Professor. 'Yes,' said Thomas. 'Some of

these peaks can be dangerous, particularly in unpredictable weather. It would be foolhardy to go alone, even with modern equipment and technology. A twisted ankle, even, and you're in big trouble. Miles and miles from anywhere. Probably not even a phone signal. So, at various times, I'd either be accompanied by my brother, or a friend.' Thomas looked around. 'Maybe someone from here.' Noah laughed: 'count me in,' he added, brightly.

Professor Morrison looked up. 'Great stuff, Thomas. How exhilarating. Any further thoughts, anyone?'

'I really see it now,' added Imogen, with a smile. 'I mean it, count me in,' shot Noah, with breathless enthusiasm. 'Thanks, that's great!' said Thomas, winningly.

'So, Noah', asked Jim Morrison, 'before or after the Munros, how about you?'

'That's easy', responded Noah, 'I want to travel to the moon.' Noah waited for a reaction, but there was none. He went on: 'I'm from Mansfield, but over the next twenty years, flights to the moon will become quite common – a regular occurrence. There'll be commercial flights, available to the general public, and it should become increasingly affordable. I want to be on one of those first flights. I want to experience the thrill of space travel, of going to another world, a world of mystery, and silence.'

'That's quite an ambition, Noah, but I'm sure it will be possible,' said the Professor. 'You have all the time in the world. You just need to prepare, and be ready.'

Sunita laughed. 'I'll look out for a planet beginning with 'C'! Somewhere beyond the solar system!'

'OK, well,' stammered the Professor, 'I'm delighted to see such imagination, such ambition. So who's going next?'

Imogen responded. 'Hi, I'm Imogen, from Stratford. Upon-Avon, that is. Apparently, someone quite famous preceded me.' There was a tinkle of laughter.

'I want to follow in the footsteps of Lord Byron, and explore

Venice – the *real* Venice. Byron lived in Venice for five years, from 1816 to 1821. His experience there was extraordinary – at once infamous, but also revelatory. I'll explore the hidden alleyways by gondola, explore dimly lit palazzos by night, and attend masked balls by candlelight.'

'Sounds incredible,' offered the Professor. 'Yes,' continued Imogen; 'and, while taking various handsome lovers, I'll complete Byron's unfinished 'Don Juan.'

'Extraordinary!' added Morrison, clearing his throat. 'Any thoughts, anyone?' 'Crikey', asked Noah, 'can I come too?'

'I think you have your hands full as it is, what with moons and Munros,' laughed the Professor. 'OK, we're nearly done. What a revelation this has been! Barclay, I think it must be your turn?'

'Thanks' said Barclay, with a sharp intake of breath. 'I've been amazed by what I've heard. Truly inspired. But I fear that I'm going to disappoint. I've always loved sunrises. And sunsets. Every one beautiful. Every one, different. Like the very first dawn – ever. Or maybe the last sunset. For me, to witness the rising sun – or the departing sun – is the most sublime experience. These events are immortal: they'll continue long after mankind has disappeared from the Earth. So, I'd like to experience sunrises, and sunsets, on every Continent on Earth – including Antarctica. That's it, really…hope it's not too bland.'

'Too bland?' asked the Professor, incredulously. 'Anything but! Any questions?'

There was a circle of blank faces. Then Noah whispered 'awesome.' And Imogen asked: 'So how many Continents are there? Stupid question, I know.'

'No, it's not stupid at all' responded Barclay. 'The number is still being debated – for example, some scientists don't consider Europe to be a separate Continent. But most scientists would say that there are seven. If you include Antarctica.'

'Many thanks, Barclay. Awesome, indeed. But thank you all so much,' enjoined Professor Morrison. 'I do hope you've all got as much out of this session as I have. I hope that your ambitions have now become real, and that you can see the way to realising them. And we'll see how they change, as we work and study together over the next three years. You have everything on your side: youth, energy, ambition, talent, opportunity…'

'What about money?' laughed Noah.

'That's the least of your worries,' smiled the Prof. 'With everything else, money will come. It is important, but not the be-all and end-all. Love, friendship, health, career choices, are key. Money will follow your dreams – don't make it your dream. And, talking of friendship, today could be a new beginning – he looked around – to make a host of new friends. OK? Shall we wrap up?'

'But Prof…Jim,' corrected Hannah: 'what about *your* very best experience?' The Professor hesitated. 'Very well,' he intimated. 'Though I'm not sure I can compete…' There was a buzz of concurrence, and eager anticipation.

'OK. You will understand that I speak about the past, rather than the future. I am, after all, 58 years of age. My chief ambition was to find my perfect soul mate. There had been a number of failed attempts – fun, but frustrating. Think about it for a second. Anyone between the ages of 20 and 30 will 'enjoy' around 86,000 physical hours, in total; of course, we will spend many of those hours asleep, or performing mundane tasks, or even working. And, at any one time, there's around half a billion – that's 500 million – young women in that age group, inhabiting this spinning planet. So finding one's soul mate – a life's ambition – provides both an opportunity, and a dilemma. So where to start? And how to continue?

Then, in June, 1990, I found myself sitting on a beach in northern Italy: in my hand a delicious ice cream – purchased from a beach vendor, seconds before. How I was looking forward to it! All around me, beautiful people, in various states of relaxation. Suddenly – and I'm surrounded by beautiful women, in swimsuits and bikinis – the most astonishing woman I've ever seen strolls on to the beach. How I know that I don't know; I just *know* that she's sensational. Though it's broiling hot, she's wearing shades and a fur coat. A full-length fur coat! And with a be-suited minder each side, also wearing shades; and trilbies.

And, guess what? She comes and sits right by me, greets me with 'ciao, baby' in the most delightful accent, then licks the top off my – virgin – ice cream.' The Professor laughs at the memory. 'Well, three weeks later, Francesca and I were married. We still are. The most extraordinary experience of my life, burned on my retina, my mind – my very soul – for all time.'

'Francesca was – is – an actress. OK,' he laughed – 'further revelations next week. Along with Kant and Wittgenstein. In the meantime, have a ponder. Reflect. It's a sound basis for life, and for living. Then *carpe diem* – seize the day!'

ELIZABETH'S CONDITION

Life was good, and I was feeling in excellent spirits; champion, in fact. My doctor had recently confirmed that Thomas Manning, then aged 32, was in tremendous shape, and would probably live to be a hundred. I had just come into a quite unexpected and life-changing inheritance, and had recently met, and fallen in love with, the most exquisite creature – Miss Elizabeth Smith. Life was just ticketty-boo. Really couldn't get much better. A template for the future. Just give me excess of it. And then some more.

I had met Elizabeth almost by chance. I was a lecturer in English Literature at a provincial college. Elizabeth was involved in an official inspection from the Government Inspectorate, and briefly joined my class – on John Keats – to observe my style, and the quality of my teaching. Apparently, she was impressed. So was I – in fact, so impressed that I could hardly concentrate on *Ode to a Nightingale*. I might well have been inspired. Put the blush into 'blushful hippocrene', as it were. In any case, I would, over time, study Elizabeth as a student of Raphael might study his glorious *Madonna in the Meadow*. Or the student of Manet might study his iconic *Olympia*. But first impressions on that first brief encounter were enough to completely enamour the young – or not so young – Thomas Manning.

Elizabeth was, by far and away, the most gloriously beautiful woman I had ever clapped eyes on. Long jet black hair, framing a perfect face with deep, lustrous, emerald eyes – 'lustrous' – ah, Johnnie Keats again! And features carved as if from Carrera marble. That extraordinary face, and flawless, glowing complexion were quite bewitching. And Elizabeth's fashionable, figure-hugging dress only served to delineate the most exquisite hour-glass figure, that hinted of unimaginable, sensory delights. Superbly shapely long legs emerged from the hem of that lucky dress.

I was not exactly a stranger to the female gender – the 'opposite sex'. Over a decade or so, I had had nine girlfriends – relationships, of various lengths – and they were all great girls – not only good looking, but fun-loving, and really genuine personalities: but I had never quite found 'Miss Right'. Now I had. Oh, yes. And, though she always dressed with immaculate taste, Elizabeth was the only woman I'd ever known who looked even better with her clothes off, than on. Garments, of course, being intended to flatter, as well as cover our modesty.

But I race ahead. We met at Elizabeth's favourite Italian restaurant to enjoy our first date. My excitement was, inevitably, tinged with anxiety. The anxiety dissipated almost immediately; Elizabeth had dressed to impress. No words of mine could amply describe the impact of Elizabeth's appearance, as she greeted me warmly, upon my heightened senses. So I hope you don't mind my borrowing a little poetry – this time from Robert Herrick – which rather proves my point – about *the* point – of clothes. Just substitute 'Eliza' for 'Julia', and forget the scan:

> *Whenas in silks my Julia goes,*
> *Then, then, me thinks how sweetly flows*
> *That liquefaction of her clothes.*
> *Next, when I cast mine eyes and see*
> *That brave vibration each way free;*
> *O how that glittering taketh me!*

One evening, after we'd had dinner at her flat, and a couple of glasses of wine – Elizabeth had then treated me to a shadowy, candle-lit striptease. The gentle candle-light revealed soft shapes and contours, undulating through light, and shade, and semi-shade, blending loveliness with mystery. It – she – was sensational. Did God really make even young, female nudity quite that beautiful? I was overcome; awed with astonishment, with wonder. When the last shreds of chiffon and lace lay breathless on the floor of our suite, Elizabeth, clad solely in her glory, embraced me, whispering: '*dear heart, how like you this?*' I caressed and kissed her, replying: 'my Lady, I like it exceedingly!' The moment was so pure, so perfect, this was not the time to demean it with what might turn out – if I under-performed – to be an anti-climax. I internalised the moment; when the time came to make love to Elizabeth, the experience would be rendered even more special; even more spectacular.

We had dated for a mere four months before I proposed. I was thirty-two. Elizabeth, twenty-four. I was a man in a hurry. While I was no stranger to sex, the sheer specialness of this relationship imbued me with a new-found charm and chivalry. While I could barely keep my hands off this delectable woman, and dreamed of undressing and possessing Elizabeth every night, I was determined to leave her pure, perfect and mysterious until our wedding night. Everything *had* to be perfect; and our wedding night unique and unforgettable. Somewhat to my surprise, Elizabeth did not make this commitment easy, in practice; many a long good-night kiss would leave me groaning with pleasure – and regret.

I had proposed to Elizabeth in nervous, trembling tones. This was an extraordinary moment; one that I was to re-live every single day of my life. For me, a huge, life-changing, life-enhancing deal. To my overwhelming joy, Elizabeth responded with a 'yes.' 'But,' she added, with that engaging smile, 'on one condition.' 'Condition?' I stammered, heart in mouth. 'Anything!' 'That you honour me, and worship my body, every single day.' 'That's a condition!' I responded, incredulously. 'I'm not sure you understand,' she continued, looking into my eyes. 'I want you to love me each and every single day. Without fail, fear or favour.' Suddenly, I understood; and was suitably excited. I glanced down at my tightening trousers, by way of confirmation. Elizabeth followed my eyes, with feigned amusement. 'That's my boy' she averred, with a smile.

Following this whirlwind romance, Elizabeth and I were married at Winchester – St Swithun's Church – one lovely morning towards the end of May. We had enjoyed barely a dozen dates. But I knew that she was the one – the only one – for me. On our second, or maybe third date, I had mentioned my new found wealth – my inheritance from a widowed, childless uncle. Elizabeth's face hardly flickered; she registered the barest of interest. As if I doubted, that had proved the clincher: she was marrying me. For me.

Our nuptials were celebrated by a hundred or so convivial guests. During the Reception, full of gaiety and laughter, my best-man – Johnny Johnson – would glance in Elizabeth's direction, dig me in the ribs and shout in my ear: 'you lucky, lucky bastard!'

Following the Reception, and a raucous, rather drunken exit, Elizabeth and I headed off, via Southampton Airport, to the Italian Lakes: to marvel at the Alpine scenery, and to revel in each other's company, in a delicious honeymoon setting. We landed at Milan airport at three in the morning, and checked into a small but luxurious hotel at Stresa, a picturesque resort on the shores of Lake Maggiore – and a short boat trip from the self-styled 'beautiful' island of Isola Bella. We were just in time for breakfast. The concierge, a young, slim man in immaculate uniform, and with elegantly coiffed hair and roaming eyes, glanced longingly at Elizabeth, before reluctantly returning his attention back to me: blowing out his cheeks, and shaking his head. 'You are on honeymoon?' he asked; more of a lasciviously-infused statement of intent than a question.

A few days later, catching me on my own, the same guy – Fabrizio – confided to me: 'Sophia Loren? Gina Lollobrigida? Isabella Rossellini? I thought they were great. But…'. He patted me on the shoulder, again shook his head, then insisted on shaking my hand. 'I'm shaking hands with a God! United with a Goddess!' he exclaimed, a tad melo-dramatically.

Elizabeth and I rested in the late Spring sunshine most of that first day, luxuriating in the warmth of the elegant terrace, and in each other's company. I will never forget the candle-lit evening dinner that followed that relaxing, sun-kissed day. Oysters. Followed by lobster. Followed by chocolate and ice cream mousse. Elizabeth caressed every single, delectable mouthful, as though it were heavenly ambrosia, while looking intently into my eyes. Delicious food and wine, and sexual arousal, go hand in hand, as it were. Add the most beautiful eyes in the world looking lovingly at me, and the most elegant foot in the world caressing my calf, and the effect was quite overpowering. As we left the dining room, a pretty young waitress slipped a phial into Elizabeth's hand. As we climbed the staircase, I asked 'what on Earth did she give you?' 'Only the finest Italian honey!' 'Why?' 'It's our honeymoon, silly!' she smiled, squeezing my hand. 'And you're about to find out!' 'And there,' she pointed out, through the windows of our suite, 'is a superb full moon, surrounded by stars! Tonight is our night, baby!' It was 10.00pm. We did not emerge until noon the next day.

Elizabeth's body was soft, smooth, silky, supple and superb. She was flawless, and perfect. Her desire and technique took me to more palaces of pleasure than I had ever hitherto experienced. We made love that night many times, in many different ways, exploiting every possible avenue of pleasure. I was astonished by my own stamina, in expert hands, and felt drunk on ecstasy. I remember quoting John Donne to my gorgeous Elizabeth:

> *'If ever any beauty I did see*
> *That I desired and got,*
> *T'was but a dream of thee.'*

No truer words ever spoken, at that moment. I was possessed of a seemingly magical woman, and an apparently magic wand. When we eventually emerged from a foetid bed, I felt exhausted, but not tired; elated, but still hardly satisfied. Elizabeth was a tigress: indefatigable, insatiable, and inexhaustible. Rather like Cleopatra – infinite variety.

The following quite glorious afternoon found us lying on sun-loungers beside the popular, rather crowded, hotel swimming pool. Elizabeth looked simply stunning in a pink bikini. A procession of too-nonchalant men passed by, in a steady stream, trying hard not to too-obviously direct their gaze at the reclining goddess.

Both Elizabeth and I had indulged in a couple of margaritas, and our heads were just a little fuzzy. Suddenly, Elizabeth reached around the back of her bikini top. 'What are you doing?' I asked, lazily. 'I want an all-over tan,' she replied. My senses returned, urgently. 'What! You want a squadron of paparazzi to descend on us this afternoon? Elizabeth: you're for my eyes only. And maybe God's, since he can be credited with the handiwork.' It was intended as a compliment, but Elizabeth flung herself back down, a tad petulantly. The other male guests continued their enthusiastic vigil, but at least my new wife was protecting the finer points of her modesty. Even so, I observed one or two semi-erect members strolling by, in their damp speedos. I lost patience. There was better fun to be had then watching semi-naked men with rictus grins.

'Come on,' I said, grabbing Elizabeth's outstretched hand – 'let's make some poetry!' I paused only long enough to order a couple of fresh cocktails, and we ran hurriedly up the steps to our room. I flung open the full-length double-windows – let the bastards get their fill! – and fell on the giggling Elisabeth, still, briefly, in her bikini. 'Now,' I whispered, 'if you want those guys to cream their pants, make as much noise as you like!' Elizabeth obliged, and played to the gallery. More John Donne followed:

'Licence my roving hands, and let them go,
Before, behind, between, above, below.
O my America! My new-found land,
My kingdom…'

Who cares? We were madly in love, and didn't give a damn who knew.

Our honeymoon was spent exploring the sensory delights of Lake Maggorie, enjoying lakeland strolls, or *passeggiati*. The early-June air was heavy with the perfume of wisteria, bougainvillea, rhododendron, and roses in full bloom. Strolling around the flower-filled, winding streets of Stresa itself, Isola Bella, and Isola Madre, with my glorious, ecstatic young wife was pure, idyllic heaven. Beautiful places attract beautiful people, and a glory, a phantsasmagoria of lovely girls might be seen enhancing the sparkling shores and beach-side promenades. But, inevitably, it was Elizabeth – however she dressed – who drew all the attention, and turned all the heads. This was something I was beginning to become accustomed to, with a mixture of pride and a touch of frustration. Elizabeth was *my* wife; but if she gave a frisson of pleasure to others, if only for a moment, then the world might be – however briefly – a brighter place. Elizabeth, to be sure, was no stranger to such attention, and had a range of mechanisms to deal with unwanted intrusion, depending on circumstances. I greatly admired, not only her person, but her forbearance and intelligence, in graciously accepting, deflecting or disarming the male gaze, and sense of male entitlement, as her judgement decreed.

On the penultimate day of our two-week sojourn of sensory delights, we were crossing the hotel lobby when we were approached by an agitated-looking Fabrizio, twisting a napkin in his hands. 'I wonder, Mr Manning, if I could ask you a big favour?' 'Yes, what?' I replied, a little hesitantly – Elizabeth and I had plans. 'Sadly, you will leave us tomorrow. I wonder, before we lose you, if I might make a portrait of the beautiful Mrs Manning? It would be a real honour!' 'Portrait?' I queried. 'A photographic portrait: I have a Canon camera, and take lots of portraits with it.' 'Well, sure!' responded a smiling Elizabeth. 'But where?' 'Possibly, on the terrace to your suite?' suggested a relieved-sounding Fabrizio, who had been anxiously preparing for this moment and, not unnaturally, was fearful of a reprimand. 'OK. And what would you like me to wear?' 'Anything you choose… at your discretion.' Fabrizio laughed; a little nervous laugh. 'Mrs Manning, you would look amazing in rags!' I looked on, a little side-lined, a little amused. What a lucky bastard I was; let's not play greedy or jealous.

That same afternoon, at four-thirty, Fabrizio turned up at our suite. The slightly reclining sun, melting into rich, golden tones, set a perfect scene on our balcony terrace. Elizabeth came out of the bedroom looking as ravishing as I'd ever seen her, wearing *haute couture*, a figure-hugging and rather daringly-cut emerald crop-top – that complemented my goddess's eyes – and that left her mid-riff bare; and coutured, hip-clinging white skirt. It was clear to me – an expert on the subject – that Elizabeth had dispensed with a bra. Clearly, a quite unnecessary garment. And also, for that matter, discarded her pants, since the skirt closely followed every contour and nuance of her hips and *derriere*.

The happy, grateful young Fabrizio accompanied Elizabeth on to the terrace, and started giving 'directions'. Clearly, in the circumstances, my presence was hardly required, and would probably have proved a dampener in the creation of 'art'. I decided to keep a low profile in our suite, reading (another) biography of John Keats. The poet had died in Rome, in 1821, at the age of 25. Food for thought. I was still thinking of Keats – and his sensitivity to beauty – when Elizabeth returned with Fabrizio. If anything, her décolleté was now even more revealing than at the outset, with the emerald garment's shoulder straps now decidedly off-the-shoulder, and the neckline verging on reckless. And I could see distinctly, through the fine fabric, the impression of Elizabeth's nipples. Both Fabrizio and Elizabeth were smiling broadly. I glanced at my watch. They'd been a whole hour – and a half! 'Thank you so much, Elizabeth, that was wonderful!' gushed the now-familiar young man. 'The best subject ever, the best photos ever!' he beamed. 'My pleasure' said Elizabeth. 'I really enjoyed it. Great fun...and I learned a few things, too.'

'Hey, Fabrizio, if I give you my e-mail address, could you forward some copies?' I kind of demanded. 'Of course, of course, Mr Manning, it will be my pleasure!' 'And we'll forget about the modelling fee,' I laughed. 'By the way, how many snaps did you take?' Fabrizio seemed offended by my slightly disparaging remarks concerning his art. 'Precisely three hundred and fifty six, Mr Manning. Exactly the number that were required – different poses, different attitudes, different moods, different scenes and props.' 'Three hundred and fifty six!' I gasped. 'It was fun I tell you!' interjected Elizabeth. 'The time flew by...Fabrizio's really rather good. And very *professional*,' she added with emphasis. At this, the young man beamed. 'And what will you do with all these images?' I asked, still trying to sound amused. Fabrizio looked pained. '*Do*? Mr Manning. Not '*do*,' but treasure them – memories of a wonderful afternoon, making art with a..a..goddess!'

'Fabrizio' said Elizabeth, in confidential tones, 'I wonder, could you please arrange for a couple of margaritas to be brought up? And so many thanks for this afternoon. We'll see you at Dinner.' And with that the young man, still in some sort of reverie, was ushered from the suite. 'We really must get a decent camera' said Elizabeth. I snatched her in my arms, and pulled down the emerald top. 'What? so I can photograph these? I suggested, kissing the top of her breasts, before venturing further. 'Mine! Mine! Mine!' I protested, peevishly.' 'All yours, baby' replied Elizabeth, giggling, and pressing my face to her softness. An image from a Lawrence poem – '*like Gloire de Dijon roses*' – sprung into my mind. Then the margaritas arrived, and we sipped the nectar of the gods.

*

I am writing this brief Memoir at the age of 45 years, a full thirteen years after these memory-seared events. I suppose I've now entered that state called 'middle age'. It's been a marvellous life so far, and I've continued to lecture, despite our wealth. As some critics love the Williams' – Shakespeare, Wordsworth, Blake and Yeats – I love the Johns' – Donne, Keats, Clare and Masefield. However, I'm still slim, and trim, and feel as fit as a fiddle. Elizabeth is now 37 years old, but looks ten years younger. She decided to give up work after we married, to 'concentrate', as she put it, on our new home, in the Hampshire countryside. Five bedrooms – all of them well used – and set in three acres. We're not overlooked, so Elizabeth loves to prance around the garden with no clothes on. If she thinks that will turn me on, she's quite right. Takes some maintenance, I can tell you; the garden, that is. Oh, and she concentrates on me, too.

At an early stage we decided against having children. For my part, I did not want to see lines etched on that lovely face.

Or that perfect body stretched out of perfection. On Elizabeth's part – although she was never explicit – I knew, there was *the Condition*. A bit odd, really, when you think that a key driver for making love is making babies. Still, this is 2020, and there's quite enough of us homo sapiens on planet Earth.

Elizabeth remains quite breath-taking – her face and figure still marvellous. She's gained just five pounds since we married, thirteen years ago, now – a small weight gain that is hardly detectable. However, I will say – especially since this is a private Memoir, written for my own amusement, and not for publication – that Elizabeth's breasts are possibly even more spectacular than ever. I could go into detail. But then I'd have to kill you. Oh, and talking of breasts – albeit very briefly – we still keep in touch, by e-mail – with young Fabrizio; though he's 37 now, the same age as Elizabeth. In fact, he's become quite a friend, over the years – and we've returned to Isola Bella several times since the honeymoon trip. Fabrizio now manages the hotel, which is like a warm old friend to us, these days.

And the pictures Fabrizio 'captured' of Elizabeth – looking so fresh, abandoned and carefree – are still amongst the finest we have: Elizabeth looks magnificent, and so, so happy, even if some of the images are a touch daring – reckless, even. With the benefit of hindsight I can say: what the hell?

I said that I still feel young and fit, and you may be wondering why. Which is silly of me, since no-one else will be reading this. But I'll indulge myself. I do a little exercise – walking, running, cycling, and swimming. And we have a private gym in one wing of the house, along with a billiard room, and a music studio. But I believe that the main reason for my fitness and flexibility is down to continuous…sex. No indeed, one couldn't make it up.

The problem, though – at least a mild frustration – is that at my age I don't always feel like it. Or up for it, if you follow my drift. Not, that is, every day. Now this may sound churlish, given

Elizabeth's charms and appetite. Like a guy in Heaven moaning about angels, or celestial music. But a day off occasionally – I mean, to rest, sleep or quietly read some poetry – would be so delightfully relaxing. But Elizabeth simply won't hear of it. She reminds me of the Condition, and my willing agreement to it. 'Every day you will honour and worship my body.' So there we go again. Every night. And most days. I can't complain – if I confided my 'complaint' to any of my male friends, they'd think I was stark staring mad. So there we are. I've worked it out that, if I live to 70, we've got another 10,000 sessions to go. Phew. And if I did happen to stick around to be a hundred…And Elizabeth a sprightly ninety-two…Maybe beam me up, Scotty. Or maybe not…

*

Elizabeth Manning takes up the story:

I found this typescript when I was sorting through Tom's stuff, about three months after I lost him. The poor guy was only 45, and he looked great for his age. As you will note from the foregoing (this really deserves to be published, along with Tom's studies of John Donne, and John Keats) Tom was besotted with me, and me with him. That John Donne was a pretty sensual guy, despite his being a man of the cloth. Still, beneath the uniform, he was still a man, was he not? As another poet wrote, 'A man's a man, for a' that.' Tom was always reciting Donne's poetry, during our love-making. Some pretty racy stuff, I can tell you. A real turn-on – not that we needed much turning on.

Unfortunately, one night, when we were very active, Tom suffered a massive heart attack, and died pretty instantaneously. When he cried out, I thought he was climaxing. I suppose he was, in a way. Well, if you gotta go, that's the way to go, baby. But, anyway, thank God I was on top, because otherwise I might have been suffocated. I suspected something was wrong a little earlier…but that's quite enough of that.

It could be that I've been a bit too demanding of Tom, especially in the last couple of years. His Memoir hints at a recent physical struggle. But, hey, I'm his loving wife – very loving, as you may have gathered – and, anyway, he never complained to me. Anyhow, what's to complain about? Tom left me the house and everything and, after the initial shock, and the funeral, I just got on with things; as you do; as you must. And it was really good of Fabrizio to come over for the funeral. The guy's been so sweet. He visits me from time to time. And we keep in touch through Zoom. It can be quite an intimate medium, I've been pleased to discover…

Of course, there's a big house and grounds, so I've called in some help. There's young Adrian, who helps me with the garden, three afternoons a week. Sometimes, when Ade's ridden round on the mower, and the lawn's immaculate, we'll share a cocktail together. He's only twenty-three. But quite a lad, I can tell you. And then there's Matt, my housekeeper, who's adept with a duster, and can rustle up a mean bolognese. Matt's mainly here in the evenings. He's great company. Somehow, with Ade and Matt's active support, I manage to get through each day.

Please think kindly of me: I loved Tom and really miss him, but I'm a thirty-seven year old widow and, people tell me, still very attractive. Tom thought I was the sexiest bitch on the planet (well, when he was excited, which was rather often). Adrian and Matt pay me similar compliments – but then, like poet and priest Donne, they are men, after all. But, I hasten to add, not 'just men'. And they never need much encouragement – just a smile; even a glance. It's just as well, really. Because we all need to be honoured and worshipped. Each and every day…

BRIEF ENCOUNTER 1:

BLACK COUNTRY DOGGING

Walking along the path home with my dog *Henry*, a familiar dog-walker, Brenda, hove into view, alongside her Labrador, *Hero*. As we grew nearer, I could see that *Hero* was equipped – well, it was approaching Christmas – with tinsel around his neck, and reindeer antlers. *Henry* looks *Hero* up and down, and sniffs; and is suitably unimpressed.

'Hi Brenda, how *are* you? You look blooming, Brenda! And *Hero*, of course! How charming!'

'We're fine, thanks. Just returning from a super walk in the woods. *Hero* almost caught a squirrel – (bending down towards *Hero*'s face) – who's been a naughty boy, then?'

'You know – hope you don't mind my asking – I haven't seen Ken for ages.'

'Well, (slight laugh) that's because he's no longer around.'

(Shocked) 'You don't mean…you've parted – after all this time?'

'No, what I mean is that, after forty years of sterling service – that is, marriage – he's gone and died. Six months ago, now. Very sudden. *Too* bloody sudden.'

'I'm *so* sorry. I mean, I had no idea…'

'No, *I'm* sorry. As I say, it was all very sudden. There were so many people to tell. And so much to do. It was all a bit of a blur, really. Now it's just *Hero* and me.'

'I do wish I'd known. I'd have come…'

'Oh, that's so kind. But it was a simple family affair. Afterwards, we scattered Ken's ashes in the local Park, next to our late dog, *Zorro*, and our cat, *Flanders*. They loved the local Park – just beyond the garden gate.'

'Sounds lovely. Ken must have loved it, too?'

'Not sure about that. He certainly loved cursing the kids when their footballs landed in the garden…But then, 'football' does start with an 'f'!'

'Even so, it must all have come as a terrible shock. And poor Ken; I always thought how fit and well he looked…'

'Well, I suppose he did, 'til the end. Then, suddenly, he wasn't. I remember it so distinctly. It was 21 June – the longest day of the year. He'd been watching *Newsnight,* and cursing every politician as incompetent morons. Then he just fell asleep in his favourite chair; at least, that's what I thought. But, to be frank, he was always moaning about something; everything. Honestly, the slightest, smallest thing. I never felt that he was happy – that I could *make* him happy. So maybe he's gone somewhere where's there's nothing to complain about. Just his regular favourites – a curry, washed down with a pint or two of Bathams.'

'But, surely, Ken can't have been very old? I remember his retirement from that accountancy firm. Maybe 62, was he?'

'He was 63. Old enough, apparently. I thought he might enjoy his retirement – but he seemed to get in a bit of a groove. Every day pretty much the same routine.'

'Well I must say, Brenda, I do admire you. You seem to have coped with Ken's loss incredibly well. It's really quite admirable – philosophical, I'd say.'

'That's very kind of you. But, in all honesty, it's opened up a whole new world for me. Though we had no money worries, and a nice house, and lovely holidays in Spain, the glass always seemed half empty for Ken. Now it's brimming over.'

'Sorry? How come?'

'Well, I always knew that Ken was a keen investor. Always had his head buried in the *Financial Times*. I used to joke that he enjoyed his little hobby better than sex. He used to laugh at that; but not in the way I intended. But we didn't discuss it much – that is, the investments. We always seemed to have more than enough, and I didn't pry further. What I hadn't realised was how canny Ken was. When our solicitor looked into our affairs, seemed we were sitting on a fortune!'

'That's great. But I'm sure it hasn't changed you at all?'

'You've got to be kidding. *Hero* and I have moved to a bigger house. And bought an apartment in Spain. And two or three nights a week, I'm out with the girls. Then there's the ladies who lunch – this lady lunches every day the sun shines!'

'But, with respect, doesn't *Hero* miss you, when you go out?'

'Not really; he's well cared for by our Filipino maid. Margherita also does the cooking, cleaning and washing. Bloody marvellous, I can tell you. Don't know how I ever found the time.'

'That's great, of course. But I thought that *Hero* might miss Ken…'

'Well, he was a bit confused for a week or two. Ken was his main walker. But, to be honest, his walks were all a bit perfunctory – a bit like our sex life…(laughs). No, dogs are nothing if not adaptable. And *Hero* loves Margherita.'

'Sounds like you've both taken things in your stride…'

'I do hope so. Have I mentioned Robert?'

'Robert? Who's Robert?'

'What a find! Robert's the young man does my gardening, and all my little jobs. You know, changes the light bulbs, or touches up the paint work. He's so obliging…And if I'm feeling lonely, or a bit bored, Robert's not averse to touching me up a bit, if you get my drift. My man Friday. I say that because he is, well, black. But who cares, these days? Or about the age difference?

Bloody amazing. Never knew sex could be so much fun. No wonder the young uns are at it like rabbits. Anyway, nice to see you, er...Steve. Sorry, I need to get back for Robert... Do give my regards to...'

'Shirley.' 'Yes, Shirley, of course! You take good care of her, do you hear?'

Brenda and *Hero* depart. *Henry* looks me sternly in the eye, with a hint of disapproval. What was that all about?

EULOGY FOR RIDLEY TULK

The demise of Ridley Tulk, aged 75, came as a surprise to no-one but himself. Not that many cared, or even noticed, Tulk's passing.

Mr Tulk, a confirmed bachelor, womaniser and drinker, had died peacefully, in bed, one evening; by his side 22-year old model-escort Rochelle. It was what Tulk would have wanted; but not yet.

On waking, Rochelle had experienced a few moments of shock, bordering on panic. The old boy had been pretty lively in the night, she recalled. However, Rochelle had the presence of mind to ring for an ambulance, before leaving the front door on the latch, as she quickly left the house. Another £500 had slipped into her bank account. All was well with the world. It was only later that day that she burst into tears. 'Poor Ridley!' she sobbed. *'Poor* Ridley.'

Tulk had few relatives, and even fewer friends. He had lived alone for 50 years in an increasingly dilapidated, cluttered, semi-detached on the outskirts of Kidderminster. A 12-year old Ford Escort stood forlornly on the drive. The old car had many stories to tell; but no-one would ever ask.

Unexpected Headache

It would be for 48-year old nephew, Jonah Smith – the son of Tulk's sister – to pick up the pieces. Although he had some insight into his uncle's lifestyle, Jonah was not looking forward to picking up those pieces, and tying those pieces neatly together. Even less was he looking forward to organising the funeral at the local church – or delivering the Eulogy. He had been a fairly frequent visitor to his uncle's home – just to check he was OK; but, despite or because of his 'lifestyle', the tough old bird seemed likely to carry on forever.

But Jonah rarely took teenagers Clare or Julie with him. Jonah's daughters were transforming into glorious womanhood. Oh, no. That ancient, wandering eye would not be given chance to gaze on that particular tempting young flesh. Clare, and Julie, were destined for University – and eager, ambitious husbands; and much more elevated, perhaps academic, Platonic lives.

Since Jonah, somewhat to his surprise, was the chief beneficiary of his uncle's Will, he undertook the responsibility of sorting through the 'Estate' – that is, 50 years of accumulated clutter: old, worn furniture, creaky beds, shelves and files full of paperwork, compact discs, plant pots, book-cases, framed photos. And God knows what other paraphernalia. But also racks of gin, malt whisky, and vintage wine. Well, that at least could be put to good use. As for selling the house itself, that would have to wait. All in good time. Jonah began to realise that, despite the short term hassle and inconvenience, his inheritance might be worth a pretty penny…

Jonah tackled his enormous responsibility in a tight, disciplined manner. First, registering the death. Then, contacting his uncle's solicitor, to keep him informed, and to obtain necessary advice. And then to instruct a firm of funeral directors. The funeral would take place in three weeks time. Let's get through this process first, thought Jonah; then tackle the house and its accumulation of history.

The Interview
In the interim, Jonah received an invite to Tulk's solicitors, to

discuss the Estate. He was greeted in the lobby by a Mr Slade, with a cold, clammy handshake and a rancid smile. Slade was tall, angular, quite bald and with thick, rimmed spectacles that seemed to be part of his physiognomy. Jonah tried to imagine him naked – a naughty little party trick – and failed.

Mr Slade and his client, Mr Smith, sat opposite each other across a wide mahogany table. 'Mr Smith, thank you for coming in this morning. Your uncle's case is quite unusual. Fortunately, he was in frequent contact, so we're up to speed with events. Your uncle would update his Will on a regular basis – maybe twice a year. To cut to the chase. Ahem. I would not say that Mr Tulk was a wealthy man, Mr Smith, but he did have substantial assets.'

'I only knew him as an electrician,' said Jonah, with some surprise. 'True, true,' said Slade. 'But for many years it seems he dabbled on the stockmarket' – he looked at Jonah feelingly – 'apparently with considerable success. Mr Tulk left an Estate of around £500,000, not including his house and personal effects.'

Jonah's attempt to speak was halted by an upraised bony hand. 'I must tell you, Mr Smith, that you are the main beneficiary of Mr Tulk's Will. But you are not the only beneficiary. Mr Tulk left £10,000 to a charity...' 'Charity?' repeated Jonah. 'Yes, your uncle was fond of birds – wild birds – so he's left a bequest to the RSPB.'

'Well, that's very fine and noble' opined a surprised Jonah.

Slade looked at him with narrow, furtive eyes. 'It seems there were a few other avian friends in Mr Tulk's life...' Jonah looked non-plussed. 'Just my little joke,' Slade smiled, in a rather pained way. 'No, it seems Mr Tulk formed...amiable relations with quite a cohort of...young ladies. Ten, to be exact. I have their names, and contact details. To get to the point, Mr Tulk has left a bequest to each of them of £5,000.' 'Five grand *each*?' spluttered Jonah, in genuine disbelief. 'Hadn't he given them enough?' 'I'll leave that one hanging in the air, if you don't mind,' replied Slade, archly.

'I know how you feel,' Slade continued, in his most sympathetic bedside manner. 'But, as you are aware, Mr Tulk had no immediate family – no wife, no children. So these women became a sort of adopted family. Apparently, he grew quite close to some of them. You may want to invite them to the funeral. Though it may be quite a brave gesture' he added, with a thin smile.

Slade noted Jonah's agitation. 'Never mind, Mr Smith, look on the bright side. Your uncle must have been very fond of you and your family to have left you the bulk of his Estate – together with his house. You're a very fortunate and, if I may so venture, quite a wealthy man. And a word of caution: don't even think of challenging the Will. It's completely sound and solid. For the main beneficiary to challenge a Will would be quite unprecedented, and open up a most unpleasant can of worms. And be most troublesome and expensive, in terms of legal costs. Seven hundred grand out of seven-hundred and fifty sounds a pretty good deal to me…'

'Finally, Mr Smith, there's the small matter of Probate approval, which may take a couple of months. But we can release funds to pay for the funeral costs.' 'Thank you,' said Jonah, sounding deflated. 'We are a bit stretched at the moment…' Slade stood up, and shook Jonah's hand. 'Congratulations, Mr Smith. Should you need any financial advice…'

'Thank you, Mr Slade. I'll give it some thought…So much to take in…'

The Funeral Service
The church was booked for May 21, and Jonah endeavoured to invite everyone who may have loved, liked, or even known his Uncle Rid. He even placed a notice in the local press. Despite everything, Jonah was determined to give the old boy the best possible send off; no trouble or expense was to be spared. It

was the least that they could do, he felt, in the circumstances. A gleaming gold and black carriage, pulled along proudly by plumed grey horses, was to provide the spirited centrepiece of the ceremony.

In the end, though, it was a patchy and pretty undistinguished cast who turned up to commemorate a life lived, if not greatly, at least, er, memorably. A few distant relatives. A struggle of leaned-upon neighbours. A scattering of 'wide-boy' friends. And a bevy of, ahem, 'girlfriends'. Ten, actually. So, a motley, press-ganged crew, with the exception of these beautiful, fashionable young women. Still, people willing to expend a few hours of their precious lives, on a sunless May-morning, in order to pay their respects to a Falstaffian old letch. Surely, not just here for a curled up sandwich and a cup of tea?

The service began with 'All things bright and beautiful' and ended with Shakespeare's 'Fear no more the heat o' the sun', with it's apposite lines: 'Golden lads and girls all must/As chimney sweepers, come to dust'. The young women – Rochelle, Caroline, Ebony, Katya, Carmen, Jess, Eleanor, Grace, Charlotte and Madison – sat like a line of budding volcanoes, that might erupt at any moment. After all, they had seen more of Ridley Tulk – in every sense of the word – than any other living person. The vicar, sounding vaguely censorious, spat out phrases like 'Heaven' and 'eternal joys' as prospects that were, at best, highly unlikely to be enjoyed by the deceased. The organist, flushed and distracted, mangled the melodies. Nobody noticed.

As for The Eulogy... No: let's call it a Tribute. And let's accentuate the positive, thought Jonah. A few, pithy, memorable phrases, that were all too quickly un-remembered...

A lust for life (call that zest). A bonhomme. Honest. Private. Discrete. Loving. Especially young people. (From the lectern, Jonah looked down upon the young woman in the fur coat. She gave him a reassuring smile. He couldn't help thinking there was probably nothing beneath the coat). *Kind. Self-effacing. Generous. A visionary conservationist...*

The Wake
At the Wake, munching his way happily through another canapé, Jonah was approached by the young woman in the three-quarter length fur coat. She smiled again. Jonah thought, 'what a face!' 'May I take your coat, Miss..er..?' 'Smith. Call me Rochelle. But better not,' Rochelle added, referring to the coat, and smiling that bewitching smile again. 'This is a bit embarrassing, Mr...' 'Smith' he replied, with his own take on a smile, 'but do call me Jonah.' 'Thank you. You know, Ridley was quite a dear. I...knew him for some years. He felt genuine affection for me, and me for him. It was so good of him to remember me in his Will. But – and I don't want to appear greedy, Mr Smith – he promised me a lovely diamond ring...I know he bought it...but Ridley passed away before he could present it to me. I wonder if you could find it for me? I'd be *ever* so grateful...' An even bigger smile. Jonah himself was beginning to feel a little under her spell. 'Just give me your mobile, Miss Smith...Rochelle. I'm sorting the house out next week. I'll take a good look. Solitaire ring, eh?' Rochelle gave him a peck on the cheek and, in doing so, her coat fell open a little to reveal a creamy, generous cleavage. Jonah felt the perfumed warmth, albeit for a moment. 'Sorry, I need to go. Client booked. You know, I'll really miss Ridley.' Then Miss Smith – Rochelle – turned on her heels, and was gone.

'Crikey!' Jonah thought, 'she can't be much older than Clare. I wonder if Clare has....'. Jonah guillotined his developing thoughts. Mental note: discuss with Maggie...

Maggie Smith observed proceedings, from close quarters, with feigned amusement. Clare and Julia had been ordered to remain in her slipstream. 'What was all *that* about?' Maggie shot at her husband.

'Oh, nothing. Rochelle – Miss Smith – just wanted to thank us for the invite. And said how much she'd miss the old boy.'

Maggie sniffed. She had not been amused to hear that ten – ten! – of old Rid's floozies had been left five grand each in the old chap's Will. Or that all ten had been invited to the funeral; and all ten turned up. Although Maggie's first angry reaction, on hearing of Tulk's bequests, had been to challenge the Will, her husband had persuaded her that this would be futile. In any case, Maggie's mood had changed during the course of this surreal morning. She had thought that these young women might bring embarrassment, even scandal, to the funeral proceedings. And she dreaded awkward questions from Clare and Julia – especially Julia. But the 'escort' contingent of ten represented nearly half of the small group of mourners. In truth, their presence had lit up a cold, dingy nave. And the young women had behaved with dignity, respect and decorum; there had been more than a few tears shed, dampening those perfect eye-lashes.

As for the money – the legacy – it represented a life-changing windfall for the Smiths. Clare was now 18, a young, willowy teenager, with a passion for art and photography. 16 year-old Julia, pretty and fun-loving, and studying for her GCSEs, was wild about history, and English literature. And, unfortunately, in her mother's eyes, also mad about the boys. Jonah, a bus driver, and Maggie, a primary school teacher, who obviously wanted only the best for their girls' future, had naturally been worried about the high costs of university education, and how these might be met. Now, Uncle Rid's quite unexpected windfall could fund the girls' university career, for a start. No mountain of debt around *their* necks. And buy them a car each, in good time. And, of course, in the fullness of time, provide deposits on their first homes. 'But let's not run too far ahead,' thought Maggie. A well-deserved family holiday in the sun was the immediate priority…

'Thank you, Uncle Ridley, you old bugger,' reflected Maggie, a touch grimly, in silent appreciation. 'May you rest happily… in somebody's arms.'

THE DISGRUNTLED MR SPEIGHT

Martin Speight put the grunt into 'disgruntled'. He was gruntled about nothing; disgruntled with just about everything. Mr Speight might have turned disgruntlement into an art form, save for the fact that he wasn't keen on modern art, either. Nor, in fact, modern society. Or modern life. Such was the pitch of Martin Speight's acute unhappiness with his lot that Mr Speight, a 70-year old married man with two grown up daughters, and three grandchildren, enjoyed – or possibly endured – a monthly session with his long-suffering therapist, in order to explore every conceivable complaint regarding the deficiencies of life in general, and Martin Speight's life in particular.

Garry Weston had graduated from the University of Birmingham with a degree in Modern History. Upon graduating, Garry had trained to become a professional therapist, and had begun his own practice, fifteen years ago, now. Garry's modest but comfortable consulting room was based in a ramshackle Victorian edifice on the outskirts of the middle-class suburbs of Stourbridge. Garry had a varied clientele: men and women of all ages and professions, and with a variety of complexes and 'needs'. But, with the exception of teenagers – a client group with a peculiar and particular suite of 'challenges' and ushered through

Garry's doors by anxious parents – most of Garry's clients were in the 50-plus age groups. Common problem areas included financial and inheritance anxieties, family relationships, marital breakdown; even sexual 'issues'.

A rather common and general type of conundrum, however – though it manifested itself in different ways, to different people – concerned the varied and intense stresses occasioned by what might be termed 'modern life'. Indeed, many of Garry's clients were quite well-to-do retired people, who had thought they had earned – and were now embarking upon – a golden age of cocktails on deck, Caribbean sunsets, and warm afternoons listening to Sinatra on a perfumed terrace. Martin Speight, a client of five years standing, was the crème de la crème of this latter type of client. Indeed, for Martin, the glass – whether of martini, or g&t – was invariably half full.

At a few minutes to ten o'clock, Garry prepared himself, both physically and mentally, for the tirade that he was about to face. Not that Martin Speight viewed Garry as the problem, exactly. But he was the sounding board, and Garry's brand of resigned good humour did sometimes tend to provoke Martin's only-too skin deep irascibility. Never mind, Garry told himself philosophically, it'll be another 60 quid towards his own retirement plan. It was precisely 10.00am on an overcast Monday morning when Martin Speight marched over Garry Weston's welcoming threshold.

Speight, looking casual but smart, even dapper in a light suit, appeared grim-faced; as though the weight of the world was on his shoulders. As indeed he felt to be the case. 'Good morning, Martin. How are you?'

'Good morning, Garry. You know, in *A Tale of Two Cities*, Dickens wrote that *'It was the best of times, it was the worst of times.'* That was the 1780s. I feel that the 2020s are, quite simply, the *worst* of times. Period. Two hundred years of progress! Blah!'

'I see,' responded Garry, with a frown. 'That is pretty forthright, Martin. Now, we've covered this ground before – in fact,' he laughed, 'we've read the book, and bought the t-shirt. But, just to keep us up-to-date, and on the ball, as it were, just remind me what's discomforting you at the present time. Let's review that state of mind. What ails thee, Martin?'

'Well, Garry, just about everything, I'm afraid. The country's vastly over-populated. People everywhere. Can't move for 'em. And rubbish – litter – everywhere one looks.. And crime – it's hardly safe to go out at night, these days. Gangs seem to have taken over the streets. And teenagers – not just snivelling, arrogant little gits – but at it like rabbits, everywhere one looks. Discarded condoms, in every nook and cranny. And that's despite the bloody Pandemic – what happened to social distancing?

'Ah, that's the life, eh, Martin? Gather ye rosebuds, and all that? Not like in your day, I'll bet!'

'You've got to be kidding. In my youth, I hardly knew what a girl was. And no thought of hanky panky. Just smile at a young woman, and you were dragged to the altar. But, as I was saying, instead of war, or Cold War, we now have this interminable lockdown. It's just driving me nuts…'

'Is that it?' enquired Gary.

'Sadly, no, I'm afraid,' continued Speight. 'My wife Sue needs a knee replacement, and the waiting list keeps getting longer. So we can't book that Caribbean cruise we promised ourselves, for our 50th Anniversary. Meanwhile, my daughter Catherine and her husband have split up, and there's all sorts of issues with money. Roger – the two-timing Roger – won't clear out of the family home, and live with his mistress. 'Cos *she's* reconciled with her husband, apparently.'Oh, and young people these days can't afford to get on the housing ladder. I really worry about our grandkids. And the cost of getting them through university!'

Garry nodded, empathetically.'Well, Martin, there's an awful lot to unpack there, and we only have an hour. So where would you like to start?'

'What I'd really like,' enthused Speight, warming to his theme, 'is to go back to a different time, a different age, and experience life as it was then. It must have been infinitely better than now. Life was so much more elegant, so much simpler, so much more refined...'

'And what Golden Age, or Ages, might they be?' enquired Gary, intrigued.

'There's three actually,' replied Martin, his furrowed face brightening a little. 'Firstly, the Regency period. Failing that, the Edwardian Era. Or finally, the 1950s. Actually, a stint in all of them would be most stimulating...most enjoyable...'

Garry Weston smiled. 'Far be it from me – your therapist – to dampen your enthusiasm, your ambition, but it might be helpful if I pointed out a few practical issues. Just to provide some context, some historical perspective, as it were...'

'OK, be my guest,' scowled Speight, reverting to his half-glass-full persona.

'Well, first of all, we don't have a time machine. We can't be in, or re-create, the past, although we do in fact attempt to re-create it, or re-cycle it – pretty badly – in endless TV and film adaptations. And, next, allow me to point out that each of the historical periods you've highlighted lasted for a mere ten years. Then, the people who were then alive, and experiencing this Golden Age, would have been obliged to have moved on; dragged kicking and screaming into the next 'age'. Very soon, that 'Golden' period would itself have become history. But, of course, these characters may not have appreciated that they were living in a rarified, halcyon historical period. The only place that the Regency period exists for ever is in the Costume Department of the BBC. Indeed, presented with a claim that they were living in a veritable Golden Age, people living at the time may well have responded that the idea was preposterous – even hilarious. Especially the poor buggars at the bottom of the social pile. I wouldn't want to labour the point, but of course all those 'fortunate' people are also all long dead. Finally, dare I say – you know I have a degree in Modern History – none of these Eras may have been quite as grand as subsequent claims makes them out to be…So where would you like to start – the Regency? That's 1811 to 1820?' Speight nodded.

'OK. We all think we know the Regency,' Garry began. 'That we've all been there. Jane Austen. Elegant carriages crunching up manicured drive-ways. Dancing in candle-lit ballrooms. Refined gentle-folk indulging in sophisticated conversation. Problem is, it's all largely a fiction – at least a pastiche. Not even Jane Austen – a fabulous realist – thought or wrote like that. Yes, there were a few hundred peers of the realm, a landed aristocracy, a few thousand wealthy merchants and business men, and an expanding middle class. And true, the population was only around eight million, so everyone had plenty of space. But ninety-nine percent of the population were so dirt poor they hadn't got anywhere to go – and no vehicle to take them there if they had. Meanwhile, the average woman bore eight children – so she was too busy to go anywhere – but most of these poor children would, in any case, die in infancy. We don't know what happened to Lizzie Bennett after she married Mr Darcy; though we can guess. But we do know that Jane Austen herself refused to become a baby-bearing machine, and remained a spinster. '*Pride and Prejudice*', and '*Emma*', are her immortal children.

The average – Regency – person, having survived infancy, had a life-expectancy of 40 years – after a lifetime of back-breaking toil on farm, in factory or down pit. And that back-breaking toil included women and children in its relentless grip. In fact, the early 1800s saw the very worst of the vile living and working conditions brought on by the early Industrial Revolution – with no health and safety legislation at all until 1802. In the House of Lords, in 1812, even Lord Byron railed against the callous misery caused by the new machine age. A few years later – in fact, 1816 – the said Lord buggered off to Italy, never to return to these beatific shores.

But to return to the general populace – those who couldn't flee – the not so lucky ones. The Napoleonic Wars raged until 1815: this represented the public's only chance of seeing 'abroad'. So you might have been press-ganged into Nelson's Navy, or forced by poverty into criminality – and Wellington's Army. With a very good chance of not returning alive, or at least of not returning with all their limbs intact. And, I hardly need to remind you, Martin, there was no state education, and no state pension provision. And no NHS. So no waiting lists! Jane Austen herself died, aged 41, from a disease that would be treatable today. And no university – at least for the vast majority of illiterate working-folk. Of course, they weren't aware that they lived in a 'Golden Age' (Gary laughed) 'though the Government did try to tell them they lived in the best society on Earth. Indeed, a society that had just – in 1806 – abolished the Slave Trade. But – note – not slavery itself. However, nothing that you might vaguely call 'democracy'. That is, no vote or representation for working people – only for what might be called the 'upper', landed classes. So, when Manchester's working public indulged in a peaceful protest, in 1819 – in St Peter's Fields – to agitate for political reform – the Government was so outraged at their ungrateful impertinence that they sent in the yeomanry, on horseback, to massacre the miscreants. With heavy irony, it's called 'Peterloo'. OK so far, Martin?'

'Well, I never,' exclaimed Martin. 'There's certainly food for thought there, Garry. Maybe we should move on?' Martin added, hesitantly.

'Good idea. Right, so where are we going next?' asked Garry, brightly. 'Oh, yes, the Edwardians. Well, we may be on slightly firmer ground here...' Martin looked up, encouraged by a change of tone.

'1901. The British Empire is at its zenith. An Empire on which the sun never set. Britain was still, arguably, the greatest power on Earth; the envy of the world. And, at home, all seemed glitz and glamour...balls, and parties, and game shooting... Downton, and all that. Meanwhile, the countryside luxuriated in endless summers, and a calm and tranquility never seen before or since. Hardly a motor car to be seen. And an enlightened Liberal Government (from 1906) that had just introduced the first state pension scheme. To cap it all, London hosted the Olympics in 1908. Britain won by far and away the most medals – 146. 56 of them were gold. It really couldn't get any better. And, in many respects, it didn't.'

'Sounds great, said Martin. When can we go?'

'Not so fast, young man. Not so fast. You know the story of the swan gliding along? While below, all is feverish activity? Well, that's the Edwardian Era for you. At the top of the pile sat a sex-mad, blood-sport obsessed monarch – Edward VII. And, while the power of the landed aristocracy was about to be broken – because this was, at last, the 20th century – for every aristocrat or millionaire upstairs, there were ten Thomases or Pollys downstairs. But the economy ran on coal, steel and cotton – and that's where most working people were to be found. Down pit; in mill – or in service. And, you guessed – they lived – survived – on the breadline. The average working man was dead at 45 – worn out by heavy work, in terrible conditions. So most people never got to receive the pension that was introduced for those reaching the almost unobtainable 65 years of age.'

Martin opened his mouth; but nothing came out. 'And that's not all,' continued Garry. 'Your Golden Era began with the deeply colonial and horribly violent Boer War. And the period was marked by serious industrial strife, leading, in a notorious case

– Tonypandy, in the Rhondda Valley – to armed intervention against striking miners. In November, 1910, one miner was killed and 500 injured – by Government forces! However, if I'm to be totally accurate,' added Garry, 'good King Edward had died in May that year; his Era was over, and a new, Georgian period, begun. But to return to my theme. There was growing conflict in Ireland – still part of Britain – that risked the outbreak of Civil War in these Islands. And of course there were protests – many of them violent – involving suffragettes, who were often incarcerated, and cruelly tortured – by being force fed. More than 1,000 women were imprisoned – essentially because they campaigned for female suffrage…'

'I think I've heard enough,' sighed Martin.

'But you've not heard the best bit,' continued Garry, enthusiastically. 'The imperial competition, and arms race, between Britain and Germany intensified, and threatened to explode into a global conflict. As we now know, that conflict did not begin until 1914. But if you were planning to be a young man in the Edwardian Era – not much fun being an old one – still no Health Service – the trenches of Flanders would be your destiny, my son. Maybe – since we know how it all ended – the *denouement* imbues the Edwardian period with a glamour it doesn't wholly deserve?'

'I think I need to invest in a good history book' concluded Martin, disconsolately. 'But not for the 1950s,' he added with a grin. 'Cos I was there!'

'OK', said Garry, with raised eyebrows. 'So maybe tell me what you remember about that fabulous decade. Though I take it you were a child at the time?'

'That's right,' Martin agreed, 'I was born in '51. My childhood wasn't exactly a bed of roses – my father was an engineer, my mother a shop assistant in the corner shop – but we had our own house – rented, of course – and I felt warm, safe and secure.

We knew all the neighbours, and the community sort of gelled. I can't remember any crime – not to speak of. And in 1960 Dad bought our first car – a Ford Anglia.'

'1960?' said Gary, with some emphasis. 'Well, yes' replied Martin. 'I suppose I regard that as the summit of our family's achievement. Before Dad died, in 1965, from heart trouble. All those fumes in his factory wouldn't have helped. Mom remarried three years later. He – Charlie – was OK, but of course it was never the same. So the 60s were a bit checkered for me – not the swingin' time most people seem to remember…'

'Right,' said Garry. 'Now, I wasn't born until 1972, but I don't suppose things had changed that much. Not that I want to puncture your rosy recollections. For, after all, your reality is your reality. And, in general terms – as Harold Macmillan famously reminded the great British public – people were becoming better off. And, at long last, the country had a National Health Service. Not to mention universal suffrage. And some people at least – unfortunately not including your Dad – were living long enough to get their pensions…'

Martin interrupted, with some impatience. 'Why do I feel there's a 'but' coming on!'

'Well, maybe, but the 'but' is in two parts. The first is, what the '50s *did* deliver. Do you remember those pea soup fogs?'

'Remember? I'll say I do! We just thought it was weather! Fog. But it was all those furnaces – and everyone – every household – burning raw coal.'

'Yes indeed,' said Garry. 'A good job they introduced a Clean Air Act in 1961! And school. What was that like?' asked Garry, with marked interest.

'School was all right' answered Speight, with some hesitancy. 'Though of course we were all factory fodder. And the bullying was pretty awful. The bloody teachers were worse than the kids!'

'And holidays?' enquired Garry. 'I mean, did you have any?'

'A few,' remembered Martin. 'Llandudno – twice – and Blackpool. We stayed in guest houses. It seemed so exciting; so exotic. I remember first seeing the sea...when I was nine. I was completely bowled over. Even though it was bloody freezing! But I mean, nobody went abroad, then. A week at Blackpool – and a visit to the Tower Circus – was as near to Paradise as we could ever hope for! But as I said, no-one was having foreign holidays at that time – apart from the rich, of course, who inhabited a different planet.'

'And what about politics, and the good old Empire?' enquired Garry.

'All I remember is that politics seemed very grey and boring – a bit like the fog. There was a succession of Tory governments. But we did have a beautiful young Queen. Every time she appeared on telly my Dad's eyes would well up. What a presence! Still, the old Empire – I remember they started calling it the 'Commonwealth' – was being wound down. It almost seemed to have become an embarrassment. But people – new people from the Caribbean, and India, mostly, were now coming to *us* – to settle in Britain. The country was booming – there was plenty of work for everyone.'

'And entertainment?' asked Garry. 'How did you enjoy yourselves?'

'Well, in 1956 I think it was, we acquired our first telly.' Speight laughed. 'It came in a big, shiny mahogany cabinet – the screen must have been all of nine inches across! – and the picture fuzzy and shaky. But it seemed like a miracle at the time. And we had one of those big Bush radios. Ah, yes, there was also the cinema – I think we visited every month or two, to see the latest block-buster – though the James Bond movies were a few years down the line... Oh, and I bought a BSR record player, to play Beatles singles and so on. But come to think of it, that would have been the '60s...'

'Telephone?' enquired Garry.

Speight shook his head. 'You must be joking. Only one of our neighbours had a 'phone – one of those black Bakelite jobs. Dad would ask to use it if there was a medical emergency – I think that was just twice...'

'Well, that's all most interesting,' said Garry, with renewed emphasis.

'What is?' said Speight, looking puzzled.

'The fact – a slight surprise – that you're keen to go back to that time...'

'Yes, but...'

'Which brings me to my other line in 'buts'' interrupted Garry. 'That is, what you *didn't* have in 1950s Britain. What you *couldn't* have. You've already mentioned foreign holidays. What do you do *now?*'

'Well, we do love a cruise every year – usually to the Caribbean. And two or three weeks on one of the Costas, or maybe the Greek islands, every Summer.'

'I see,' said Garry, gravely. 'And entertainment? – I mean, now.'

'Yes, I confess I do enjoy our plasma TV screens. Sky is a bit expensive – we have Netflix, too – but they do provide a plethora of choice.'

'What about the Internet?' Garry asked, mischievously.

'What about it? We've got wifi, like everyone else. A bit slow, sometimes, though. And smart phones – though I wish the local signal was better.'

'And I believe you own your own home, now?' enquired Garry.

'Well of course,' answered Speight. 'Fifty years a home-owner – though three separate houses. Currently – probably our last – a four-bed detached, in rural Worcestershire.'

'And I presume the Ford Anglia has been up-graded?'

For the first time, Martin Speight laughed. 'Kate has a

BMW Sports. I make do with my old Jag.' He laughed again. 'Can I make a plea for mercy, Your Honour? I'm beginning to see your point. I think nostalgia, and old affections, have made me into a silly old sod. The past is the past. It has to stay there, even if we remember it with fondness, even affection. It has helped make us who we are. But we can't drag all our modern conveniences, all our comforts, into that historical straightjacket. What a Frankenstein's monster we'd create! We have evolved and, though things could be better, they could also be a lot worse. Maybe time to reconcile myself with the new reality...'

'I believe so,' said Garry. 'And maybe time to enjoy life – I mean, every minute of every day. You know, Martin, it might be best, all round, to reconcile ourselves to the life we have, and the time we're in, since this seems to be a one-shot game. Escapism is great fun but, in the end, it's exactly that. But, of course the past has helped shape who we are – so every era is critically important. Yet what it teaches us mainly is how very far we've come. So, for every sliver of downside, there's at least one big juicy slice of upside. I think our time is up, for now, Martin. Assuming you still want to meet, what would you like to cover next month?'

'Maybe how I should respond to my daughter's situation. I know Catherine's 40, now, with grown up children of her own. But, what with Roger and the kids, and the prospect of losing her home – not to mention the family's main income – she's in a real crisis...'

'Indeed, indeed,' said Gary wearily, while opening the door. 'We'll just need to consider whether it also has to be *your* crisis...'

SEPARATION

Mal and Mary Bell have been married for six years, now, and have two young children. They live in a semi-detached, in deepest suburban West Midlands. Mal works at a butcher's shop in nearby Kyleford: 'Hancox Finest Family Butcher'. Mary is a teacher at a local Primary School, Belle Vale.

Mal is tall and affable, with a mop of jet black hair, and a ready smile. He's proud of his wife and family, and eager to make them all happy. However, he is a traditionalist, keen to maintain family values, despite his laddish manner, and blokey sense of humour. He had 'hankered' to be a butcher since the age of five, when his mother, Dawn, took the young lad shopping for the first time: he was fascinated by the pigs' trotters, laid out in neat rows in the window, and the rings of black-pudding hanging from hooks on the wall.

Mary is serious, bright and loving. Mary's mother, Sally, tragically died when Mary was only ten years of age. She had been brought up by her devoted father, Geoff, who had never re-married. Sally had been a teacher, too. During Sally's last illness, Mary had promised – there had been no parental pressure – that she would follow in her mother's footsteps. Although she teaches a range of subjects at school, her specialities are History and English. Mary is pretty, and shapely, in a way that every 26 year old woman is, to a teenage boy. She is aware that some of the 10 year-olds in her class are already attentive in a way not always justified by the subject matter, or even Mary's inspiring teaching style. Mary imagines that, at around the same age, Mal would have been cheeky and irreverent, with his future already mapped out. And, already, firm views on the qualities needed by his future wife – down to the colour of her eyes, and her cup size. Especially her cup size.

The couple's much-wanted, and much-loved, children are Rebecca, aged three years; and Miranda, aged three months. Married life to date has been ultra-busy, but fulfilling; even exhilarating. Mal and Mary fancy themselves to be still in love, and enjoy an active social life – and sex life. Mary is currently on maternity leave, following the arrival of Miranda.

Mal's mother has, until recently, been Rebecca's main carer, during working hours. However, Dawn has dropped the bombshell that she no longer feels able to cope with these pressures. She is sorry; but she is no longer as young as she was, and the responsibility is causing too much anxiety.

These stresses of family life have caused tensions in recent weeks; ripples beneath the generally calm facade of relations. However, neither Mary, nor Mal, has any serious thought that their relationship is about to undergo an existential crisis…

One calm, uneventful Saturday afternoon, Mal and Mary relax over a cup of coffee. A rare moment to savour; to just chill. But, given the congenial domestic atmosphere – infant Miranda is fast asleep, and Becky is playing with her dolls – Mal seizes the chance he's been waiting for. He's been anxious about this moment, but he really can't wait any longer. There'll never be a better time...

He's unusually serious, for Mal; and Mary, seeing Mal's unsmiling face, is unusually flustered. 'Mary, we have something serious to discuss. I've been going through the figures, again and again, and I really don't think we've got any choice. When you finish your maternity leave, you really need to become a full-time carer. Look after the kids. And me, I suppose. But the kids are the priority. You'll need to leave your job, I'm afraid, at least until Miranda starts school. We'll miss the money, of course, but I can't see any other option. We'll manage, I'm sure. I'll volunteer for extra shifts...'

There is a moment's silence, that Mal knows doesn't bode well. But he is still surprised at the unambiguous response. 'Mal, are you joking? Where's this come from? Leave my job? My job! Mal, I'm a *teacher*. It's not a job. It's a profession. A vocation. A career. I'm trained for it. It gives me respect and satisfaction. I enjoy it. No – I love it. I've already achieved a great deal. I'm already Head of Year. I'm highly respected within the school. I've got my sights on a Deputy Headship in the next five years. If I interrupt my career at this point, I'd be starting from scratch in five years time. You're asking the impossible of me!'

'Well, what are we going to do, then? Professional childcare – even nursery – is bloody expensive – at least £25 grand a year. That's nearly as much as I earn!'

'Exactly. So why don't *you* look after them? You didn't have any trouble creating them!'

Mal smiled. 'You mean...'

'Yes, I mean. I know the exact date. The time you wanted to do doggy style. Well, it worked just fine. But we did want to create a baby, so there. And I can't remember any fanciful calculations while you were doing it!'

Mal was pleased to turn the conversation to more congenial

areas. 'That's a point. Funny thing about men. While they're at it, everything else flies out of their mind!' Mal smiles. 'Doggy style, eh? Bet that would turn-on your ten year old lads, eh?'

'Don't be smutty. Anyway, these things are covered, in a sensible way, in their sex education classes.'

'While we're at it,' mused Mal, and while you're so fit, do you think we could do a home movie? (Smiling knowingly) we have the equipment; and we have the technology…'

'Not if the words 'movie' and 'Internet' come within a million miles of each other. Mrs Bell with her knockers out is not an image that would go down well with the School Governors. In all honesty, I don't think some of those old chaps have ever seen a woman without her clothes on. They'd have the shock of their lives!'

'Don't you believe it!' responded Mal. 'Rumour has it that that Mark Wearing is a bit of a paedo…'

'Mal – I'm being serious, just repeat that allegation anywhere outside this house, if you want to wreck my career – and our future.'

'Well, you could wear a mask…'

'Not on your frigging nelly. I thought we were having a serious discussion, not indulging your fantasies?'

'OK. Let's get serious. You can't possibly expect me to give up my job at Hancox's. I've been there ten years, now, and I'm Deputy Manager. I want to be Manager. If I leave now, I'll look a right pratt – 'specially if I give 'em the truth. And I'd start right back at the bottom in three or four years time. Sweeping the bloody floors, cleaning the counter, scrubbing the block – minimum wage stuff. There's none of my friends given up their jobs to look after their kids. It's just not done!'

'But you're a good dad. And, if we're being practical – and don't take this the wrong way – I earn more than you. And if I become a Deputy Head, my earnings will go up by about 25%.'

'I thought you'd fling that in my face. We can manage on my wages. Especially with your careful management of our money. Bringing up our kids in a safe, happy environment has got to be the priority. You can use your teaching skills to prepare Becky and Miranda for when they start school. While all I could teach them about is different cuts of meat! No contest!'

'That's just silly. You're asking me to give up my future, *our* future, for short term considerations!'

'Like your children?'

'*Our* children. They're your children as much as they are mine!'

'But you're their mother! It's different!'

'No: we have to decide what's in our family's long-term interests. If Dawn feels she can't cope any more...'

'Don't bring my mother into it!'

'Well, she is only 50. And she is their Grandma!'

'But she's said she *can't* cope any more. We need to respect that!'

'I do respect it. But none of this means that I have to sacrifice my career.'

Mal sighed. 'There's an important match on telly. Can we sleep on this, and talk again tomorrow?'

'I suppose so. But you need to know that I'm upset; upset that you seem to think so little of my career. I hope 'doggy' and 'style' don't enter your vocabulary tonight.'

Mal sighed again, and shook his head. 'That's not fair.'

'Fair doesn't come into it. I don't feel valued, that's all. I'm going for a walk.'

'Why?'

'To clear my head. And think.'

'Isn't all this a bit melodramatic?'

'Melodramatic? No – I'm happy to talk it through – but it can't always be on your terms. *Au revoir.*'

Three months of almost constant argument followed. For three months, Mal employed every possible tactic and manoeuvre known to him to wear down his wife's moral courage, and impose his will on her. For three months, Mary tried everything in her power to find some compromise, consistent with her self-worth, and passionate desire to continue her career. Over those three months, the relationship suffered a deep and ugly fissure. Mal and Mel began to dislike the sight of each other, such was the expectation of endless, fruitless bickering and dissent. An air of depression hung over every room, like a thick, grey pall. Both Mal and Mary came to realise that they were deeply, almost unbearably, unhappy.

Mal went out most nights, to escape the tension, and to avoid his – he thought – unbelievably stubborn wife. Much better to share a few beers, and have a laugh with his mates. Often, he would not return home until the early hours, or even at all. Mary would watch some TV, after bathing her daughters, and settling them to sleep. She began to be suspicious of Mal's long absences, and checked for tell-tale signs of an affair. She would sniff Mal's shirts for perfume, and examine them for smudges of lipstick. She would pore over his clothing for foreign hairs – of any description. And she would conduct forensic examinations of Mal's discarded underpants, for incriminating stains. But, despite all her efforts, Mary found nothing. Somehow, this only made the situation worse.

But there was one further avenue to explore. Mal was always leaving his smart phone lying around, and it was an easy thing to check for unusual numbers. But Mary felt guilty doing so. Had things come to this? As it turned out, there was only one unusual number and, when Mary checked it out, it belonged to a young woman called Melody, who worked at a local Estate Agent's.

SEPARATION

What the hell did they need an Estate Agent for? Otherwise, the phone merely bore evidence of a scattering of porn. 'Amateur Busty Babes' indeed. What the fuck did he need that crap for, when he had a responsive young wife at home? Well, he had had. For God's sake, they all looked a bit like... Perhaps she needed to try again...

Mal rarely went out on Monday evenings, and today was a Monday. In bed that night, Mary cuddled up to Mal in a particular way, that she knew he enjoyed. 'What the fuck do you think you're doing!' Mal turned away, hugging the bedclothes tightly. And that was that.

There seemed to be no end in sight; no resolution that was acceptable to both husband and wife. Very soon, they pretty much stopped all communication, since the arguments had become exhausted, along with their emotional resilience. Even bed was a cold, comfortless place.

Then, one day, finding herself alone with Mal for the first time in a week, Mary blurted out: 'Mal, I think we should separate, at least for a while.' To Mary's surprise, Mal agreed, with almost indecent haste. He was gone the same day, leaving Mary with the children.

In due course, the separation became permanent, and the house was placed on the market. Melody handled the sale. Mary had been pleased to meet her. Melody seemed smoothly, and confidently efficient. But, judging from Mal's choice of porn, definitely not his type. She turned out to be boyish, and independent minded. Boyish was clearly not Mal's type. And independent-minded, Mary reflected bitterly, was definitely not his type, either. But even the sale of their lovely family home, in

Melody's capable hands, would bring little comfort. Very little equity had built up: there would be no money for new deposits – just enough to repay the bank.

Mary, Becky and Miranda went to live, at least temporarily, with Mary's father, Geoff. Although very sad at 'developments', he was primarily concerned with the welfare of his only daughter, and his grandchildren. Geoff had recently retired as a police officer: his every waking moment would be devoted to his daughter's needs. He knew she was emotionally traumatised but, in the fullness of time, he would help Mary to secure a new home – either contributing to the rent, or finding a deposit for a house. His pension lump sum would see to that. As for child care, when Mary returned to work: well, it was only a matter of money, and they would find it, somehow. Following her maternity leave, and months of emotional trauma, Mary was eager – as never before – to return to her School, and to resume teaching.

As for Mal, one fine day he turned up on his mother's doorstep, with only a holdall, and an apologetic smile. 'Hi Ma, I've come home!' Dawn looked horrified, then adjusted her face. 'Very well, but I can't possibly be expected to look after both you and Bernard!'

'Who the fuck's Bernard?'

Be careful what you wish for.

HEAVEN SENT

'It is easier for a camel to pass through the eye of a needle than for a rich man to enter Heaven' proclaims the Biblical proverb. I would challenge the sophistries of the most dexterous barrister to get out of that one. Or so I thought. After all, 2,000 years ago, a camel was a camel. Even a baby one was pretty hefty. And, though needles come in various sizes, I've never seen one that could admit passage to a large quadruped. Of course, in this digital age, anything can be 'fixed', manipulated or atomised into different sizes and shapes. But I think we have to give the august writer due credit: his – or her – rather graphic metaphor was meant to focus minds. And, over the millennia, focus minds it has.

Andrew Carnegie, the 19th century industrialist and magnate, famously said – and no doubt with the Biblical reference in mind – that no man should die rich. So Carnegie divested himself of his enormous wealth before shuffling off his mortal coil. Great exemplar. Great insurance policy. Since you can't take it with you, why not book a safe place in Heaven? A bloody good investment in the future, if you ask me!

So why am I telling you this? Well, I was 90 years of age and, until the age of 80, had built up considerable sources of wealth. It wasn't planned that way; it just sort of happened. Property. Pensions. Investments. Savings. It wasn't on the scale of Carnegie, of course, but it all added up to a pretty penny. So when my wife died unexpectedly, and we were childless, I thought it high time to dust off that insurance policy by ridding myself of all material encumberments.

Enid would have been furious, but one thing I've learned is that, once dead, you simply don't count. If she'd been a man, Enid might have been Ebenezer. She just loathed spending money. She ended up as one of the richest guests in the graveyard. Quite an accolade.

To be honest, once you *start* giving, it's easy. And everyone's suitably grateful. At least, that's what their letters proclaim – evidence to show St Peter. Charities, old friends, and nephews and nieces all benefitted from my generosity, as my largesse showered upon them in the years before my demise. And, in truth, it was heart-warming to get all those acknowledgements of thanks; and all those hugs and smiles. There are tax implications, of course, so you'll need to employ a good solicitor to minimise that particular bill. Strange, in a way, but the one body I didn't want to benefit from all my hard work was Her Majesty's Government. No, young Will could buy his Porsche, and Mary could have her round-the-world jolly. But the Chancellor wouldn't be rubbing his hands with anticipation any time soon.

And then – just in time – I died, aged 90. Nice round figure; and I was prepared – not in the middle of something complicated, like a new relationship, or a holiday coming up. Not caught off guard. Or spent it on cruising, which was the pleasurable alternative. And 'just in time' because I'd given everything away. By the way, I'm not supposed to be telling you this, because it's highly confidential. But, in what seemed like a flash, seamlessly, effortlessly, my soul was whisked to Heaven; and an audience with St Peter.

*

HEAVEN SENT

The Pearly Gates glimmered and shimmered, floating in a vast, vague nothingness. Flights of Angels, similarly floating, sang in the background. 'Welcome to Paradise, Peter!' beamed St Peter. St Peter, transparent and formless, but still instantly recognisable, likewise floated before me.

'I never expected the Pearly Gates to be real, just a metaphor! Not to mention Angels!' I exclaimed, instantly impressed.

'Well, we aim to please; and keep up appearances,' replied the Saint, smiling. 'Always been one of my favourite names, Peter. Glad the mortals are sticking with tradition. Of course, we see far more Mohammeds these days. No matter – anyone and everyone is welcome here. After all, there is only one Heaven. Mind you, if your name *was* Mohammed, Mohammed himself would have welcomed you. People of all beliefs and persuasions – and non-believers – are all greeted most warmly. Though I can tell you, we get more than a few raised eye-brows. That's if they had any eye-brows to raise...' St Peter laughed at his own joke. He never tired of it, and had refined it over...time. 'I remember that Pope...' he continued, 'had quite a shock. We're all the same, here, Peter. Kings, Emperors, Presidents – makes no difference. Anyway, Peter, we hope you enjoy your stay – because of course it's forever. Right, Peter. That'll be a five grand non-refundable deposit, please.'

'*What?*' I blundered. 'I thought this was Paradise! And, if you haven't noticed, though in spirit form, I'm naked! Nowhere to hide even a debit card!'

St Peter smiled. 'That's OK. Not to worry. We do have our running costs, you know. Heaven wasn't built on a wing and a prayer. 'The other place' doesn't charge, to be honest, but you wouldn't want to be going *there*...'

'But how on Earth – Heaven – am I supposed to pay? I've given everything away, like a good Christian!'

'Oh, dear, are they still peddling that nonsense? How

bizarre!' Peter – the other Peter – smiled. 'There are ways. We just need your permission. Please fill in this form, Acs 34 – it's a long form (though formless) but you have all the, er, time in the world – and we'll arrange things for you. Do take it to your pod – number 1324576890 – and fill it in over a nice cup of tea. Well, metaphorically speaking, since you no longer have a mouth, or...'

'But I still don't understand. I have nothing! I've given it all away!'

'The form will explain everything. To complete it, you just need to think upon it – easy peasy. But, basically, we take a cut – sorry – tithe – of your late assets.'

'There's two main means we employ. First, inflation. You've heard of inflation? Money just evaporates – into thin air. It comes here! And everyone knows that money falls down cracks and into holes – that's why there's always more month than money. So all those beneficiaries of your Will will find that the money doesn't go as far as they'd hoped.'

'But what do *you* do with it? I mean, I presume there's no shops or restaurants here?'

'Think of it as a cryptocurrency, or gold. Intrinsically worthless. But a store of value, just in case. A kind of insurance policy. Any further questions at all at this stage? We appreciate there's a lot to take in...'

'Yes, when will I meet God?'

'God?'

'Yes, when will I meet him?'

'Him? You'll 'meet' the force you call 'God' bye and bye...'

'And is he as Almighty as people say – he can do anything?'

'Yes, I'd say so. Except reform the human race. That's a hopeless case. In fact, it's a cause of some regret that it was ever created. Bloody graceless, ungrateful bunch!'

'And what about my wife, Enid? Where is she?'

'I'm afraid Enid is in the other place. She refused to pay the fees...'

'Oh my G...I mean, could I help in any way...to make up the shortfall?'

'Fraid not. Spirits commit, and commit for eternity. Not to worry: Elsie – your Guardian Angel – will be here in a jiff. We only say 'she' as a courtesy, because she was a woman in her mortal life. Elsie will show you the ropes, the lie of the place, and patiently answer any further queries you may have...See you later with that form...'

'One more question. What do we do all day?'

'Do? Not 'do'. Just 'be'' replied Peter with a smile. 'Chill and relax. And remember there are no 'days'. Right, here is your Guardian Angel, Elsie, a pure spirit. Elsie will guide you to your pod.'

Elsie floated before me, diaphanous, almost transparent, but with a kind of inner glow. We set off. Elsie – though a spirit, still having the impression of womanhood – drifted in a kind of glowing ether, passing many other spirits, and guardian angels, along the way. We eventually arrived at 'my' pod, a kind of globular gossamer form, of indeterminate space. We passed through the apparently immaterial walls. The internal space, if it was such, was completely bereft of any material items. No bed. No TV. No shower. No food.

'OK, the bad news first,' Elsie began. 'Your pod will cost you £100 per week. But the rent is fixed forever.'

'That's quite reasonable, I suppose,' I muttered, staring blankly into the empty space. 'But what do I actually *do* with my time?' I asked, a little petulantly. Elsie smiled. 'That question again. 'Time' doesn't officially exist. But the answer is: anything you like.'

'Well, what about TV? I was quite partial to a bit of Netflix, and the odd soap...'

Elsie smiled again. 'All you have to do is *think* of something, and it will happen. Example: when I was a woman, I enjoyed gardening. In fact, nurturing and picking fruit and veg for my Lord and Lady was one of my duties. So I enjoy 'Gardeners World'. And here it is…' Suddenly, figures appeared before us… Monty Don…Carol Klein…a Golden Retriever…flowers and vegetables…Quite nostalgic, really. 'Or maybe 'Bargain Hunt', or 'Escape to the Country', if that's your thing. Or any Spurs match that's ever been played.'

'That's great!' I said, genuinely impressed, and impressed, also, that Elsie knew I was a Tottenham fan. 'So I can look at anything? No control, or censorship? Any sport, for example, or game shows, or those Italian housewives?'

Elsie laughed. 'Really, anything. We're here forever. There's no-one to judge you. No harm to be done, either by or to you. Eternity is a long… time, so settle down and try to enjoy it!'

'So what about the opposite sex?' I asked, throwing caution to the winds.

'We're all spirits here. You can commune with whoever you like. You can talk, mix, mingle or whatever, but physical relations are no longer possible. I can assure you, you won't miss it. Always been over-rated.'

'But I can look up famous people – I mean spirits? Helen of Troy for example? Napoleon? Mozart?'

'That's no problem. You'll find them all keen to reminisce and tell their stories. And they all have a semblance – the impression – of who they were, so you'll easily recognise them, floating around. And remember Heaven really is your oyster: anything that's ever happened can be revealed before your…senses. Pompeii, for example. Or the court of Henry VIII. Or, yes, the Trojan Wars. You just have to think it, to *will* it to appear…'

'Well, that sounds like fun. I'm just a bit surprised Napoleon is actually here. I mean, he caused quite a few problems in his time.'

'I think you'll find we're pretty non-judgemental, here. You'll find Boney-that-was quite effusive about Marengo and Austerlitz. But if Wellington appears, 'he' gets a bit animated… Anyway, let him without sin etc…So long as they pay the fees…'

'Yes, that's another thing. I don't get this money thing. This is supposed to be Paradise. I wasn't expecting an echo of capitalism!'

'And that's the point. The spirit you call God got fed up dealing with complaints. Like, 'God, I'm bored!' Or 'Call this Paradise? And there's no fish and chips?' Or, 'Where on Earth can I get the wind in my hair, ride a horse, climb a tree, eat a steak?' So God decided to charge 'people' for their stay. Quite simply, so they'd continue to appreciate what they have, and not take it all for granted. But there is an important caveat: only those who can afford to pay are charged. Paradise is free to the poor. But it's the same Paradise for everyone. So – as a spirit – you can do everything a spirit can, go everywhere, do everything, do anything…'

I was already wondering what that 'everything, anything' amounted to, but decided to keep mum. Time would tell. Except there was no 'time'. Mmm…no food. No sex. No physical being. Were they freedoms, or constraints? Did they imprison us, or release our true selves…?

And that reminded me. I must catch up with The Bard. He'd have a view or three about this Brave New World. 'Elsie, I expect Will Shakespeare is here, somewhere? And that he's churning out plays like never before?'

'Well, yes, his spirit *is* here,' replied Elsie, hesitatingly. 'But, last time I met him, he seemed a bit 'down'. Silly, really, but apparently he's been complaining about 'writers block'. Whatever that is!'

I reflected on Elsie's words. 'Elsie, do you think people – spirits – are happy in Paradise?'

She laughed, or at least made a pleasant sound. 'That sounds like a contradiction in terms. Happiness is a human concept and condition, and probably defined by its opposite – unhappiness. Here, there is no poverty, no disease, no hunger. And no war, conflict or violence. As for happiness, I'd say that we're in a different state; an exalted and more stable state. The extremes of human emotion may no longer be possible, because the drivers of those states are absent. But we exist in a wonderful, benign pool of calm, where all possibilities – save those appertaining to flesh and mortality – are available. But you need to experience for yourself. You have all the time – sorry, I don't know what else to call it – in the world…and more…'

'So how *big* is this place?' I asked Elsie. 'Only I haven't seen any roads, or fields, or sky, or horizon. There's no perspective. It just seems to go on forever!'

'Well, that's right!' she replied. 'Heaven is infinite. You can travel anywhere, forever, but it's really all the same. No risks or dangers – just carry on drifting, and greeting, for as long as you wish. Then just will yourself back to your pod!'

'But is every day the same, then?'

'Peter, there are no days – or nights. Things just carry on as they are, for all…' Elsie stopped in mid-flow. 'Really,' she continued, 'you'll soon get used to it! Some spirits never leave their pods. Some rarely come home, they're so busy conversing with friends, or historical figures they're keen to meet. The possibilities are infinite…'

'And is that it?' I asked, a little ungraciously. 'We can't travel to 'the other place', for instance?'

'Oh dear goodness, no. Here all is light and air, peace and freedom. The other place is dark and hopeless and, besides, horrible beyond even our imagination.'

'And are there no other Heavens? I asked. 'I was hoping to catch up with my old dog, *Buster*.'

Elsie's countenance seemed to melt into a frown. 'I have

heard rumours, that I hope are true. But, whether or not, we're in Heaven and (Elsie made a tinkling sound) that's it, baby!'

'Phew. But is there nothing here you regret, Elsie? Nothing you miss?'

'Well, they're two different questions. We always prayed for eternal life, and here we have it. How great is that? As for missing anything from my life on Earth, I really don't think so. Certainly not my mean, brutal, vicious husband, Edward. Or my professional life as a domestic servant to Lord and Lady Whatsit. Or the terror of becoming pregnant, or ill, without a Health Service!'

'Hold on!' I cried, 'that means Enid is with Edward! How amazing!'

'Well,' said Elsie, archly, 'if that's the case, she'll wait a bloody long time for a drink! He always had short arms and long pockets. Now he has neither! But to continue: here in Paradise I feel free, content...my own self. And I know that those delights will last forever. Don't you feel the same?'

'Generally, yes. I certainly don't miss being a creakey old git, aged ninety. But, maybe, I'll miss the sky, and the sea, and fields with dancing buttercups, and being in love. And the odd cool pint.'

'I do understand' said Elsie, feelingly. 'But those memories will fade, over...OK, time. Or rather your *feelings* towards those memories will fade. I do urge you to give this place a chance... we're all rooting for you.'

'Thank you, Elsie. I'm sure you're right. My thoughts are all very transitory, I agree. It's nothing. I've not been here long, so I can still remember – still have that sense of nostalgia for the physical, for the material, for the *changeability*, for the surprise each day brings. If I'm honest, this spiritual life – even though back on Earth we all hankered for it – all sounds a weeny bit bland. But, yes, this is the 'future'. I suppose I'd just better get used to it...'

LOVE IS ALL YOU NEED

Joel and Johnnie were neighbours, certainly for two weeks, since they occupied adjacent 'cottages' in a holiday village in northern Brittany. They had also, over a handful of days, become firm friends; though whether they would remain friends, only time would tell.

Joel and his wife Lottie hailed from Antwerp, Netherlands; Johnnie, and his wife Lola, from Andover, Hampshire. Both couples were easy-going and gregarious, and their friendship, fuelled by these virtues, similar ages, and similarity of outlook, was further hastened by the Dutch couple's fluent English.

The two men in particular bonded quickly. They both smoked, for instance – for Johnnie, perhaps the most racy, *dangerous* activity in his life; Joel preferred hash. They both loved to laugh and joke at the absurdity of life, even if Johnnie's assumed confidence disguised an underlying social unease. They both loved sunshine and barbecues. And they both loved the finer things in life – like wine. And women: (though Johnnie's reputation rested solely on his spectacular success with Lola – it quickly became clear that Joel was the acknowledged expert in *that* field). And song: surprisingly, perhaps, Joel and Johnnie shared a passion for poetry – especially, oddly enough, English Romantic poetry.

Joel was the senior guy, at 36; the less socially-confident

Johnnie, with his narrower horizons, was easily impressed by his older friend's broad, urbane philosophy to life, his larger-than-life persona, and his casual, roguish nature.

Joel and Lottie
Joel, a software engineer for a multi-national company, seemed to have done everything, to have experienced everything; indeed, he seemed at times to be a little world-weary, before re-collecting himself, and re-asserting his almost permanent smile. Joel was tall and slim and vital, with a mane of shoulder length hair that made him appear younger than his years; only his goatee beard, streaked with grey, gave away the biological truth. In fact, Joel was beginning to suffer from 40 anxiety – masked by a slightly forced exterior bonhomie – and determined to extract the maximum possible pleasure from each and every day.

For some years now, Joel, and his wife, Lottie, had had an open marriage, permitting each other different sexual partners. They had both indulged this freedom, and the arrangement had worked on a practical, real-time basis. Though Joel pursued his freedom far more readily, and far more energetically, than Lottie, their emotional relationship continued almost unchanged, and the institution of marriage, at least in a formal sense, remained intact.

Joel had been married to Lottie, his childhood sweetheart, for 17 years, now. Indeed, they had a 17 year-old daughter, Imogen. Lottie herself was tall, slim, long-limbed and angular – with blonde, curly locks and startling blue eyes, set in a strikingly attractive face. If not conventionally beautiful, 34-year-old Lottie had undeniable presence, accentuated by her lithe, supple – almost feline – grace. In fact, Lottie looked, and moved, like the erstwhile athlete she was – specialising in the 400 metres and long-jump, and representing Groningen University. Professionally, however, Lottie was a primary school teacher. She worked hard all year, for herself, and her family. This was her major summer holiday; time to relax, and enjoy.

Daughter Imogen, a beautiful, but self-conscious, and self-willed, young woman, had not travelled with her parents, preferring to holiday in Nice with her boyfriend Mohamed's family. Her parents were upset and annoyed at her behaviour; she was too young, and too headstrong – even for her loving father. But, heck, what could liberal, open-minded parents do? And Imogen's absence – as they frequently reminded one other – at least gave the still youngish, fun-loving parents space to enjoy their holiday as they desired – and deserved.

Johnnie and Lola

Johnnie, 33, was deputy manager of a bank branch in Andover, where he'd been based, working his way steadily up the career ladder, for the last seven years. It was not the most exciting life, but it paid the mortgage, and funded holidays like this. The couple owned a prim detached house, with manicured garden, and two new cars on the drive. Not bad for 33, thought Johnnie, when he had those rare moments of self-doubt, and stirrings of an inadequacy he struggled to define.

Johnnie was accounted handsome by his acquaintances: of medium build, with short, dark hair, and regular, pleasing features. There was the merest suggestion of the beginnings of a paunch. Lola sometimes teased him – to Johnnie's embarrassment and annoyance.

Johnnie's wife of nine years, Lola – the 'baby' at 31 – was petite but vivacious, with flashing emerald eyes, natural bee-stung lips, and long, auburn tresses that framed her perfectly symmetrical face, and shimmered on her tanned shoulders. Her light, elegant clothing casually, but artfully, revealed a fulsome, voluptuous figure. Lola, a self-employed beautician, was flighty and vaguely dissatisfied with her life, and had few apparent interests other than maintaining her perfect persona; and this she performed with admirable effect. Ah, beauty! Skin deep, maybe, but so dazzling its impact on humanity that it readily obscures or disguises less visible qualities. And so it was that Lola's hidden depths of personality and intellect remained largely hidden – even to her husband. Certainly, Lola's most obvious attributes – a slim, slight, but awesomely shapely figure, and a face that might have been drawn by Raphael – were the product of Nature's beneficence; her beautician's artifice only enhanced an already almost over-wrought provision. For better or worse, Lola's glowing appearance conditioned – and perhaps constrained – the substance of every relationship she enjoyed with friends and acquaintances.

Not surprisingly, Lola was extremely popular with her clients. Bubbly, chatty and witty, a beauty therapy session with Lola was always a delight. A standing joke – whenever Lola enquired what treatment the client fancied that day – was: 'whatever treatment you've just had!'

Remarkably, for a girl already popular – indeed legendary – among the young bucks at college, it was the handsome, studious Johnnie who had attracted her attention. Lola could, literally, have had her choice of any – indeed all – the guys at college. But, instinctively shrewd, if not 'clever', she chose Johnnie. Johnnie was different – and she knew he was serious. She also knew that Johnnie was ambitious, as well as handsome, and would help her achieve the life-style to which she aspired. And, yes, they now had the 'dream' house, and manicured garden, and the complementary cars. So Johnnie had been Lola's only partner – and only lover.

Though the couple had been married for nine years, now, love-making continued on a regular basis. But, in truth, Lola found little pleasure in Johnnie's attentions. She found the whole pantomime rather disappointing, but did not quite know why;

Johnnie represented her totality of experience. Lola wanted to be *loved* – passionately; completely. While she could not fault her husband's frantic, perfunctory efforts – which he sometimes blamed on her beauty – their sexual activity seemed a bit predictable, a little one-dimensional, a touch monotonous. And, when Lola was honest with herself, deeply unsatisfying.

This was a struggle for the young wife: materially, socially, she had all that she desired. And Johnnie still sometimes said he loved her – but, generally, when supplicating his wife for sex. Lola had a keen sense of her attractions, and desirability – of *self-worth* – and sometimes thought she deserved better; *more*. So, at times, she felt somewhat less than happy; at other times she shrugged, and thought, in the scheme of things, she really *must* be satisfied with her lot.

Johnnie and Lola had no children; Lola had been alarmed at the very idea. But, if life was not terribly exciting, Johnnie had always been a solid, dependable kind of guy. Johnnie himself felt that his life was set in aspic, its course unchangeable and set; a prospect that sometimes inspired smug satisfaction, and sometimes its very opposite.

Surreal Scenario
Almost a week had passed, a week of enjoyable easy living and conviviality, with an underlying, undeniable sexual *frisson* in the air. The couples had already spent a large, sun-lit slice of each day in each other's company, and five of the last six evenings (on the third evening, Lola had been overcome by a nervous migraine). Everything was fresh, vibrant, titillating; arousing. They ate, drank, swapped stories, and exchanged tantalising details of their respective lives, interests, and hopes for the future.

Friendships quickly deepened: Joel liked Johnnie. Johnnie liked – and admired and looked up to – Joel. Joel liked Lola. Lola liked Joel. Johnnie liked Lottie. Lottie liked Johnnie. Lottie liked

Lola. And Lola liked Lottie. The magic, blessed circle seemed complete. Though their habits and preferments made for easy, relaxed relationships, each party was attracted and fascinated by their respective differences: of personality, temperament, lifestyle, culture; and appearance.

The athletic Lottie loved tennis, and was an exceptionally talented player. Since Joel loathed all unnecessary physical activity, Lottie was delighted to learn that Johnnie shared her passion – if not her ability. The couple had already played three games that first week. Although Lottie had quickly toned down her natural game to around 70% of capacity, in order to spare Johnnie's blushes, she still comfortably out-classed him in every game. In all honesty, Johnnie hardly minded losing to his delectable, graceful opponent. Lottie wore a red bikini, then blue, then white, on their respective playing days. Johnnie complained, teasingly, that he was being unfairly distracted – whether Lottie was serving, crouching at the net, or racing to return a shot, Johnnie always saw more bikini than ball.

At the conclusion of the third game – another 6:2, 6:2 win for Lottie – Johnnie asked if she might wear the blue bikini, the following afternoon: 'I find it a little less distracting,' he laughed. 'Fair enough,' replied Lottie, with her trademark smile: 'And I promise not to remove it while we're playing. That really *would* be unfair!' Johnnie could only hope. And believe.

Joel was surprised to find that Lola shared his love of board games – particularly *Scrabble*. While his wife and friend enjoyed *their* game, Joel would spend a couple of hours sitting opposite Lola – delighting not only in her intelligent play, but her quick, earthy humour – and her mesmerising presence. Joel appreciated every physical expression and nuance of the casually under-dressed Lola with the expertise of a Renaissance master. This was the closest to heaven to which he could aspire, he told himself. Well, almost. Joel's natural composure and concentration quite deserted him; his thoughts were elsewhere. Lola understood, and felt flattered; she could not be ignorant of her impact on this sophisticated *bon viveur*.

As far as *Scrabble* was concerned, the honours were shared – two games each. Joel complained, smiling, 'I don't think any woman's ever beaten me before.' 'Well, Joel Nielsson, I'm not *any* woman. I'm Lola Harcourt!' 'Lola Harcourt?' reflected Joel. 'Phew, that's a tough one. What about 'Curt Hoar?'' he laughed. 'But I could do with a couple more consonants – maybe those found in the word 'consonant'' he added, slyly. During one – for him – purple patch, Joel had opportunistically added I-S to Lola's 'PEN', and, triumphantly, fronted C-L-E-A-V to Lola's 'AGE'. Only Joel knew whether or not he had cheated; they both dissolved in fits of giggles. Lola responded by transforming 'ROBS' into 'THROBS', and Joel's predictable 'SEX' into 'SEXUAL'. But the competitive spirit seemed to be subdued and submerged beneath a glorious swoon of sun and sensuality: enjoyment – and revelation – was all.

The Breton weather had been on its very best behaviour, and each and every day proved a delight of blue and gold. On this particular afternoon – not for the first time – the two couples had relaxed and sun-bathed together; the men bare chested, stretched out on sun-loungers, in sculpted shorts. Lottie, for her part, lounged easily in the red bikini that set off her blonde curls and lithe, lightly tanned limbs. Lola wore a gold bikini, which complemented her skin tones and moulded to her curves. Everyone enjoyed everyone's presence, delighting in small talk, and risqué but good natured comments about appearance, physicality, and future hopes and plans. Alcohol and afternoon sun relaxed the foursome further, until they entered an almost trance-like state.

Joel made a teasing aside – complimentary, but ripe with suggestion and innuendo – concerning his wife's figure; causing

Lola to raise her eyebrows. 'You don't believe me?' he said. 'You want evidence?' Joel nodded to his wife, who dutifully, deftly, took off her bikini top, flinging it in her husband's face. Johnnie gasped, 'Christ!' and rolled over. The confident Lottie arched her back on the recliner, as if to demonstrate the veracity of her husband's ribald comment, before slowly subsiding into a delectable, sensuous, pose. Johnnie shot an anxious glance at Lola. Understanding, she smiled and, not to be outdone, slowly, oh so deliberately, removed her top. Joel groaned in astonishment, before turning on to his front.

Following – for her – act of unprecedented bravado, Lola thought it judicious to lie face down – pillowed upon those lately-revealed – but, for some, all-too-briefly revealed – exquisite breasts – and to ask Johnnie to oil her back. A moment or two later Lola felt her shoulders being massaged, in short, sensuous sweeps. She relaxed – melted – beneath the strong but gentle hands, until the insidious, roving fingers reached inside her bikini bottom. Though the caress felt thrilling, something felt different, indeed *very* un-Johnnie like. Looking round, she saw Joel kneeling above her, wearing only a big grin – her gaze met his semi-erect penis. Lola's body convulsed with shock, then shook with uncontrollable mirth. The whole party joined in. Joel himself howled with laughter, took a big swig of rum and coke from his tumbler, and placed himself, carefully, face down on his lounger. His bare, taut white bottom gleamed in the sun. 'What a cool dude!' thought Johnnie. 'And what an awesome gal!' – meaning Lottie.

That evening, a merry barbecue ensued, of course master-minded by J & J, and washed down by copious amounts of beer, wine, and gin and tonic. The ring of laughter, sometimes bordering on hysteria, rang out across the campsite meadows, and across the shimmering sea, as the day softened, cooled, and faded to twilight.

It was already past midnight when Lottie was invited to

Lola's chalet, for yet another night-cap. The two women left arm in arm, embracing and giggling. 'What's the fucking joke?' asked a heavily inebriated Johnnie. 'Not a clue, old chap!' replied the equally sozzled Joel. 'But Johnnie, what a fabulous wife you have! You're the luckiest bastard in the world!'

'Yep, I think so,' Johnnie agreed. *But,* he added, 'Lottie is the *most* desirable woman…She's totally irresistible…'

'I know, I know,' said Joel, winningly. 'But we've been together for 17 years. It's a long time…As you know, a few years back we agreed to have a more open marriage. Let others in, as it were. Keeps us eager, and feeling alive. It's not for everyone. But it suits us. Just sex, mind – we'll always have feelings for each other, always have a deeper commitment.'

'But you're not jealous?' asked an incredulous Johnnie. 'Your wife? Screwing another man?'

'Jealousy is for wimps' replied Joel. 'Besides, *my* screwing Maggie or Martha generally takes my mind off it,' he laughed. 'But tell me, old chap, is it *really* true that you've *only* ever been with Lola? And no-one else?'

'That's about it' averred Johnnie. 'We met, got together, and got married. In the traditional, time-honoured way.'

'Don't get me wrong' hastened Joel. I shouldn't have uttered the words 'only' and 'Lola' in the same breath. One of the great poets, John Donne, described his mistress as 'my kingdom', 'my America', and 'my empire'. Same with Shakespeare and Cleopatra…'infinite variety'. It's only *now* that I really get what they meant.'

'Bloody hell,' said Johnnie. 'It'll be Byron next. So tell *me* – since this is cards on the table time – how many women *you've* had?'

'God knows' responded Joel, shaking his head. 'I stopped counting when I reached a hundred.'

'Good God!' cried Johnnie. 'A hundred! What's *that* all about?'

'It's not *that* difficult, you know. And it's been over eight years or so – I remember we'd been married for nine years at that stage. I don't count the women who came before the…arrangement. Really, we're all sexual beings, at the end of the day. We *all* want some fun – without commitment. Its just fucking sex! But I tell you what: in all honesty, I haven't met anyone who's a patch on Lottie.'

'So why do you bother…why do it?' asked Johnnie, with a mixture of curiosity and something approaching awe.

'Well, I could quote what climbers say, when they're asked why they climb a mountain: because it's *there*. I can only say that everyone is different; every situation is exciting; every encounter full of eagerness and expectation. It just makes me feel alive. Lottie feels the same. But I always come back to Lottie…'

Johnnie swallowed hard, and coughed, unsure. Joel made it all sound so easy, *so* natural. And the alcohol had loosened his tongue. 'So could *I*, you know…Lottie?'

Joel looked him squarely in the face, though he was swaying slightly, from side to side: 'This is man to man. I'm her husband, not her pimp. Lottie's not vain, but she is proud. She makes her own choices. You'd need to approach her, and sweet-talk her… nicely. But Lottie likes you. So it's a start. And I could put in a good word for you…that is, do my best. If…'

'If?' echoed Johnnie, instinctively comprehending, his mouth suddenly dry.

Joel saw an open goal and seized his chance. 'Lola. You know I want her. Fancy her like hell. What a spunky girl! What an angelic face! What a fucking fabulous figure!'

Johnnie gulped. 'Phew. I dunno. *She's* only ever been with me. And we've never done that kind of thing. Ever.' He chuckled, grimly, in an alcohol-fuelled fug. 'I mean, she can be a feisty bint. Doesn't always do what *I* want…mmm. Tell you what, I'll run it past her in the morning. Do what I can. But don't get your hopes up. She'll probably do her nut. It ain't a done deal…'

'No probs. I like feisty. And I'll do what *I* can for you with the athletic, flexible Lottie!' Joel reminded him, underlining 'flexible'.

Be-fuddled as he was, Johnnie could see how things lay; the *quid pro quo*. He was no fool; only a drunk with a fire in his pants. The two men hugged. That was quite enough ground covered for one day. Tomorrow should, to say the least, prove interesting.

The Deal

That morning, still in bed around nine, and still recovering from the excesses of the night before, Johnnie nervously addressed his wife. The gist was – 'honest, straight conversation, don't get shirty – Joel and Lottie have an open marriage. We both like Joel and Lottie. Joel really fancies you. Well, what about it? If it's just sex, don't worry – I won't get heavy.'

Johnnie was taken aback by his wife's furious response. 'This is about Lottie. Just so you can fuck her, without repercussions! You must think I'm an idiot!'

Johnnie tried to re-assure his wife. 'Look, it's not about Lottie, though yes, I admit I *do* like her. Of course I do. But we're in a new place…spiritually. A totally new experience. It's all so different, so exciting, with these new, freedom-loving friends. Look, do *you* want this? If so, you have my blessing…'

'Blessing? You know, most men would want to put me on a pedestal. But you – *you* – want to share me out! What's got into you? The boring banker! Become a bonker! Or maybe a wanker!' Lola *knew* that the bastard was lying. He was pimping his wife. Though not a fool, he *was* a fucking idiot. Who knew where it might lead; where it might end?

'Look,' fumed Lola, incandescent, 'if your dick needs an outing, *fuck me!*' Perversely, on uttering those words, she pulled the duvet protectively around her bosom.

'No, no,' said Johnnie, wincing from the onslaught, and shaking his head. Though he *was* sorely tempted by the *apparent* seductive offer – anything to quell the storm – Johnnie knew that any attempt in that direction would result in his being struck dead. 'You know,' he said, in his most soothing, placatory tone, 'over the last week, Joel's become almost like a brother. You like him, don't you? You *seem* to like him a lot. And we know that Joel and Lottie have a very civilised understanding. This last week has really opened my eyes. Just this once, maybe *we* can relax and enjoy life. We're on holiday. In a week or two's time, we can live on the memories, and maybe benefit from a little life experience…put a little pep into our own love-making.'

His wife listened silently, with arms folded. Johnnie's words were beginning to soften her, despite her fierce denial. Lola was gripped by a cruel internal struggle. She listened to her husband – her touchstone, her mentor; her man. And it was true – she *did* like Joel. Joel fascinated Lola: he was a strange, smiling, sensual beast of a man. And she knew, oh she knew, that he was besotted with her. Her female curiosity *was* aroused, and maybe her vanity at being appreciated, truly, as a woman. Lola had *felt* the attention of the charismatic Joel. She had felt flattered, like a flighty young girl, again. She felt the animal attraction fixed upon her. She felt Joel's pure, pungent, urgent desire for her. Lola sensed that, at last, she was being accorded her true deserts.

Still, a nausea gnawed deep in her belly, at the idea of *giving* herself to a stranger. Of strange hands upon her; doing what they would to her. Lola shuddered at the *idea*. What would the *reality* be like? Even so – her imagination freed from normal constraints – a new, surprising idea had just arisen unbidden to her mind. But she knew this leap into the unknown was inextricably linked to satisfying Johnnie – and Joel.

Johnnie prattled on, relishing the silence. 'Listen, all I'm saying is that if *you* really want to, I'll not stand in your way, or play the jealous husband. We're all grown ups here. It's just sex! Just a bit of fun! I'll still love you, as always...' His voice trailed away.

There was another long silence. Then: 'OK,' Lola said at last, almost despite herself, and subduing a sigh.

Johnnie only heard the echo of continued opposition. 'Lola...I really think...'

'I said I'm up for it!' Lola repeated, in a sharper tone. 'If it's going to happen, the sooner the better. Let's make it tonight.'

Johnnie's face lit up with surprise and unimagined delight.

'But on one condition.'

'Condition?' echoed Johnnie, who had thought he'd crossed the finishing line.

'Yes. If you're having Lottie, I'm having her too!'

Masterplan

Following a hasty breakfast, Lola hurried over for a confidential chat with Lottie – a dialogue characterised by passion, but also practicalities. Joel had already briefed his wife, and made it clear what he expected of her.

Joel took the opportunity for a diplomatic stroll along the cliffs, feeling very satisfied with his plans. Heaven seemed to collude with his every move; the stars were conjoined. Joel congratulated himself, chuckling, that he had set *the* heavenly bodies in motion...so that heavenly bodies could be set in motion. Lottie and Lola would play the role of high priestesses – Isis and Artemis – primed to reveal and execute the Will of the Gods. Everything seemed to be coming to fruition, just as he had hoped, dreamed and planned. What a prospect lay ahead! What wild ecstasy!

Joel's plans, as he presented them and urged them on his wife, were, as he had foreseen, acceptable, even agreeable, to Lottie – she welcomed the prospect of sex with Johnnie; though she read

Joel's motives with some disdain. If Joel had master-minded the strategy, Lottie and Lola perfected the detail. It was agreed that, that night, the boys and girls would pair off, in the coupling they all seemed to desire, if with varying degrees of enthusiasm. But that, the following evening, it would be the girls' turn. It was Lola who set the pace, and suggested the precise arrangements, though Lottie well knew who had set the master-plan in motion. Lottie listened, intrigued and delighted with her new friend. 'Very well. Let's get it on. Just one thing before you go, my love…'

Lola hurried down the chalet's steps, one strap of her dress loose on her arm; the curve of her breast revealed, trembling, as her feet tapped lightly on the wooden steps…

Reflection
Over coffee, the morning after the eventful night before, Joel decided to break an awkward silence. 'So how was it with Johnnie?' he asked brightly, trying to simulate interest.

'Meaning what?' exactly, replied Lottie, defensively. 'You've never asked me before.'

'Well, I'm just curious. Is his dick bigger than mine?'

Lottie sighed, then decided to laugh. 'Don't be stupid. But, since you ask, he's certainly a close fit. And' – Lottie hesitated, then blurted, not entirely truthfully – 'Johnnie really knows how to satisfy a woman.'

Joel looked up, perhaps surprised. 'And how precisely did he do that? Are you saying he's a better lover than me?'

'No, of course not. But all men are different. And' – raising her eyebrows – 'all women, too. I only meant that Johnnie was thoughtful, and attentive. You're not getting jealous, are you, after all this time?' She rather hoped that he was. 'It's only sex, remember? Good sex, but only sex.'

Joel was not in the least bit jealous. But he had reasons for making Lottie think that he was. 'Tell you what, to prove I'm not jealous, rather than you and Lola getting it together tonight, why don't we enjoy a foursome instead? Would be fabulous fun!' He emphasised 'fun'. Joel was taken aback by the vehemence of his wife's reaction.

'Absolutely no fucking way! I want to discover Lola for myself. Properly. Intimately. I want quality time with her, woman to woman – like you've had. Not to be treated like a porn star, and plugged by two guys at once. Besides, softly softly catchee monkey. You seem to forget that, until last night, Lola had only known Johnnie. Now she's had her eyes – and God knows what else – opened by you. Another profound new experience awaits her tonight. I really don't think she's ready for anything else – she'd freak out.'

Joel knew when he was beaten; and not to push it. At least not yet. 'Good point' he answered slowly. 'Let's do it your way, as planned. Johnnie and I can have a few beers and a chat…I can't wait.'

Lottie hissed: 'You can fuck *him* if you like!'

Joel smiled. He knew not to rise to the bait.

Reflection, too.
In the adjacent chalet, a similar conversation was taking place. Johnnie stared afresh at his wife: Lola had lately emerged, damp and desirable, from the shower. She was wrapped tightly in a white bath towel; another, smaller, towel, was fashioned like a turban on her lovely head.

Lola sat down, sipping a coffee.

'You haven't mentioned last night,' said Johnnie, a hint of accusation in his voice.

Lola shrugged her shoulders. 'We had sex, that's all. I presume you weren't playing Scrabble?'

'Very droll. But what was it like? What was *he* like?'

'Sorry,' Lola said, taken aback. 'What do you mean, exactly?'

'I mean, what did you fucking get up to?'

'Johnnie, that's a very indelicate question. This was *your* idea, remember, not mine. Until last night, the only man I'd ever been with was *you*. To be honest, when I left here I felt sick, and embarrassed. Did *I* really want this? Would he even like me? Not just the *idea* of me. I felt so horribly anxious, in those few yards I thought of turning back. But we – well, you – had made a deal.' She laughed. 'We'd *made* our bed. But Lottie met me, and gave me a big re-assuring hug on the steps. She whispered to me to relax, that Joel was a considerate, tender lover, and not to worry. I had her blessing, I think she said. Everyone seems to give me their fucking blessing – to get what *they* want. And then she left – for you. As for Joel, he was quite the gentleman – considerate, patient – not rushing. Asking what *I* wanted, how he could please me. But if you're asking about the actual sex – and you've got a nerve – it just got better and better…'

Johnnie said nothing, but waited for his wife to continue, as he knew she would.

'But, Johnnie! God! He has such stamina! We were at it all night long! I saw the sun rise – over the sea – from the bedroom window…It must have been 5.00am. And, you know what? Joel was reciting poetry. Byron, I think it was. It was all so beautiful…'

'Byron, eh? It would be,' Johnnie said, wincing. 'Just tell me one more thing, then I'll shut up.'

'OK,' Lola said, resigned. 'Anything.'

'When you saw the sunrise, was it upside down?'

'I hope you're not getting off on this,' said Lola, testily. 'No, Johnnie, my face and eyes were the right way up. There was the sky.' With deliberation: 'on top. Then the sun. Then the sea. Though the Earth did move,' she giggled. 'Actually, quite a lot!'

'Johnnie,' she sighed, 'he never….' Lola hesitated.

'Go on.'

'He never seemed to have enough of me…'

Johnnie was silent for a while, before mouthing, sulkily, 'Well, glad you enjoyed it. Since you ask, Lottie was fucking fantastic! But, as you say, it was just sex.'

'Great!' snapped Lola, with finality, 'something for *me* to look forward to – tonight.'

Lovers and Losers
That evening, as the girls were 'discovering' each other, the boys leaned over Johnnie's chalet's balustrade, beers and reefers in hand.

'Well, I hope they're enjoying themselves,' offered Johnnie, with a hint of irony.

'No doubt at all. They're great girls,' opined Joel. 'You know,' he continued, 'I suggested a foursome to Lottie, for tonight. But she wouldn't hear of it. Pity. Would have been fun.'

'A foursome?' echoed Johnnie. 'Wow. I think I'd have been up for that. Can't vouch for Lola, though. Maybe a step too far.'

'I'm not so sure,' said Joel. 'She's *your* wife; so you should know. But I think you – and Lottie – under-estimate her. She's a *very* game girl. Very game indeed. And what an ass!'

Johnnie bridled, suddenly uncomfortable. 'You mean you…'

Joel shrugged his shoulders. 'Everything's fine between consenting adults.' He dragged hard on his reefer.

'But *we've* never…' began Johnnie, heatedly, before checking himself. He was confused, upset even; but he wanted to maintain the *sang froid* of a man of the world. 'All's fair in love and war, I dare say,' was all he could muster.

Joel lowered his voice, conspiratorially, anxious to move Johnnie on. 'You'll find Lottie very…passionate,' he suggested. 'She's imaginative. Experimental.' He gave Johnnie a knowing look: 'Very accommodating, if you follow my drift. Perhaps, tomorrow, you can continue to explore…'

'Thanks for the advice' said Johnnie, already alive to a range of options in his mind. 'I'd like that. Very much. And, Joel, before

I forget, what's with the poetry thing?'

Joel looked sheepish. 'Oh, that,' he grinned. My hero Byron. '*Don Juan*'; Haidee's and Juan's Feast. I'm sure you know it. Sensuous, sensual, and deliciously rhythmic!'

'Phew!' said Johnnie, swallowing hard, and wishing he'd never asked. Seeing the shadow clouding his friend's face, Joel added: 'Let's face it, old man, it couldn't have been Wordsworth, could it? Maybe STC!' he added, with a wink.

'You mean Samuel Taylor Coleridge?' asked Johnnie, his mood lightening.

'No, I mean Sex Trick Crazy!'

Johnnie shook his head, in disbelief. 'You know, Joel, you're a special guy!'

'Thanks,' said Joel, with a smile. 'I know.' He glanced at his watch. It was 10.45pm. 'If I know Lottie, I think the girls will be a while yet. I've got some interesting films inside. Might take our minds off the action next door, and give us a few new ideas. Care to join me?'

Johnnie grinned, slapped his friend on the back, and replied: 'why ever not?'

Foursome Frolics

'*Foursome Frolics*' was nothing if not full-on.

'It's in Dutch!' exclaimed Johnnie.

'No, it's in universal,' said his friend. 'But if you need a translation, just let me know.'

Johnnie had never seen such ferocious coupling. He took a great swig of beer from his glass and asked, amazement in his voice: 'Do you think the guys *take* anything to perform like that...viagra or something?'

'Maybe', said Joel, observing closely. 'But if you were faced with women like *that*, would you need a pill? Anyway, who do you fancy?'

Without hesitation, Johnnie replied: 'the blonde, leggy one.'
'Figures.'

'And you?' asked Johnnie.

'All of 'em!' said Joel, with rapt attention. As if to prove his point, he tugged on his crotch, and grimaced. 'My cock is hurting. I need to give it some air!' Without further ado, he released his burgeoning penis from its confinement.

The bemused Johnnie recoiled at the vision before him… 'God, I wouldn't want you anywhere near my arse!'

Joel laughed. 'Don't worry old man. This is purely for the girls!'

Johnnie thought instantly of Lola, and shuddered, despite himself.

Joel noticed his discomfort, and guessed the reason. 'Johnnie, Johnnie, none of this would have been possible without you. You're a brick, I think you English say. I'll be forever in your debt!' he added quickly. 'All water under the bridge, now. Nothing to worry about. Everything to enjoy!'

Joel placed his arms behind his back, and looked admiringly at his member. 'You know, it's not too late to crash the party. They might be more receptive, now, and wanting what we can provide!'

Johnnie shook his head. 'No. Not tonight.'

'But what's the problem? Don't you want to? If it helps, I'll concentrate on Lottie, and you on Lola. We are fucking married, after all!'

At that juncture, Johnnie wasn't sure that any combination appealed to him. Perhaps not for the first time, he felt irritated with Joel, and his inane persistence. 'Look, Joel, I gave Lola my word. It was part of the Deal. She'd go fucking nuts. If you want to buggar your prospects, just carry on. But maybe, if only for one night, don't let your dick do the talking.'

'OK. Keep your shirt on, old chap. Just a thought.' Joel was soothing, unctuous – but couldn't resist a sting in the tail. He looked again at his resting member: 'I'll just concentrate on building my strength. For tomorrow night.' He smiled, before carefully returning his penis to its sheath, and patting his trousers; then stretched his arms again in quiet contemplation.

'Now, old man,' Joel added. 'Just relax and enjoy the film. Watch and learn. And think of *all* that *fun* we're going to have!'

More Reflection

Lola woke at eleven o'clock; in Lottie's arms. She felt relaxed and happy. She kissed the sleeping Lottie, tenderly, stretched her body, and rose.

Half an hour later she was chewing a croissant, deep in thought.

'Dare I ask?' smiled Johnnie. 'Was it any good?'

'Any *good*? Not good. It was incredible. Unbelievable!'

'Really?' said Johnnie, incredulously. He felt a slight to his manhood.

'I felt my body – me – worshipped. It was simply glorious. I never knew sex with a woman could be like that! It just felt so instinctively natural.'

Johnnie felt uncomfortable. He could not equate with this experience. And he felt annoyed; a night of passion – with Lottie – had eluded *him*. So he changed the subject.

'You know, Joel wanted a foursome last night…'

'Yes. Lottie told me. She apologised that all she could offer was herself, when two rampant cocks were desperate for my ass…So what did you two studs get up to?'

'Well, we just watched one of Joel's porn movies. '*Foursome Frolics*', I think it was called.'

'And was *that* any good?.

'I suppose so. But just made me hanker for the real thing.'

'So you had sex, then?'

'Don't be ridiculous.' He looked embarrassed.

'You *did?*'

'No, of course not. But at one point Joel said his cock was hurting him – because of the film – and would I mind if he took it out for a minute?'

'And?'

'Jesus! I've never seen such a monster!' He squirmed. 'I think he calls it Bertie…'

'Tell me about it!' said the knowing Lola. 'It's becoming part of the family.'

'It was at that point that Joel suggested crashing your party, and joining in. I said no – it wasn't part of the Deal.'

'Very wise,' said Lola. 'Yes. Lottie told me that, if Joel insisted, she'd go through with it, if only to protect me. She wouldn't have put up with the alternative – a *ménage a trois*, involving *just* Lola on the menu. But that an orgy would have been the end for her and Joel. Lottie and I were in a private moment. A crash course would have been disastrous.'

'Sounds a bit melodramatic. And what about you?'

'What about me?'

'Well, might *you* be up for it? A foursome, I mean. Not the other thing. But by arrangement. If *I* protected you?'

'I'm a woman, Johnnie. And a wife. Not a piece of meat.'

'OK. OK. I get it. But we're still alright for tonight?' he asked, anxiously. 'I mean you and Joel? Me and Lottie?'

'I suppose so. But only if it's what *you* really want, Johnnie.'

'And what *you* want, too, Lola.'

Lola turned her face away, to avoid revealing the tears that had come, suddenly. She felt a quick, deep stab of jealousy pierce her breast.

And More Reflection

In the neighbouring chalet, a parallel conversation was taking place.

'You know,' said Lottie, 'you may feel I'm sexually experienced. But I've never had sex with a woman before.'

'And what was it like?' asked Joel, feigning interest. He was interested only in news of Lola.

'Well, as you know, Lola is perfect. And not just her heavenly body. She was so tender. So loving. I just came and came...'

'Good God!' exclaimed Joel, appalled.

'You know, I've never experienced anyone quite like Lola,' Lottie added. 'No,' thought Joel, to himself, 'neither have I.'

'So what did the pussy-less Joel and Johnnie get up to?' enquired Lottie, brightly.

'Not a lot, in the circumstances. We just watched a porn vid.'

Lottie laughed. 'So a lot of drinking. And a lot of wanking!'

'No' said Joel, annoyed. 'You know I don't go in for that sort of thing. Especially with another man present.'

'"Man"? repeated Lottie. 'You were friends enough to offer him your wife!'

Joel's irritation surfaced: 'That's why I suggested crashing your party...I'd still really appreciate that foursome...it would be awesome. I'll show you the film – it should turn you on: '*Foursome Frolics*'.

'Maybe the film. They're pros. But not the foursome, thank you. I think I could persuade Lola. She'd do anything for me. But I couldn't persuade myself. I'd *know* that it wouldn't be about Lola and me. Just you and Johnnie. And maybe not even Johnnie. Just fucking Joel. I think it would finish us, Joel.'

Joel laughed, uneasily. 'OK. Phew. No need to get heavy. But, otherwise, we're still OK for tonight? I mean, Lola and I? And, of course, more japes with Johnnie...'

'Yes, I'd like Johnnie again,' Lottie said, absently. Then sighed. 'But,' she said to herself, 'it's not the only game in town...'

Later that evening, Lola was preparing herself for the short trip to the adjacent chalet, and for the long night ahead. Johnnie had never seen her looking so ravishing. For the first time, the husband felt a pang of bitterness and regret, verging on shame. He was eager for Lottie's arrival, but felt nauseous at the prospect of Lola's leaving. 'Lola,' he said with feeling, 'if he hurts you, I'll kill the fucking bastard!'

Lola nodded, smiled, and then was gone. Moments later, Johnnie heard the sing-song of women's voices as Lola and Lottie exchanged greetings, in passing. Then, suddenly, Lottie was upon him, with her shining blonde locks and broad, blue-eyed smile. Those blue eyes shone with desire.

Desire and Despair
No-one would have admitted that that evening was not a success. It was very good, sex-wise. Bordering on phenomenal. Any inhibitions had been cast aside, and a new confidence and eagerness was expressed by the English couple, with their respective partners. It was no longer the case of teacher and pupil: Johnnie knew what he wanted, and the ever enthusiastic, passionate Lottie willingly, joyfully urged him on. At one point, when their love-making had taken a surprising twist, a startled Lottie, panting, shrieked: 'is this your idea, Johnnie, or are you obeying instructions?' 'Mine, all mine!' Johnnie responded, through gritted teeth. Lottie was oblivious to the grin that stretched across his face.

Lola, a few metres distant, in Lottie's bed, approached her performance – since that was how she viewed it – like a tigress, exerting control, and challenging and stretching even Joel to the limits of his strength. 'Jesus Christ!' he yelled. 'You're killing me!'

Yet there was a sense of *deja vu* in the air; an energetic, frenetic, but mechanistic quality. If Johnnie amazed Lottie with his endless desire, and terrific energy, and Lola challenged – and astonished – Joel with her ferocious demands on his resourcefulness, there was nonetheless a desperation in their love-making. This desperate quality was fuelled by the realisation that their holiday, and their physical closeness, would be abruptly terminated in only three days time. And tectonic plates were shifting, though not in ways that had been envisaged; or in ways that anyone yet understood.

This sense of acute uncertainty was heightened, for Lola, by her bitter self-knowledge that she was falling out of love with her husband. The scales had well and truly fallen from her eyes. Tonight, for the very last time, she would play the whore that her husband had demanded. And, for Lottie, her disillusion with Joel was almost overwhelming. She gave herself completely, utterly, to Johnnie, not because she loved him, but because she wanted to lose herself in uncontrolled passion, and to forget the husband who was abandoning her so shamefully.

Johnnie, for his part, realised that he was falling in love with Lottie. At the presumed end of their love-making he lay, exhausted but still energised, and kissing her breasts, before declaring: 'Lottie, you know I'm in love with you?' It was not what she wanted to hear. She needed to end a long relationship with a man. She hardly needed another. 'I wish I had a euro for every time I've heard that,' she sighed. 'You'd be fucking mad to give up Lola. And you hardly know the *real* me. Get over it my boy. Now, have we done, or are you ready to go again?'

Something similar was happening in the adjacent chalet. Perhaps it was the balmy, almost sultry, July air. Or the sense of holiday abandon. Or the energy generated by an encroaching, painful reality. During a pause in proceedings, Joel asked Lola to be his, alone, forever. He was crazy about her, like no woman he had ever known. Lola burst into tears, her breasts heaving with the emotional effort. 'I'm so grateful to you, Joel. I've become a changed woman. I've learned so much – not just sexually. Though I never knew sex could be like this. The last few days have been an unbelievable, roller-coaster, life-changing experience. There's so much for me to think about...'

Joel responded, desperately, bitterly: 'What's there to think about? Do you still love Johnnie? If so, why are you here?'

Lola may – until then – have been naive in the ways of love; but she was not naive in the ways of men. There was a new note of harshness in her voice. 'I'm here *because* of Johnnie. The Deal. My arse on the plate!' But, despite herself, she *was* flattered to have captured this charismatic man. Lola's voice softened as she said, teasingly, 'But I wonder, in all honesty, how many women you've told *that* story to?'

'OK, so I'm a serial womaniser. I don't deny it. But that's how I know you're special. And it's not gratitude I'm looking for. I'm offering to give up everything for you. My marriage. My home. My comfortable life. OK, I've sprung this on you suddenly, I realise now; it's too much to take in. Let's sleep on it…' Lola began to relax, feeling sure that they had done. She was tired. She was confused. She needed time to think things through. The performer, and the alter ego, returned, exhausted, to their box.

Daybreak was already arriving – although without sun – and the emerging light softly sculpted the woman's glowing contours. Lola suddenly became aware of her nakedness. And her vulnerability. As did Joel. She glanced around the room, anxiously seeking her clothes. Joel forestalled her, took hold of her slender shoulders, and glared into her fearful face. 'Lola, you've been awesome. Insatiable. But we're not finished yet. Now for something *very* different. Let's see if we can't bang some sense into you…'

Lola did as she was bid. But there was no longer any joy in it. Any feelings Lola may have had, any love for Joel – or any hopes Joel may still have had – died with those words.

Denouement
Dark, ferocious clouds descended on the holiday camp; literally, and figuratively. Incessant, driving rain rapped like a tack-

hammer on the chalet roofs, sluiced over every surface, and penetrated every crease and crevice. And dampened still further the already despondent spirits within. Spirits riven with anger, and bitterness. Pure rage, accusation, and harsh recrimination, passed among them; a swirling storm of bile and hatred. But spirits denuded and enervated, nonetheless. Like still-simmering volcanoes, all sexual activity ceased, as suddenly as it had erupted; replaced by seething steam and smoke. This was the reckoning; the final, ugly, denouement. The trajectory of several lives had terminated, abruptly; and egos irreparably punctured.

Lottie spoke truth unto Joel. And Lola to Johnnie.

A rejected Joel blamed Lottie, more even than Lola. A rejected Johnnie blamed Lola, even more than Lottie. Joel cursed Johnnie, and Johnnie cursed Joel, for failing to deliver on a tacit understanding. Despite his own complicity, Johnnie's anger towards Joel was fuelled by the gnawing sense that he had been lured by the nose – or the dick – into a trap. He recalled his own words: an *irresistible* trap.

But rain is also renewal. At the end of that week, Joel returned to Antwerp, alone. And Johnnie to Andover; also alone. Lottie also returned to Antwerp – but with Lola; arm in happy arm. Lottie and daughter Imogen rarely saw eye to eye; she had too much of her father in her, thought Lottie. Never mind: the bitch could either like it or lump it. She could always move in with her doting father, in his tiny company flat.

Lola cared for nothing of this. She felt happy at last; only time would tell if this was destined to be a deep, lasting love, or a passing phase. Beautiful, beatific beauticians could make their way in life, in Andover, or Antwerp – or Anywhere.

THE DUDBRIDGE PROJECT

Following extensive media reports on the increasing importance of the grey vote, the grey pound, and the silver surfer, 'A' level tutors at Dudbridge College in the West Midlands decide to create an exciting research project for their Sociology students: to interview a selection of 'pensioners' of the 'baby boomer', 'Third Age' generation – in order to discover more about their interests, priorities and lifestyle.

Mary Evans, 18, has arranged to interview Mr Ken Downs, and Mrs Eileen Downs, in the comfort of their own, Dudbridge, home. Mary is a second-year A level student, studying English and Economics, as well as Sociology. She is diligent and punctilious. Mary, an only child, lives at home with parents Mo and Milly, and pet dog *Spike*.

Mr and Mrs Downs have happily given consent for the interview – scheduled to take around thirty minutes – to be recorded. In fact, Mr Downs – aged 68, and Mrs Downs – aged 66, feel quite chuffed to be selected by the College to discuss their 'affairs'. It is 2.30pm on a Friday afternoon. The doorbell rings on cue, and Mary is welcomed, and ushered into the house, by the kindly, smiling Mrs Downs.

'Thank you so much for coming, Mary.' Mr Downs held out his hand. 'May I call you Mary? Do call us Ken and Eileen. It's not everyday we're interviewed by a genuine college student. How can we help?'

'Thank *you* so much, Mr Downs…Ken. We're intrigued by people's lifestyle in retirement. By interviewing around 100 couples and analysing the results, we aim to learn a great deal more about the activities of, er, pensioners. Rather, people in the 'Third Age'. We will publish the results, but anonymously, of course; no names or personal details will be included. You will receive a bound copy of our findings, our final Report. Everything you say to me will be held in the strictest confidence. May we begin?' Mary invited.

'No problem,' smiled Ken. 'OK, Eileen?' Eileen nodded. 'Please. Fire away!'

'Well,' began Mary, 'I think you've been retired for about three years, now. What difference has retirement made to your lives?'

Ken laughed, and nudged his wife. 'Well, Mary, I used to be an accountant, and was always very busy. But, I can tell you, I'm at least as busy, now. I'd never have believed it! Rushed off our feet! Barely a minute to live! I hardly know where the time goes!'

'So,' said Mary, 'how do you spend your time? I mean, what do you *do*, exactly?'

'I think we structure our time pretty carefully,' said Ken, very deliberately. 'Otherwise, we'd never get through it all. Isn't that right, Eileen?' Eileen nodded.

'Could you give me some details of your daily life, please?' continued Mary.

'OK,' said Ken. 'We structure every day to get the most out of it. Squeeze every last drop, as it were. Discipline and structure is what's needed. Otherwise, life just drifts. Too much telly, too much chat with the neighbours. Don't get me wrong, they're all salt of the earth, but people can steal your time…'

'Well,' prompted Mary, 'could you possibly take me through your daily routine?'

'Of course,' said Ken. 'Feel free to chip in, dear, if I miss anything out. Right. Monday. As you can see, we have a fairly spacious house. Four bedrooms. Two bathrooms. It takes a lot of maintenance, I can tell you. So Monday is basically washing and cleaning day. I suppose we are fairly house proud, and we wash our bed sheets every week. And clean the whole house. And windows – at least inside. We have a guy who does the upstairs, outside. And that's about it, really. By six-thirty we're bushed. A well deserved gin and tonic, and a spot of Netflix, are in order. But Eileen cooks a delightful supper, before we settle down in front of the telly. Oh, I quite forgot: Mary, can we get you anything? Tea, coffee or whatever?'

Mary assented to a cup of tea. 'Eileen?' said Ken. Eileen rose and headed towards the kitchen.

'Very well,' considered Ken. 'Tuesday. Tuesday is basically car cleaning day, at least for me. We have three of the blighters. I run a Volvo Estate, and Eileen has a Fiesta. And for my sins I maintain a vintage TR6. Immaculate. Costs me a bloody fortune. Anyway, by the time I've cleaned them all, I'm buggered. If I can summon the energy in the afternoon I might tackle the lawns. But that's a pretty full and satisfying day, I can tell you…'

Eileen returned with a tray of tea. 'Ah, dear, there you are,' observed Ken. 'I was just telling Mary about Tuesdays… Phew!'

'Thanks very much indeed,' said Mary. 'May I ask, er, Eileen how you spend your Tuesdays?'

Eileen pondered, her mauve hair gleaming in the sun. 'Well, mainly pottering about in the garden, I think,' replied Eileen. 'I mean, all those pots and trays take some watering. And of course I prepare all our meals.' From *scratch*', added Ken, with emphasis.

'I see,' considered Mary. 'Sorry, what does 'scratch' mean?'

'I prepare the food from the basic ingredients,' said Eileen. 'You know, vegetables, rice, pasta, and so on. Cooking them as necessary.'

'Sounds great!' enthused Mary.

'You must join us one evening,' invited Ken. 'As our guest!'

'Thank you so much,' said Mary, 'that would be very nice. Could I ask about Wednesdays, please?'

'Ah, yes, that would be our shopping day,' affirmed Ken. 'Sainsbury's all morning. Then touring the malls in the afternoon, hunting for clothes, or researching future purchases. A lot of leg work involved – and we're not getting any younger! But if we do get home a bit early, I might do a bit of hoovering, that sort of thing.'

'Super. We're on to Thursday, I think?' said Mary.

'Ah, yes, Thursday,' affirmed Ken. 'Thursday is sacrosanct. It's my golf day, at my local club. I'm a member. Eighteen holes with a few select friends; still trying to reduce that handicap. Then an hour or two at the nineteenth hole!' Ken laughed at his own joke.

'Handicap?' asked a perplexed Mary.

'Strange term' agreed Ken. Basically, it means trying to reduce your score over the 18-hole golf round.

'And nineteenth hole?' persisted Mary.

'He means a few drinks in the bar,' smiled Eileen.

'Oh, I see!' laughed Mary. 'So sorry for my ignorance. So what do you do, Eileen?'

'Well, Thursday is bin and re-cycling day. I need to make sure the bins are put out, and then collected back in again. And then thoroughly cleaned and disinfected. It's a bit of a military operation, I'm afraid. Otherwise the neighbours are prone to a bit of tutting…unsightly bins, and all that…'

'But after all that,' confided Eileen, I'm afraid it's a bit of me time. Ladies who lunch. I meet friends every Thursday, and we have a hoot! A variety of venues, a nice lunch, and one or two drinks. Dry white wine, in my case. Sally normally drives, 'cos she doesn't drink. Though there's seven of us in total – we arrive at the venue in two cars. We all dress in our Sunday best. To be honest, it's the highlight of my week…'

'Great!' said Mary, with a smile. 'It sounds most enjoyable. So I suppose we're on to Friday?' Mary asked, with a brightening smile.

'Friday is a bit different,' mused Ken. 'After the social whirl of Thursday, we normally have a quiet – but busy – day, catching up on paperwork, and contacting absent friends. We have a few friends and relatives in distant places – such as America, even Australia. Must say, that Zoom's made things so much easier. And I need a bit of time to catch up with the papers, and particularly the business news. What, with the Markets all over the place. So much to take in…'

'Eileen? How about you?'

'Well, as Ken says, Friday is really our catch-up day. As well as planning for the following week. But I do have my hair done every Friday morning. A nice lady comes round on Fridays, at about 10. And we have time for an interesting little chat. Barb knows all the local gossip – who's up to what.' She giggled: 'it's enough to make your hair curl…'

Mary laughed, urbanely. 'Well, we're nearly there! Thank you both for being so helpful. This is really fascinating! So: we're on to Saturday…'

'If the weather's fine,' confided Ken, 'we do enjoy a trip into the countryside in the Volvo. Shropshire and Worcestershire have some lovely countryside, you know. Gorgeous right from April through to October. So we find somewhere – a little pub, maybe, or a cosy restaurant – for lunch. We always order fish and chips, and then rate the different venues out of ten. It's quite fun.' 'Yes,' interjected Eileen, 'though no-one has yet *quite* earned a ten. I think nine point five is our best, so far. Though the venue's a secret – we don't want *everyone* heading there!' 'Anyway,' added Ken, 'then we enjoy a leisurely stroll. Nothing too taxing mind, not since we lost *Bobby*…'

'Bobby?'

'*Bobby* was our Labrador – a great lad; loved a brisk walk on the Shropshire Hills…'

'Oh, I'm so sorry…'

'He's been gone three years, now. Very sad…just as I retired. How time flies!' ruminated Ken.

'Did you ever think…?' hesitated Mary.

'Of getting another? No,' said Ken, with a shake of the head. 'There was only one *Bobby*.' Eileen, her eyes glistening, squeezed Ken's arm.

'Anyway, that's Saturday…' sighed Mary. 'So, Sunday follows, I suppose,' she smiled, though beginning to feel a touch fatigued.

'Yes' said Ken. 'I'm afraid Sunday is our down-tools day. Maybe even a little boring! Just relaxing with the Sunday papers, followed by a roast lunch, and a nice bottle of wine. Then an evening in front of the telly. The end of a very busy week. Then, before you know it, it's Monday again!'

'Thank you so much!' gushed Mary. 'We really are nearly done. Just a few, final questions, if I may. Do either of you pursue any interests or hobbies, other than those you've already mentioned?'

Ken's smile was so broad his face almost split into two. 'Model railways,' he confided, as though sharing the secret of the Universe, and providing all the explanation required. 'One of our bedrooms has a sophisticated track, with stations, fairgrounds, bridges, and dozens of people lining the route. But centre stage are my GWR trains and carriages. I tend to give the locos a good run between eight and nine most evenings. I have special, limited edition models of both *'Flying Scotsman'* and *'Mallard'*.

'GWR?' enquired Mary.

Ken looked almost offended. 'Great Western Railway,' explained the mortified Ken.

'Oh, I see. How interesting,' hastened Mary.

'*Very*,' underlined Ken. 'I'll show you the railway complex before you go…'

'Thank you. I would like that,' re-assured Mary. 'Anything else?'

'Mmm'...offered Ken, who felt he'd just offered the crown jewels, and seen them rejected as paste. 'I did take up Spanish when I retired, as we've always enjoyed relaxing holidays on the Costas. But after a term or two I called it a day. Just too much like hard bloody work. You know, I don't think we English are naturally cut out to learn other languages. I mean, most people can barely speak English these days!'

'Thank you. Eileen, do you do...anything?'

'Yes, actually I love baking. Bread, cakes, biscuits and so on. I do provide special cakes for birthdays – even the odd wedding – but I've never found the time to turn it into a proper business.'

'Thank you,' said Mary, a touch relieved. 'And do either of you do any voluntary work at all? I mean, in the community?'

Ken and Eileen looked at each other; then Ken looked at his watch. 'Well, as you've heard, Mary, we are incredibly busy people. Time is of the essence. But, once a month, we do make time to go out with neighbours to do a local litter pick. Quite amazing what we find! Far too grim for delicate ears! But the work is very satisfying – seeing the hedgerows and grass verges looking clean as a whistle. But, before you know it, the problem starts all over again! Mainly young people, I'm afraid,' stated Ken, sternly, before adding: 'but not nice young people like you Mary I'm sure!'

Mary smiled; she hoped, for the last time. 'Thank you. We're nearly done. Just a couple more questions, please. You've both been so helpful, and I'm afraid I've already taken up too much of your valuable time. But do you contribute to any charities at all?'

'Charities?' said Ken. 'Let me think. Yes – last year we lost Bill, suddenly. Bill was one of our golfing buddies. So we had a kind of memorial send off at the golf club, and a whip-round for his widow, Jo. Think we raised a couple of grand. In fact, Jo went on a cruise with it. It helped her to recuperate, apparently. Then we all contributed to charity at the funeral – one of those heart or cardiac charities. They all do great work, I'm sure.'

'Eileen?'

'I'm really glad you've asked, Mary. The Ladies Lunch Club adopts a charity each year, and we add on 10% to each of our lunch bills every week, then send the proceeds off at Christmas time. This year is in aid of Dudbridge Hospice. We should raise a few hundred pounds, I think.'

'Finally,' smiled Mary, 'I don't want to pry into your personal finances, but I'm sure you've both heard of the cost of living crisis. What impact is this having on your own lifestyle, and life choices?'

Ken looked at Eileen. She hesitated. 'It's definitely a big worry. Gas, electricity, fuel, and food prices, all going through the roof. There doesn't seem to be any end to it. We are considering fewer trips into the countryside – maybe just one a month – and cutting down on foreign holidays. Perhaps just once a year. Other than that, we may need to rely on our savings to carry us through it.' Eileen looked back at Ken.

'I suppose we're lucky,' added Ken. 'But, to some extent, you make your own luck. I started work – as a boy – working in a shop – from the age of 14. And, after school and college, worked solid till 65. And Eileen always worked part-time, doing accounts and payroll, in an office. So we were able to build up savings and investments as we went along. Sorry if that's boring, but it's the unvarnished truth. There's no magic solution.'

'Thank you both so much!' enthused Mary. 'You've been a great help. And thanks so much for the tea, Eileen. As I said, everything will be kept confidential, under data protection laws. But we will provide you with a complimentary copy of the Final Report. It should provide some absorbing insights into the lifestyle of our 'Third Age' community.'

'Oh, Mary,' queried Ken. 'What about you? What are your plans for the future?'

'I plan to go to Uni next year, to study English. Then maybe train to be a teacher. Or possibly a researcher?'

'Never forget, Mary' said Ken, earnestly, 'that the world's your oyster. Stay ambitious, and achieve what you can. Always remember that.'

'Thank you so much, Mr Downs!' Then – all smiles – Mary shakes hands with Ken and Eileen, and is ushered to the door. 'Bye!' 'Bye!'

'Well, I thought that went well,' said Ken, puffing his cheeks. 'Only too glad to help. Pretty little thing, too. Blast! I forgot to show her the model railway!' 'Indeed,' added Eileen. 'Maybe when she comes round for dinner..?'

'Yes,' said Ken. 'Goodness, Eileen, that's taken me back! Mary reminded me of you, at the same age. God! I wish we could have our time over again!'

'Do you, dear?' said Eileen, and hugged him. 'And would you change anything?'

'Not a thing!' smiled Ken, kissing his wife. 'That reminds me! It's Friday. Our special night…now don't forget that new lingerie set!'

'Get away with you!' teased Eileen, smiling, coquettishly. 'Thank God you didn't start blabbing about that kind of thing, to Mary!'

'Perhaps I should have done. It's one of the few things we don't need to pay for!'

'And you'll have all the neighbours talking, if you carry on like last time!'

Ken laughed. 'Only if I leave the curtains open again!'

Mary was glad of the two-mile walk home to clear her head. Were all older people like that? She wondered: did they still do *sex*? And shivered at her own preposterous suggestion. If only she'd been given a bird's eye view, through the chink in those curtains…

This had been Mary's first interview. Only another nine to go! She couldn't wait to get back to the faithful *Spike*, and delight in his smile, and his wagging tail…

THE SISTERS

Not even Harry Hayes' oldest friends – not even his wife Harriet – would have accused Harry, 45, of being 'handsome'. Indeed, if he had not been handsome in his youth, his thinning hair, podgy complexion and puckered face would hardly argue the case, now. Wife Harriet might, out of friendship and loyalty, be accorded the term 'handsome', but Austen aficionados will know that that epithet contains more than a soupçon of coolness; even disdain. Perhaps, euphemism; perhaps, damning with faint praise. Harriet's lank grey hair, dull grey eyes and sallow skin argued that, even at nineteen, she had possessed few features that might accrue into a beautiful outcome.

Since, as we know, beauty is in the eye of the beholder and, as we also know, is generally regarded as merely skin deep, perhaps love had conquered all – had seen through the plainness, on both sides. Perhaps. Or perhaps money, proximity, and the lack of alternative partners in a quiet, sleepy little town in Lincolnshire had brought Harry and Harriet quietly, inevitably, into each other's anxious orbit.

If Harry was not handsome, his large, detached, six-bedroom almost-mansion was clearly handsome. His Jaguar Estate was gleaming and handsome. And his golf handicap was certainly handsome. Harry ran a plant hire business that was extraordinarily successful – making handsome profits – in an era of frenetic build-build-build. Harriet, meanwhile, was a successful portrait painter, who had achieved at least regional reputation and renown; she painted the distinguished, the famous, the beautiful and, yes, the handsome. Clients arrived at Harriet's studio from far and wide in order to be immortalised; or, for an extra fee, she would travel to their home, or preferred setting, to set down their likeness in water colours, pastels or oils, for their and their descendants' delectation.

Harry and Harriet enjoyed two daughters: Cheyenne, 18, and Cordelia, 16. These girls were not accounted handsome – either in the Austen sense or otherwise. They were, in quite different ways, startlingly, astonishingly, beautiful. Genetics is nothing if not an odd science. Quite how Harry and Harriet could have produced such paragons was rather beyond their ken – or indeed ours. But such it was; ours not to reason why, but only to record, and recount.

To tell truth, Harry did not value, did not *believe in* beauty; aesthetically, as a *quality*, as a *gift*. He was the quintessential, sober, sartorial, cynical businessman. Rather, Harry saw beauty as a commodity: to be bought, or traded. Harry and Harriet had drifted apart, physically, after Cordelia was born – it had been a difficult labour – and Harry had become accustomed to seeking, and finding, his pleasures elsewhere. Harry's business dealings – for *Hayes Plant Hire* – led him to Norwich two or three times a month, where he would stay in a local hotel, and utilise the services of the local escort girls. Harry's favourite – Lisa Taylor – was a real beauty, and sympathetic to his every need. Three – or sometimes four – hundred quid did the job perfectly. Cash for beauty, served with a smile. Everyone was happy. Everyone, that is, except Lisa's pimp.

Mark Deighton was the most suave and subtle of operators. No stranger to pin-striped suits and fast cars, Mark abhorred the idea of physical violence. He regarded himself as an entrepreneur;

the service he and his girls provided was no less ethical than the roguery and corruption of the punters – politicians, councillors, businessmen. Mark's business provided a superb service – that was also discreet and safe – and it demanded respect and compliance. But he also knew that many punters were more powerful than he; and that upsetting one or other might result in him ending up behind bars, or even spending eternity in a concrete coffin. He could not be sure that Harry Hayes fell into this camp; but he was taking no chances.

The irritating fact was that, despite a fixed menu of prices, Harry Hayes often left Lisa less cash then Lisa's – or sometimes Cindy's – services required. £300 might melt to £280, or even to £260. £400 might unaccountably shrink to no more than £360. Harry would joke that he was a little short that week, or that the duration of service was, well, less than he had been expecting. Not my bloody fault, thought Lisa to herself. He also sometimes 'forgot' to wear a condom – another requirement. Riding bareback was not a 'house' service. Lisa always smiled, apologetically; she did not want to antagonise a regular and powerful client.

A couple of twenties here or there was, of course, nothing to Harry. Loose change. But he liked to get a bargain. And he liked to win. Getting a five-star service for a three-star price turned Harry on; gave him orgasm plus. Mark vetted his girls' clients – health and safety assessments were part of his service – and he knew that Harry was a wealthy man. Lisa also shared sensitive information with Mark. For Harry was fond of bragging whilst shagging – about his success, his business, his lifestyle, his fabulous daughters. Lisa did not lie back and think of England; she absorbed everything spluttered in the heat of passion, whilst thinking of palm-fringed beaches in the Caribbean – with boyfriend Mark.

Mark Deighton had sent Harry a couple of texts, reminding him politely about the house rules, and Harry's failure to comply.

Harry was furious about being contacted by – as he called him – 'that slimy worm', and had replied simply with emojis – dismissive, even insulting, in tone. Despite Mark's urbane demeanour – he knew that Harry regarded him as a parasite – Harry's behaviour began to get under his skin. Mark was determined to get even; to teach Harry a lesson he would not forget.

Of course, Harry knew that his daughters were beautiful, and was proud of it; as though he had personally created works of art. But the worth of Cheyenne and Cordelia would be weighed in hard cash. Cheyenne and Cordelia had been brought up as ladies; had been sent to the best all-girl schools; had studied music, deportment and languages, as well as maths and science; and had been steered clear of involvement with boys. Boys – those little shits – were always trouble, and must be kept at bay. The girls must be shielded, until they were ready for marriage. Harry knew – or thought he knew – his daughters' true value; they would be sold to the highest bidder; that is, to put it more diplomatically, they would be introduced to the sons of only the best, most prestigious, local families. Harry was keen to build a dynasty, to leave a legacy, and was busy establishing alliances with the families of the leading building contractors in the county. He was sure that, in the end, his girls would thank him for it.

However, Harriet *did* value beauty, and delighted in her daughters. She basked in the reflected glow, and painted portraits of Cheyenne and Cordelia on numerous occasions as they grew from childhood to glorious womanhood. These paintings were displayed prominently throughout the house; they would never be sold. Harriet wanted only the best for Cheyenne and Cordelia, so did not demur from her husband's grandiose ambitions. Harriet knew – from bitter experience – that money did not buy happiness; but she also knew, from a penurious childhood, that lack of it made people perfectly miserable. The girls grew up looking at themselves adorning the walls; but they were easy in their beauty, and lacked pretension and vanity. But they *had* begun to yearn for the company of boys. What was all this hair-styling, make-up and *haute couture* – not to mention deportment lessons – *about*, if it was not connected to mingling, to socialising, to *being with* boys?

The Davenport family owned and operated the largest residential construction business in the county; its operations – and its concrete footprint – spread across Lincolnshire and Norfolk, and were beginning to invade neighbouring counties in the East of England. Harry had met the – now controlling – son of the founder, Chris Davenport, enjoyed regular contracts from him, and was mightily impressed with Chris's business acumen and vaulting ambition. What Harry did not know – he might have grinned knowingly – was that, despite his impeccably respectable domestic establishment – Chris Davenport was also a regular client of Mark Deighton. And Lisa Taylor.

Chris and Claudia Davenport lived in a crenelated 18th century castle – a folly – a few miles west of Skegness. They had two sons – James, 19, and Wills, 17. Claudia doted on her offspring. James and Wills had the family business in their blood, and had joined it upon leaving boarding school. The family business consisted largely of building four and five bedroom mock Tudor houses on prime greenfield sites in Lincolnshire and Norfolk. James and Wills took to the family business like proverbial ducks to water. They were rich; arrogant; totally spoiled; wild; and thought the world their plaything, to do with as they might. They had just as much education as was required to provide the exact sense of entitlement needed to succeed in the family business – buying up farmland, steamrollering planning permission, and building handsome houses – while squeezing contractors and suppliers. Oh, and the boys were handsome; and lived a princely life.

James already drove a Porsche Boxster. And Wills had been

promised an Audi TT for his 18th birthday – on 10 May, three weeks hence. A guest list consisting of the great and the good had been compiled, and invitations issued. In all honesty, the Hayes family might not have made the cut, had Mark Deighton not aimed a well-timed, thoughtful e-mail to Chris Davenport, with an attachment showing photos of Cheyenne and Cordelia Hayes. The outcome was a gold-rimmed, effusive, stiff-card invitation to Wills Davenport's brilliant, glittering coming-of-age party.

If the Hayes seniors were delighted to receive the invitation – and acknowledgement of their social status – their daughters' response bordered on euphoric. Parties! Wealth! Glamour! Excitement! *Boys!* New dresses, new hairdos, and new shoes awaited the desperately excited Cheyenne and Cordelia. This would be their 'coming out'. Their day in the sun had arrived at long last. Even better, this party would span three whole days – from the opening Reception at 6.00pm on Friday – champagne and canapés – to the final – opulent and over-flowing – brunch, on Sunday morning.

Harry Hayes thought it advisable to brief his daughters, in a light-hearted, informal kind of way. Had they heard of James and Wills? Met them, even? Very handsome, apparently. And they'd inherit the family empire. Cheyenne and Cordelia remained silent. Their father dropped gold into the void. 'They're worth millions. *Many* millions. Worth thinking about…' shrugged their father, a smirk playing across his florid face. Cheyenne rolled her eyes at Cordelia, but with a smile. Their father's hints were a bit gross, a touch embarrassing. But, whilst suggestion was laid on with a trowel, the girls were genuinely intrigued. They *wanted* to meet people – boys included. Welcome to the real world – the adult world! All that education and grooming would, at last, have a purpose.

One fine morning, over breakfast, the Davenports' discussed

the guest list. The – positively – handsome, and elegantly, elaborately equipped Claudia pulled a face. 'Did we really need to invite those Hayes people?' she asked, peevishly. 'I mean, he's so vulgar, and so full of himself! Although I understand that his wife is quite artistic? I hope that's right. Not *autistic?*' Claudia sniggered at her own joke.

'Well,' responded her husband, 'Harry Hayes provides a lot of the plant for our projects. He usually quotes the keenest prices. And, yes, Harriet is a talented artist. And *I* understand that their daughters are quite sensational!'

'I dare say,' offered his wife. 'But you're not proposing them for James and Wills, I hope? Beauty is all very well, but we certainly don't need an alliance with *that* family. I couldn't stand that man as a brother in law. I mean, God forbid!'

'Of course not, dear' replied Chris, soothingly. 'But the boys may find the girls amusing company for the weekend. They need to play the field a bit before they settle down.'

'Play the field?' said Claudia, raising her eyebrows. 'From what I see on their Facebook accounts – not to mention their smart phones – they've been playing in lots of fields for some time now…'

'Boys will be boys…' shrugged her husband. 'Shall we move on?'

James and Wills were close, had similar temperaments, and acted as a unit; a – literal – band of brothers; a partnership, with James the senior partner. The young men were intelligent, in a cunning, supremely self-interested kind of way. So they, too, discussed and planned for the forthcoming big bash. There were three anticipated highlights. Booze. Business contacts. And 'broads' – girls. The brothers trawled through photos of the invited girls on social media, and put together a shortlist of women they wanted to meet – and get to know. Cheyenne and Cordelia were top of the list. No question; no contest.

James had had a series of girlfriends – young women mostly found in bars or clubs, or trawled on the Internet. Many girls, apparently, were attracted by James's film star looks, flash lifestyle and cool sports car. None had lasted more than a few months, before James became bored, and moved on. They would never know what a lucky escape they'd had. James' latest crush was Cindy Perks, a waitress in James's favourite watering hole – *Spanners*. Cindy had been deterred from the forthcoming Party; James needed maximum freedom of manoeuvre; maximum opportunity for pleasure.

Despite his youth, and lack of independent 'wheels', Wills, too, had already enjoyed – I use the term advisedly – a couple of girlfriends (one, Chloe, had been a James cast-off, though she came highly recommended). Wills' attitude and approach to women closely resembled that of his brother, whom he looked up to as a role model. Though most of Wills' sexual exposure to date had been via *Pornsub*, and similar salubrious sites, he now had a hankering for the real McCoy, as it were. Women were, generally, regarded as commodities; to be consumed, as and when required. And, like James, Wills' appetite required more and more. As a discreet rite of passage, Wills father had arranged for the young buck to visit one of Mark Deighton's 'best' girls – just as James had done, a couple of years earlier. *Don't* mention to your mother, he was told, sternly. Wills was looking forward to this top-notch experience. But, first, there were the delights of the Party to anticipate; oh so keenly...

A day or two before the extravaganza, James and Wills sat down to study the 'form' – they had assembled pictures of all the young women invited to the Party. Of the 120 or so guests, around 20 consisted of eligible young women: daughters, grand-daughters, or nieces – or even 'partners' – of the key invitees. Two pictures stood out from the rest: those of Cheyenne and Cordelia. Some time before, James had sent out 'feelers' to his wide range of 'mates' and acquaintances. The outcome was that, while Cheyenne and Cordelia were known *about*, they were not *known*. Fresh meat. 'Corkers', opined James, with the customary expletive. 'I really fancy the dark one,' said Wills, adjusting his trousers. 'Dark one?' queried James. 'Oh, you mean hair. That'll be Cordelia. Great body. Good job for you I prefer her sister!' he smirked. 'What a face. And what legs! I wonder if she's a natural blonde? Here's to finding out!' he laughed. 'But, bro, remember, they're only here for two nights…We need to act fast…'

The day of Wills' Grand Coming of Age Party duly arrived. Reception: 6.00pm. The Jags and Mercedes dispense their glittering occupants. Although there are a smattering of Davenport relatives – grandparents, aunts and uncles – most of the guests are attracted – like iron filings to a magnet – by the Davenports' power and wealth. But, if they knew the celebrated young hero at all, the guests knew Wills as a young man on the make – a scallywag and disruptive spirit, who promised only trouble to anyone who crossed his path.

Chris and Claudia greet each distinct party. 'How are you, Harry and Harriet!' beamed Claudia. 'So lovely to see you!' Air kisses. 'And this must be Cheyenne and Cordelia? My goodness! How perfectly gorgeous you are! I must introduce you to James and Wills. I know they're dying to meet you…' As the girls made suitably polite replies, the subjects of the conversation – as though choreographed – immaculately, meticulously groomed, and smiling their most engaging smiles – stride up to the Hayes family to make their first, sunny, introductions. Vigorous handshakes for Harry Hayes. Polite pecks on the cheeks for Harriet Hayes. Respectful hugs for Cheyenne and Cordelia Hayes. These boys knew you didn't get a second chance to make a first impression.

120 smiling guests assembled on the rolling lawns. Marquees specially erected. Uniformed waitresses serving Krug and canapés

from silver trays. The whole scene bathed in a honeyed glow from an obliging, slanting sun. A perfect setting. The majority of guests would spend Friday and Saturday nights at a Travelodge, five miles away. However, twenty or so especially honoured guests would overnight at Crendall Castle. At the urging of the guest of honour – Wills – these special guests included the Hayes family.

James and Wills gallantly invited Cheyenne and Cordelia on a candle-lit tour of the 40-room mansion, with its brick-lined galleries and vaulted oak ceilings. How could the girls not be impressed? 'It's said that the castle is haunted by young women in white, who can be heard screaming in the night,' claimed James. 'Really?' said Cordelia, slightly shocked, but intrigued. Though a smile played around James's lips, the claim did not seem too far-fetched.

On Saturday, the foursome played, talked, walked around the walled estate, and discussed their future plans – and dreams. Cheyenne already worked in her father's business, as receptionist. She was also 'the face' on the firm's publicity material, helping to introduce new business; there was a none-to-subtle link with the images of Cheyenne, and the company' purpose – '*Hire*'. The younger Cordelia, currently studying for her 'A' levels, was unsure of her future direction, though she'd dabbled in modelling. 'I've thought of modelling,' she confided to James and Wills, 'but it seems I'm too…too…' 'beautiful,' interjected Cheyenne, tactfully. 'Really?' said James, artfully. 'I know the boss of a modelling agency. Consider it done!' '*Really?*' repeated Cordelia, her lovely face lit by a radiant smile.

'That would be great!' Cordelia was ready to be influenced by events. Maybe opportunity, through James and Wills, beckoned. James and Wills themselves had no doubts, no uncertainty: they wanted to develop *Davenport Homes* into the country's biggest house-builder. 'The country needs the houses, and we need the money!' laughed Wills, gleefully. 'We want to be Lords of the

Universe!' added James, hysterically. 'And have everything!' 'And do *anything*!' frothed his brother, sinking into the sofa.

How could the girls not be impressed by all this splendour, power, confidence and certainty?

There was a final, Grand Dinner on Saturday evening, complete with choice wines from Chris Davenport's well-stocked cellar; followed by meaningful, slightly emotional speeches from Wills' father, and the young hero himself. Undoubtedly, a sparkling, successful, future lay ahead.

As a final act in the day's drama, guests gathered in the immaculate gardens for a 20-minute, professionally managed, spectacular firework display. Then, finally, the guests were free to do as they wished: crash out on soft sofas, drink and chat in earnest little clusters; tour the delicately illuminated gardens, or wander around the mansion itself; or – if they were lucky – sink gratefully into a soft bed. Harry and Harriet Hayes, gorged and satiated by too much good food and drink, fell into this latter category. But most guests departed around 10.30pm, escorted by an army of taxis to their hotel 'Lodge' five miles away.

Suddenly, the castle was quiet; and calm; and empty. Apart, that is, from the sound of laughter, and giggling, and high-spirits, in the far-sitting room, where James and Cheyenne, and Wills and Cordelia, held Court; continuing the process, earnestly and intimately, of getting to know each other. A range of wine bottles, quite conveniently, littered the coffee table in their midst. Though unused to alcohol, Cordelia had somehow managed to surreptitiously sip her way through three – or was it four? – glasses of chardonnay. Cheyenne was a little too far gone herself to notice. Still, they were all young and passionate. Why waste time? It seemed there was no time to lose.

In fact, it was well past midnight when Cheyenne and Cordelia finally succumbed to the blandishments of too much flattery, too much flummery, some heady if vague promises, and the effects of too much wine. In the adjoining bedrooms of James and Wills Davenport, the bed-sheets would bear testimony to a night of feverish activity. In all honesty, the next morning, neither of the young women could remember giving consent; at the same time, they could not recall making any complaint. At 7.00am on Sunday morning, the sun already filtering through half-open curtains, James climbed on top of the naked body of Cheyenne. Suddenly, the world seemed different. Clearer. Frightening. 'What are you *doing?*' asked the half awake, surprised Cheyenne. 'You were so great last night, I thought we'd go again!' James asserted, confidently. 'James, I'm really tired. This has been quite an experience for me. I really need time to think!'

'What the fuck is there to think about?' replied James, petulantly. 'You were all for it last night!' 'Sorry, but it's different, now. I need space! I need to talk to my sister!' James rolled off his intended conquest, with barely concealed irritation. His penis did not attempt to disguise his intentions. James looked down on his erect, proud member. 'Your sister's just through that door,' he nodded. 'But' – looking down – 'what the fuck am I supposed to do with this?' Cheyenne shrugged, grabbed some clothes, knocked gently on the door, and was gone.

Cordelia and Wills were still asleep. They had their backs to each other, and were separated by a chasm. Cheyenne noticed tell-tale blood-stains on the bed-sheets. Cheyenne gently touched, then kissed, her sister, who opened her eyes. Cheyenne noticed some reddening, and a little puffiness, around her sister's emerald eyes. She had been crying. 'Cordelia, do get up, love. It's time to go!' Young Wills stirred. 'Jesus. I'm in fucking heaven. What a birthday present! A threesome!'

Cheyenne ignored the unwelcome invitation. 'Get dressed, Cordelia!' urged her sister. Cordelia hurriedly dressed, though she could not find her knickers. 'See you later, Wills', smiled Cordelia, weakly, before kissing him on the forehead. 'Sorry we have to go!' 'Sure,' replied Wills, before adding 'fuck!' as the girls gently closed the door. Then Wills smiled as he recalled something, before retrieving the knickers that he'd hidden beneath his pillow. They were white, and lacy, and soft. Wills gave them a big sniff – their scent was pure essence of Cordelia – before wrapping them around his erect member...

The weekend's celebrations were rounded off with a sumptuous brunch – served with Buck's Fizz – where Harry Hayes, with his highly developed antennae, was quick to spot urgent whispers, and signs of hurried intimacy, between Cheyenne and James, and Cordelia and Wills. Harry was over the moon. 'Bloody fantastic!' The weekend had been a stunning success. Harry was already looking forward to marrying his own empire with the Davenports. In business, this was called 'vertical integration'. He was proud of his girls. They'd done great! There couldn't be a better match, in either case.

But Harriet was disturbed, dismayed even, by her girls' body language, which betrayed confusion and distress; and irritated by her jackass husband's artless self-deception. It was clear that something profound had taken place; but that the experience may not have been overwhelmingly positive. She could not wait to get her daughter's home, for an urgent de-brief.

Manic, rictus smiles, and vows of eternal gratitude made, before the Hayes' longed-for departure. Harry was in jubilant mood, and was perplexed by the tight-lipped silence of his female contingent.

The promised de-brief was frustrated by Cheyenne's and Cordelia's emotionally-closed unresponsiveness to their mother's probing enquiries. Both girls had experienced a dizzying range of emotions over the last 48 hours; they themselves were anxious and confused, perhaps embarrassed. They could share these secrets and anxieties only between themselves. They had thought themselves to be in love; and loved. Now, they couldn't be sure.

Harriet became increasingly angry; but not with her girls. She suspected that, where affection and tenderness might have been expected, there had only been coldness and calculation, from two self-entitled young men on the make. Her daughters' affections and trust – and their beauty – had been traduced – and trashed. Harriet, too, blamed her greedy and grasping husband's stupidly selfish ambitions. And she blamed herself – the mother, who should have done more, much more, to guide and protect her daughters.

All week, the girls waited for calls that never came. For the Davenport brothers, these were one-night-stands. Fun; memorable; but not meaningful. James was still occupied, at least for the moment, with Cindy Perks. And Wills was looking forward to his rendezvous with one of Mark Deighton's girls – Alice Goodwin. Then the bombshell – rather, bombshells – fell. An anxious friend rang Cordelia. Did she know? Know what? That her knickers were being auctioned on a well-known worldwide website! Horrified, Cordelia bid for and eventually secured her own underwear, to prevent their falling into the hands of a stranger or pervert. The £120 was a small price to pay.

But neither sister could do anything about the videos that appeared on a popular porn website. Several minutes of 'choice' footage, uploaded for the world to view. Why? The boys' idea of fun. Plus, James and Wills harboured a grudge that, though they'd tasted paradise, they had not been able – had been denied – the chance to drink their fill. The footage attracted more than 100,000 'hits' before, a week later, Harriet's frantic efforts managed to get the material taken down. Cheyenne and Cordelia were distraught; traumatised; overwhelmed. They would not go out, leave the house, see anyone. The scales had fallen from their eyes. Indeed, Cheyenne had noticed a flashing green light on the ceiling of James's bedroom. But how on earth could she have known it was a camera? What had they done to deserve this horror, this humiliation?

Everyone – well, almost everyone – was furious. Harry Hayes seethed with anger at the antics of those young bastards. As guests, his daughters should have been safe under the roof of someone he regarded as a friend. But he was uncomfortably aware that his own vaulting ambitions may have contributed, if not to this abuse, at least to creating the opportunity. And he had failed to check on these guys characters; he had only checked their bank balance. He could not, in all conscience – Harry was surprised that he still had a conscience – continue business relations with Davenport Homes. It would seem like an admission that he'd been pimping his own daughters. That would mean a 30% hit to the bottom line. Serves me right, he thought, bitterly. From a casual remark made by Chris Davenport at the Party – 'By the way, Mark Deighton sends his regards' – he was also uncomfortably aware that his visits to Deighton's girls – girls not much older than Cheyenne – might somehow be connected to these vile events. 'Mark Deighton?' Harry had replied, ashen. 'Yes, Mark Deighton,' Chris had added, pointedly. Harry would never visit Lisa Taylor again.

Claudia Davenport suffered the anguish of an indulgent mother who has seen her uncritical love cruelly betrayed and thrown back in her face. She had known that her sons were self-willed and wild, and revelled, if a little uneasily, in their high-performance jinks. If they'd *just* screwed the sisters – of course consensually – she would have been coolly satisfied. Her boys, on top of the world. But, at the end of the day, she, too, was a woman. She was ashamed for her family – and for herself. This behaviour was totally beyond the pale. Unforgivable, in fact. And after all that expense! The ungrateful little shits!

Chris Davenport was seriously embarrassed. He had brought up his sons to be ruthless, to be successful, to be strong *men*. He had not appreciated that he was nurturing two monsters. He had misread their outrageous business methods: misread lies and duplicity for street-craft and cunning. He now deeply regretted introducing his sons to Mark Deighton's girls. All the wrong signals; and instilling all the wrong values. Adding fuel to a wildfire.

Even the reprobate James and Wills were furious. That is, with everyone else. 'Lighten up, guys!' was their theme. It was just a fucking joke! If the videos help guys 'get off', we've done a public service! 'We didn't force them into bed!' opined Wills. 'And it *was* my birthday!' The desperate tactics fell on deaf ears.

The elder Davenports had a serious, stark discussion that sealed the fate of their sons. Fundamental parental mistakes were admitted. This was painful. Lessons would need to be learned, and pride swallowed. Humble pie was a new and unpalatable dish for the Davenports to force down. But this behaviour was quite beyond the pale. Utterly unacceptable. James and Wills were summarily sacked from the family business. As well as abusing two innocent young women, they had bought shame on their family. Perhaps worse, they had tarnished the brand. Although, thank God, the police had not been involved, Chris arranged for James and Wills to undertake 400 hours each of community service, as a starter for ten. In cold anger, Chris personally ripped the recording apparatus from his sons' bedrooms. Chris and Claudia swallowed pride, and eschewed vanity, and wrote a grovelling letter to Harry and Harriet Hayes. Only time would tell whether their miscreant sons might be rehabilitated, and accepted back into the family fold. The parents were realistic: it might be a *very* long process.

But not *quite* everyone was furious. Mark Deighton flew to Barbados, with Lisa Taylor, for a fortnight's well-deserved hedonism. If revenge is a dish best served cold, Mark preferred his served on a hot beach – with a fabulous woman, and a pina colada.

But Harriet's was a cold, hard fury. An Exhibition of her art work was taking place at a Lincoln City gallery in June. The Exhibition was publicised throughout the county and beyond. Harriet's work had begun to attract serious attention in the art world, and the gallery would be packed every day of its two-week run. Harriet set to work on two new portraits that would form the Exhibition's centre-piece: two bold, full-size, full-frontal male nudes. There were no discreet folds of material, or shading, or pixelling, to hide the naked truth. Just two young men – who were readily and sharply recognised – with silly grins. And very small penises.

Cheyenne and Cordelia were persuaded to attend the opening Reception. They saw, for the first time, the startlingly accurate portraits of their tormentors. And burst out laughing. Their lives had not ended, after all. They were still young, and still beautiful; only now somewhat wiser. Indeed, their lives had only just begun…

In a modern variant of self-flagellation, Claudia Davenport purchased the portraits of her sons, and hung them – she would have preferred to have hanged them – in pride of place in the family sitting room.

Harry Hayes never recovered from the twin blows to his pride, and his business, and he suffered a debilitating stroke a short time later. The business was revived by – who else? – Cheyenne and Cordelia, who had no qualms about renewing the business relationship with Chris Davenport. Chris was delighted to oblige. Hayes Plant Hire is thriving, and one of the most pre-eminent businesses of its type in the UK.

Davenport Homes, too, continues to thrive, and its tentacles have now spread throughout the South East, and into the Midlands.

Mark Deighton and Lisa Taylor are now married, and have left the escort business behind. They now run a successful hotel complex in Bridgetown, Barbados, close to Lisa's parents.

And what of those heroes, the younger Davenports? Who cares? You may well ask. Literature and life can be equally creative; equally astounding. James and Wills are reformed characters. It did not take too long for them to appreciate the error of their ways. And to recognise that they were the losers. They were not only ashamed; they experienced agony. They had rejected Paradise.

With their father's support, James and Wills started a branch of the business based in Stratford-upon-Avon. These guys know the planning and building business, and Davenport Homes is now a familiar name throughout the Midlands.

Oh; and they married Cheyenne and Cordelia. The rapprochement wasn't quick. It wasn't easy. And it wasn't pain-free. But these guys were nothing if not resourceful, and the girls – beautiful and sensitive – were also intelligent and forgiving. Even Harriet eventually gave her blessing. And, in due course, the couples' cup of joy ranneth over – with Charlene and Jonathan; and Candice and Walter: beautiful grandchildren, doted on by Harriet, Chris and Claudia. As a son of Stratford once wrote: 'All's Well That End's Well.'

Brief Encounter 2:
MORNING IN NORMANDY...

The sun rose on a perfect Normandy morning in mid-July.

James Fulford awoke early, the bright, buttery sunshine – streaming through his Velux windows – warming his smooth, pink face. James was soon enjoying orange juice, coffee and croissants on the terrace of his remote, granite *maison de vacances*. It was 7.30am; Mary was still asleep in their opulent bed. She looked so lovely, so peaceful; so happy. James kissed her softly, and whispered that he was leaving shortly – to *faire la course* – buy the weekly groceries. Mary smiled in her sleep, as James brushed his lips on hers.

James felt he was a lucky man. At 32 years of age, James, a self-employed graphic designer, divided his time between England and France, with homes in both countries. He and Mary, 28, had been an 'item' for only six blissful months. After two or three relationships that might be termed semi-serious, James was sure that Mary was *the* girl for him. She was a primary school teacher – but the opposite of the starchy caricature: for Mary was a life-force: fun-loving, life-loving, nature loving; a real zephyr of pure, free, ion-charged air. A happy and generous being. And pretty, too, with dark, flashing eyes and tumbling black curls; and mysterious – possessing a dark, proud, gypsy-spirit.

James smiled to himself. He sometimes crooned the *caballero* from Carmen when they made love; what a wild, natural essence she was! Mary, too, had had other relationships – who hadn't these days? thought James, shrugging his shoulders. And who *wouldn't* want her? Yet Sam – her last 'flame', and a young vet – had turned out to be a complete bastard. At first, Mary had been thrilled at the relationship with the flame-haired, frenetic Sam – and all that passion for afflicted cats and dogs. But Sam was intense and insanely possessive, and quickly sought to subdue Mary – to control every aspect of her life and being: her money, her freedom, her body; even her soul. Mary had fought back, like the proud, quick spirit that she was; she would not be Sam's object, his *thing*. Mary's experience and ordeal had traumatised her, and she had left Sam after yet another furious argument – this time over a dress she had bought online, that Sam thought too revealing – and, worse, too expensive.

Even after the split, Sam had continued to pursue Mary, with batteries of telephone calls, texts and insinuating posts on social media. A restraining order finally put a distance between Mary, and her former partner; but Mary had remained wary – and scared. Mary's escape and new freedom was James's great good fortune. He had found his true soul mate, at long last. But Mary had been frightened and scarred, emotionally; it was James's mission to make her feel safe, to make her feel loved, again; but also to give her the space she needed, and to encourage that confidence – and that sunny smile – to return to her daily life.

James started the engine of his VW Golf, and pressed the play button on the CD player. Almost immediately, Ella began pouring forth…'*Summertime*…' James proceeded cautiously along the narrow, twisty lane leading from the ancient *maison*. Though few vehicles might be expected at this or indeed any other time of day, James knew that that very fact encouraged some drivers to travel at reckless speeds. And that the marguerite daisies, harebells and foxgloves adorning the hedgerows concealed deep drainage ditches on either side of the road, that posed a danger to carelessly guided, 'off-piste' vehicles.

The mellifluous Ella was reaching the climax of her story when, suddenly, out of the blue, on a blind bend, a speeding car burst into sight. The only option open to James – to avoid a head-on collision – was to slam his foot on the brakes – sending CDs, phone, shopping bags, and wallet, flying noisily around the car, before settling shambolically in unceremonious little heaps.

Shaken, James stared through his windscreen. A portly woman of around 50 – with a broad, florid face stuck on a thick bull-dog neck, grey hair swept back into a bun, and spectacles wedged on a flat nose – stared back. Angrily. She gestured to James to reverse, since there was simply no space to attempt a passing manoeuvre. James looked behind, down the road. The nearest passing place was at least 70 metres further back, along the winding road. Bugger. A tricky manoeuvre, indeed. Ella was switched off, ungraciously, in mid flow. James needed to concentrate. The florid woman, immobile in her seat, continued to stare angrily in his direction.

As James began to work out his best line of trajectory, his protagonist revved her engine to an angry whine, and moved the battered grey car menacingly closer to the Golf's bonnet. The two cars were now mere millimetres apart.

An exasperated James began to reverse and, with every metre travelled, was tracked by the woman wedged in her impatient silver steed. At the very moment that James had edged into the passing place, the woman's car, like a furious wasp, buzzed past, almost shaving paint from the impeccable Golf. As her car came parallel to the Golf, the 'lady' made a vulgar, and unmistakable, gesture in James's direction. Then she was gone.

Shaken, but pressing forward again at last, James noticed that there was a convenient passing place a mere ten metres behind where the woman's speeding vehicle had lurched to a spectacular halt. James continued his journey, without further incident, but his equilibrium had been disturbed; what had been a perfect morning had now been marred and disfigured by behaviour that could only be described as mean, un-called for and plain rude. Did that woman think that she owned the bloody road? And that the normal rules of civilised behaviour did not apply to her?

James had not been aware that the French employed *that* particular gesture – the old Anglo Saxon code, signifying: do something very painful to yourself. Ironically, the gesture had first been employed by Henry V's archers at Agincourt, in 1415. Captured archers had their two bow-string fingers amputated – thus preventing their using a longbow in anger ever again. This 'V sign' to the opposing French forces, on the field of battle, indicated that these archers' digits were intact – and presaged the bloody carnage soon to be inflicted on the French cavalry.

Still mulling darkly over the incident, and arriving at the supermarché, James grabbed a 'chariot', and stormed into the emporium. This was the weekly shop, and all that anticipated pleasure – all that glorious fresh food, and all that cornucopia of choice – had now shrivelled into a miserable chore. Even so, it was a full forty-five minutes before James approached the checkout. He was the rearguard of a small, orderly queue. As the client immediately ahead of James was served – her goods piled on the conveyor belt – the cashier turned her till light to red: indicating that James would be her final customer, before a well-earned break. 'Thank God for small mercies!' he muttered to himself.

James unloaded his array of goods – wine, bread, fresh meat, cans, packets, and ice-cream – on to the track. There it all was; a whole week's provisions. A couple of hundred euros worth. What an eye-watering, sumptuous pile of goodies it was! Almost an art-work in itself! It was only then, when he paused for breath, and looked up from the 'sumptuous pile', that James glanced at 'his' cashier. She had a broad, florid face jammed into a thick neck, grey hair swept tightly into a bun, and spectacles wedged on a flat, podgy nose. If James had hackles secreted anywhere on his person, they rose, now. *'Bonjour!'* offered James, through gritted teeth. Then, *'au revoir!'* James raised his two fingers to the woman – but in a defiant, Churchillian gesture – and darted past, and out of the shop. Minus all that shopping. His tormentor, suddenly recognising James, waved her arms in the air, before swivelling in her seat, and shouting *'merde!'* at the departing figure of James.

A bevy of nearby customers looked on, shocked but fascinated at the unexpected turn of events. The already florid face appeared as big and bright as a pumpkin; the apoplectic, embarrassed cashier sat helpless on her stool, like a becalmed whale.

'Let *her* have the inconvenience of cleaning up!' thought James, 'and explaining to her supervisor about the mad Englishman. And, hopefully, missing her coffee break!' As soon as James arrived home, he would send an e-mail to the store manager, explaining all. 'Harassed and abused by a member of your staff! Why do you employ such vile people?' It occurred to James that, while he had taken the scenic route to the supermarket, his protagonist – no doubt late for work – was speeding through the most direct route possible; and in no mood for compromise. Although leaving the shopping behind entailed a certain amount of inconvenience to James – on a day marred by inconvenience – James could not help but feel a certain satisfaction at the *denouement* of a morning that had begun so perfectly. The incident even brought a smile to his face. Funny thing, life! The look on that woman's face! What a treat!

James visited a rival superstore five kilometres distant. He would need to hurry, if Mary and he were to enjoy that planned trip to the beach, that afternoon. And he knew for a fact that the store did not sell Mary's favourite ice cream – magnums. Never mind. *C'est la vie*. What the hell – other decent brands were available.

Mary would understand. Indeed, James looked forward to telling all to Mary; she relished a rakish, *dangerous* tale. Mary was such a wild girl, with an impish sense of humour and vivid imagination. When he told his morning's story, she would be beside herself with shock and awe…*'Good God! How could she? What a bitch!' Wish I'd been there!* Then she would look into his eyes and kiss him, and soothe away the morning's memories. James reflected that not all people were good. In fact, some were positively evil. That woman, for instance – her badge had read 'Florence'. Some bloody nightingale she'd proved. Not to mention St Francis – that is, that discarded bastard Sam.

But *he,* James – would always love, would always cherish – Mary. For, every day, in every way, Mary was *very,* very good…

SLICES OF SAM

'Sam?'
'Mmmmmm...'
'Are you awake?'
'Ohhhh...'
'Sam, let me in...'
'What...?'
'I'd like to make love to you...'
'Don't think so...'
'Promise I'll be quick!'
'Mark, it's late. I'm already fucked.'
'What?'
'Knackered. Burnt out. Had it. A long day. *Another* long day...*Please!*... Just go to sleep.'

Mark turned over, like a beached whale, and sulked himself into sleep. It *was* after midnight. Maybe tomorrow morning... After all, tomorrow was Saturday.

When Mark awoke at 7.15am, thoughts of passion still urgent in his head, it was to find a warm but empty space next to his body. Damn! Sam had risen early, had a shower, made herself a coffee and begun preparing for breakfast. And greeted and patted *Ben*, their chocolate Labrador dog. *Ben* responded by furiously waging his tail. He's the only buggar in this house that appreciates me, thought Sam. No work at the Surgery today, thank God. But the twins – Abigail and Tom – would no doubt emerge at some point, and they were always hungry. And Mark always enjoyed a bacon sarnie on Saturdays.

Sam went through the day's schedule in her head. Preparing breakfast, lunch and their evening meal. Well, that was an unalterable given. Shopping, at Tesco's. Before that, she needed to put the washing machine on – for the third time this week. She'd change the bed sheets when everyone had vacated their respective sleeping places. After that, Sam needed to clean the lounge and dining room thoroughly. It was April, now, and time for a real Spring clean. Then – if there was time, before lunch – the whole house needed to be vacuumed. Again.

Usually, on Saturdays in Spring and Summer the family would go for an afternoon drive into the Shropshire countryside – around Bridgnorth, or maybe the meres at Ellesmere. But not today, pondered Sam, grimly. Not today. She had other plans. Sam looked through the window: it was quite light, now, but murky and grey. A bit like her life, she mused, bitterly.

Sam caught sight of herself in the mirror. God, she looked tired and lined, for 38. *These* really should be the best years of her life. She would be 40, shortly. Then 50. The kids would be at University. Then beginning their own adult journey. While her own life – the vital years – would be drawing to a close. Jesus, was this *it*? Was this all there is? No. Things had to change. Drastically. She did nearly all the heavy lifting – in addition to a demanding full time role as a nurse at a local GP practice. Mark walked the dog – *Ben*. And mowed the lawn. Abigail and Tom did…what, exactly? Emptied the dish-washer – *very* grudgingly.

But the times they were a changing, baby. Sam had endured fifteen years of drudgery. She was tired – physically, and emotionally – of a life of apparent servitude. She felt like Sisyphus, rolling that bloody rock uphill. Continuously. For ever. There was never any end in sight. The daily, weekly, yearly routine would continue until she was old and, like a draught horse, put out to pasture. Or shot – and turned into dog food and glue. But, in the meantime, she was expected – and without thanks – to be a drudge in the house, a slave in the kitchen, and a whore in the bedroom. Always on fucking tap.

We were in the last chance saloon, thought Sam. If today's honest chat did not lead to serious change, she might well take the nuclear option. The family often spent their holidays in France – Brittany. Well, qualified nurses were always in high demand; could always secure a job. Roaming around the Breton countryside, being greeted by grateful patients in their own homes, had a certain charm; a certain appeal. A certain *piquancy*. But could she *really* contemplate leaving Mark and the twins? thought Sam to herself. Not really; not at an age when they needed her most. At the same time, she could not imagine months – even years – of this mindless, endless drudgery. Let's not box yourself in, girl. Let's just see how this afternoon's medicine goes down…

Sam took out the printed A4 notices she had prepared a couple of days before, and pinned them to every door in the house. They read:

Buckley Family Summit:
2.00pm, Saturday 3 April 2022
'The Times They Are a Changing!'

Minutes later, the eleven year-olds Abigail and Tom – tall, good looking and already showing distinct signs of adolescence – dashed into the kitchen and, without a word, began to eat their personal choice of cereals. Tom orders beans on toast for his next course; Abigail, a croissant. Then, with mouth still full, but vacant mind, Tom said: 'What's this Summit thing about, mum?'

'We need to discuss how we all live together. To make the

most of the precious time we have – me watching and helping you grow up. And mummy and daddy enjoying our free time together.'

'But what's wrong with how we are, now?' enquired Abigail. 'We have a nice home. Everything seems to work just fine.'

Sam smiled. 'Well, maybe it's not so fine for all of us, darling,' she said, gently. 'Anyway, here's your father.' And, to the twins, a touch conspiratorially, 'I'd better put the cooker on.'

Mark appeared – fresh and clean-shaven, following recent ablutions. He looks lithe and carefree, his face smooth, with just a trace of grey in his hair. Mark is a car salesman at a local dealership, where he's a respected, experienced member of the team. He's recently enjoyed a promotion; he's now 40, but life is going swimmingly. Apart from last night, that is. Mark had wanted to celebrate his promotion, in the best way he knew. 'Summit, eh?' He winks at Tom. 'Sounds exciting. Anything we need to know beforehand, love? So we can think and prepare?' Another wink – this time directed at Abigail. Abigail turns away, embarrassed.

'You guys all need to know – to understand – that my workload is simply too great. It's unsustainable. I seem to do practically everything around the house. I feel permanently knackered, and it can't go on. I'm not criticising anyone. I'm just saying that things have to change. Big time. I really feel that my time is being cut into a hundred slices. That there's no space for me – to be *me*. So, at two o'clock, we can sit down and have a serious four-way discussion. Tom, Abigail, you're old enough now to have a say. But I'm looking for solutions, not excuses. The status quo is unacceptable. So I hope that gives you all food for thought. Ready for that bacon sarnie, Mark? By the way, sorry about last night…'

The twins look thoughtfully at their mother, then at their father. Mark blushes, and coughs, before spluttering: 'No probs.

I hadn't realised things were so bad. Let's have a good chat, later. Maybe we'll still have time for a trip out with *Ben*.' Mark tucks into his sarnie, every disappearing mouthful eyed anxiously and jealously by waggie-tail *Ben*.

Breakfast over, the twins retire to their rooms; in Tom's case to play computer games; in Abigail's, to practice piano. Mark hurriedly slurps down a coffee, before taking *Ben* for an overdue walk. On that walk he ponders Sam's words. Are things really *that* bad? he asks himself. Is Sam just a bit tired and emotional at the moment? Welcome to marriage, Mark says to himself. And kids. And fucking life. Did anyone ever promise a bed of roses? Still, he reasons, I'd better humour the old girl. Or that postponed shag might never happen. Mark returns home, and braces himself for that fun trip to Tesco's.

A few minutes before two o'clock, Sam takes a break from the endless chores, and ruminates on her family. Mark, her husband of 15 years, is OK, she decides. He's been a good husband overall; a good provider, and a loving father. There was just that brief fling with the office girl, five years ago. Bendy Brenda they called her. She had set herself a personal mission of going through all the married men at the dealership. And they had all fallen like ninepins – Mark included. In the end, she had proved such a disruptive influence – jealous male colleagues barely speaking to each other – that the owners had palmed Brenda off to a rival firm. They couldn't believe their luck: a modern version of the Trojan Horse.

Young Tom was growing up fast; he would soon be as tall as his Dad. He was proving to be a little vain – the family spent more on his hair and various gels than Sam spent on her own. Tom was very bright, if a little nerdy. Technology was his thing. Girls, and GCSEs, had not arrived on his radar, yet. But they would soon, reasoned Sam. Especially girls. If he's anything like his Dad.

Abigail was a serious, sensitive girl. She was entering puberty, and was developing breasts – just like her mother, at the same age. Abigail was acutely self-conscious about this, and lost herself in her studies, and her music. But Abigail was developing into a particularly pretty young woman. She seemed scarcely conscious of the fact; but Sam knew that, in only a year or two the landscape would begin to change, as her daughter's attractions became obvious, and the boys came round to play.

Sam *knew* that she needed to be there, for her son and daughter: to help, support and guide them, through the most important years of their young lives so far – the pressures and stresses of growing up; emotional trauma and mood-swings; hormonal changes; school work and exams; sexual challenges; financial issues. University. Career choices. This was all vitally important, but everything was concentrated into a few brief years. Blink, and you missed it. Miss it, and there would be a lifetime of regrets. Opportunities missed, never to be regained. And Sam couldn't fulfil her role properly, fully, if she always had her head in the oven, or down the bog. She steeled herself for the meeting. There could be no rowing back.

The Summit
At 2.00pm precisely, all four members of the family took their places around the dining room table. *Ben* sat on the fringe, vaguely expectant. Mark had made what he hoped would be a propitiatory round of coffees. 'Well,' began Sam, brightly, 'this is the first time we've all sat down together for a chat in many a month. So it's not before time. But I'm really looking forward to it. OK. I've already explained the problem. So over to you. Suggestions, please.'

Tom adored his father, and thought he'd act the *agent provocateur*. 'Mum, I'm still not really sure I understand the problem. I mean, everything *works*.'

Sam sighed. 'I know everything works, Tom. Because *I* make it work. Shopping. Cleaning. Cooking. Washing. Ironing. It's all me. Every single thing. Meanwhile, you're spending 20 hours a week on your play station!'

'But I am only eleven!' countered Tom, defensively. 'And, anyway, isn't it what parents *do*?'

'You're nearly twelve. You're both growing up quickly. You need to learn some important life skills. And we need to share the family burden – the workload: the workload created by all of *you*. I'm simply not doing it any more. I need to be there to help you grow up; I can't do that if I'm the domestic slave. Remember that I also have a demanding full time job. Of course, I could give that up to be a skivvy. But my job – my *career* – is one of the few things I actually enjoy. I'm good at it; it gives me satisfaction; and I feel appreciated. And, if I were to give it up we'd all be – what's that four letter word? – yes – *poor*. So we all need to do our bit – a very considerable bit – to keeping this home going. You'll appreciate it one day. The *bottom*-line – literally – is this: who's going to wash your pants?'

'Mum, I'd be happy to help in the kitchen. It's time I learned to cook,' Abigail offered, in placatory mode.

'And I'd be happy to clean the house once or twice a week' smiled Mark.

'And I'll do the dishwasher every day…' muttered Tom, before realising he'd suffered a rush of blood to the head.

'It all sounds great' responded Sam. 'Except that we've been here before. And, as we all know, after an initial burst of enthusiasm, and the gurning of martyred souls, you all revert to type. And, within weeks – zilch.'

Mark shifted uncomfortably in his seat. 'So, do *you* have a solution, dear?'

'Glad you asked' said Sam, looking Mark squarely in the eye. 'It's simple. We contract it all out.'

'What! You mean we pay for *strangers* to do all the housework!' said Mark, incredulously. 'It'll cost a fortune!'

'Indeed. But that's the hidden cost of all that I'm doing. I've been researching local companies, and what they charge. £250 a week should cover it. And think of all that extra time we – I'll – have. To get fit. To get creative. To provide parental support to my growing family. And start enjoying life to the full…While I still can.'

'Yes…but it's still an awful lot of income draining from the family budget…' muttered Mark.

'Don't worry, following your promotion, you can afford it!' countered Sam. 'However, there is an alternative…Because,' said Sam, a tad mischievously, 'if you feel the competition is too pricey, put in your own counter offers – and be paid for doing stuff in your own house. For your own benefit. But on a contract basis. Thus, keeping the money in the family.'

'That's a thought!' Mark responded, brightening.

'But the quid pro quo is: if standards slip, you'll be given notice to quit. And *Fairy Dust* cleaners hired instead.'

On that basis, since Sam's earnestness was clear to all, and even Tom could see the benefits accruing to him, all tasks were agreed and shared between family members. Mark would clean the house twice a week – including toilet, shower and oven. Abigail would learn to cook, and help her mother in the kitchen. In a new development, Mark also offered to cook the evening meal twice a week. In addition, each family member would choose and prepare their own breakfast. At least once a week, the family would buy in a takeaway. Tom would both fill, and empty, the dishwasher every day. Everyone would be paid, according to the type of work required, and its estimated duration.

Since no-one volunteered for the chores of washing and ironing, this was to be contracted out to a local firm. As well as retaining some of the cooking duties, Sam agreed to do the family shop – stipulating doing this on her own – once each week. She had never really appreciated Mark's impatient charging down the aisles, and the time saved would free him to indulge his favourite hobby – golf. Besides, Sam was aware of admiring glances from the male shoppers whenever she shopped alone. She may be a wife and mother of two, but Sam was not above harmless flattery. Especially at times – like now – when she was feeling so low. Sam had retained an admirable figure; the new regime would permit a fortnightly visit to hairdresser and beautician.

Within an hour, all was sorted; all agreed; and everyone, apparently, happy. Tom thought eagerly about the new computer games coming his way. And Abigail realised that her longing for a cello might now be realised in a matter of months. Mark thought about his freedom on the golf course. Not even *Ben* was forgotten. Sam, Tom and Abigail would all exercise with the happy lad in the local park, while Mark cleaned the house. Money management skills – and exercise – and teamwork – were unexpected bonuses arising from Sam's serious foot-stamping.

'Thank you darlings,' said Sam with a big smile. 'Now, if you don't mind, your Dad and I have something important to discuss...' Abigail and Tom were relieved to get away. But, with his analytical mind, Tom was already considering how to complete his tasks – his contract – in the most energy and time-efficient way possible.

'Here's a word,' Sam ventured. 'Sex'.

'What of it?' said Mark. Then the penny dropped. 'You mean you want me to *pay* for it?' he spluttered. From being Mr Smug, a few seconds ago, he was suddenly shaken; and ashen, the colour draining from his cheeks.

'I've been looking at the rates charged by escort agencies. Their average day rate – or should that be night rate – is 500 quid...'

'But...' objected Mark.

'You mean they're young and pretty?' anticipated Sam. 'Try 'em, if you really want. I mean it. Give me a break. But, well, I'll give you my very best for £250. And I'll be *really* energised… And, after a year, I'd have saved up enough to take us all on that cruise…'

'This is getting interesting…' said Mark. 'Like, win-win.' Sam lent over, licked his ear, and whispered:

These boobs are made for kissing,
And that's just what they'll do…
And one of these nights these boobs
Are gonna smash right into you…'

'Tell me,' enquired Mark, suddenly alive to new possibilities: do you take cheques, or is it cash only?'

'Cash only, sweetheart. And up-front – on my bedside table. Not that I don't trust you. But I won't disappoint. Promise!' Sam laughed: 'You can call me 'Samba' in the bedroom!' (She had neither forgotten nor forgiven Bendy Brenda for leading her suggestible husband astray). And with a snarl beneath the smile: 'anything goes, baby!'

The whole family was renewing and refreshing itself. Everyone was more focused. More energised. Having more fun. *Ben*, too – with his multitude of walks and walkers. Even Sam was hopeful that France – Brittany – could remain on the back burner; at least, for the time being. There was – surely – now, only one direction of travel: towards a brighter future for them all. Onwards and upwards.

TEN TIPS FOR A LONGER LIFE

There was an air of excitement at Grimsthorpe Care Home, South Yorkshire. It was the morning of 30 June; and Stanley Smithson's 100th birthday.

Bunting had been erected in the large, airy sitting room; a hundred birthday cards placed carefully on every shelf, table and mantelpiece; and a telegram from the Queen displayed in pride of place. A large chocolate cake – Black Forest Gateau, no less – and festooned with 100 candles – had been specially prepared in the Home's bustling kitchen. And – to cap it all – the local press had been invited to interview Stanley, in that pregnant interval between breakfast and lunch.

Stanley had lived at the Care Home for five years, now. He'd lost his wife of 70 years, Elsie, when she was 91 years of age. Wisely, Stanley had hired a gardener, and a cleaning service, and the gallant old chap had coped manfully on his own – there were no children – cooking, cleaning and shopping – until a fall, while climbing steps in the garden – had incapacitated him. Stanley's lovely, and much-loved, home had had to be sold to pay for the care costs – but he knew in his heart that there was no possibility of returning there.

Dr Smithson, as he was still known, had worked hard in his profession – a GP – in his local community, for more than 40 years. He had retired at the age of 66; the couple had then enjoyed a comfortable retirement. Stanley and Elsie had travelled the world, luxuriating on cruises to the Caribbean, and Mediterranean, and stayed – and dined – in some of the UK's finest hotels and restaurants. Such a grand life had gradually petered out, as age and infirmity had increased their grip. But, overall, there was nothing to complain about. Even so, Stanley had keenly missed the company of women. At least, in the Care Home, there were people to talk to; to reminisce with – and smiling staff – mostly women – to converse with, even flirt with, in an innocent, unassuming way.

The centenarian remained in rude health for his age, and was looking forward to his interview with the local journalist. He'd had a special wash and shave that morning, thanks to Care Assistant, Wendy, and a comb-over for his thinning hair. But his ruddy cheeks and sparkling eye revealed an elderly gent who was still trying to get the most from life, despite his dwindling capacities.

Stanley felt proud that morning: proud to be alive, still, and grateful for all the fuss and attention. He sat comfortably in his armchair, his embossed walking stick by his side. The young journalist – Simon Lane – from *The Yorkshire Echo* – dutifully arrived on time. 'Great to see you, Dr Smithson!' gushed Simon. 'And congratulations! Tell me, how does it *feel?*'

'What? To reach a hundred?' replied Stanley. 'Well, better than the alternative, I expect! Oh, and do call me Stanley. Everyone else does.' The old man's eyes sparkled with amusement. 'So, to what do you attribute your longevity…er, Stanley. Is it your medical expertise? Or perhaps your excellent care, here? Or maybe your positive outlook on life? Oh, can I take a picture or two? Maybe one with the Queen's telegram? And another with you holding a glass of something? Possibly champagne? And maybe one with your splendid birthday cake?'

Stanley looked towards his carer, who gave a thumbs up, and hurried to fetch champagne from the fridge. Moet; just the job. And, of course, the exceedingly grand Black Forest Gateau, with its 100 candles.

Wendy arrived with the gateau, champagne and two glasses. Everyone looked on, as the comely Care Assistant, in her immaculate uniform, lit the candles. It took Stanley four attempts to blow out the profusion of little flames, but he was quite delighted when his lung-power overcame the flickering lights. All one hundred assembled residents and staff cheered and applauded the 'grand extinguish'.

'Will you care to take a glass with me, Simon? And enjoy a slice of cake?' 'Well…I'm driving, but, go on, just a small one…And a small slice, please, er…Wendy.' Then, photo opp. completed – a beaming Stanley, glass raised, and a sumptuous gateau poised before the main man – Simon took a swig from his glass and, with his silver spoon, dived into his gateau. Simon paused to admire Wendy, before asking a further question; but, possibly owing to his distraction, really repeating his first. 'It's quite extraordinary, Stanley. I've not met a 100 year old before. I mean, what's it all about? Are you still enjoying life?'

'It's certainly a strange thing; a strange feeling,' replied Stanley. 'Maybe there are many elements, contributing to the whole. But, in my long career, I've known many patients who died far too young – victims of excessive smoking, or drinking. Or maybe poor lifestyle choices. But I've also known many patients struck down by terrible illnesses, diseases, or viruses – way, way before they'd lived decently lengthy lives. So luck comes into it; though sometimes you make your own luck. I don't believe there's a magic prescription, in any sense. Just some sensible rules that one can follow. Then continue to enjoy, and keep your fingers crossed…'

'That's really fascinating' said Simon, taking another sip of

Moet, following another mouthful of cake. 'You've obviously thought deeply about this.' 'Well,' laughed Stanley, 'I've had plenty of time!'

'But what about your own case, Stanley? What have *you* done?'

Stanley paused. 'Well, I've been blessed. I was married to a wonderful woman for 70 years. I had a fulfilling, purposeful career. And I developed a comfortable lifestyle. So I was lucky, if you like. But, as I've said, sometimes you make your own luck. I've found that, if you enjoy every day, you're likely to have more days to enjoy. And, though my life has changed pretty dramatically of late, I've carried some core principles into my new life, here.'

Simon looked surreptitiously at his watch. The next job could wait awhile. 'Do please elaborate, if you will, Dr…I mean, Stanley.'

'Well, there's a key word for me, and that's 'hot''. Simon raised his eyebrows. 'Ten activities that, if you include 'hot', can transform one's life. At least, they've transformed mine.'

'Do go on, if you will' urged Simon, before emptying his glass – and his plate.

'OK. So, at least three times a week, make your body hot, while exercising in warm clothing. You must exercise, or run – or, in my case, walk – until your body gets pumped up and hot – a little breathless in fact.'

'I see,' said Simon, a trifle disappointed.

'Next,' continued Stanley, 'enjoy at least one good, hot meal every day – but particularly over the winter months.'

'Then, drink at least three or four hot cups of something every day – especially when the weather's cold. I recommend tea, or coffee. Or, if you prefer, hot chocolate, or Ovaltine. Even Bovril.

'Again, for at least six months a year, enjoy an old-fashioned hot water bottle.'

Simon stifled a yawn, and glanced again at his watch.

'Fifth, listen to some hot music, and read some chapters of a hot book, every day. It doesn't matter whether it's Beethoven or Beyoncé, Strauss or Sinatra, so long as it turns you on – makes you *hot*. Same with the literature – Dickens, Dostoyevsky – or Drivel. It just needs to zing energy and life!'

'Sixth – I think – enjoy a holiday in a hot resort at least once a year. Sadly, it's no longer the Caribbean, but we went on an exciting coach trip to Hayling Island, last Summer, and I'm looking forward to Torquay, in July. New scenes, new sights, new stimulation – and hot sunshine.'

'Then, drink a hot toddy every night, before bedtime.'

'I'm afraid we're running out of time,' Simon said, this time not quite stifling a yawn. Stanley appeared not to notice.

'I think we're at number eight. We have Sky TV here. There's really some pretty hot stuff on, these days. You just have to flick through the channels. I recommend it. All those beautiful young things. Don't think we old 'uns don't notice any more, young man. Quite mind expanding, and life enhancing.'

Simon loosened his collar.

'OK, nine. Have at least three hot baths every week. I look forward to mine every other day, ably assisted by the lovely Wendy.' Stanley smiled in Wendy's direction.

Simon pictured the scene in his mind. His collar became looser.

'Ten, finally, I do think that female company is most important; most stimulating. Don't you? So a young lady visits me each week; for a nice, cosy chat. She has a marvellous face and figure, and a beautiful persona, and keeps an old chap exceedingly happy.' Stanley followed this up with a wink.

'Thank you so much, Dr Smithson. How stimulating! How very absorbing! I may have to do a bit of editing, of course, but I look forward to telling your fascinating story – and sharing your advice – in next week's *Echo*. All the best! And thanks for the drink! And cake! Goodbye, and all the best!'

Simon hurried to his car, again looking at his watch. 'Bloody Nora! So *that's* the secret!'

Simon hadn't heard Wendy's fleeting footsteps, until she arrived beside his car. The unexpected presence gave Simon quite a jolt, though not an unpleasant one. 'Thank you so much Mr Lane,' she gushed. 'Stanley's a splendid old gent. But he does have a lively – one might say over-active – imagination. And a mischievous sense of humour. But you do need to take his stories with a pinch of salt...' Wendy smiled sweetly, gave Simon a parting wink, and was gone. Simon watched her shapely *derriere* disappear back into Reception, and sighed.

Stanley settled into sleep, a smile playing on his flushed face. Wendy walked up briskly, her starched uniform rasping against her motion. She plumped Stanley's pillows, playfully. 'Stanley,' she smiled, 'you *naughty boy!*'

THE GIRL AND THE GUY

It was a sunny, expectant morning in mid-April. They met – the girl and the guy – and introduced themselves.

A moment earlier, the taxi had disgorged the human equivalent of an exquisite Faberge confection. Mike had dashed over to pay, and tip, the driver. 'Thanks, mate!'

'Lucky bastard!' the driver had said, under his breath. He had subjected his mesmerising – but apparently modest and monosyllabic – 'fare' to a machine-gun barrage of questions during the half-hour journey – scrutinising her constantly in the rear view mirror – and had arrived at a conclusion based on a long and cynical world-view. The passenger had parried his intrusive questions with studied nonchalance. 'Are you not supposed to be driving?' asked the girl, archly, at one point. Greasy, sweaty and balding, the cabbie could not help repeating to his over-heated self: 'so near, yet so fucking far!' As he sped away, eyeing-up the girl for probably the last time, the driver mouthed: 'give her one for me, you old buggar!'

'Hello, I'm Olga,' she said, simply. 'And you Mike? Mike I like…'

She had smiled the smile of smiles, and proffered her hand, proudly but demurely. He had raised the delicate hand to his lips, and brushed it gently. She had teased: 'you English Romantics! Full of bullshit!'

He had laughed at her teasing. 'Olga?' he repeated, though he already knew. 'And you're really *Russian*?'

She nodded in assent. 'Does it matter? As you can see, I'm all woman. But, yes, I am Russian. I grew up in Moscow.' There was a pronounced Russian accent.

'So why are you here?' he added, a touch stupidly. Did it *really* matter?

'That's a deep question,' she smiled. 'Why are any of us here? But if you mean, why am I not in Russia, it is because men tried to control me. They frightened me. Here, I can be free, and make my own decisions.'

'Oh, well, Putin's loss is my gain!'

She frowned. 'You must not joke. There are eyes and ears, everywhere!'

He looked around. They were sitting on a park bench, in the middle of a park. A lone dog walker, and a young woman wheeling a pushchair, was all that he could see. No men in shades, or wielding long lenses.

Mike looked from the young woman with the pushchair, clad in jeans and t-shirt, to his new companion. The contrast hurt his eyes. If the pushchair girl was a woman, Olga was woman alpha plus.

'Phew. So: come back to my place? Now?'

Olga looked down to Mike's trousers, and suppressed a smile. 'Yes, but not yet. I am yours for the day. There is plenty of time. No need to rush. It would be nice if we got to know each other a little. Then the sex will be better…Is there anywhere we can get a coffee?'

The couple climbed into Mike's waiting Audi tt, and headed for the nearest Costa Coffee. They were silent in the car, except for a brief exchange:

'Did you have a good journey?' asked Mike, with exaggerated courtesy.

'Yes, very pleasant, thank you, though the driver was a wanker.'

'May I commend your command of English?' laughed Mike, a touch ironically.

'No problem; maybe commend Russian education system.'

'I'm happy to commend any system that's produced *you*.'

On arrival, Mike quickly commandeered an unobtrusive corner table in the quiet cafeteria. Over an Americano (for him) and expresso (for her) the exchange of information flowed easily, and without embarrassment.

'Anyway, Olga, really great to meet you. Tell me, how long have you been here?'

'In the UK? About twelve months. I got a visa, looked at a map, took advice from friends, and caught a plane to Birmingham!'

'But why Birmingham?'

'A big city. Lots of potential business, but less than half the costs of London.'

'Fair does. Have you been in this line of work – that is, modelling – for very long?'

'About three years. I started when I was nineteen. Before that I worked in a big supermarket. But it was boring, and the pay was, how do you say? Well, shit. And the bosses – and their bosses – kept pestering me. Eventually I decided, if they want it that bad, they can pay for it – big time.'

'And did they?'

Olga giggled. 'Oh, yes! But it's not easy in Russia. Always people who want to 'protect' you – control you. And beat you if you don't like. England is different – my life, my decisions, my money. And if I don't like a guy, I say no.' She added, brightly: 'but I like *you* Mike!'

Mike beamed, in appreciation. 'But you must have a boyfriend, Olga – a girl like you? What does he think?'

'No, not regular boyfriend – *boyfriends*. Easy come, easy go

– before they get controlling or jealous. I love my freedom – I don't need a regular guy to boss me around. But what about you, Mike? You look quite young. A full head of hair. I mean, some of my clients are *really* old!' She laughed. 'I have to help them, if you know what I mean…'

Mike shifted in his seat. 'I'm 44,' he averred. (He was 47).

'You look younger,' said Olga, a touch doubtfully. 'But tell me more, Mike. About you. You married?'

'Yes, but separated.'

Olga's smile returned. 'All clients say 'single' or 'separated'. But it not bothers me. You are single for today; today you are mine. But why you separate? You did bad thing?'

'Sarah took exception to my fondness for other women. It was me or them, she stamped. No contest, then,' he laughed.

'I see,' shrugged Olga. 'And your work? What do you do?'

'I run my own business; I'm a gas engineer.'

'So you are a businessman? You make money from hot air? I like that. I'm a businesswoman. I like making money, too: from hot fantasies. But I also like making love. And giving full satisfaction. And do you do this often, Mike, being with women?'

'I wouldn't say, 'often'. I've had relationships with women… but generally, with women around my own age. Sometimes it works; sometimes not. But it always seems like *hard* work. Everybody wants so much – not just money, and all that, but time. And commitment.' Mike sounded strangled. 'What can I say? This is different; this is special. This is non-committal and, dare I say, Olga, *exciting*.'

'Thank you, Mike. That's very nice. But do you have any other interests? Apart from sex and money?'

Mike laughed. 'Why, yes. I like music – mainly easy listening, and jazz. Sinatra, Basie, Ellington – that kind of thing. And I enjoy running – hence my amazing figure.' Mike grinned at his own joke. 'Oh – don't laugh – I'm into bird watching.'

Olga did laugh, but briefly and engagingly. Mike was a valued and valuable client, and she needed to massage his ego.

'And what about you?' asked Mike, with feigned interest. 'What are *you* into?'

'I like reading the Russian classics – Tolstoy, Dostoyevsky, Chekhov. So full of life and humanity. And I like English Romantic poetry – Byron, Keats, Shelley. And I like music. I'll surprise you – Sinatra, and a guy called Matt Monro: *'From Russia with Love…'*

'Wow,' said Mike, a little breathlessly. 'We have stuff in common! And I don't mind a bit of poetry myself. Any other likes?'

'Yes. I love to dance. And I love to cook. Olga turned on her dazzling smile: 'I'm really an old fashioned kind of girl!'

'Blimey,' gasped Mike, 'I'm surprised you find time for, er, this.'

Olga shrugged. 'I make time. OK. Tell me, Mike, you've seen my photos online, but now you've seen the *real* me. What do you like about me most?'

Mike laughed – a gargled, nervous laugh. 'Maybe discuss again later, when I've seen and experienced all of you? But from where I'm sitting, I'd say that I like everything – from your hair and eyes to the tips of your toes.' He smiled. 'Not forgetting, of course, your sparkling personality…'

'Oh, that's great, Mike. You know how to flatter a girl. Some men just seem to like my 34 double-g boobs,' Olga whispered, confidentially, while leaning provocatively over the table.

'Well,' replied Mike in the same vein: 'I wasn't going to mention it, but I *had* kind of noticed them.' He felt empowered to stare deliberately, acutely, at Olga's voluptuous curves. 'Tell me honestly, Olga, are they for real?'

'You think they're fake?' replied Olga, with mock outrage. 'I promise you, everything about Olga Pereshkova is real!'

'I didn't doubt it for a second,' smiled Mike. 'Another expresso before we go?'

*

When Mike and Olga left the cafe, it was already past noon. Mike felt excited; elated, as he strode to the Audi, arm in arm with Olga.

'Mike, I'm feeling hungry. No time for breakfast. Anywhere we can go for a spot of lunch? We don't want to make love on an empty stomach…we'll need lots of energy…'

'Er, there's a Rando's in town…I'd recommend the bolognese…or maybe the goulash…'

By 12.45, the happy couple were ensconced at a corner table in the restaurant. Olga ordered an aperitif: double vodka on the rocks. What else? Then – the restaurant was busy, and service was delayed – she ordered another. But Olga ate heartily. Where did it all go in that svelte, hour-glass shaped body? Three courses – oysters, steak and fries, and crème brulee – were washed down with several rather choice glasses of claret. Mike made do with a ham salad, and a glass of coke.

'Christ, this is turning out to be an expensive fucking day!' thought Mike, as he watched those luscious lips closing over yet another juicy slice of steak. 'And I haven't even seen any action, yet!' Meanwhile, every eye – men, women, waiters, waitresses – was trained on the exotic Olga as though they were iron filings to her magnet. She looked stunning; sensational; and utterly sensual in her style.

It was now 2.15, and Mike paid the bill, while Olga headed on the path towards the car. Then Mike heard a shriek, and dashed towards the source. There was Olga, sprawled on the path; though she'd fallen elegantly, she had not fallen painlessly. She'd stumbled on the uneven slabs, she explained, breathlessly. The tight red dress and high heels hadn't helped. Neither, possibly, had the alcohol, on an empty stomach. It seemed that Olga had sprained her left ankle. It was OK, she offered, by way of apology: in her line of work – mainly horizontal – ankles were expendable. Mike was profusely attentive, and concerned: he'd invested a great deal in this venture, and was anxious to protect that investment from further harm. Leaning on her beau, Olga hobbled awkwardly – and apologetically – to the waiting Audi. Mike felt the warmth and softness of her breast through his shirt. Jesus; let's just get her home.

'Straight home, I think?' said Mike, soothingly. 'We'll need to have a look at that ankle…'

Olga meekly assented. Home was a good 30 minutes away. They should get there for 3.00, Mike thought. Wrap her ankle in a compress, give her some suitably re-assuring words… then bingo. They were half way towards the leafier environs of Wolverhampton when Olga – who had been noticeably quiet – exclaimed: 'Mike, I feel sick!'

Mike looked desperately for a lay-by on the dual-carriageway but, before it could be reached, Olga threw up over the dashboard. 'I'm so sorry, Mike!' spluttered Olga, her beautiful lips still frothing with a residue of unctuous matter. It must be the oysters, she groaned. They must have been off!

Mike mouthed a few expletives as he steered into the lay-by. He chaperoned Olga from her seat, and set about cleaning his beloved Audi. 'How do you feel, now?' he asked, not sounding terribly concerned.

Olga was about to utter a few re-assuring words when her countenance altered, and she threw up again. There was a further retching, before the distressed girl – looking pale though still exquisitely beautiful – announced that she was ready to complete the journey. Unfortunately, the vile effusion had stained her dress. Olga burst into tears. 'Just look at my dress! It cost three hundred pounds!'

'Let's just get you home. It can always be dry cleaned. And I can lend you some clothes...if you really need them...'

The Audi reached Mike's drive without further incident, and Mike helped the subdued, hobbling, Olga into his capacious detached house, sitting her in a favourite armchair. A glass of cool water seemed just the ticket, to calm that debilitated system. Unexpectedly, and without warning, Olga emitted a rancid stream of bile, that perfectly ruined her expensive new dress.

'Oh my God, I'm so sorry!' she spluttered. 'I'll make it up to you. Promise. But now I need to rest!'

'Of course, babe.' Mike showed her into a bedroom – not the master, he wasn't taking any more chances – and advised her to have a nap. Olga thanked him, kissed him on the lips, and retired to bed. Mike wiped his mouth. Jesus! And checked his watch. It was already fucking four o'clock. Mike's spectacular hopes were deflating faster than a punctured balloon. Would the girl be able to perform, before she had to leave? he asked himself, churlishly. Mike poured himself a stiff drink, and waited, impatiently, for Olga to emerge. He ruminated over his Glennfidich: was this just the most endless, exhausting tease? The most beautiful girl in the world – who never did sex?

At 6.30, Mike began to lose patience, and slipped silently into the bedroom, his gentle knocks having gone unheeded. Olga lay on the bed, asleep. She was naked. Mike emitted an involuntary gasp. A gasp of disbelief. He had never seen – *felt* – such beauty. My God. Perfection. Could he – should he – touch her? She had come to his house, entered his domain, for sex. He was rewarding her handsomely. So why not? Even if she *was* asleep? No doubt she would wake, when his fingers caressed her; and when he began to kiss her. He felt himself; he was more than ready, ready to exert himself, to satisfy himself, upon that living, breathing, vision of soft, warm loveliness...

But then he collected himself. What kind of man was he?

Really? I mean: *really*. No, sod the money. And – looking down – sod *you*. His luck might change. Time would tell. But now was not the time.

Olga opened her wide almond eyes, and smiled. She took him in with an experienced glance. 'I know what you are thinking. Feeling. If you wish, you can have me. You have paid for me. But it will not be the best of me. I do not feel well. I promise that I will make it up to you, Mike. Can I stay tonight, please, and rest? Then we will see. In the morning. And, Mike, is it true; I need to know?'

'Know what, sweetheart?' Mike asked, tenderly.

'Whether you are separated?'

'Yes, it is true. Sarah and I parted two years ago, now. We haven't divorced as yet, but there's no way back.' The words that he uttered next seemed to come from his lips without having first engaged with his brain: 'Especially now I have you…'

Olga smiled deliciously. 'Thank you, Mike. Please kiss me, and then leave me to rest.'

Mike did as he was bid. It was a brief, chaste kiss; though delicious in Olga's response. Mike closed the door softly. Then burst into tears; he knew not why; just an overflow of high, confused emotions. He gathered himself together, poured himself another stiff drink, meditated deeply upon his strange new situation, and went to bed. On his own. It was still only 9.30. But the day was complete. It was a beautiful sleep; his conscious unconsciousness filled with Olga.

*

Mike awoke. Olga still filled his mind. How was she? Mike found himself strangely concerned; frightened, even. Maybe she'd left during the night? He looked at his watch. It was 8.00am. Time to get up, and look see.

Mike heard sounds emanating from the kitchen, and found Olga preparing breakfast. A fry up – eggs and bacon sizzling in the pan. She was moving easily, fluently, the pain in her ankle having eased overnight. Olga gave him a big smile, and a big kiss. She was wearing a pinny and, it seemed, little else, apart from a pair of pink pants. Mike playfully caressed her sumptuous *derriere*.

Olga looked at him sternly. 'Now sit down please, and we will eat while hot. And there's orange juice. And coffee.'

'Quite the little lady!' said Mike, delight in his eyes and voice.

'Please eat!' commanded Olga. 'Today, I am good! You can sex me, if like!'

Mike observed Olga closely. In truth, he could not take his eyes off her, even while he ate. But he teased: 'Maybe,' apparently weighing his choices. 'If you play your cards right. But first I have to tell you something. I'm actually 47. Old enough to be your father!'

Olga shrugged. 'I don't care. You could have had me. You have respected me. You are good man. I like you.' She sighed. 'I think I…like you much…Eat, Mike, and then we make love. Not sex. Love: with heart and soul.'

'But first, Mike, I have to tell *you*, you have very nice house. Two downstairs rooms. Four bedrooms. Two bathrooms. A big kitchen. All just for you?'

'I suppose so,' shrugged Mike. 'You've been exploring?'

'Yes, exploring. Nice breakfast, Mike?'

'Very, very nice,' agreed Mike, still studying Olga's every movement with a forensic fascination. Olga smiled broadly, in appreciation, and kissed him. 'So, let's explore some more…'

*

An hour later, Mike and Olga parted, physically: regretfully; and oh so reluctantly. The love-making had been intense, seismic, glorious, fabulous. There were no words that would suffice; even the most overblown. Olga began to sing, sweetly, absently: '*From Russia with Love…*' before convulsing into a fit of giggles.

The giggles quickly subsided, and Mike began kissing her again. Olga pressed a finger to his lips. 'Mike? Was I worth it?' asked Olga, plaintively.

Mike thought for a moment. 'Worth it? 'If you sat on a pair of scales, and the other scale was filled with a pure gold, gleaming model of you, there would still be no contest. Your worth is beyond gold, let alone pounds or roubles.'

'Then I – give myself – as a gift. To you. But tell me,' Olga persisted, placing her arms around Mike's neck, and kissing him softly: 'was it *really* good? Was it good *enough*?'

'It was unbelievable,' answered Mike. 'Truly unbelievable. But good enough for what?'

'So that you ask to marry me? To make an honest woman out of me?'

'I've never met such an honest woman,' laughed Mike. 'And I've never heard such an incredible proposal. You are truly out of the box. Any fucking box. But return the favour, Olga: what do *you* most like about *me*?'

Olga composed herself. 'Very well. She widened her eyes: 'apart from big cock? Well, nice house. Nice kitchen. But most of all: very nice, kind man. And good lover! Oh' – Olga looked serious: 'and no return to Russia…'

Tears came to Mike's eyes. 'Olga Pereshkova: will you do me the honour of becoming my wife? At least, when I'm actually divorced!'

'Yes, my darling! Until then, if you like, I will stay. Not to worry: I have money. I have sparkling personality. I have love. And my body is for you, only. And I will cook and bake in that big kitchen. But please: do not clip my wings. If I am me, you will love me more. Is that enough?'

'More, much more than enough, my love. You will make me the man I always wanted to be. Everything I have, and everything I am, is yours. Truly. Honestly. Irrevocably.'

'What is 'irrevocably'?'

'It means that I am yours. And that it cannot change. *'How do I love thee…Let me count the ways…'*

'Is that John Keats, to his lover, Fanny Brawne?' asked Olga, intrigued at the poetic turn of events.

'No, it's Elizabeth Barrett Browning, to *her* lover Robert Browning. Olga, my love, let us count the ways…'

Olga laughed delightedly. 'You English Romantics. Full of bullshit…'

OLGA SMILES AGAIN

Olga Peters – neè Pereshkova – dared not recall a time when she was not happy. She was blissfully happy with husband Mike, who adored her. She was happy in her detached, modern home in Perton, Wolverhampton. And she was happy in an England which, for all its faults – scruffy, quixotic, and backward-looking – was – certainly compared to her Russian homeland – surprisingly safe, and remarkably *free*.

In the six years or so since she and Mike had first met, Olga had not rested on her laurels – whatever *that* meant, she reflected. She had perfected her English – though retaining a delightful Russian accent – and had learned to drive. She enjoyed shopping – particularly for antiques, in those charming Cotswold villages – dashing to and fro in her Golf gti. And she had entered local 'society' – making friends, and learning to dance. Olga's Argentine tango – in tandem with her dance partner, Dmitri (a Ukrainian) – was the subject of local legend. Poor Mike had two left feet, and watched admiringly – and not without a pang of envy – from the side-lines.

Money did not seem to be a problem, and the couple lived handsomely; but Olga did not want to be a kept woman. She craved freedom, and independence; and she wanted to make herself useful – not just a decorative ornament, to be shown off at parties to Mike's friends and golf cronies. She fancied

– not becoming a model – a *proper* model – but of starting a classy model agency. This was a line of business that she felt she instinctively, profoundly, understood. But Mike quietly dissuaded and discouraged her at every turn, protesting his need for her, day and night. They had plenty of money, he said. Why waste time and energy on unnecessary stuff, that would distract her, even exhaust her? And take her away from him? So Olga sighed, and side-lined her eager ambitions, hopes and dreams.

As for Mike, he lived in and for the moment. A gas fitter by trade, he applied himself less and less to fitting boilers, and more and more to enjoying quality time with Olga. Roaming the Staffordshire, Shropshire and Worcestershire countryside with his beautiful young wife, and introducing her to secret, scenic spots; jetting off to exotic destinations: the Cote d'Azur, Ibiza, Marbella; and showing her off at the best restaurants the Region had to offer. Then there were theatres – amongst them the Royal Shakespeare Theatre, since Olga loved Shakespeare – and even the Russian ballet. All in all theirs was an enviable life, and a thoroughly enjoyable lifestyle, though it left Olga, deep down, feeling vaguely unfinished; incomplete. Yes – *unfulfilled.*

The couple had recently celebrated their fifth wedding anniversary when, one sultry August night, Olga's world fell apart. They had retired to bed and, unusually, Mike had complained of feeling weary. That day, they had browsed and hunted for antiques – a writing slope, and a couple of landscapes – in Broadway, Burford, and Chipping Campden – and had completed their mission; returning home for an Olga special – sirloin steak and fries, with sauce béarnaise – at around 7.00pm. A degree of fatigue after such an active day was to be expected and Mike was, by now, 53 years of age. Unusually, too, Mike was too exhausted to contemplate sex with his divinely beautiful wife. 'Just wait 'til morning, my delicious Olga…' Those were Mike's last words. Olga awoke around 6.00am, and touched her husband's cold body; she recoiled in shock, before trying desperately to revive him. Her frantic efforts – and those of a paramedic team, 20 minutes later – were in vain. Mike was pronounced dead at the scene.

Olga, in a state of disbelief, was plunged at once into grief and despair. But, in a country that still, for her, retained a slightly alien otherness, she had – and quickly – to marshal reserves of resilience and spirit, and assert her practical, no-nonsense nature. She, alone, was now in control; and needed to assert that control. Everything she did, she did for Mike. Olga registered the death, with the Registrar; she notified Mike's friends of his passing (his parents were both dead, and he was an only child); she gave instructions to a local funeral director; she arranged for a burial plot to be available; and she made an appointment to see Mike's solicitor, regarding the Estate, and Probate. Olga was the very model of focused, disciplined efficiency.

*

The young widow breezed into her interview with Mike's solicitor – 'Gold & Grey, Family Solicitors' – in a business-like and confident manner that bordered on *insouciance*. Surely, this was a – mere – formality, if a necessary formality? Though Olga had very little money that was genuinely her own – it was now nearly six years since she had last 'worked' – she knew that Mike had left everything to her in his Will. Mr Grey the solicitor – Grey by name, and grey by nature – was dry, factual, and straightforward; but nevertheless empathetic and as helpful as he could be – in the circumstances. For he had a bombshell to drop on his black-suited client.

'Mrs Peters,' he began. 'I'm so sorry for your sad loss. Mike was a very good and kind man. He was far too young...' Olga smiled her practiced, young widow smile. 'I loved my husband very much, Mr Grey. I hope that I will do him due honour in his funeral arrangements, and in my future life and conduct. It would be most helpful if you could explain my financial position, so that I can start planning for that future.'

Mr Grey rubbed his hands. 'Mrs Peters, I can confirm that you are the sole beneficiary of your husband's Will. There are no secret children or hidden mistresses' – he laughed at his own joke, but cut short when he looked up at his client's deadpan expression. Grey continued: 'however, your husband's circumstances were unusual, and you may not be fully aware of the nature of these?'

'Please go on,' Olga pressed, with a sudden anxiety in her voice.

'While there was no mortgage on your husband's property – the inheritance he received from his parents paid off the mortgage – a year or so before your marriage, Mr Peters decided to go down the route of Equity Release...'

'Equity Release? Excuse me, I don't understand...Please explain.'

'I see. Let me do exactly that. Equity Release is an arrangement whereby, in exchange for a lump sum from a financial institution – such as a bank, in this case Croyds – an individual signs up to giving that institution rights over their property, upon their death. In the meantime, they can live in that property – rent free – until their demise. In your husband's case, he received a lump sum of £200,000, in the expectation that – with no dependants, and many years of life ahead – he could enjoy life to the full for decades to come.

Unfortunately, two highly significant events occurred following this arrangement coming into force.' Mr Grey forced himself into a smile. 'First a certain Olga Pereshkova came along. And, sadly, Mr Peters, most unexpectedly, died. Regrettably, that means – because of the roll-up of interest – that there is little equity left to his beneficiary. That is, your good self.'

Olga swallowed hard. 'About how much?' she enquired. 'Assuming that the property sells at around its valuation, £450,000, there'll be about £60,000 left to you,' replied Mr Grey, gently. 'I'll ask the bank in question for their final account. 'Yes, around 60 grand will be available to you, after Probate. I'll try to hurry it through, but you should expect to wait around three months.'

'Three months!' bemoaned Olga, to herself. How on earth was she supposed to manage in the meantime? And what would 60 grand buy? A suburban garage?

Olga suddenly brightened. 'What about the 200 grand?'

Mr Grey sighed. 'I'm afraid there's very little of that left.' He lowered his eyes. 'It seems that someone's been having a high old time...'

Olga felt a shock of realisation that looming money worries might have contributed to her husband's death. Why hadn't Mike told her? Could he not face reality? Or did he think that *she* could not face reality?

Mr Grey seemed to read her unease. 'I'm sure that we can advance a loan, if you wish...Although there would be conditions...'

Olga recognised the glint in Mr Grey's eye. 'Oh, no, not another old fucker!' she sighed. 'Thank you, but I'll manage... But what about the contents of the house?' Olga recalled. 'Are they mine?'

'Why, yes, Mrs Peters, yours to dispose of as you wish. Since there's no Inheritance Tax to pay..'

'Glorious young woman,' pondered Grey, as his client swept from the office. 'Bet Mike died happy,' he mused. 'Pity about *Mrs Grey*' he added, before dismissing the suggestion with a wave of self-contempt. Silly old buggar!

Olga arrived back at 'her' house to find that a 'For Sale' board had already been erected. It read: 'For Sale: G&T and Partners.' These guys didn't let the grass grow under their feet! What on earth was she supposed to do? How earn a living? How carve out a future? Return to Russia? She'd rather die. Return to escort work? She'd rather starve. There was a half-way house – maybe soothe old guys' egos in a so-called 'Gentleman's Club'. No; she'd progressed beyond all that; put it behind her. She had become a respectable member of British society. Olga laughed at her own pomposity. Had she, indeed? Then the dream re-surfaced in her mind: the modelling agency. Of course! Sixty grand should be enough to fund the start-up costs – the web-site, the auditions, the photo-shoots, the marketing…Then we would see!

For now, Olga needed to focus on the funeral arrangements, to give her husband the best possible 'send off'. The service was held on the 3 September, in a cavernous Victorian church that seemed to belittle the eighteen or so mourners. The service was simple; dignified and fitting. Olga herself gave the Tribute, from the pulpit. A glorious, late-summer sun streamed through the stained glass, that fractured light into streams of red, gold, and violet, and highlighted Olga, in her black hat, coat and skirt, in an ethereal glow.

Mike was a lovely man, she said; gentle; generous; loving. Everything a man should be. He had been taken before his time. He had loved the finer things in life – beautiful things; poetry; music; art. And, yes, (she laughed) women. And he had lived – really *lived* – a full life. We were all God's children: in the end, God's will must be respected. Olga ended her 'eulogy' with some lines from Shakespeare that she knew were among Mike's favourites:

> *Fear no more the heat o' the sun,*
> *Nor the furious winter's rages:*
> *Thou thy worldly task hast done;*
> *Home art gone, and ta'en thy wages.*
> *Golden lads and girls all must,*
> *As chimney sweepers, come to dust…*

The catch in her voice at 'chimney sweepers', heard by the collected multitude as a sob, was Olga's cheekily replacing the words with 'boiler fitters' in her mind. Yet Olga spoke calmly, and with deep feeling. And, as she spoke, she became aware of a startlingly beautiful young woman in the congregation. Instinctively, she guessed the relationship to Mike. Could this be an omen?

At the 'Wake' – held in one of those local hostelries that specialise in catering for the signal ceremonies on life's journey – christenings, weddings and funerals – Olga introduced herself to the young woman. My God, she was fantastic! It was as though Olga and Rhondda had known each other for ever: though Rhondda was English, and a couple of years younger than Olga, the women were like two peas in a pod. Each perfect, in their own style. The women reminisced fondly about Mike: there's no need to be embarrassed, soothed Olga. I know how needy Mike was; and you were there before me! And then she told Rhondda about her model agency plans: would she like to be involved? Would she!! 'Can you come to my place tomorrow?' Olga urged. 'Yes. Of course!' Olga kissed Rhondda quickly on the lips, and hugged her. She must cast off her widow's weeds. There was no time to lose.

*

Rhondda rang the bell at 10.30am promptly the following morning. Olga welcomed her warmly, and made Rhondda a coffee, bidding her make herself comfortable. Then Olga explained her own background, and how her relationship with Mike began. How many times had Rhondda met Mike? 'Three times,' replied Rhondda, looking Olga directly in the eyes. 'He was very sweet. Very caring.' She giggled: 'And very generous!' Olga nodded and smiled, appreciatively.

'What did Mike die of?' enquired Rhondda, gently, tears starting in her eyes.

'I think we wore the fucker out!' responded Olga. The women laughed. And laughed; with tears of joy and relief.

Then Olga explained her plans. A new modelling agency – an enterprise that would be different; bold; special. With a truly unique selling point. Quite simply: the most beautiful girls in the world. From every region in the world. It would be called : '10'. Code named: OPPRA: Olga's Perfect Pearls R Art. Perfect girls provided for premieres, fashion magazines, high-profile events, photo-shoots: any legitimate, legal purpose.

'It's a risk,' added Olga. 'I'll pay you what I can, but we're starting from scratch. It will be exciting, but demanding work. The faster we grow, the more you will be able to earn. Maybe we need *you* to model, but mainly we need you to help drive, help develop the business. What skills do you have?'

'IT. Marketing. Selling – before I became a model.'

'Excellent! Just one more thing...' Olga began to shed her clothes. Within seconds, she stood before Rhondda, naked. She smiled, and turned slowly. Rhondda stared – silently, admiringly; speechless.

'Your turn!' smiled Olga. Rhondda obliged. As expected, Rhondda was perfect; faultless.

'Rhondda, my love, you are simply fabulous!' exclaimed Olga, in genuine amazement.

'Yes, but what about the sex?' enquired Rhondda, in curious disbelief. 'There's always a downside. That is, men. Photographers. Agents. Movie moguls. Fat business oiks...'

'Strictly, there'll be none of that. Olga's Perfect Pearls will be untouchable. Exclusive. And chaperoned. I want to change the world! I want to change women's lives!' Olga laughed. 'And I want us to be rich!' she exclaimed. 'Men will be on merit, not on their money!' Olga kissed Rhondda, tenderly. 'Besides, any sex will be strictly between *us*...'

Rhondda left, with a heart brimming for Olga, and a head brimming with instructions: website, research, competitors, market-place, fee-structures, 'feelers'. This was a crowded market; '10' needed to be unique, providing access to the *crème de la crème*; and to 'hit the ground running'.

Since, inevitably, there would be starting costs – and bearing in mind that Olga would shortly be homeless – she began to mobilize some ready cash. The house was rammed with – quality – antiques: clocks, furniture, porcelain, pictures. Olga contacted the plethora of Cotswold galleries, and advertised on specialist sites. And she was a tough, as well as persuasive, negotiator. Though it galled her to let go some prized possessions, this was *necessaire*. Items that had cost – retail – around twelve grand, two, three, four years ago, she now re-sold for eight. It was, after all, a fire sale. Money was needed to generate money; and she might be homeless within weeks.

Olga threw herself into her new life with intense focus, and a kind of natural frenzied fury that, maybe, had been submerged for too long. The next move – every move – was planned with friend Rhondda, whose skills and talents perfectly complemented her own. Olga was 'front of house'; the public face; the influencer; Rhondda, the organiser, the backroom 'doer'. The women registered the company, with the name '10'. Olga was obliged to invest a few grand to secure the worldwide rights to '*10 – the most beautiful girls in the world.*' Rhondda created their website, and created Facebook and Instagram pages. And they secretly planned a global recruitment campaign, through a world-wide Competition: to find '*the 100 most beautiful girls in the world.*' The soundtrack to the website could not have been more apposite: Frank Sinatra's exuberant, snappy take on Rodgers' & Hart's classic '*The Most Beautiful Girl in the World*' – an Olga favourite.

The Competition would be launched on 1 January, closing for entries on 31 January; it was open to all young women between the ages of 18 and 25. Entry was by way of a standard form, authenticated photographs (all images *sans* make-up) and a two-minute video. The prize? An award confirming 'most beautiful girl' status, and an initial 12 months exclusive contract, that guaranteed minimum levels of work, and a fixed percentage of the fees earned: 75% to the model; 25% to the company.

*

The launch of the Competition generated world-wide interest, and Olga and Rhondda were in hot demand across global media sites. Olga quickly secured a slot on a regional TV programme, covering the West Midlands. This was rapidly followed by an appearance on prime time TV. Despite a generally favourable – indeed smooth, unctuous interview – towards the final segment Olga was bowled an attempted 'yorker'.

She had been expecting exactly that…

'Mrs Peters, some people might say, doesn't this Competition merely *commoditise* women?' asked the smiling interviewer. Despite herself, Olga bristled. She knew all about being treated as a commodity.

'No. It's about empowering women. So that they can be the best version of themselves that they *can* be. Optimise their potential, and their God-given talents; realise their ambition – their personal mojo. And it's voluntary; a question of choice. But I recognise it's not for everybody. *Obviously*. If some young women prefer to perfect the piano, or concentrate on rally driving, or rock climbing, or cordon bleu cookery, then good for them!' She gave the interviewer a 'stop this nonsense' smile.

'But…'

'I should emphasise,' Olga interjected, with another winning smile, 'that this venture is also about truly *honouring* beauty. Since the dawn of history, humanity has celebrated beauty. But, as the Bard would say, 'sometimes more in the breach than in the observance.' It's about bringing a little joy to this troubled world, and to allow women from varied backgrounds to have hope, and a fulfilling, stimulating, life.'

The interviewer, the elaborately-coiffed David Darcy, couldn't resist a last-ditch googly at Olga's aspirations: 'Surely, Mrs Peters, trying to identify the world's most beautiful women, from many millions of possible candidates, is a mad-cap venture? A quite impossible task. How can it possibly succeed? While some people I've spoken to regard the whole project as a publicity stunt...'

'Really? I can assure you, Mr Darcy, that we are in deadly earnest; and entirely serious. This is not a stunt of any kind; though your help in raising public awareness is of course most welcome. We have planned for a professional Competition. Of course it will be a challenge; such an ambitious project has never been attempted before. But what in life *is* worth attempting, if it's not challenging? This might well be an impossible enterprise – if it was being directed by *men*. But a team of experienced women are managing this ground-breaking venture.' Olga added, drily: 'And – I wonder, Mr Darcy – would you be putting these questions to me if I was a man?'

Darcy shifted uncomfortably in his seat. 'Thank you so much for your candour, Olga. Er, Mrs Peters.' Darcy's Steinway grin widened, on reaching the interview's *denouement*. 'Well, it's been a great pleasure meeting you, Mrs Peters, and exploring your exciting plans. We wish you every success, and the very best of luck!'

Thank *you* for *your* interest, Mr Darcy. And your time. But I intend to make my own luck!'

In the (hospitality) 'Green Room', prior to the interview, Darcy had singled out and smooth-talked Olga, with his (he thought) most winning manner: 'Hi there! Mrs Peters? Do you know who *I* am? Darcy; David Darcy. *Very* pleased to make your acquaintance!' 'Yes' replied Olga brightly – 'Peters; Olga Peters. So very excited to meet the famous Mr David Darcy!' 'Anyway,' Darcy continued – delighted by Olga's obvious infatuation – 'what a fascinating idea! You know, it really might take off! And what a *fascinating* lady! So what's your background, my dear Olga? Where did all this come from?' Olga's attempt to respond was quickly interrupted by an invitation to dinner at an exclusive restaurant. Olga had laughed it off. 'But Mr Darcy – David – I understand that you're a married man…Oh, you're *separated*? I'm so sorry, but I'm sure you'll understand that I'm dreadfully busy at the moment…preparing for the Launch. Perhaps some other time…' She had brushed his cheek with the suggestion of a kiss; Darcy had slyly slipped her his business card; a silent marker of intent.

Earlier that afternoon, beside the water-cooler, Darcy had asked an Assistant: 'Milly, what do we know about this Olga Peters – I mean, apart from this model competition malarkey?'

'Only,' shrugged Milly, 'that she's 27, and originally from Russia. And an absolute stunner, apparently…Oh, and she married some old guy; but recently became a widow.'

'Why am I fucking not surprised?' muttered Darcy, sipping his water. 'Mil, you do know you're the only girl for *this* old guy?'

Milly rolled her eyes.

*

Despite or because of Darcy's prime-time Show, suddenly, Olga was hot property. That unique blend of stunning looks, style, charm, intelligence, vision – and that exotic Russian mystique – were intoxicating to the media. Perhaps the hint of controversy added to the mix. The story took off – such a simple, such an exciting – concept, that the public could readily grasp, enthuse about, and get behind. So, too, the media – TV, radio, the press, Internet channels – all beat a path to Olga's door.

Investors, too – rich dudes who scented loads of money – offered their services in surprising numbers. Mostly, of course, men. But Olga found herself to be an astute businesswoman. She negotiated an unsecured, interest-free loan of £500,000 against the future income of the business, but that did not give up an iota of the business itself: *that* was owned 50:50 by herself and Rhondda. The 'business angel' in question – Debbie Franklin – injected not just finance, but support and expertise: Debbie brought with her a plethora of contacts in the worlds of fashion, hospitality, and entertainment. In truth, Debbie, 48, had been overwhelmed by her meetings with Olga. Such an impressive young woman! Debbie was buying into the Olga brand. Let's see where it led. It was sure to be an exciting ride! With Debbie's capital in place, Olga purchased their 'office' – her Wolverhampton home – from the bank, Croyds. For Olga, this was a most satisfactory outcome, and concrete testimony of her vision and early success.

The foundations, as it were, laid, and her base secured, Olga, and Rhondda – who had moved in to the 'office' – could focus fully on the Competition Launch.

1 January arrived. At mere seconds past midnight – of course, time zones differ, depending on whether one lives in the US, Brazil, India, Malaysia or Australia – the applications came flooding in. First, from Australia and New Zealand. And the South Pacific Islands. Then from the Far East. Then, from around Europe. From across the breadth and depth of Africa. And, finally, from across the Americas – North and South: the US, Canada; Brazil, Argentina, Colombia. Hundreds of applications. Then thousands. Then tens of thousands. From every Continent – save Antarctica. And from more than a hundred countries. There were the usual suspects – many thousands apiece from the USA, UK, Germany, Switzerland, Sweden, Italy, Spain

and France (whose current Miss France was amongst the first applicants). But also from Olga's Russia. Also, as expected, the usual failures to engage: Afghanistan, Iran, Saudi Arabia, Syria, Somalia; North Korea. Old guys rule; OK?

Since this was an unprecedented venture, Olga could not know in advance what the response might be. Even so, early world-wide interest in the Competition had convinced her that the response *might* be phenomenal. In anticipation, Olga and Rhondda had assembled multiple teams of women – artists, photographers, beauticians – of all ethnicities – to sift through the applications. By the end of January, a total of 136,725 applications had been received. There were relatively few time-wasters. A smidgen of spoilers. A small injection of transgender activists. A scattering of Drag Queens. And a sprinkling of women whose 'body art' obscured their body's true art. For the vast majority of applicants, every face, every feature, every figure, was special, unique; and discriminating between them no doubt highly subjective, and fraught with difficulty. But, surprisingly, the 'judging' process was as smooth as it was fascinating – and remarkably straightforward.

By the end of February, a short-short list of 1,000 finalists were passed to Olga and Rhondda – and their 'angel', Debbie. Only now did the process become challenging, and the judges become aware of the weight of responsibility and expectation upon their shoulders; but also, so terrifically stimulating. The three judges felt confident that they were almost uniquely qualified to make these final, potentially life-changing, decisions.

Olga and Rhondda were sifting excitedly through these final 1,000 candidates one day when Olga suddenly exclaimed: 'Rhondda, you're not here! Why ever not? You would have been a contender!'

Rhondda threw her friend a defiant look. 'I *knew* that the standard would be incredibly high. And it is! And I didn't want any conflict of interest. And this is just *so* exciting! I mean, it's like opening an old shoe box and finding it crammed with diamonds, rubies, sapphires!'

'And perfect pearls!' smiled Olga.

'Yes, perfect pearls indeed. But, ultimately, I thought that my time would be better spent, here with you, running the business. We're going to be extremely busy – like, 24/7. Plus, we have complementary skills, and I think mine will be crucial to our success. Olga, what a *team* we make!' Olga was about to reply, 'Rhondda, darling, you're quite right!' when her words were smothered with a kiss.

For Olga, the personality of each candidate was genuinely important: *personality* complemented and enriched an individual's physical and moral being. Olga was looking for confidence, and independence of mind. And, as well as genuine physical beauty, character, charisma, and *attitude* – since these girls would be starting a new life – in the public spotlight; travelling; away from home; outside their usual comfort zones. Was each candidate happy to be nominated? Why did they put themselves forward? What were their goals in life? What were their expectations, and their anxieties? Were their family and friends supportive? And what language skills did they possess – since, inevitably, most of the 'work' would be based in Europe and the US. Following several weeks poring over photographs, and two-minute videos, and intensive Zoom interviews with each of the short-listed candidates – assisted by language-translation technology – the white smoke finally emerged from the Perton chimney.

Olga envisaged a global empire – made possible by slick organisation, smart marketing, and a powerful brand. And the personal touch – constant personal contact with 'her' girls. All underpinned by an integrated, secure, software network – directed from an office in Wolverhampton. During March, the successful candidates were each congratulated by e-mail, and embossed Certificates sent by registered post. And, of course, 900 short-listed candidates notified of *their* success – and placed on a list of finalists. The authorities in each 'successful' country – which included Russia, the US, Brazil, India, Sri Lanka, Indonesia, and Senegal, as well as the UK, Germany, Italy and France (Miss France – a hairdresser) – were notified, and invited to give their winning applicant a highly-promoted public acknowledgement and official Reception. Basking in the reflected glory, most countries were delighted to oblige. But the working heart of the operation would be Europe, and the US: where safety and security could be managed, and monitored. While some of the most beautiful young women might be drawn from Russia, or Venezuela, or Nigeria, business would not be conducted in mobster states, where the gang, the gun and the gulag dominated national life.

*

As a prelude to opening for business, all 100 young women recruited by '10' were invited to a three-day Launch and team-building Conference in the heart of Paris. Olga did not know Paris – though, in times to come, she would enjoy regular trips to the *Louvre, Museè d'Orsay* and *Museè Rodin.*

Thankfully, Debbie Franklin already knew the City well, and was familiar with a wealth of business contacts; Debbie helped secure a charming, fashionable, 18th century establishment in central Paris – on the *Rue de Rivoli* – that was happy to indulge in lappings of free international publicity. Meanwhile, Debbie's remaining 50 grand covered the travel costs of the successful contestants.

Only six months before, in front of a pulpit, and bathed in a celestial light, Olga had made her heart-felt tribute to Mike;

but had felt only unutterable despair. Now, stood in front of a lectern in the hotel's *Grand Salon,* and bathed in the purity of a Parisian spring morning, Olga's opening address exuded hope and optimism, as she looked out upon a sea of sensational faces. Olga's carefully chosen words were inclusive, inspirational, and spoke of momentous times to come: 'Welcome, one and all! You amazing young women – from across the breadth of our planet – are the faces of '10'. You are all, already, winners, and you can look forward to a really life-changing journey ahead! I – we – are with you on that journey, and will guide and support you all the way. Whatever your background, whatever your experience of life to date, you can look forward to the future with confidence. We are family – in the words of Alexandre Dumas, we are 'all for one, and one for all!' Over the next three days we will be briefing you all, individually and collectively, and embedding our vision. We look forward to getting to know you all, personally, and to a transformative, wonderful future for every one of you!'

The Conference in itself generated global publicity. Paparazzi – who hardly needed encouraging – were permitted to attend the Conference at set times, to photograph '10's' most precious assets – it's 100 astonishing women. Oh, the oxygen of free publicity! Was such a 'collection' of beautiful women ever before assembled together, in a single place? Olga thought not: the spectacle was awesome; the luminosity, breath-taking. These girls had been waitresses, shop assistants, beauticians, bank clerks. Now they would start new lives – exciting lives, where the sky was the limit – as the honoured guests of respected professional clients.

Olga made it her priority to meet, and get to *know,* every one of her 'Perfect Pearls'. It was an unforgettable gathering of the '10' sisterhood, conducted in a febrile atmosphere. Olga, and the young women, forged a strong bond, based on personal charisma and a commonality of interest. For perhaps the first time in her life – possibly excepting her relationship with Mike – Olga was respected, was admired, for *who* she was, rather than for *what* she was. Olga and her girls would quickly become a band of sisters, and their strong personal relationships – and mutual respect – would underpin the efficacy of the '10' brand. If there was a problem – and given the strong ethos of the brand, there were remarkably few – Olga would be on hand, day or night; this was *her* vision, and it would not be compromised by anyone's – man's or woman's – off-message behaviour.

Olga's venture, '10', was an extraordinary success, from the outset. The requests for services, and the offers, snowballed and, once or twice in those early days, the '10' website itself was overwhelmed. But planning, preparation, a strong global brand, the energy and enthusiasm of the founders – and Olga's singular vision – were to prove critical to the business's long-term success.

Major players – fashion houses, *couturiers*, cosmetics companies, luxury lingerie makers – all hammered on the – open – door of '10'. And luxury jewellery, perfume, wrist-watch, 'accessory' (handbags and scarves) and beach-wear brands were soon advertising their wares on the '10' website – their opulent, lusted-after products enhanced – and rendered super-exclusive – by featuring on the perfect features of '10's' exclusive Pearls. Within months, a number of the 'Perfect Pearls' were amongst the world's most famous and familiar faces.

Of course, there were endless practicalities. Passports; visas; contracts; travel arrangements to engagements; accommodation; safety and security. But a focus on well-established corporate clients, and a system whereby '10' handled contracts, travel arrangements and all financial incomings and out-goings, served to drive business efficiency – and profitability. Within two years, Debbie Franklin's initial loan had been gratefully repaid; although Debbie remained on the company's Board, as a trusted adviser.

Shortly after this step change in growth and profitability, the company received a multi-million dollar takeover offer. Olga and

Rhondda – as the owners – conferred; and involved Debbie in the decision making process. But this venture was, if nothing else, about Olga realising her dream; and Rhondda, and Debbie, had bought into that dream. Why jettison it now, just as the dream became self-fulfilling? Why ditch the fun, the excitement, the fulfilment, just for a shed load of cash? At the same time, Olga and Rhondda were supporting a hundred young women, from every region of the world, who were enjoying an exciting – and stimulating, enriching – lifestyle. The takeover offer – and others yet to come – were respectfully rejected. This was not about price; about quantity. Rather, Olga's venture was about *quality:* about creating a hugely fulfilling, daily-enriching lifestyle – where every day was demanding, but every day a joyous exposition of life.

And there was a further development: as it became increasingly apparent that success bred success, and the business model proved strong and not easily replicable, '10' launched a charitable foundation – dedicating 10% of its profits to tackling female poverty, and enabling business creation, in developing and 'emerging' countries. Olga and Rhondda – enthusiastically supported by Debbie – were determined that 'The 10 Foundation' should and could help thousands of women world-wide to escape grinding poverty, with the promise of independence, and a dignified future life.

But we race ahead. Olga and Rhondda flew back to Wolverhampton, from glamorous Paris, via Birmingham Airport; arriving at Perton in Olga's Golf gti around 5.00 in the afternoon. The women were exhausted, but exhilarated, intoxicated, with the crystallising of the original vision into almost surreal reality. Olga and Rhondda had each shared Mike's bed, in the past. Now they shared it again, together. Blissfully happy. A little later, Olga remembered her personal mobile; (her '10' phone was a 24/7 operation). There were three – increasingly desperate –

messages from David Darcy. Olga giggled in bed, and caressed the recumbent softness of Rhondda, while assuming her best Sinatra baritone: *'the most beautiful girl in the world...'* Who said one couldn't have it all...?

She would deal with David; all in good time. Olga knew, from bitter personal experience, that life could lurch unexpectedly towards a terrifying abyss; become suddenly frightening; gut-wrenchingly uncertain. But when life was good, it could be very, very good. And this was *her* time. Olga and Rhondda looked to the future with excitement and optimism. '10' would transform many women's lives. Including their own. And all for the better.

THE DEAL

John Sands had been a lucky man. John enjoyed a comfortable home and lifestyle, was enveloped by tasteful artefacts and luxuries, and was married to Sue – a delightful, dedicated, and, it must be said, devoted woman.

Having surfed, indeed even rode, his luck over an enriched lifetime, John was now seventy years of age. And that was the problem. It was not that he hated being seventy – though he did. It was that the life – the descent – would not stop there, but continue to eighty, even to ninety. And decrepitude: physical and mental decrepitude, illness, dementia and decay. And then eternal oblivion. And *that* fate, he thought to himself bitterly, awaited him if he was *lucky*. If he was unlucky, oblivion might await him, might ambush him, at any time: tomorrow, next week, next month, next year.

John brooded on these thoughts so that, despite his twice-weekly visits to his golf club, his bi-annual cruises, and his beloved Netflix subscription, John became morose. Wife Sue noticed the change in his mood, and did her best to keep him content, if not cheerful; did everything she knew to take John 'out of himself'. But all was in vain. For at bottom John was a changed man. All that effort! All that work! All that striving! And for what? For *nothing?* John visited his GP, who prescribed anti-depressants, but these could not provide an antidote to John's morbid fear of the ageing process. He loved life too much to lose it but, ironically, the shadow – the *knowledge* – of morbidity blasted the very life that John was trying to nurture and protect. Even on a cloudless, brilliant day in June, John saw only the wisp of dark cloud lurking on the horizon.

Sleep became fragmented and intermittent. John's sex drive withered on the vine: the couple's private 'pleasure palace' crumbled to dust. John began to lose weight, and stopped enjoying the hearty meals lovingly prepared by Sue. A Caribbean cruise was scheduled for September, a mere six weeks away. But why bother? It was all fuss, stress and inconvenience. Every task – every possible pleasure – became a *further* inconvenience. Cutting the lawn – again. Painting the kitchen. Watching another drama, uncannily like the last. Really, what *was* the point?

Then, one sleep-interrupted night, John had a dream. It was an intensely-vivid dream, and seemed to last for *ages*. John had never had a dream like this, and never would again. Indeed, it changed John's life. For, in his dream, John spoke with God.

'Explain your problem' said the voice. John saw the figure before him. And knew he was being addressed by God. But he was unafraid. Dutifully, he explained the root cause of his troubles.

And God replied: 'All men are mortal. They cannot live forever. Tell me, what is it that you crave?'

John spoke of his unhappiness. Ahead, he saw only decay and dissolution, illness and disease. Invisibility, followed by death.

God answered with a radiance that cannot be replicated with words alone. He spoke in different dimensions, in multi-colours, in harmonies, in an indescribable warmth and richness of meaning. He spoke of the wonders of Nature, of the joys and fruits of the Earth, of friendship and love, of the sweet, subtle pleasures of life – pleasures heightened by awareness of their fleetingness, their transience…

But then God said: 'How long would you wish to live, John?'

And John said: 'One hundred years. In decent health...'

God laughed. A big, booming laugh. Even in his dream, John thought: 'how very like Brian Blessed!'

'John Sands, you will be aware that the average longevity for men in the United Kingdom is 82 years of age. Some men live longer; others not so long. And very few people enjoy robust health until their dying day. So why should John Sands' destiny be different? Or, put another way, why do you deserve a different – maybe a superior – fate?'

John's rather garbled, and quite desperate, response was child-like in its simplicity. He would 'do good'. He would help his fellow man. He would be kind and generous. He would help to protect the environment.

God listened, then said: 'In other words, you would do what you should be doing already? What every half-decent member of humanity *should* be doing. As we speak, there are many people *doing* good; and many people who *are* good. But very few live the extraordinarily long lives that their extraordinary goodness deserves!' Even in his glorious, radiant voice and awesome presence, God sounded a touch exasperated.

Then God spoke, and gave his judgement: 'Very well, John. You will live to be one hundred years – maybe a little longer. And in good health. But there are conditions...'

'Anything!' exclaimed the excited John Sands, in a state of almost ecstasy.

'My demands may surprise you. But, although you humans call me God, I have little influence in Earthly matters. It is a matter of no little regret to me... But enough of me. First of all, you must carry out two days voluntary work each week – helping others in your community, or helping to improve the environment. The exact nature of the activity will remain your choice.'

'Great!' said John. 'I accept with alacrity. Anything else?'

'Oh, yes!' replied God, with a smile. 'Second, you must give £10,000 each year to a charity, or charities, of your choice. There will still be plenty left, to be determined by your Will.'

'I look forward to donating!' responded John.

'Third, you must make peace with your daughter, Sally, and your son, Simon.'

John's face dropped, and his mouth fell open. 'But how? We've hardly spoken for years, now…'

'Exactly. Be creative. Use your diplomatic skills. Leave no stone unturned. Just do it! Maybe invite your family on your cruises, or share your future plans with them. No more bitterness and puerile, festering feuding. You must create lovely, unforgettable memories, with your children – and their children, Alice, Tom and Zandra – that will cascade down the generations.'

'Of course' replied John, deferentially. 'God knows – pardon me – it won't be easy, but I'll give it my best shot,' said John, with emphasis.

'Yes, you will!' God replied, a hint of sternness in his demeanour. 'Fourth, you must learn a new skill. Maybe learn to play a musical instrument.' He smiled. 'A harp might come in handy. Or violin, or piano. Or perhaps take up painting, or bread making, or embroidery. Anything, really, that will, to use the jargon, take you out of yourself. Take you *beyond* yourself.'

'That's great!' enthused John. 'I've always fancied learning the piano. And Sue might appreciate me baking fresh bread…'

'Yes, it does make sense, doesn't it? Fifth, on at least two days each week, you must cook the evening meal, and serve it to your wife, Sue. Of course, you will need to practice…'

'Er, that will be fine,' said John, a touch hesitantly.

'A problem?' asked God.

'No, not at all,' replied John, hastily. 'But, as you know, cooking's always been Sue's sphere. I'll need to leave my comfort zone.'

'That's the whole point. Push the envelope. Smash the comfort zone. Surprise people. Make a real difference to your – and other people's – lives!'

'Sixth, practice humility. Every person – every human being – can make a huge difference to society but, sadly, individuals too often see themselves as the centre of everything, and want society to serve *them*; to revolve around *their* interests. Listen to Mozart and Beethoven. Read Shakespeare and Austen. Understand true greatness – and appreciate how it differs from ego, arrogance and vanity. As you become a more *humane* human being, your capacity for helping others, for changing things for the better, will only increase.'

'Thank you so much!' replied John. 'It will be an honour and privilege to undertake such a mission!'

'Use your time wisely and well, John Sands. It will pass sooner than you think. And be prepared: as your journey is long, you may face grief, loss, and sadness along the way. You may not always enjoy the presence of a loving family, as you do now. Happiness may prove elusive. The time may even come when you curse me for my beneficence. But I have broad shoulders...'

'Finally, do not come to me again, in supplication, when you are ninety-nine. Be satisfied. Having led a useful and worthwhile life, resign yourself to retiring to this peaceful and perfect place. I look forward to seeing you on completion of your journey on Earth. But I will only see you again if you fulfil your pledges. The experience of Heaven is very different to life on Earth. Every Spirit is content; nay, blissfully so. But the one thing Spirits can't do is *do*. So do it now!'

John was on the point of thanking God profusely when a cloud of mist obscured the radiance...and God was gone. John awoke, and found himself staring at a half-full whisky tumbler, on the bedside table. But he was not fooled. No – what he had just experienced, dream or no, was a revelation. He could not explain it, could not rationalise the vision, and would speak of it to no-one. But from today, life would be very different. Very different indeed. John glanced at his bedside clock. It was 6.30am. Then he looked tenderly at his sleeping wife, and touched her soft arm. John sighed. Whatever *had* he done? Taking care not to wake Sue, John rose. Whatever: God's will must be done. It was time to make a fresh start…

RETIREMENT RANKLES

Malcolm Merryweather and Ken Fisher had been firm friends for nigh on half a century. Malcolm, 69, had now retired from 'active' employment. After leaving school, and a couple of false starts – in a factory, then a warehouse – at the age of 19, Malcolm had landed his plum job – as a gardener, in Stourton Council Parks Department.

Ken had joined the Department as a YTS (Youth Training Scheme) trainee, with the (now) 21 year-old Malcolm as his mentor and chief trainer. Though only five years senior to Ken, that age gap seemed huge, in terms of social and professional experience. Young Ken looked up to his mentor, and was eager to learn. The two young men bonded almost immediately and, when a full-time vacancy appeared, Ken was quickly taken on to the main staff.

For more than 40 years, the two men worked in partnership – cutting lawns, pruning rose-beds and shrubs, cleaning up leaves, and planting flower beds. And they became close friends, and quite inseparable: they were 'best man' at each other's wedding – Malcolm to pretty, petite Clare; and Ken to the ravishing Sarah; and they were, respectively, godparents to Wayne (Malcolm's and Clare's son), and Ken's daughters, Emma and Julie. And they commiserated with each other when, on the eve of his retirement, Malcolm lost both his parents, Ron and Enid, to sudden, terminal conditions.

Some years before, Malcolm had also 'lost' Clare. It had been a long but not very happy marriage. Clare blamed Malcolm's wandering eye – and hands – while Malcolm blamed Clare's love of the cosy domestic life, when he valued excitement and adventure. For her part, Clare thought she was being castigated for creating a warm, rich, loving home. Surely, every marriage, every man, needed that? But Malcolm always agitated for more than 'just' a loving home. The couple rubbed along uneasily until young Wayne conveniently departed to Liverpool Uni, and then separated, by mutual consent. But, if anything, this sad event – if indeed it was sad – only seemed to strengthen Malcolm's and Ken's relationship.

So strong did the friendship appear that a rumour began to spread around the gang that the pair were gay. When, one sultry afternoon, Malcolm over-heard Ben Jones whispering rumours to a colleague in the canteen, he flew at Jones, and grabbed him by the collar: 'If I hear crap like that again, Jones, I'll ram something even worse than a dick up your arse…' Malcolm and Jones were uneasy, suspicious 'partners' from that time forward, and spoke rarely. Malcolm continued to regard Ben Jones as a troublemaker; but, at least, the 'queer' rumours were heard no more.

The friendship was entirely as it seemed – friendship. Malcolm and Keith spent their time together, almost in harness, from early adulthood, through life's trajectory, and then to Malcolm's retirement, at age 65: and their friendship continued into and following that retirement. Ken was saddened by Malcolm's decision to retire; working life would, henceforth, never be quite so enjoyable. But Ken loved his job and, physically, certainly for his age, remained hale and hearty.

Though married to Sarah, and with daughters Emma and Julie both now married – and with children of their own – Ken's gardening role remained central to his sense of well-being; his sense of self. And, in all honesty, in recent years his relationship with Sarah had cooled to the degree of hard frost. Still, Ken reckoned that, with his experience and knowledge of every aspect of the horticultural role, he was pretty well irreplaceable; and indispensable. And that, his domestic life being somewhat less than blissful, he might be rudderless, and all at sea, without the discipline, distraction and structure provided by his green and pleasant working routine.

Despite the absence of Malcolm from the daily round, the friends continued to be intimate, meeting regularly in their favourite pub, *The Red Lion* – and socialising as family units, with Ken's still head-turning wife Sarah – at fun days out, and dinner parties. But the years passed quickly, and, suddenly, 'young Ken', as Malcolm continued to call his friend, was 64 – and a half. In all honesty, Ken was not obliged to retire at age 65. He could continue until ill-health or old age frustrated his ability to carry out his role. Nevertheless, 65 represented a watershed, and an opportunity to retire on beneficial terms – with an impressive five-figure lump-sum, and generous final salary pension.

In the months leading up to his 65th birthday, Ken became increasingly anxious about the looming decision to be made. His employer became insistent that they know his intentions, in order that arrangements be put in place – for Ken's pension, and – if necessary – for his replacement. The totality of the decision – a decision that admitted no compromise, and no time-shift – began to cause Ken unremitting stress; it was continually on his mind, affected his sleep, and weighed on his spirit. What to do? There were such cogent, persuasive arguments on both sides; it was all so finely balanced. Sarah proved diplomatically unhelpful; it was Ken's decision: 'your life; your choice.' So Ken decided to seek advice from a friend who commanded his affection and respect: Malcolm.

The two friends met one evening in June, in the beer garden of

RETIREMENT RANKLES

The Red Lion. Ken looked stressed and drawn; Malcolm, tanned and relaxed. Malcolm knew they were in for a long evening. He caught the eye of his favourite barmaid, Sally. 'When you see an-almost empty glass, love, just bring us another. I won't have time for idling at the bar tonight. And, oh, do treat yourself.' Sally happily complied. 'Right,' thought Malc, 'let's get on with it!' He pitched straight in.

'The problem, old mate, as I see it, is that you're faced with a binary choice: carry on working; or retire. You can't do both, by definition. But, while the choice is binary, the arguments for each choice are finely balanced: they may be 60-40, or even 55:45. And, when you've made the decision, you're stuck with it. It can't be changed. Regrets may happen, but there's no turning back. So, there's benefits to continued working. And benefits to so-called retirement. But you can't have them all. Simple as…'

Ken took a long swig of his beer, but looked glum. 'Mate, is this supposed to make me feel better?'

'Just setting out the key issues. Mate. We have to start at the beginning. And I need to stress that, of course, this has to be *your* decision. If you feel that I've influenced you, and that the decision turns out to be wrong, you'll feel bitter about it.' He laughed. 'More bitter than the beer. So I can only set out the facts, and tell you my own experience. And then it has to be down to you – and Sarah. But, whatever you decide, I'll support you all the way.'

'Thanks,' Ken said, with a rueful smile. 'I appreciate that. So what are the pros and cons? You know how I love my job…But you've experienced both sides of that dreadful dividing line…'

Malcolm looked again at his old friend. Old, indeed. The grey, thinning hair. The red face, with broken veins on the cheeks. The baggy eyes. The fleshy, loose jowls. What had happened to that golden lad of fifty years ago? Exactly: 50 years had taken their heavy toll. Malcolm hoped that, though five years older, he had aged a little more elegantly. In retirement, he had retained a lithe and youthful figure – as well as that twinkle in his eye. But his love of gardening itself had waned; he had cut quite enough grass, thank you. Enough for eternity. There was more to life than digging and hoeing; Malcolm now employed his own gardener.

'Well,' began Malcolm. 'You know, work has a great deal to offer. It provides a sense of purpose. And a keen sense of satisfaction. That rose bush you just planted should – vandals permitting – still be flourishing in forty years time. While you're working, you're also exercising – your body, and even your mind. But the main thing about work is that wonderful sense of well-being that comes from being with a close-knit group of mates – that warm, elating camaraderie that is so hard to replicate. I've been there; seen it, and felt the vibes. Except for that buggar Ben Jones, that is. But still, nothing like it – save for the love of a good woman, I'd say.'

'I think you've sold it to me!' laughed Ken, before finishing his beer. His glass was swiftly replaced by the obliging Sally.

'Just hold on' cautioned Malcolm. 'We've only just begun! There are two sides to every story, and this story is no different!'

'But it sounds as though you've some regrets?' queried Ken. 'The things you mentioned – retirement doesn't offer them?'

'No, it doesn't' agreed Malcolm. 'But that's life. We can't have everything. We can't have two wives, for instance. At least, not at the same time.' Malcolm laughed at his own joke. 'We just have to grab the best wife – I mean deal – that we can. As for regrets, to quote Mr Sinatra, of course I have a few. But then again, too few to mention…'

Malcolm's flow was pleasantly interrupted by a smiling Sally, who leaned pleasingly over their table, with a tray of drinks. Even Ken gave her an admiring glance. 'My God!' thought Malcolm. 'That Jude Jones is a lucky bastard!' Jude was the son of that other 'b', Ben. Malcolm looked longingly at the retreating Sally, and felt a twinge of jealousy. Then shrugged, took a good draught of ale, and smacked his lips.

'Really, Ken, you need to think about doing this job, day in, day out, in all seasons, and in all weathers. How long do you *want* to do it for? And how long can your body *do* it for? Three years? Five years? Before you're ready for the knacker's yard? You already have Type 2 Diabetes. And your hip's giving you jip. They're warning signs, mate. That grass will keep on growing long after we're dead and gone.'

'There's plenty of life in the old dog, yet!' protested Ken. 'So tell me, what are these vaunted benefits of retirement? What can I look forward to, besides boredom? And what on earth do *you* do with all that time?'

Malcolm laughed. In the interval, he luxuriated in a rather private joke. Then he continued: 'Let's stop calling it 'retirement' for a start. Think of it as a new life, a whole new beginning. You've given the best years of your life to Stourton Council. To the community. Now it's your turn to live, to enjoy, while you still have the prospect of health and fitness. *Your* time – to do precisely what you want, while you still can! And time to pamper Sarah...'

Ken pulled a face. 'Not sure about that,' he replied, moodily. 'We haven't really got on for years, now. Just don't seem to see eye to eye any more. Do we really want to spend all that time together? In the house? On a cruise? And as for our sex life, just don't ask...'

Malcolm's eyes widened. Sally re-appeared. 'Any more for any more, guys?' she smiled.

'Sorry, mate, I'm feeling knackered,' apologised Ken. 'Like it or lump it, it's time for home. And maybe bed. But thanks for the advice. I'll think about it some more.'

Malcolm smiled at Sally. 'Thank you, Sal. I'll come and settle up.' Turning to Ken, he stressed: 'Not advice, mate. Just information. Based on personal experience. In the words of Mr Mac, 'I'm lovin' it!'

The two friends gave each other a hug, said their goodbyes, and went their separate ways: Ken's demeanour spoke of his barely abated mental torment, while Malcolm walked home with a spring in his step. He knew that Ken was a contrarian, and would probably make a contrarian decision. Oh, well, he'd done his best. Conscience salved…

*

Malcolm was right. Ken opted to continue working as a gardener. Only twelve months following Ken's fateful decision, he was diagnosed with a rare form of cancer, and died three months later. There was the usual wailing, and wringing of hands.

The band of brothers – fellow gardeners – formed a guard of honour at the entrance to the church, as the funeral cortege arrived. Even Ben Jones had turned up, though he could barely suppress a face-splitting grin. Predictably, 'That's Life' was blaring as the coffin entered the church; 'My Way', as it left.

Sally – who had long since slewn off the suave but salacious Jude Jones – was the star turn, with a heartfelt rendition of 'Amazing Grace'. For his part, Malcolm wrote and read the Tribute – the Eulogy – to his old friend, at the fulsomely attended service. Ken's remarkably well-preserved parents, Bill and Esther, provided a dignified and sober presence.

All the way through his reading, Malcolm gazed intently at the tearful Sarah. The glistening eyes, and the elegant black dress, made Sarah appear vulnerable, and even more desirable. Malcolm looked forward to consoling her, in a way he had already been enjoying for the last five years…

GOD WILLING

'Hello, is that James Drinkwater?'
'Yes, who's calling, please?'
'It's an urgent call. From God. Actually.'
'God? Is this some sort of wind up? If so, get lost. Look, I just don't have the time!'
'That's prescient. Best not to beat about the bush: the fact is that you have exactly 14 minutes and 30 seconds to live.'
'Are you for real? How can I believe you? What's supposed to happen?'
'To answer your questions in order: Yes. You'll believe me very shortly. You're going to suffer a fatal heart attack…in 14 minutes precisely.'
'Well, if you get off the 'phone, I'll call for an ambulance…'
'Too late, I'm afraid. It'll take 32 minutes to arrive, by which time you'll be very dead indeed…'
'Phew. Is there really nothing I can do? I'm only 71. The average life expectancy for men is 82. Seems so bloody unfair. I'm slim and fit…watch my weight, go to the gym three times a week. I don't smoke. Drink pretty moderately. I mean, why *me*?'
'Listen – people are always trying to solve that puzzle. But there isn't a puzzle. Just the luck of the draw. Whether it's 50, 70 or 90, nobody's happy about being called. That's life, I'm afraid. Love it or loathe it…'

'Assuming you're for real, has any of this being 'called' connected to my having 'sinned' at some stage?'

'Goodness, that sounds remarkably old-fashioned, even for me. You may have noticed – but amazingly few people seem to have done – that whether saint or sinner, king or commoner, rich or poor, atheist, Christian, Hindu, Jew, or Muslim, it always comes to this. That is, shuffling off one's mortal coil. Always has, always will. The only difference is in the *destination*. There is either a beautiful new beginning, or a buggary new beginning...'

'But I've got so many plans... Is there really no *good* news?'

'Yes, of course. There's always good news. Firstly, your Will is perfectly valid. So your eye-watering bequest to your mistress, Chelsea Smith, will be honoured. Your wife will be furious, but you'll be past caring. Secondly – despite your cheating – you seem to have been quite a good egg, on the whole, and your absent friends have been rooting for you... let's see – Mike Sewell, Dave Reynolds, and Mandy Jones... your *former* mistress. So the *great* news is that – though a pretty borderline case – you're coming to join us, in Heaven.'

'That's wonderful news, of course. You didn't mention Geoff Myers? I was pretty thick with him at one time. And my old mucker Chris Blackstone...'

'Ah, Sir Geoffrey Myers, MBE. I'm afraid he's not amongst us. We're pretty liberal, you know – we don't come down heavily on 'cakes and ale' – but, despite Geoff's charitable activities, we do take a dim view of the white slave trade.'

'Good G... I mean, goodness gracious – I did wonder about Geoff's wealth. A few manky nightclubs didn't seem to add up to a millionaire lifestyle.'

'As for your old mucker, Blackstone, I know my opposite number had advanced plans to welcome *him*. For an accountant, you've certainly had some odd bed-fellows – mistresses excepted.'

'Yes, that Ponzi scheme was bound to unravel at some stage.

Luckily I decided to wash my hands of it pretty darn quickly. Got out by the skin of my teeth. But it'll be great to meet up with Mandy again. The poor girl was only 45 when we lost her. So bloody unfair. I look forward to a nice chat with you about all that...'

'No probs. And, yes, you can meet some of your old friends – at least those who are our guests – including Mandy, and reminisce about the good times. No hanky panky though, I'm afraid. All our guests exist in pure spirit form – and that spirit's got nothing to do with alcohol, I should add. Of course there's no eating or drinking. And no gyms – I know you've been a big fan. In fact, nothing material, at all. We just don't need it.'

'Ah, that's a point. Phew. I don't want to sound ungrateful, but it all seems a tad, er, boring. Even disappointing. I mean, what *do* we do all day?'

'*Disappointing*? Heaven is supposed to be what everyone longs for. It promises, and provides, everlasting life. It's the ultimate goal and experience. If it's good enough for *me*...'

'I'm sure it will be fine. Given the circumstances...the choices are pretty limited... '

'Well, the other option – if you wish – can easily be arranged...'

'I suppose it's a no-brainer. You know, coming back to planet Earth for a moment – since I only *have* a moment – my wife will be horrified when she returns from Sainsbury's, to find me dead on the floor...'

'Maybe. Maybe not. Does a trip to Sainsbury's, and a coffee with the girls, really take all day? Wendy has long suspected your strange absences, and your vague excuses. And she is 12 years your junior. So she's taken her own lover – Sam Snelling.'

'Sam!! How could he! Sam is – *was* – my best friend. I trusted him! And he's been married to Jane for 30 years! What a cheating bastard! And *my* wife! How could she do that to *me*!'

'Well, maybe this isn't the ideal time for a homily about marital fidelity…'

'Fair play. So what do you suggest I do in these final moments? Thinking of those who'll deal with my mortal remains, might a shower and a change of clothes be, er, considerate?'

'Perhaps forget that. The last moments are always a trifle messy. Dying alone's not the most dignified experience. Can't be helped. You'll be beyond embarrassment. But with everything to look forward to. Still, maybe a brief note to Wendy…possibly asking her forgiveness. Since not only have you 'strayed' big time, but you've made Chelsea a wealthy woman. And, since there *is* an emotional attachment, Chelsea may wish to attend your funeral. And I'd suggest a prayer or two. Seeking *my* forgiveness. And my love. Just in case – since talking with you – I've changed my mind…'

OLD MAN KNOCKING

It was 8.45 on the morning of Monday 27 December, and an old man – though Eric Grant would have bridled at the 'old' – had just opened his eyes, stretched his arms wide, and yawned. Before muttering: 'Oh, my poor head!' He sighed. Strange. He usually woke up with an erection – a consequence of erotic dreams in the early hours. But not today. He sighed again. Then he remembered last night – at least, the bare bones of it. 'The neighbours! What a party! What a bloody din!' Time to get up and put the kettle on.

It was true that Eric, 66, looked pretty young for his years; maybe late-fifties he thought, hopefully, catching himself in the mirror. But others had thought – and said – so, too. It wasn't just vanity. Slim; a full head of hair; a smooth, unlined face. Eric looked down. And, yes, still pretty active… At least, generally. But, oh, my poor head!'

Eric reached for a couple of paracetemol, and swallowed them with his first mouthful of tea. He looked out of the kitchen window, to the lawned front garden beyond. It was a grey, dreary morning, with a spattering of rain carried on a mean breeze. Eric's attention was drawn by a small transparent object lying on the pavement, just beyond the garden. What was it? mused Eric, annoyed at the idea of detritus within his eye-shot. A discarded tissue? A handkerchief? A surgical glove? A pair of knickers, even? Eric took another slurp of tea, and walked down the garden path, to investigate.

What he discovered, lying limp and translucent, reminded him of a dead jellyfish he had once found, on a beach in Cornwall. But this was no jellyfish. Since the *thing* seemed pure and clean, Eric picked it up to take a closer look: then quickly dropped it again, grimacing, and wiping his hands on his trousers. My God! It was a female condom; with a splurge of semen deposited at the far end, and streaks lining the fabric. Eric hurried back into the house, thoroughly discomfited. He would clean it up later, using thick gloves, a dustpan and brush, and a bin bag. He thought for a moment: it must have been from the party last night. God; disgusting…

Eric didn't remember much about it. The party, that is. Odd; because he'd been invited by those new young neighbours, Sam and Samantha. They'd only moved in six months ago. How Eric envied their youth and energy! And, in Samantha's case, her beauty. Lucky young sod – Sam, that is. Strange lifestyle, mused Eric. Margaret – Eric's late wife – would have loathed them, thought Eric. '*All smiles and wiles*,' she would have said. Eric grinned. Margaret's voice still rang faithfully in his ears, a full 18 months after her passing. And it was true; they didn't seem to *do* anything. Like *work*, that is. Sam seemed to enjoy cleaning his car – a white Audi sports – and Samantha pottered around in the garden. Good job they didn't need to work, thought Eric – they kept such late hours. Maybe they lived off an inheritance, or a trust fund? Who knows? Who cares? Bloody lucky – they couldn't be older than their late 20s.

Then, one day, Sam had dropped out that they were 'in business.' Samantha spoke fluent French, and they often visited France – on business trips. What kind of business? enquired Eric. 'Just wheeling and dealing,' shrugged Sam, enigmatically. There was no further explanation, except, 'Well, we are in Kent – France is closer than London.'

Eric thought back to another day, late July, soon after the couple had moved into the semi next to his. Eric had heard the sound of laughter, like a tinkling, crystal stream, emanating from the garden next door, and was drawn to peep over the fence. It was Samantha, giggling at something Sam must have said. In truth, Eric had *thought* he'd heard the word 'Eric', in Sam's resonant tenor tones, carried to him on the breeze. Still, he laughed, it might just as easily have been 'dick', or 'prick'. But what he saw banished foolish thoughts. Samantha was lying on a recliner, with her arms extended behind her head. She was topless. Eric quickly looked away – then, aware that he couldn't easily be seen – took another long, hard stare; drinking in the scene. God, she was *properly* gorgeous. It was from that moment that Eric witnessed the return of regular erections. Thank you Samantha, thought Eric, with no little satisfaction.

Although, sadly – for him – there had been no repeat of the topless incident – the weather since had hardly been conducive – Sam – and the divine Samantha – *had* been quite friendly towards Eric, thought Eric. But, he supposed, there was method in their madness – they lived a pretty bohemian lifestyle, with lots of racket – shouting and loud music – most evenings. And Eric supposed they'd only invited him to the party to prevent any possibility of complaint. How could he possibly complain, if he was *at* the party? He remembered going round at 7.30 with a bottle of wine…What else? He remembered being greeted by Samantha at the door: all smiles and tits, squeezed into a tight black dress. She had kissed him on both cheeks. He didn't mind in the least. Flattered, even. If you've got it, flaunt it, baby. Eric had then been shown in by Samantha, and introduced to the other guests.

The least of many surprises that evening was that, compared to Eric's spacious and extended semi-detached, that had a separate lounge and dining room, the adjoining semi had had the internal wall removed – 'knocked through' – leaving just one rectangular, capacious space. The guests were seated, two by two, on five – or was it six? – soft leather sofas. Eric tried to remember who all the guests were. Certainly – apart from him – they were all young – and all exceedingly attractive. Five couples – not including Sam and Samantha – all casually, but artfully – and expensively – dressed. The group was completed by Samantha's younger sister, Serena – hardly less beautiful than her sibling. And of course Eric. Suddenly – he remembered – he had felt old. And alone. And slightly uncomfortable. But also cheered – to be surrounded by so much youth and beauty.

Samantha had guided Eric to a seat next to Serena – at the same time introducing him to her sister. Eric, who had lacked social contact since losing Margaret, was eager to swap social chit-chat with these fascinating young adults – though the effort had been frustrating, since the music – Beyoncé, he remembered, and Rhianna, maybe, were being played – very loudly. And, thought Eric – Shakira – yes, that was it – *Hips Don't Lie.*

Gradually, over the course of the morning, the clouds fogging Eric's brain began to lift, and he recalled progressively more. One couple – was it Clare and Jake? – 'dealt in' fine art. Another – possibly Donna and Dave – 'traded' top marque cars – like Ferrari, and Aston Martin. Yet another couple – was it Mark and Emma? – 'did' banking, via the Internet. Eric dredged his memory – yes, one more: Grant and Gemma – they were 'investment experts.' 'Need to make money on the stockmarket, Eric?' The entry point was ten grand. 'No pressure. Here's my card.'

The discussions were perfunctory; spasmodic. But Eric was left with the impression that these young people lived fast and exciting lives. At one point Samantha had teased him, smiling: 'Eric, darling, is this an interrogation?' – shutting his mouth with a kiss. Another surprise. 'And what can I get you to drink?' Eric replied, submissively, 'oh, a glass of dry white, please. Any chardonnay?' 'Only French, darling. Burgundy. We don't do that Aussie shit!' Such was Samantha's smile and charm that Eric had simply grinned and nodded his assent.

Eric remembered having more success with his 'partner', the gorgeous Serena. 'I'm a retired family solicitor,' was Eric's opening salvo. 'What do you do, Serena?' He had guessed fashion model. Or maybe actress. Serena smiled, winningly. 'A solicitor? You must be very clever...er, Eric. But I'm glad you said 'retired" she giggled. 'I'm an escort,' she said, widening her eyes, knowingly. Another surprise. 'What does that involve?' asked Eric, his throat suddenly dry. 'I accompany rich dudes to dinners and premieres – and so on...' Eric suddenly felt conspiratorial: 'Does it involve...you know?' 'You mean sex?' Serena replied, apparently artlessly. 'It's optional. Depends.' 'On what?' pressed Eric, riding his luck. 'On whether I want it. And whether he can afford it!' She laughed. 'And is it lucrative?' Eric asked again, peering towards Serena's cleavage. Serena extended her left hand: the index finger was decorated with a terrific solitaire diamond ring. 'It's two carats,' she added, a trifle unnecessarily.

Then she loosened the *décolleté* around her ivory throat, easing a long amethyst necklace from the dark, delicious recesses of her cleavage, and the voluminous bloom of her bosom. The glittering violet of the jewels complemented Serena's eyes, framed by that blonde sweep of her hair. Then Eric caught a whiff of Chanel No. 5. Serena smiled: 'Dear heart, how like you this?' 'Extraordinary,' whispered Eric, caught up in the moment, and peering beyond, between and below the necklace, before returning to those wide blue eyes. Finally, Serena extended her right hand, to display a diamond-studded Rolex watch. 'I see,' said Eric, simply. 'Blimey!'

A perfect moment was interrupted by Samantha's reappearance, rather dramatically clutching a sprig of mistletoe above her head. 'Now, darlings, time to kiss your partner! It is

Christmas!' Serena smiled, a touch coyly, whispering to Eric: 'I guess that must mean me!' Serena hugged her bosom with her arms, in an apparently unconscious, perhaps nervous, gesture. Eric felt compelled to take a long swig of his chardonnay. It must have been his third glass by now – it seemed to re-fill of its own accord. Another surprise.

Serena squeezed herself towards Eric, and embraced his face with her small, soft hands, before launching into a breathless kiss. Eric responded, and felt a stirring in his loins. Jesus, this was incredible! It was delicious; it was ridiculous! He held Serena tightly around the waist, and again returned her kiss. Time went by – God knows how much – when Samantha interrupted proceedings with her customary tinkling laugh: 'I think that's enough guys! Variety is the spice of life! Time for a different partner!'

Dutifully, the guys and dolls all smiled and shuffled the pack, the guys all moving to the next sofa, in a game of musical chairs that seemed to be synchronized. Samantha waved her mistletoe. 'Get on with it, guys!' Eric looked around him, in amazement: the kissing had resumed. Should *he* resume, with Serena?

'I guess you'll have to do with little old me!' laughed Samantha, provocatively, in Eric's direction. 'Serena, do you mind? But do stay, babe, in case I run out of gas!' Another surprise: where was *Sam*? Certainly, not in the room. 'Take a good swig of your wine, babe. Then you'll taste even better!' Eric did as he was bid. Jesus, was he fucking dreaming? He looked around: guests were beginning to undress: he saw a man – Jake, was it? – kissing Donna's breasts. But his head was becoming fuzzy, and it was hard to focus his eyes. Despite himself, a drowsiness was overpowering his being. He remembered Beyoncé crooning *'If I were a boy',* and remembered Samantha's hot breath, as she whispered: 'you're in my hands now, baby!' then kissing him, and of hot hands all over him...Then: nothing.

It was now mid-day on Monday 27 December. Eric had been wrapped up all morning in his thoughts and recollections, and his struggles with his own memory. All that had passed his lips that morning were two cups of tea. Suddenly, Eric felt hungry. The headache had dissipated. 'Better pop to Sainsbury's for a loaf,' he reasoned. 'What a wild night! Pity I can't remember how it ended!'

Sainsbury's Local was a five minute stroll away, so Eric shoved his wallet in his pocket, and set off on foot. It would help clear his head and, hopefully, refresh and restore memory. Had he, you know, done *it* with the gorgeous Samantha? Or even the fab Serena? Back to reality: Eric approached the counter with his wholegrain loaf. 'Hi, Sandra. Just this, please, for now.' Eric presented his card. 'Sorry, Eric, it's been refused,' said the incredulous Sandra. 'Ridiculous!' exclaimed Eric, and presented the card again – this time using his PIN. Refused again. 'Madness!' spluttered Eric. He rummaged in his pockets and found a fiver to spare his blushes; then hurried home, in a state of some agitation.

Eric 'phoned his bank. The young lady was most helpful. After leading Eric through the security minefield – or mind-field – Eric was advised – would she drop that fucking sing-song voice! – that the contents of his current account – £9,653 – had been transferred to a different account at 11.02pm last night. The transaction had been completed via the Internet; PIN, account details, Passwords and security checks had all been successfully negotiated.

'But it wasn't me!' howled Eric. 'I'm coming down *now* to see Kevin!' (Snodgrass – Manager), he barked. In his confusion, Eric couldn't find his car keys, but located the spares. It didn't matter: when he arrived at his garage, his racing green Jaguar was notable for its absence. Another fucking surprise! Shocked to his core, Eric booted his computer. He checked his investments – mainly cash ISAs. They'd been looted, and the proceeds transferred. £120k!!! Gone!! The fucking mother of all surprises!

There were still gaps in Eric's memory, but the structure of the story was now becoming crystal clear. It was now 1.00pm. Even *they* should be up by now! He banged on the neighbours' door. The knocker echoed, vacantly. Eric looked through the windows: no sign of life. The Audi, and Samantha's sporty Peugeot, were gone, too. Another bloody surprise. Don't be surprised any more, you fucking moron!

Eric 'phoned the police, who – yes, surprise – came hurtling round to Eric's house. The two officers listened and conferred, then soberly confirmed what Eric already thought he knew. 'I'm afraid that your drink will have been spiked,' opined Sergeant Spencer. 'And your car is probably in France, now, with new plates. As for your money, that's probably beyond the reach of UK jurisdiction. A very bad – and clever – sting, I'm afraid.' Only yet another surprise: the house had been rented, and Sam and Samantha were two months in arrears with their rent.

The police departed – with grimly shaking heads – and repeating fears that Eric's stolen chattels would never be recovered. Though, on the trip back to the Station, their mood was brightened by the idea that this clever and intriguing scam – with its glamorous women and decadent climax – might provide the genesis for a rather racy police training video…

Soon after the self-satisfied duo left, Eric received a text:

'Thank you, babe. You were awesome. Samantha & Serena XX.'

Suddenly, Eric felt a nausea in the pit of his stomach. That condom, outside. The most expensive fugal frolics. Ever.

TOM AND HARRY DISCUSS THE FACTS OF LIFE

'As you know, Dad, I'm nearly nineteen years of age. And about to start my University career. But I'm beginning to have serious doubts. In fact, I'm beginning to wish I'd never been born. My generation is facing ruin. What a shit legacy you're leaving me!'

'Phew. Why not tell it as it is, Harry? But, no, I don't think so. On the contrary, my belief is that yours is the most fortunate, blessed generation in human history. And the most prosperous. And with the most to look forward to. So what's brought all this on?'

'It's simple. The planet is dying. We have climate change. Mass extinction. Global pollution. Resource depletion. Then there's University – it costs a fortune! And, now, even the jobs are disappearing! And don't even mention getting on the housing ladder! Just impossible. What's to like? What's to enjoy? It seems like we just have to *endure*.'

'Well, there's an awful lot there to unpack, son. You're sitting comfortably, a cup of coffee in hand, a giant plasma screen to your left, a wifi and Zoom-enabled laptop to your right. In front of you is a photo of you and girlfriend Julie on Bondi Beach. For your grandparents, it was Bognor Beach, at best. Not too bad for Armageddon, I'd say!'

'That's a low shot. You haven't rebutted a single thing I've said. The whole world is collapsing…'

'With respect, *your* world doesn't seem to be collapsing. You have your own centrally heated bedroom, complete with TV – and another laptop – and, thanks mainly to your mother, eat royally at least three times a day. As for the planet itself, it's now managing to support more than eight billion people – most of them in a better state of health and nutrition than at any time in history. Over the face of that planet, disease, if not abolished, is in serious retreat. While poverty, too, seems to have receded in the rear view mirror for billions of our global fellow citizens.'

'That may be true, but it all sounds a bit glib. We're on the very cusp of global disaster…'

'So I hear. And we can discuss all that in a moment. But first we need to get a little historical perspective. For most people on this planet, from the year dot to almost the present time, life has been – as Thomas Hobbes's pointed out – 'nasty, brutish and short.' Struggling for food. Struggling against oppression. Struggling in war. Struggling against illness and disease. Struggling for equality. Even struggling to get yourself heard – because the 'right' to democracy, and to free speech, didn't exist. In fact, for the 'lower orders', the right to *anything* didn't exist. So, pray tell me, what era would have suited you better than the present?'

'That's easy – yours. Loads of jobs – *good* jobs. Free university tuition. Affordable housing. Checkmate, I believe?'

'Not so fast, young man. The reason university education was free was that very few working class people could afford to apply – they needed to work, and couldn't afford the 'luxury' of study. And, of course, their time in education finished when they were 14 or 15. They weren't able to acquire even the entry qualifications they needed. They were all destined for factory, pit or warehouse – blue collar jobs. Or, if they were women, destined for sweat shops or domestic service. On top of that, they had the drudgery — and risk — of bearing babies year after year. But yes, there were loads of jobs — dead end jobs. Incredibly, now, half of all young people — girls and boys — progress to university, and enjoy an eye-watering range of career choices!

'It was my generation — and those that preceded it, through two cataclysmic World Wars — that began to change, even to break the mould. Now that mould is shattered, and opportunity is everywhere. In theory, if you have the ability and desire to work hard, you can enter any profession. As for the housing market, well, it's never been easy. Always a struggle. But if I'd asked my father for financial help, for a deposit, he'd have laughed. 'Stand on your own two feet!' he'd have said. Tough love, they called it. So I didn't bother to ask. So your mum and I saved, and struggled, and eventually climbed that housing ladder. Whereas, when you're ready, you can call on the Bank of Mum and Dad. Or, possibly, just Mum...'

'But why bother with any of it? When the very planet is going down the tube, what's the point of *anything*? What's the point of ambition, when we're all going to die?'

'Well, as the man said, we *are* all going to die. Eventually. But right now, people are living longer than ever. Did you know, a man's life expectancy in 1900, in the UK, was 45? Now it's well over 80. According to the scientists — guys and gals not much older than you — your generation is headed for a life expectancy of at least a hundred. Because of better nutrition. And sophisticated medical technology. And a life-style even my grandparents could barely have imagined. They never enjoyed — never knew — colour telly, with almost limitless choice. The wonders of the Internet. The excitement of international travel. Food brought in from across the globe. Free universal health care. So I could say, what's not to like? It's everything Man has ever wished for. But with your mind set, you probably think that such a life-span, enjoyed in un-heard of prosperity, is no longer nirvana, but pure purgatory...'

'But, surely, that's the problem? All this 'stuff' – 'prosperity' you call it – is suffocating our very life source!'

'Well, if it is, maybe set an example. Put off that trip to India, or Brazil. Get rid of the gadgets – the laptops, the iPhone. Don't buy a car. Get your clothes from charity shops. Turn down your central heating. Turn vegan – by growing your own veg in the garden. Don't have any kids. You can *choose* to do your bit. The choice is yours. Previous generations didn't have such choices. Maybe make a start by having a litter pick in the lane? I wonder who's throwing away all those coffee cups and fast-food cartons?'

'God! Where am I supposed to find the time! I'm off to Uni, to study Eng Lit, in a couple of weeks! But, Dad, I really don't think you're taking this seriously. It's OK for you – you'll probably be dead before all this happens. You'll escape the worst…'

'Lucky old me, lying oblivious in the churchyard. I do accept that there are massive problems. Life has never been – nor ever will be – perfect. It's called 'the human condition'. But let's not begin from a position of despair. But of optimism and hope. Things – attitudes, actions – are beginning to change. And your generation will soon be in control – will seize the levers of power. I really don't think it's too late. But don't blow the opportunity. I hope to be here when you're explaining to my grandchildren just why your generation – like the last – has continued to let things slip and slide. Addicted to consumerism. Obsessed with foreign 'travel'. And sex. And money. And power. Marx said that religion was the opium of the people. Now it's stuff – consumerist stuff. Fashion. Cars. Gadgets. The risk, of course, is that you will all be quickly distracted by the pressures of work, relationships and life, to change course. Wife, mortgage, kids. 'Events, dear boy, events!' as Macmillan famously said.'

'And then that's another thing – social media. Facebook, Instagram, TikTok all adding to the pressure on my time…obliged to keep up with all my friends' amazing lives and experiences! It's such a frustrating, endless burden of expectation!'

'I agree. Of course, we never experienced that 'burden'. We just had a telephone. And TV. I'm not here to advise you, Harry, but you could just make a grand announcement to the world – and switch it off!'

'I think you're being far too...too...'

'Complacent? Possibly. But I'd say, read a good history book. Read about real poverty. About violence and war. About slavery. About cruelty. About life throughout history, for the vast majority of people who chanced, naked and blinking, on to this seductive, scary, spinning planet. People who needed to spend every waking minute just *surviving*. And then think: how am *I* going to live my life? How use my time? How make the right choices? How make a difference? You are fortunate – you have a world of choice and opportunity before you, as hardly any generation has ever known. And you're going to be around for a *very* long time. Far too long to be wringing your hands in despair – in a kind of wish-fulfillment. Stand up and *do* something!'

'OK. I can see you're trying to be helpful. Suppose it's a start. Anyway, there's a match I'd like to see, in my bedroom.'

'Bedroom? There are two TV sets down here...'

'Julie's coming over...'

'Ah...that's another thing: sex. In my day, you'd need to be married to enjoy all the benefits, as it were.'

'Dad, I've told you it's not sex...'

'Sure. That came right out of the Bill Clinton School of Sophistry. Is that what they'll be teaching you at University? Anyway, give Julie my love, if that's not too telling a phrase...'

'Maybe come back to all this later?'

'Anytime at all. I appreciate you're very busy right now. Shall I get you that history book for your birthday? Maybe Kindle version? Or are you still thinking about that new camera...'

MUDDY WATERS

Graham Mudlark was a strange man. In many ways, Graham was strange in ways that most men are strange; in others, his strangenesses were very much his own.

Graham, a startlingly handsome and active child, was brought up in the middle of nowhere – the suburbs of Reading – the only offspring of his mother, a Doctor, and his father, a tax lawyer. Graham was not a 'wanted' child, and was seen as a major impediment to his parents' hedonistic lifestyle. The parents were – both – extremely busy people, and perhaps too busy dealing with patients, and clients – and making money – to take much notice of young Graham. Not that their son minded; he had the space, freedom and opportunity to do pretty much exactly what he chose.

So, although well dressed and well nourished, young Graham never flushed the toilet, or washed his hands; nor did he socialise much, enjoy walks in the countryside, or pursue healthy hobbies. From a young age, violent computer games were his passion and, when the young man felt in need of further diversion, a pot shot at the local bird population, using his air rifle, kept him hilariously amused.

At the age of eight years the engaging young thing was packed off to an all-boys' Independent School a few miles distant. His parents, Chantal and Charlie, would have preferred him to have been a boarder – his daily demands were so inconvenient – but baulked at the fees. So Graham continued to return home in the evenings, arriving, like an unwanted, alien asteroid, by scheduled taxi each evening.

Over the years, Graham's peers – and his school-masters – tried hard to convince the now adolescent lad that he was gay, or – like his hero the sixth Lord Byron – bisexual; or else trans. But Graham refused all of these persuasive blandishments. At the age of 12, Graham discovered a copy of Casanova's *My Life* in the school library – it was not part of the formal curriculum. Young Mudlark devoured the book with growing fascination and excitement. Graham decided that henceforth he was interested in only one thing. And that thing was girls. But could late 20th Century Britain offer the same opportunities as dissolute 18th Century Venice? Only time would tell. Graham, though intelligent and inquisitive, became increasingly disinterested in his lessons, and barely scraped enough passes together to qualify for University. But, at the age of 18, the tall, maturing young man attended Reading Uni, as a fresher, to study Psychology.

If Psychology was the means, it was not the end. For the main object of young Graham's studies at University was women; particularly young women. Graham had hardly met any girls, or women, up until this time. Except, that is, for his mother who, despite her dismissal of her son, remained an object of fascination for the adolescent Mudlark. For Chantal remained wild at heart, carefree, and deeply sensual. But, otherwise, there had been a drought of women, and the female gender remained a mystery to Graham's inquisitive spirit. Now, suddenly, there appeared a glut, a veritable over-flow, of young women in their first flush of youth and beauty. There was a cornucopia of riches, a treasure chest overflowing with all that Graham so earnestly desired. Graham was fascinated; absorbed; captivated. He did not want a woman. He did not want a girl-friend. No; he wanted every female on campus.

Graham set about losing his virginity with indecent speed. He quickly learned to make adjustments to his habits, in order to produce a favourable impression. For example, to bathe occasionally; to wash his hands before a date; to take more care of his appearance; to dress fashionably. Even to flush the loo. Graham kept a diary, in order to record his experiences, and his conquests. He became a man on a mission.

For Graham, a girl was a girl was a girl. Our Graham was a quick learner, and soon learned that the most beautiful girls were not only the most desirable, but the most sought-after, the most in-demand – with a level of competition that absorbed a great deal of time, trouble, and sheer hard work – but with little prospect of tangible reward. Though young Graham was handsome and well-heeled, the competition remained frustratingly ferocious.

So Graham concentrated on that strata of the female market – in a 'market' where there was a 1:1 male/female ratio – where the girls, whilst clearly still attractive, and fully valuing themselves – might nevertheless welcome Graham's attentions; a market where Graham – already a 'dish' – might also be considered a 'catch'. These young students might be blonde or brunette, or tall or short, or skinny or plump, or attractive, to a varying degree, or verging towards plainness. But, to young Graham, each and every young woman appeared as a virgin America: rich, redolent; a mystery ripe to be explored. Graham knew that his target audience were – by definition – all female; all young; and – in the main – looking for a man. And – possibly – overlooked by other suitors, who yearned for the poetry of beauty.

Graham did not need to wait long for his first conquest. Pamela was a second year English student, from Wolverhampton. Pamela boasted a proliferation of rings through her ears, and large tattoos on her forearms. Further tattoos might be found lurking around Pamela's fulsome nooks and crannies. Though some people might also have considered Pam a smidgeon or two overweight, Graham shrugged – such qualms meant nothing to him – and he proudly escorted Pamela for a chat and drinks in *The Kings Head,* only minutes from the campus. But Pamela found her beau a bit nerdy, and a little over-wrought – his main topic of conversation being psychology theory – and was disinclined to give him the benefit of her person, the first time around. Pam didn't consider herself to be 'that' kind of girl.

A few cheesy texts, some smarmy calls that dropped in hints of his parents wealth, and a box or two of chocolates, were all required before Pamela was enticed back to the pub. This time around, Pamela was quite prepared for the consequences. Around 9.00pm, Graham found himself – for the first time – in bed, in his student flat, with the said Pamela. The inexperienced, but dreadfully eager Graham, was hardly required to demonstrate expertise: Pamela was both experienced and voracious, with sufficient experience to compensate for her partner's novice groping. Graham gratefully forgot the tattoos, and the multiple earrings, and enjoyed Pamela's opulent young flesh. He was delirious with pleasure and, though Pamela mumbled something about an early start the next day, insisted on an early-morning encore. Graham was hooked. He was drugged. He was intoxicated. He was addicted.

The nineteenth-birthday boy celebrated in style with Pamela. Graham already had an excess of stamina; with Pamela, he quickly gained in confidence and technique. Over the coming weeks – do excuse the pun – the 'experiments' in positions and techniques that had long exercised young Mudlark's brain now exercised – and energised, and exhilarated – his young manhood. Sometimes, such were the sensations coursing through his frame, Graham felt that his eye-balls might burst out of his head; and, in return for this exquisite pleasure, that that outcome may have represented fair recompense. As Graham's prowess grew, Pamela became more compliant, acquiescing quickly – though hardly quietly – to her lover's urgent and implicit – and increasingly explicit – demands.

Most of Pamela's previous sexual partners had been young 'wham, bam, thank-you-mam' types. At first, Pam had hoped there might be a chance of a serious, long-term relationship with young Mudlark; but quickly reconciled herself to an exciting, purely sexual partnership. Sadly, while the gung-ho Mudlark had shown every conceivable attention to Pam's quivering young body, he had displayed next to no interest in Pamela's longer-term aspirations.

Although, over the weeks and months, Graham began to regard the willing Pam as a tad tedious, he did not ditch his muse; not only was she his first 'love', but she was reliable, and she was the ideal learning 'vehicle'; Graham's term. And she had a range of connections and contacts that Graham could cultivate, with future conquests in mind. Besides, the young stud could use his leisure to pursue more girls; if he could 'run' two or three at a time, why ever not? Graham decided that he needed sex every day. If Pam – or no-one else – was available, Graham would trawl the surprisingly vibrant streets of his native city, and find a willing – perhaps desperate – working girl. Bung her a 'pony'; and everyone's happy.

Although Graham continued to pursue his formal studies, his main pursuit – in fact, his main object of study – was the female gender. His studies here were relentless, and exhaustive, and verging on obsessive. Graham matriculated with a 2.1 in Psychology. But he was far prouder of his informal studies, that had connected with a phenomenal 365 women.

Despite his professional qualification, Graham displayed no interest in the psychological make-up of women, except insofar as this gave him an edge in their pursuit and 'conquest'. He was not remotely interested in a woman's interests, or her hopes, or her fears, or her ambitions. That is, he was not interested in a woman – the woman – as a *person*. Yes, maybe, he wanted to please them; *needed* to please them, in order to attain his goals. But that was all; the fascination was in the physicality, the sensuality, the orgasmic pleasure available in each and every individual. What a devious creature, God, or Nature, was! To have created this divine, animal, desire and attraction! What was football, or cricket, or music, or art, compared to this?

Surprisingly, perhaps, for a young man with often vulgar, oafish habits – except when putting his best foot forward – that is, on the prowl – Mudlark had no interest in pornography. This disinterest was unrelated to ethical niceties. No; what was the point of two-dimensional representations, whether via magazines, TV, video or Internet? And even if the actors and performers *were* enjoying themselves, *he,* Graham Mudlark, was a mere spectator. Left out of the fun – except as a voyeur. No, thank you: give Mudlark a real, live, full-size, warm, responsive, satisfying woman, any time – and every time.

Graham calculated that there were around 18 million women in the UK between the ages of 16 and 60. Enough, even for him. Yes, many would be married, or in some aspect unappealing. What the heck? Though he started his professional life as an assistant in a private practice – his parents were only too happy to help their 22-year-old son to purchase his own apartment out of town – Graham was free to spend his leisure time indulging his only hobby. He had long since become bored with computer games and shooting little birds. Now he was grown up, and his only study was Man. Well, Woman.

Graham Mudlark was too, well, sex-obsessed and self-absorbed to hold a job down for long, or to establish a 'proper' career. Instead, Graham migrated to wherever his 'research' led him to believe the best 'action' might be found – whether in Derby, Dudley or Doncaster. But his experience and modest salary expectations meant that he had little trouble finding office work, and his working life in the thrumming heart of a bank, hospital or corporate entity – institutions enjoying a high percentage of young female staff – provided yet more opportunity for the indefatigable Mudlark to hone his craft. These fertile hunting grounds supplied a rich diversity of 'game' to a hunter with a quill always replete with fresh arrows.

Mudlark's parents, fearful that their son might crash back into their lives – parachuting in like a Nazi storm trooper – provided a generous monthly allowance to cut off that potential danger. So the young – and increasingly not so young – Mudlark, led a highly focused, but increasingly chaotic, 'lifestyle'.

Graham Mudlark was now 38 years of age – on the cusp of middle age – and living in Leeds. Reading had all-too quickly become too small for him; he had mined and exhausted its treasures. And Birmingham. And Dudley, Derby and Doncaster. So, too, Wolverhampton – Pamela's home town. Indeed, he became re-acquainted with the young woman to whom he had gratefully surrendered his virginity. Pam was now divorced, and a respectable, and respected, primary school teacher. She was familiar with Mudlark's animal tendencies, and his borderline aggression – but *she* could use, as well as be-used.

And then on to Nottingham – reputed to be the home of England's prettiest women. Graham tested out the theory, to his own evident satisfaction. And so to Leeds. Different places; different styles; different cultures; different ethnicities (there wasn't a racist bone in Graham's body); different body shapes; different techniques; different expectations; different attitudes to casual sex.

Fortunately, from the outset Graham kept a diary of his exploits. Who. Where. When. How. Otherwise, the whole crazy adventure would have morphed into an enormous, amorphous blur. And a photographic diary, to boot. A face – sometimes more – sometimes much more – to paste alongside the diary entry.

Graham's obsession had sometimes skirted with trouble. Give this guy an inch, and he would assume one meant a mile. Where does one draw the line between consent, and abuse? Between respect, and excited, vigorous immersion in the moment? Between 'yes' and a drunken smile? Between urgent, no-holds barred sex, and further sexual penetration in the small hours, when the partner is asleep or unconscious? Between 'normal' sex, and a sudden descent into unexpected kinky sex 'games'? Between sex-play, and physical pain? Graham crossed these lines, and more, on many occasions.

But no one – not a single woman – complained, even when they felt a line had been crossed; when norms and boundaries had been breached. Was it acceptable? Was it abuse? Was it rape? Though individual women might feel uncomfortable, though they felt taken advantage of, who would possibly believe them? What proof had they that consent, once given, had then been denied? What evidence had they of refusing consent? Did they *really* want to re-live every moment of what had become an unpleasant, upsetting, distressing, even painful, experience? Who would take them seriously? Who would *listen*? Who would *do* anything? Most often, the victims concluded that a formal complaint would simply rebound on the complainant, bringing with it acute embarrassment, vile flashbacks, hassle and angst – but with no expectation of a positive outcome. Every woman – from Barking, from Birmingham, from Burnley – shuddered at the prospect of entering a police station, and being confronted by a dick-on-a-stick: 'So, Miss…you went out for a meal with this man? Of your own accord? And you went back to his flat? Of your own accord? And you went to bed with him? Of your own accord…?' So, even if ruefully, regretfully – bitterly: put it behind you, and just be more careful, next time.

One certainty – Mudlark's positive spin on his rigorous approach – was that any and every woman would be guaranteed

Graham's complete, ardent attention. Of that there was no question. This guy had trained as a Psychologist, and knew well that he had a clinically recognised 'problem'. An addiction. Compulsion. Let's call it 'sexual compulsion disorder.' But Graham did not regard his 'problem' as a problem. It was not as though he had a terrible desire to put his hand in a fire. Or drink himself to oblivion. Or mutilate himself. Or starve himself to death. No: he just wanted to screw women. As many and as frequently as possible. If it *was* a problem, it wasn't a problem to him. A challenge. A burning desire. Yes, a compulsion. But, problem, not a bit; not a smidgen. Not a scintilla. And there seemed to be an endless supply of these objects of desire…

At 38 years old, Graham Mudlark suffered a tragedy – of sorts. His parents – Chantal and Charlie – were returning to the UK, from luxurious holiday on the French Riviera – when Chantal fell asleep at the wheel. The BMW ploughed into the back of a truck, and the couple became history. Their son dutifully arranged their funeral; and that was that. Graham washed his hands of them – at least, figuratively speaking. The couple died Intestate – they had no intention of dying any time soon – but, following the Probate process, their Estate was showered on their non-showering son. Graham became a millionaire overnight. He no longer needed to work for a living, and gleefully gave notice to his employer. The parents would have been horrified that this strange man – of their creation and upbringing – should have inherited the fruits of their own addiction to work and wealth. But so it came to pass.

Graham Mudlark had long indulged himself on fast food, fast booze and, as we know, fast women. So, by this advanced age of 38, the cracks were beginning to show: Graham had put on shed-loads of weight, his face was bloated and podgy, and his movement become ponderous and slow. Despite the influx of newly inherited wealth – the Porsche, solid gold necklace and rings, and opulent new home in the leafy suburbs of Leeds – Graham was no longer viewed as a 'catch', and found it increasingly difficult to interest and attract women. The whole process was becoming too protracted, too exhausting; too much like bloody hard work.

So, more and more frequently, Graham found himself frequenting the seedier precincts of the urban sprawl, and securing the services of the City's apparently endless supply of 'working girls'. No need to charm them; no need to amuse, flatter and cajole. No stress, hard work or hassle. 'Just tell me what you want, and give us the ffing money, dude!' Simple, practical, time-efficient. Job done. A different girl, most nights. Except that Graham now 'found' Chantal. Strange – the same name as his mother. But – as well as being beautiful – Chantal *had* something different, physically, that brought Graham to a paroxysm of orgasmic pleasure. Whatever Chantal had, Graham couldn't get enough. In his frenzy, and in order to achieve Chantal's earnest compliance to his desires, Mudlark started to brag about his lifestyle, and his wealth.

Then, on maybe his twelfth visit – Graham really should have insisted on Chantal coming to his own home – the obliging Chantal beckoned him in, and the door was quickly slammed behind them. Graham was bustled into a chair by two burly guys, and roughly tied by the legs and arms. The guys – and Chantal, who appeared tearful – then left the petrified captive to his own devices. All night. At seven the next morning the even more than usual stinking Mudlark was shaken and slapped awake by one of the masked guys. Graham groaned. Despite the mask, it was clear that this brute meant business.

'What do you want?' moaned Graham. 'Everything, bastard!' replied the masked man, patting Graham's soaked trousers. Graham suddenly became terrified, sensing the danger he was in.

Urgent, but muffled, cries emerged from the room next

door. The masked man kicked the door open. Chantal lay on a creaking bed, her face distorted; her eyes bulging; her mouth gagged; her wrists tied. A heavy man – the muscles of his back and buttocks pulsing and straining – jammed into the helpless Chantal – just as he pleased. Her desperate eyes seemed to cry out to Graham; but to no avail. Mudlark wouldn't have helped the bitch, even if he could.

'Look, bastard. Do what we ask. Or that's a taste of what you're in for!' The masked man took off his mask, cackled insanely, and eased his gorged crotch.

'Please don't hurt me! I'll give you anything!' cried Graham.

'Yes, yes!' smirked the tormentor. 'Of course you will, bastard, you're in our hands, now!' Mudlark did everything that was asked of him. And gave all the personal and financial information demanded by his captors. But it made no difference. These were not men whose word could be trusted. The *denouement* did not – to say the least – make pleasant viewing, or hearing. It was mid-afternoon when the perpetrators had completed their work on Graham Mudlark. They had long since extracted his bank details, and secured his house and car keys. When he had nothing…he had nothing. Except his body. Then the brutes completed their 'fun'. The last words heard by Mudlark were those of the sobbing, blood-spattered Chantal: begging his forgiveness.

After his murder, Mudlark simply disappeared. And no-one noticed the absent man. His identity was transferred to one of the gang, and possessions – house, car, bank accounts – all liquidated, or sequestered. Without friends, and with no immediate family, it was as though the loner Graham Mudlark had never existed. Certainly, for two thousand, four hundred and sixty five women, Mudlark's existence had been real enough; though his memory hardly brought unmitigated pleasure.

Ironically, several weeks after the real Mudlark's disappearance, a woman called Anne Roberts complained to the police of rape.

Anne and Graham had 'met' on the Internet, some months earlier; she was 32-years old, warm, bubbly – and buxom – and a divorcèe. After they had 'regular' sex, a couple of weeks later, Mudlark had indulged in his standard practice of penetrating his sleeping partner. Anne's cries of protest only served to spur on the frenzied 'lover'. Mudlark would have shrugged in surprise at Anne's belated response. She was far too delicious to just leave alone. And a bit bloody late in the day to keep yelling 'No!!' Anne had agonized about making the complaint, but her experience had left a deep trauma that time would not assuage.

When police officers banged on the front door of 2, Milton Rise, to arrest 'Graham Mudlark', they were shocked by the appearance of the wretch who confronted them. The bald, tattooed, muscular barrel of a man bore little resemblance to the detailed description given them by Anne Roberts. Still, the man – who identified as Graham Mudlark – was charged with the crime. Even the police were appalled by this overpowering, foul-mouthed horror of a man and, their suspicions aroused, they dug deeper. The identity 'ruse' was quickly exposed, and the genuine names revealed. These guys had real form. Chris Bull – and his accomplices, who included the coerced Chantal – were charged with extortion, fraud, grievous bodily harm (GBH), modern slavery, rape – and murder. True: Chris Bull had not raped Anne Roberts but, given the chance, he would have done so, without a second's thought; and there were many other victims of Bull and his partner, Steve Pratt, besides Graham Mudlark himself. To her credit, the pimped, abused Chantal sang like a canary. The jail sentences handed out to Bull and Pratt stretched almost to eternity.

Maybe sensing that the trajectory of his life was about to change dramatically, drastically, and irrevocably, the real Graham Mudlark had, only weeks before his demise, transferred his voluminous secret diaries to a bank vault. Perhaps, one day, that vault would be opened, and its secrets revealed. What would the world of 2072 – a world unimaginably different to our own – make of this peculiar, obsessive record? Indeed, would it still be possible for the strange Graham Mudlark to find a space in that brave new world?

Perhaps yes; perhaps no. If no Mudlarks, certainly no Bulls or Pratts. But it cuts both ways. If no Mudlarks, which of us, too, would 'scape a whipping?

BRIEF ENCOUNTER 3:
BRITTANY – HARRY'S FRENCH LESSON

France. Brittany. July. Waking to shimmering blue sea and sky, croissants, coffee and fresh orange juice. Paradise.

The holiday chalet, nestling in its own shady nook only metres from the sea, sheltered Harry, his partner Sarah, and their dog, *Harry 2* – a play on words and meaning that, over the years, had become a touch tedious.

Yet, here they all were enjoying their two weeks away from Croydon, in the piercing Breton sunshine. 'Shall we go down to the beach this morning?' asked Harry. 'You know, the one we passed the other day on the way in? It looked quite informal, and delightful. Just the thing for a dip…'

'Yes, why not?' replied Sarah, absently. (She was busy finishing a croissant). 'We can pop into that supermarket on the way back,' she added, practically. '*Much* cheaper than the camp shop.'

It was already 10.30am – how time flies when you're happy! Their rising – I use the word advisedly – had been delayed that morning by Harry's wheedling and pleading – brought on by an excess of sunshine, and the surfeit of tanned, taut, bikini-clad *mademoiselles* draped around the camp-site – for some urgent physical therapy. Harry had been rather vigorous and, er, demanding that morning. Sufficiently so for Sarah to raise an eyebrow; not that Harry had noticed. *Harry 2* had noticed, however. He had noticed *indeed,* and was annoyed that his early morning constitutional had been delayed by a full six minutes. In his irritation, *Harry 2* had not over-looked the smug, self-satisfied look on his master's face, and was certain to make amends. Determined to re-assert his right to Harry1's attention, the *chien* duly squatted and delivered himself of the largest possible poo, right in the middle of the service road. 'Buggar, I've forgotten the poo-bag!' moaned Harry.

The small pimple on the bottom of paradise duly sorted, the three English musketeers entered their chariot – Volvo V60 – and set off on the five-kilometre stretch to their chosen beach. There it was: an exquisite, sandy cove, just beyond a *petite* metalled car-park. No facilities, as such, apart from a white-washed toilet block. A glorious sun smiled benignly from a full blue sky; a disc of fine, golden sand, a gentle, sparkling sea, and a sprinkling of fellow revellers melded in perfect harmony to welcome the happy threesome.

'I'll stay in the car if you don't mind' said Sarah. 'It's a great view, and I wanted to make a few calls to mum and dad, and Alice,' (Sarah's sister). 'You know, the baby's due any day, now.' Harry looked afresh at his own girl. She was thirty, suddenly, but deceptively good looking, with a fine, firm, full figure. And kind of blonde, in a bob. His thoughts turned to this morning's main event, and he saw Sarah's naked form again in his mind's eye. 'I thought you might want to sun-bathe in your bikini. Or even out of it' he joked, glancing at the shapely breasts that appeared beside him, partially sheathed in a saffron summer dress.

'I think you've had quite enough of that for the time-being' replied Sarah, coolly. *Harry 2* whined, impatiently. 'Do take *Harry* on to the beach – you know how he loves a swim in the sea.'

Harry laughed. 'Your wish is my command,' he said, slightly disappointed. 'Come on boy, time to play!' With one bound,

Harry 2 – a chocolate Labrador, who had been thumping his tail against the car's rear-window – jumped from the car, ran towards the beach, and dived into the inviting pulse of the incoming tide. Harry brought *Harry 2*'s obligatory ball, and an inviting stick. Within seconds, the pair were immersed in a frolic of innocent fun, as they chased about in the gentle, lapping waves, glancing silvery and shining on the cool, smooth sand.

A child, in a fedora, perhaps sampling the sea for the first time, screamed when he saw *Harry 2* darting through the waves in his direction. *Harry 2* saw only his ball, dancing on the crest of a wave. *Harry 2* swam past a stately woman with silver hair reaching down her back, and figure barely concealed by a tangerine bikini. Though almost immersed up to her thighs in the voluptuous water, she appeared to glance disapprovingly at *Harry 2*. But *Harry 2* was in his bubble. People did not concern him. He barely noticed *them*. He was, in fact, the gentlest of creatures, but sea and sand excited him, and he enjoyed rough sport with his ball, and his stick. This was *his* time.

Harry, too, was in his own bubble. He was 32, and had recently left his job as a marketing manager with a publishing company. He had a new position to start, on his return to Croydon – with a competitor – but the last few months had been unsettling. And he was no longer *quite* so sure about his partner of six years. Harry was worried that he and Sarah seemed to be growing apart. Sarah had different interests and views on life, and the couple often clashed about silly, trivial things. Even sex – not that sex was a trivial thing. Physically, matters were OK, but it was all becoming a bit routine. And Sarah wanted kids; Harry didn't. But as Sarah often reminded him, at thirty, the clock was ticking. 'I mean,' he thought, 'we have the bloody dog! Do we need anything else?' It was *the* point on which *Harry 2* agreed with his master.

Harry looked across the beach, at the girls sunning themselves on the edge of the soft sand – singly, or in small groups, on their backs, or their fronts – and at others jumping into the cool waves, and screaming with pleasure. How desirable, how delicious, how delightful they were! My God, these French women! Even the girl on the till in the campsite's Superette looked like Bardot! Harry strode purposefully into the waves, so that his boxer shorts were covered by the gently cooling sea. Enough. 'Come on *Harry*, time to go!' Enough? Could a dog ever have too much fun? *Harry 2* delivered a disapproving look, and shook himself furiously, divesting himself of half the ocean in the process. Reluctantly, and sulkily, and carrying his ball, he followed his master back towards the Volvo. '*Why?*' was his only thought.

An old man in a straw boater, his big belly uniformly round and bronzed, was attempting to manoeuvre a large, shark-nosed, bright yellow canoe down a gully on to the beach. He looked at Harry and shook his head. Puzzled, Harry continued towards the waiting car, but a man in uniform blocked his way. The uniform read: '*Police Municipale*'.

The man in uniform addressed Harry, in French. 'Bonjour. Dogs are not allowed on the beach.' Harry understood, and his mouth went dry. 'Pardon, officer,' he said, suddenly aware. 'But I really didn't know. Where are the signs?' The suitably bulky policeman merely shrugged his sturdy shoulders. And continued to eye Harry with both barrels. This was a much larger pimple on the *derriere* of paradise.

The old man in the straw boater grinned: 'He says that dogs are not allowed on the beach!'

'*Merci*, I know what he said,' replied Harry, in passable French, and clearly annoyed. Turning to the policeman, Harry continued: ' I have seen no sign or notice about dogs. How was I supposed to know?'

'It is the law in France. It's about health and safety. Everybody knows,' he said laconically.

'*How?*' continued Harry. 'I knew that some beaches were

banned, but thought that smaller, unpatrolled beaches were OK? Especially if there were no signs,' he added, with a hint of exasperation.

The officer made no response. Harry had a sudden brainwave. 'Tell me, were you *already* here, or did someone on the beach call you?' The policeman swivelled his eyes towards the old chap in the boater, who continued to hover, alongside the evil-snouted yellow canoe.

'Here is a penalty ticket for €100, the standard fine,' said the policeman, with a flat finality. You have 14 days to pay.' He turned nimbly on his heel, leapt quickly into his striped Renault, and sped off.

The old man stood grinning, his boater pushed back on his head. Harry turned to him: 'As for you, you old bastard, that canoe is likely to smash somebody's head in, when you launch it. So much for bloody health and safety. Let's just hope you fucking sink without trace!' And with that, he tore the boater from the bald, wrinkled head, and cast it into the waiting waves.

'*Merde!*' exclaimed the suddenly discomforted walnut figure, commencing a volley of abuse, and throwing up his arms in fury.

'Come on *Harry*, let's go somewhere where we're actually wanted!' *Harry 2* hesitated, then pee'd loudly against the plastic side of the canoe, before bounding into the rear of the Volvo. Harry chuckled 'that's my boy!' and quickly followed, before slamming his door, and handing the fine to Sarah. 'Fucking French!'

Sarah had observed the scene with growing excitement and indignation. She was fuming, quietly, though the urgent motion of her saffron-framed bosom betrayed her agitation. 'Don't worry, my darling, I saw and heard everything!' Sarah reached down, and pressed Harry's damp crotch. Not for the first time that morning, she raised an eyebrow. 'The power of the sea!' she whispered, turning to Harry, in a fusion of query and surprise. 'Tonight, my darling, you may have your every desire...'

THE CHIP SHOP CAPER

Jake and Jane Weatherall have always loved their fish and chip supper. They had bought their fish and chips from the same favourite eaterie – a traditional chip shop, with Victorian glazed tiles, and engraved windows spelling out '*Smith & Sons*' – every Friday night for the last 25 years.

Generally speaking, Jake considered himself to be a very lucky sod. Jane, now 45 years of age, remained a happy spirit – gregarious, fun-loving and full of life. Moreover, whilst a mother – of two daughters – Jane retained a trim, athletic figure. Regular jogging, and twice-weekly tennis with friends contributed to her slim, fresh-faced appearance. If Jane had acquired hints of silver in her dark bob of hair, Jake would not have known; such was the twice-monthly art and mystery conjured by Jane's long-term hairdresser in the village.

And, generally speaking, Jane considered herself a very lucky woman. She loved Jake, and felt loved in return. She *felt* his love. Jake was still pretty trim, and retained a rich surfeit of hair – even if it was now mainly silver in appearance. Rather distinguished, Jane thought. At least as important, Jake was a decent, level-headed, hard-working and thoroughly dependable and *decent* husband. If that were not enough, Jane had a nice, comfortable home – though a little empty since her wonderful daughters – Rachel and Emma – had departed for university.

Jane also enjoyed a variety of interests; mainly sporting interests – including golf, and tennis. And she still loved her Friday evenings; so *different;* so special; and knew that Jake did, too.

Jake, 47, was a manager in a warehouse that stocked and distributed widgets. Jake didn't let that fact interfere with his love of football and golf (partnering his wife). Jane worked in the local library, and had the pleasure – which she prized highly – of speaking with, and helping – perhaps a hundred or so local people every day. It all added colour and substance to her life. She could write her own book about her experiences. Maybe, thought Jane, one day she would.

Today happened to be Friday 13 October, and, as it happened, they – and everyone else – were in the midst of a global Pandemic. Never mind. Life must go on. 'What would you like this evening, dear? Cod and chips, plaice, haddock, or what?' asked Jack, mischievously. He knew very well that Jane always ordered cod; with battered chips. It was her weekly indulgence.

'Think I'll have haddock for a change' said Jane, nonchalantly. Jack expressed surprise, creasing his brow. 'Haddock? he said in amazement. 'Haddock? Really?' 'Only joking,' laughed Jane. 'I'll have cod – of course!' Jack's face relaxed into a smile. All was well with the world, and on track. Because Friday night was fish and chip night. And sex night. Tasty fish and chips, washed down with a bottle of chardonnay, and followed by a good film – say *Notting Hill,* or *Love Actually* – put them both in the mood for a bit of love-making. Such a happy combination made Friday night their special time of the week. Every other day was an anti-climax, so to speak.

'Well, I'll be off then!' Jake muttered, looking at his wife with puppy eyes. Jane kissed him, lingering in the moment, as a token of what was to come. 'Don't be long, darling. Oh, but don't forget your mask!' Jake closed the door; something warm within him was already stirring.

Jake drove to the village – actually grown into a busy town in the 25 years since their marriage – in his trusty, ten-year old Volvo, parking in a favourite spot a short distance from the chippie. It was 6.45, and already growing dark.

Because of the threat of Covid, only three customers were allowed inside the shop at any one time, and a queue of perhaps half a dozen people waited sullenly outside, in the gathering gloom. Jake sidled up to them, bade the small snake of a group 'good evening!' and waited patiently for his turn.

Five or so minutes later, the queue – all men – in front of Jake had hardly moved, and had become restive; muttering and shuffling their feet. At the same time, perhaps another half a dozen guys had joined the snake-like throng, and were noisily expressing their frustration. Jake peered through the large window, into the garishly lit interior. It seemed that one customer was hoovering up the entire supply of fish and chips, and that a new batch would need to be fried. More delay. The customer in question emerged from the shop, his back bent, his arms weighed down with bulging carrier bags, and scurried away with his booty. Narrow, jealous eyes followed him to a waiting car.

The 'lead' customer entered the chippie, to wait his turn for the new batch to fry. Another five minutes, then. Jake was getting nearer to the entrance now, and his nostrils twitched with the smell of frying fish, and malt vinegar.

Another customer entered the shop, as another one – now two – quickly departed. There were only two customers in the chippie, and Jake was free to step inside. The customers behind Jake were becoming increasingly irritated and vocal at the unusual – and to them unacceptable – delay in being served. They included one very harsh, noisy gentleman, of stentorian girth, his florid face apparently smothered and gleaming with grease fat, and his fleshy lips twisted in anger. The unkempt grey hair did not prevent the shop's harsh lights catching a scar – a deep gash – along his forehead. It reminded no-one of Harry Potter.

Another customer left the shop, laden with his steaming supper. It was Jake's turn – opportunity – to enter. As his right foot alighted on the steps of the shop, the last customer to enter the chippie – perhaps overcome by the pervasive smells – began to sneeze uncontrollably. Jake could actually see the cloud of moist droplets shining in the air, like beads of phosphorescence, beneath the arc lights. Jake hesitated on the step. Better not to enter a confined space, with possible infection lurking so near.

'What yo wertin' for!' hollered the large, florid gentleman, his girth bulging from an inadequate leather jacket. 'We aye gor all night!' It was clear to Jake that his hovering on the step made no difference to anyone's waiting time. There were only two staff serving, and they were already serving two customers. Jake peered through the window: there was a sign that read: *Abuse of our staff or other customers will not be tolerated.*' And there was a large fish tank, containing tropical fish, also displaying a sign: '*Do not tap on the glass, as this is distressing our fish.*' Jake smiled; oh, the irony!

Jake pondered. Whether he went in, or stayed out of, the shop, really made no material difference. He tried to explain to the florid gentleman, who was stood some four metres away. But this, too, made no difference. Jake's words fell on deaf ears. 'Get in that fucking shop, you stupid bastard!' he screamed. 'We're not 'ere for our 'elth!' Clearly not, thought Jake. But there were mutters of assent for the florid gentleman from the ranks of the frustrated queue.

'There's really no need for that,' replied Jake, sighing, but annoyed by the vulgar rant. 'I'll go in as soon as I can get served...'

'You'll fucking go in now, or else!' screamed the even more florid man. Jake looked at him; he was indeed bursting with a quite unnecessary and over-the-top fury. Then Jake surveyed the chippie. He still couldn't be served, and was most reluctant to enter the doorway, with infection still lingering within its confines. He turned to the man and shrugged his shoulders, apologetically.

This was too much for Jake's tormentor, who rushed at Jake with quite surprising speed and, grabbing him by the shoulders, tried to manhandle him into the shop. Jake resisted. 'Get off me, you maniac! Sod off!' A moment later, Jake screamed, and fell to the ground. Within seconds, his shirt turned crimson with arterial blood from a stricken heart. Two onlookers quickly grabbed the perpetrator, and wrested a hunting knife from his grasp. Someone called for an ambulance. Someone else called the police.

Fifteen minutes later, there was a firm knock on Jane's front door. She opened the door with a smile, already mouthing, 'Goodness! Wherever have you been?' But it was not Jake.

A Trilogy: I
BETRAYAL

Matt and Mel Barlow have been married for three years. Matt, 32, is a professional accountant; Mel, 29, is a nurse, in a GP's practice. The couple live in a leafy suburb of Newbury. There are no children, and Matt is disinclined to start a family. Matt is proud of his pretty young wife, but remains jealous of her freedom. He himself enjoys a strident social life; but is meticulous in ensuring that his wife observes a correct and strict code of conduct...

Hearing a slight disturbance, Matt awoke just in time for one eye to glimpse a pair of shapely pale thighs heading nimbly towards the bedroom door...

'And where do you think you're going?' he asked, peremptorily.

'Just going to have a quick shower,' replied Melinda, softly.

'And then you'll come back?' he queried, drily. But his words did not seem like a question.

Melinda paused, her large hazel eyes looking at her husband, plaintively, like a captive animal. Matt stared back, unblinking: the short, almost diaphanous, nightie outlined his wife's sculpted breasts and slender figure. Melinda sighed. 'You know, Matt, we have a busy day ahead. There's the weekly shop this morning, and this afternoon we're invited to Wayne and Samantha's wedding anniversary 'do'. And this evening – Saturday night – you always look forward to a Big Mac, and a couple of pints with the lads...'

Still staring at his young wife's body, Matt felt a sensation of firmness invading his loins. His hand moved towards his groin, and confirmed what he already knew.

'It's Saturday. Our time. We can change anything; everything's flexible. Go take that shower, but come back soon.'

Within minutes, Melinda returned to the bedroom. A green towel was knotted around her head, and a large green bath towel wrapped tightly around her bosom. The early morning May sunshine filtered through the bedroom curtains, and glistened on the beads of moisture that still sat on the exposed tops of Melinda's breasts.

'I thought we'd agreed you wouldn't cover yourself like that?' challenged Matt, irritably.

'Matt, I've just come out of the shower! I'm a touch cold...'

'You know we've just had a gas bill?' asked her husband, apparently changing the subject.

Mel's face froze. 'How much is it for?' she asked, a little nervously.

Her husband grinned in Mel's direction. 'It's not too bad, actually. More summer than winter. Just over £200 quid. Do you want me to pay it?'

Mel gulped. 'Of course. There isn't any choice, is there? Only, if I had my own bank account, I could pay it myself, with my own money!'

Matt shook his head, impatiently. 'You know we agreed that I'm best suited to run our financial affairs. Otherwise, what's the point of being a qualified accountant? You don't want to worry your pretty little head about money matters. Anyway, you get a monthly allowance. I think it's pretty generous. All my friends say so... Anyway, the gas bill... you know what that means?'

Mel considered, her face in a deep frown. '£200?' I suppose that means twenty minutes love-making?'

'No suppose about it!' retorted Matt. 'But let's call it what it is: sex. I've set the timer. Let's get on with it!'

'But Matt,' pleaded Melinda with feeling, 'Sainsbury's will be packed...'

'I really don't care about frigging Sainsbury's. Not 'til we've finished. No time like the present – drop that towel, and get into bed!'

Mel obeyed and, with a thin smile, asked: 'So, what position would you like me to do, Matt?'

'Let me count the ways,' answered the husband, rather tartly. 'Twenty minutes gives us loads of scope.'

Twenty-three minutes later, the couple lay prone in bed, silent and separate. Sweat sat heavily on Matt's brow, and he breathed in deep gulps. His exposed, pale torso appeared flushed with recent effort. Mel's head rested calmly on her pillow, the rest of her body wrapped closely in the duvet.

'That was pretty good' said Matt, as if to no-one in particular. 'Just, next time, try and put a bit more oomph into it...'

'I'll try,' replied Melinda, faintly. 'S'ppose I just got a bit tired.'

'Matt,' said Melinda, in a distant, trembling voice.

'Yes?'

'Do we have to do *that*.'

'What?'

'*That*. You know I don't like it.'

'Well, I don't like going to Sainsbury's. Sometimes, we just have to put up with things.'

There was a pause, then Matt added: 'You know, I'm not sure about this afternoon. I know they're friends, but I think Wayne fancies you.'

Melinda laughed, perhaps a tad nervously. 'What on earth makes you think that?'

'I've seen the way he looks at you. His eyes seem to want to undress you. Dirty bugger. Isn't Samantha enough for him? I might go there on my own. You've got all that ironing to do...'

'Oh, no, please Matt – I've hardly been out all week – and it is their anniversary. I promise I'll dress very plainly, and stick to your side…'

'OK, then. If you promise to behave. So while I'm out tonight, what will *you* be up to?' enquired Matt, critically, but with barely perceptible interest.

'I'll watch '*Casualty*' I suppose. And maybe a film on Netflix. Relax, after a busy day.'

'That's OK. I'll give you a couple of calls, just to make sure you're enjoying yourself.'

'There's really no need,' replied Mel, quietly. 'I'll be relaxing at home. No worries.'

'No, I *insist*,' replied Matt. 'Least I can do. OK, then, Sainsbury's awaits. What fun.'

*

That Saturday afternoon, standing perilously close to the suspicious Matt, Melinda merely observed the social graces, and exchanged mild pleasantries with Wayne and Samantha Wentworth. Wayne, an investment banker, and rather corpulent and puffy, is already 'well-oiled', and leers clumsily towards Mel. Great globules of sweat pock-mark his prematurely creased brow, that somewhat overshadows little piggy grey eyes. Already, at the age of 35, thin red veins are evident in Wayne's gorged and bloated cheeks. However, the husband's crisp cream suit, gold Rolex watch, and carefully groomed black hair, flatter and help to redeem an overblown and boorish presence. Samantha, slender, willowy, and elegantly turned-out, is the most gracious host, and consciously overlooks her husband's indelicate manners. Samantha is attractive in an austere sort of way – her main attributes being a liquid natural elegance, and the cascade of rich auburn hair that flows down her slender shoulders.

It is, though, the house that is centre stage: a sparkling,

brand new, pristine, beautifully furnished detached home: and Samantha invites Melinda, glass of champagne in hand, for a personal guided tour. Matt nods his approval, and the pair sally forth on their venture...

With the 'girls' departure, Wayne mused on seeking his friend's advice on his impending divorce...on the grounds of what...boredom? This anniversary celebration had been all his wife's stupid idea. Some nonsense about re-energising their marriage. Though he couldn't bear the idea of giving up half of his hard-earned wealth to his wife, who had contributed...what, exactly, to the marriage? But, on reflection, since this *was* their anniversary, even Wayne had thought the moment inauspicious to discuss his plans with Matt. Especially as he had not yet broached the subject even to his wife.

Besides, Wayne had an inkling that all may not be exactly harmonious in the Matt-Mel camp. And he had urgent designs upon the nubile Mrs Barlow. He even fancied that, as a close friend – and a *wealthy* close friend – he would be best placed – indeed, in pole position – to offer solace to the marvellous Melinda. A favourite subject with both men – money – was overlooked, since Matt not only detested the investment banking world – all those guys in braces, shouting and screaming at computer screens – but also detested the fact that Wayne earned four times his own salary. So, instead, these august silver-backs turned to their default option, and engaged in earnest sparring on the universal male fixation of football...and... football. They were both self-acknowledged experts, and would brook no opinion other than their own.

'What a lovely new home you have!' exclaimed Melinda. 'So spacious, light and airy! I do envy you and Wayne...what a super couple!'

'Easy on!' laughed Sam. 'It is our seventh anniversary, so we're rather old hands, now. And, to tell the truth, it's not all been a bed of roses…or plain sailing…Maybe the house, all this luxury, is a substitute for something that's lacking. Like sex. You must tell me what it feels like,' she joked, bitterly. 'I'm only 31! Christ, what's wrong with me? I think I have all the right bits and pieces. You know, I sometimes think I've made the wrong choices. And wish that my life had gone in a different direction…'

Samantha closed the bedroom door, as a sign that she wished to exchange confidences. 'Did I ever mention about Wayne and his Secretary…?'

'No!' whispered Melinda, conspiratorially; 'do tell…'

'Well, she wasn't the first, and I daresay she won't be the last,' Samantha began. 'A few baubles, and they just seem to fall into bed…There was a time when Wayne played a lot of rugby. Now he just seems to play a lot of women!'

The confession over, Mel felt emboldened to enquire further, regarding Wayne's predilections. 'Sam, can I ask you a personal question? Don't answer it, if it makes you feel uncomfortable…'

'Fire away!' answered Samantha. 'Really, anything!'

'Well,' began Mel, hesitantly. 'Do you think Wayne fancies me? Only Matt thinks he does, and I don't want to be the cause of any problem, or misunderstanding.'

'Darling, I'm afraid that Wayne doesn't let me into his confidence, where the fairer sex is concerned. That said, he'd be a fool *not* to fancy you. He does seem to like his women petite, dark and buxom. Rather like you, in fact. To be frank, I can't think of any fucker in his right mind who *wouldn't* fancy you. And quite a few non-fuckers, too, if you get my drift…'

'Thanks,' said Mel, flushing slightly. And then added: 'So why…?'

'Why did he marry me?' Sam shrugged her shoulders. 'I was young, and passable, I suppose. And I'm an only child' – Sam laughed – 'and my parents owned a chain of hotels in the South West. My parents actually gifted us £250k to help get us going.

And remember, when we met, Wayne wasn't much more than the errand boy at the bank.'

Samantha felt empowered to ask Mel about her own marriage. 'You know, you guys seem so well suited. Matt's a handsome, caring husband. Hardly lets you out of his sight. As for you, Mel...you know, I've always thought you the best looking, as well as nicest, friend I have.'

Mel laughed, shaking her head. And then: 'So why don't I feel happy?' Suddenly, her big eyes filled with tears.

'Out with it!' demanded Samantha. Mel ventured, as delicately as she could, to suggest the causes of her unhappiness.

'No – seriously? *Seriously*! If he's not treating you right, he should give you up to somebody who can! What you're suggesting is abuse. And control. I can tell you now, it certainly ain't love. What a bastard! I had no idea! You don't have to put up with it. Girl, you have *class*! Such a pretty face, framed by that bob of hair. And perfect little snub nose. And boobs to die for! Can I ask *you* something personal?'

Mel nodded, and smiled. Samantha coughed, and nodded in the direction of Mel's breasts, before simpering: 'Are they for real?'

Melinda fell about on the bed, giggling, her tears spilling on the sheets. Then she looked seriously at the waiting Samantha, and unbuttoned her blouse. 'Please do have a feel...'

*

A week or two later, and Matt returned home rather later than usual from his favourite haunt, *The Fox and Grapes*. For once, Matt had failed to phone home that evening to check on Mel. Since it was half-past midnight, Mel had retired to bed, but was finding it hard to sleep. Matt entered the bedroom noisily, clumsily.

'Are you alright, Matt?' she asked, anxiously.

'Course I'm bloody alright. Why shouldn't I be?' he demanded.

Mel looked at her dishevelled husband, who appeared to have a slight smudge of lipstick on his cheek.

'Night out with the lads?' she enquired, suddenly interested.

'Yep, with Charlie and Ben. And a few laddesses!'

'Laddesses? How come?'

'Well, we three were just chatting, when in barged a hen party, dressed as St Trinians. After making a big splash, they settled down with us, and we offered to get them a few drinks.'

'Why, how many of them were there?'

'Let's see – yes, there were twelve tits in all, so that makes six. Bloody accountant's training!'

'And what happened next?' asked Mel, looking accusingly at the smudge.

'Happened? Fuck all happened!'

'You appear to have lipstick on your cheek!' Mel persisted.

Matt rubbed at his cheek, then peered at his hand. 'Oh, yeah, we had a few drinks, and one thing led to another. We were outnumbered. Vicky and Ronnie came on to me…I fought them off pretty gallantly, I think…'

'Matt, *I* think you're a bit the worse for wear, and smell like a brew-house. How about a shower? Then come to bed. We'll talk about it after a good night's sleep.'

'Shower? Sleep! Listen to *her*! Did I tell you about the lecky bill? 250 smackers! Are they taking the piss, or are you leaving that immersion heater on all day? Anyway, you know what that means…Nearly half an hours worth! Off with 'em, sweetheart!'

'I'm not your sweetheart tonight! Go and find fucking Ronnie!'

Mike blundered into bed, almost crushing his wife. Her frantic cries of hurt and anguish fell on deaf ears.

Something in Mel died that night.

*

A few weeks later, Samantha inadvertently picked up an incautious 'phone message from a local Estate Agent, regarding a new valuation of their house – the home they had bought barely nine months before! Understandably upset, Sam confronted a sheepish Wayne, who blustered that he needed a valuation, for possible capital gains tax purposes. Sam sensed this was a mere yarn, meant to deliver false comfort.

For Samantha, it was the final, bitter straw. Her marriage was built on crumbling foundations – on betrayal, lies and deceit. And, she knew, she would soon be facing the final humiliation – of rejection by a philandering husband. She could see the future clearly now. She must chart her own course, and seize her own opportunity for happiness.

*

A month or so later, in mid-August, Melinda is seen exiting a black cab at Newbury rail station. She is enveloped in sunshine, smiling broadly, and, despite the stilettos, hurries up the stone steps to Platform 4. There is an aura surrounding Mel this morning, and other passengers, men and women, weave sideways to allow her free passage. With a yelp of joy she races towards a waiting woman, a woman with a shock of auburn tresses, and dressed elegantly in pastel colours. 'Good morning, Mrs Wentworth! Fancy meeting you here!' Mel hugs her, sobbing gently. 'Everything's fine, Mrs Barlow!' assures her companion. 'The hotel's booked, and we leave first thing tomorrow morning from Heathrow…Palma, here we come! And, to get the ball – or should I say balls – rolling – I've instructed my solicitor to file for divorce…on the grounds' (she laughed) 'of everything, really. And don't worry, I've emptied the bank account. I've got bags of cash!'

Mel remembers, with a frown of anxiety: 'Just before I left, we got an enormous water bill in the post…My doing, I'm afraid. Ever since Matt's St Trinians' episode, I've been leaving all the taps running every Saturday night…Matt will be livid!' Both women dissolved into a fit of giggles.

'He'll be even more livid,' said Sam, her face close to Mel's, 'when he realises he'll have to screw himself!'

Melinda's wide eyes, still moist in joy and greeting, looked earnestly into the face of Samantha; seeking re-assurance, and finding it. Mel stood on tip-toe, held Sam's face in her hands, and kissed her passionately.

Minutes later, the train arrived on schedule, screeching to a halt. Sam opened the door to the First Class carriage, inviting Mel inside. Seeing the panting train and open door, Mel shivered with the shock of finality.

Starting suddenly, she asked: 'But what about the boys?'

'What about them?' answered Samantha, archly. They both laughed: excited, happy – and free.

A Triology: II
ROSE TINTED

As mean, as miserable, as Richard Rose was with money – Richard himself would have used the terms 'careful', and 'prudent' – his wife, Rose, was warm and generous – as warm and generous as a duck-down-filled duvet.

Richard and Rose had been married, now, for twenty-one years. They were comfortably off – Richard was a middle-ranking civil servant in the Home Office; Rose, a librarian in the nearby town's central library. The couple lived quietly, in a rambling old Grade 2 listed, 17th century cottage in Sussex. There were no children; a source of no little regret to Rose Rose.

Richard had few hobbies or interests other than safeguarding, and growing, the family fortune – that is, *his* fortune. He had, from earliest times, been a saver and, since early adulthood, a serious, and serial, investor. Indeed, Richard discovered that he had a talent for investing, and spent hours each week poring over the financial press, company reports, and viewing financial TV channels and websites. The stockmarket held no fears for, and no secrets from, Richard Rose. So successful was Richard at generating and accumulating wealth that the couple's net worth, and income, far exceeded what might have been expected from a middling civil servant. But this accumulation of wealth was a kind of cerebral game to Richard, appearing to have no end but itself. The largesse funded no charities, no expensive hobbies, and appeared to have no purpose into the future. At 45 and 43 years of age, the Rose's had plenty of future left, reasoned Richard: plenty of time to think about legacies, and other innovative ways of spreading excess wealth beyond the date of their demise.

Rose, on the other hand, was as generous as Richard was parsimonious. She was a gifted amateur artist – mainly painting landscapes, in watercolours – and a keen photographer. The two interests were complementary, and Rose enjoyed travelling to new sites, and exploring exciting topography: an atmospheric churchyard in a rustic village; a sunrise over a bay – perhaps the Seven Sisters, or Bexhill-on-Sea; or a mist weaving through an ancient woodland. But Rose also took a keen interest in her charitable activities – mainly connected with nature, and animal welfare. Although she only earned around £25k per year, for many years now Rose had earmarked 10% of her earnings for charitable good deeds.

Frankly, Richard – and he had no hesitation in articulating his views to his wife – thought charitable giving a waste of time. Richard earned £45k per year, and was rather irritated that anyone earned more. This upright man had done his research, and he knew that it was not uncommon for the senior staff of larger charities to earn six figure salaries. 'What's charitable about that!' he would exclaim, with brusque finality. Rose gently protested that large, complex charities required expert, experienced management. But Richard was unrepentant. His organisation – the Home Office – employed 10,000 staff. Only a handful earned more than £100k. 'You do surprise me...' commented Rose, rather enigmatically. The inference didn't escape her husband's shrewd attention.

Rose would not have described herself as happy. On the other hand, she did not feel *unhappy*. She must be satisfied with her lot: she had a decent lifestyle, and a decent, undemanding husband, who generally left her to her own devices. She felt in

Goldilocks country: not too hot; not too cold. Luke warm and OK. Well, that's life, brother. Let's just get on with it.

One fine morning in late April, Richard announced that he intended to take up golf. 'But you've never shown any inclination to take up *any* sport!' replied his wife, rather surprised. 'Well, it's time I did,' said Richard, flatly. 'None of us is getting any younger, and the exercise will do me good. Besides, the peace and calm will allow me to ponder investment decisions. It's my birthday next week,' Ronald continued, 'could you possibly get me a set of golf clubs, and a quality bag?'

'Of course,' smiled Rose. 'It will be a pleasure. But where will you play?' she asked.

'I was thinking of joining St Dunstan's. It's reputed to be a friendly Club, and the fees are reasonable. And it's only seven miles away.'

'Well, that's settled then,' said Rose. 'Always good to take up a new hobby!'

A week later, a new set of golf clubs duly appeared, wrapped in red and gold greeting paper. Richard was chuffed, and began pushing golf balls around the lawn, with his new putter. Richard expressed himself delighted with his present, pecked Rose on the cheek, and made preparations to begin his new golf career.

From that day on, Richard would disappear every Saturday afternoon, to practice his new hobby. The new diversion suited Rose, in all honesty. She felt free to pick up her paintbrush, or look through her photos, in order to get ideas for the next project. But Friday 13 July – a day she would never forget – changed that sunny equilibrium to a more agitated and uncertain state of being.

Richard had been late for work that morning – possibly due to inconveniencing his wife during the night – and, in his hurry, had forgotten his mobile phone: an omission that had never occurred before. Mid-afternoon, Rose heard the phone's ringtone. Thinking that the call may be important, in Richard's absence Rose looked for missed messages. The caller had sent a text: 'See you tomorrow – same time xxx.' Odd, thought Rose. The sender – called Charlie – must have been referring to the golf session. But why the kisses? She had thought Richard's golf partner was a man. Even if Richard embarked on those 18 holes with a female partner, three kisses seemed a bit over-the-top. Rose was a loyal, trusting wife, but the mystery – and uncertainty – continued to gnaw at her for the rest of that day.

In fact, Richard returned home earlier than usual that afternoon, and in a state of some agitation. 'Have you seen my phone, Rose? Ah, yes, there it is!' Richard hastily checked it, then put it in his pocket. The rest of the evening passed quietly. Rose decided not to mention the text. She thought Richard might raise the subject; but he didn't. Instead, they watched the usual anodyne mix of news, cooking and antique-based shows, and some gentle comedy, before turning in. Unusually, these days, Richard – similarly to the night before – pestered Rose for sex as soon as they had undressed for bed. Unusually, too, he was insistent – and persistent. 'I can't remember him doing *that* before,' she thought to herself. And it was after midnight when, accompanied by various oaths, Richard climaxed in his wife. Rose was exhausted; but not satisfied. Thank God it was over. 'I love you, Rose,' Richard said, before turning over, heavily; irritatingly. A few minutes later, Richard was snoring, loudly. Rose couldn't sleep; though her body ached, her mind was racing. Today's events posed an awkward challenge. At last, at long last, Rose hatched a plan for the morrow.

On Saturday, on the dot of 2.00pm, Richard picked up his car keys, and his golf clubs, and bid his wife 'bye!' 'Should be home for 6.30, or thereabouts,' he added, reassuringly. 'OK, have a good time. Oh, just wandering, who's your lucky partner today? I mean, you could stay for a drink at the 19th hole, if you wanted…' 'Charlie Smith', said Richard. 'First class guy. Good idea about that drink…Maybe 7.00ish, then – but you know I always look forward to supper. Bye, then!'

Rose watched him go; jauntily. Ten minutes later, Rose got into her own car, and headed in the same direction. She arrived at the golf club car park, and parked the car in a discreet, shaded corner. Looking out, Rose could see Richard's Volvo Estate, neatly parked. But wait: weren't those his golf clubs, still sitting in the rear of the car? Odd. Rose stepped out of her car, to take a closer look. There was no sign of Richard; but his clubs were definitely there. Perhaps he would return to collect them – maybe he'd gone for a chat, or popped to the loo. Rose decided to wait a while, and returned to her Fiesta.

Half an hour went by – slowly. No sign of Richard. Perhaps he – and Charlie? – had gone straight to the 19th hole, for that friendly drink? An hour passed. This was ridiculous. Rose walked straight into the Clubhouse Reception, and asked after her husband. The smart young woman on the reception desk smiled brightly at Rose, then looked confused. '*You are Mrs Rose?* Yes, Mr Rose is here…somewhere. Is he not out on the course? No? Let me see…I don't think I can help you…Mrs Rose.' The girl delivered an enigmatic smile. 'You might want to enquire at The Lodge…some members book rooms for stay-overs and so on… The Lodge is only a short walk away – the building with the flag flying from the roof…' Rose thanked the smart young thing, and walked briskly to The Lodge.

Another smart young thing on Reception. Similar white blouse, and two-piece suit. 'Mrs Rose?' The smart young thing's eyes widened. 'I'm afraid I can't give details of our guests. This is a Private Club. It's confidential information. If there's an emergency or something, you'll need to contact the emergency services.' She smiled broadly, with an air of finality – displaying her perfect teeth – and a little too much cleavage, Rose thought, testily.

What to do? Go bloody home, Rose mused, and start supper? Hell, no! She would wait. And wait. Eventually, Richard's car would call out to him, would reveal what needed revealing. Sure enough, just after 6.30pm, a *very* smart lady materialised from the double-fronted doors of The Lodge, followed by an earnest Richard. Richard looked around, perhaps anxiously, before accompanying the lady to a Mercedes sports. He held – Charlie's – head, and kissed her on the mouth. The moment was caught perfectly by Rose's 300mm lens. A few warm words of farewell, and the slim, smart, dark-haired woman was gone. Richard adjusted his tie, smiled smugly to himself, and strode to the waiting Volvo.

Rose's Fiesta was well hidden, behind luxuriant vegetation. The vegetation had parted for long enough for Rose to take that long lens shot of the happy couple. Rose had seen enough to convince her of some devious, duplicitous – at least – behaviour. Though Richard departed in some haste, Rose knew that her preferred back-routes would bring her home several minutes before her husband.

'Charlie, eh?' thought Rose. 'But what now?' Such a shock. 'What have *I* done?' Rose asked herself, bitterly. 'What have I *ever* done? To deserve this? But I need a plan!' She had no evidence that would stand up in court. 'Bet his bloody dick would stand up in court!' she grimaced. When Richard appeared, a full five minutes after Rose, he was full of *bonhomie*; cheerful and playful. Rose was peeling potatoes. 'Good round of golf, Richard?' she enquired. 'Bloody terrific. You know, I've lowered my handicap. Charlie is such a help. All to do with my grip, apparently, and my swing… And all that healthy exercise… I'm feeling famished, now. What's for supper?'

'I thought steak and chips would be good. It *is* Saturday evening. And a decent bottle of claret.'

'Excellent!' declared Richard. 'This Charlie must be quite

a guy,' enquired Rose. 'I'd love to meet him. How did you two meet?'

'It's a long story,' shrugged Richard. 'Well, we have all evening,' Rose suggested, shrugging her own shoulders. 'Nothing much on telly...'

'Well, we met at my office. He's a lawyer who specialises in migration. Just happened to mention an interest in golf – a hobby I was thinking of taking up. It all just clicked, really.'

'A local guy, is he?' continued Rose.

'Yes, he lives near Hastings, I think. He's married, with a teenage son.'

'About our age, is he?' Rose suggested.

'I'd say so,' hesitated Richard. He laughed: 'maybe a bit younger. Hard to tell with us grizzled old men...'

'Maybe invite him to dinner one evening?' Rose added, brightly.

'Maybe' shrugged Richard. 'But I wouldn't describe him as a bosom buddy. Just a casual golf partner.'

'Not a *bosom* buddy?' repeated Rose.

Richard suddenly felt uncomfortable. Where was all this going? 'Tell you what, shall I fix us a drink? The sun's definitely sunk over the yard arm!'

Rose assented. She had completed her interrogation. For now. Suddenly, *Macbeth* entered her mind. Her husband was so deep in the proverbial that, in no time at all, he would drown in his own duplicity. Richard might think he was being clever; but he was just digging a bigger slime-pit...

*

A whole week later, at 2.00pm precisely, Richard departed, golf clubs in hand, for a rendezvous with his new hobby. Ostensibly, that was golf. But, thought his wife, the new hobby was Charlie.

In truth, Richard's steps as he shut the front door were not so jaunty as hitherto; he felt a touch anxious; a little uneasy. But, he thought, he must be imagining things. What could Rose possibly know? What suspicion could there possibly be?

Richard reflected on his life. He had been married – of course, there'd been ups and downs – for more than 20 years. He was not unhappy but, after so long a time, not seriously *happy*, either. He was 45 years old; and had met the love of his life. Charlie – for the first time in many years – made him feel special – amazing. Richard reckoned he was due a final flourish from this shitty life. And Charlie represented quite some flourish! No longer did he feel like a boring, middle-aged guy with his life on hold. No; he felt like a teenager again. Alive. Vibrant. In love with life.

Was he – Richard – *really* under suspicion, or, in his exalted state of being, was his imagination running wild? He had been so careful. He'd even ramped up his sex life with Rose, to make her feel special again. He hoped she was suitably grateful. It was strangely thrilling screwing two women within hours of one another. And practically everything Richard had told Rose about Charlie had been true – apart from the sex – that is, gender. And of course the sex itself. Charlie was indeed a lawyer who specialized in migration issues – particularly claims for asylum – and at first Richard had found her to be a pain – if a particularly attractive pain – in the ass. But he'd invited her out for a coffee – and, perhaps surprisingly – she'd accepted. And things had developed from there; delightfully easily, smoothly; excitingly.

Richard had never met anyone like Charlie. She was beautiful, intelligent, witty, fun. And deliriously adventurous in bed. Charlie was, Richard told himself, the love of his life. Charlie meant more to him than anyone he'd ever met, and anything – well, almost anything – that he possessed. But things were complicated: not only was Charlie married – to Chris –

but they had a fourteen-year-old son, Sean. Not a good time for disruption, and the breaking up of the family home.

No matter, thought Richard. While they waited for young Sean to grow up and bugger off to University, *he* could have his cake, and eat it. Or should that be, eat his cake, and still have it?

Richard's Volvo turned into the entrance to St Dunstan's Golf Club. There was Charlie's Mercedes, with the beautiful, long-haired brunette inside. Time for more cake. And another flourish.

*

A jubilant Richard arrived home at 6.30pm, on the dot. Sweet smells wafted from the kitchen. Scents of chilli con carne. Nice with a bottle of shiraz. Richard went to kiss his wife but, though she smiled, she turned her face so that his lips brushed her cheek. 'Telly looks interesting tonight,' Rose said. 'A charity extravaganza. Starts at 7.30.' 'Charity again? What's it in aid of, this time?' Richard groaned. 'When will it ever end?' 'Nonsense!' Rose replied. 'It's in aid of vulnerable young children. I'm determined to do my bit, this time!' Rose smiled inside. 'Tonight is payback time, Dick, you old bugger!' (Richard hated being called 'Dick', but Rose thought it suddenly appropriate).

The 'Show' began, with glittering celebrity hosts recounting moving stories of illness, poverty, courage in adversity, and heart-warming, inspirational tales of triumph and success. 'Please dig deep! Every pound makes a difference!' beamed the household name, with his famous tanned smile. There was the usual blend of popular singers, comedians, various 'athons' to twang the heart strings, and little cameo performances to season the sometimes distressing, unpalatable real-life stories. Every fifteen minutes or so, an electronic scoreboard provided a glittering running total of the donations raised so far.

Rose got to work with her laptop, looking determined and earnest. In just ten minutes, it was done. Mission accomplished! 'That's me done!' exclaimed Rose, to her own evident satisfaction. 'How much have you parted with?' asked Richard, with clear disdain. 'Two-fifty,' Rose replied, simply. 'Two hundred and fifty quid! Waste of bloody money!' Richard spat out, with some finality.

At that moment, the elaborately coiffed, apparently embalmed, Steinway tooth'd celebrity presenter performed a St Vitus jig, and bellowed, excitedly: 'I'm delighted to announce that a private donor has donated two hundred and fifty thousand pounds to the Appeal! Thank you SO MUCH! Absolutely fantastic!'

'What a bloody fool!' Richard shouted at the screen. 'More money than bloody sense!' He seemed personally affronted that anyone – *anyone* – could have been so utterly stupid.

Suddenly, Rose beamed at her husband. 'And *I'm* delighted to announce that it was me, Richard. The donor, that is. Or rather, *you*. It's all come from your account!'

The blood drained from Richard's face, and his features became contorted. 'You must be fucking joking!' he gasped. 'No. Deadly serious!' Rose confirmed, helpfully. 'You mad bitch!' Richard screamed. Rose ignored the insult. 'Well, that's my job done. How exciting! And all that good work, *noble* work, you're funding! The local press will soon be round to congratulate you, and hear your story. Great! I think it's bed time!'

'But *why*?' Richard yelled, at his departing wife. That £250 grand had been ear-marked as a deposit on a house for him and Charlie – to start their new life. Now gone; all gone. When, after three or four *very* stiff drinks, Richard wearily climbed the stairs to his bedroom, he was confronted by a full-size photo pinned to the bedroom door: the image showing him in passionate embrace with Charlie.

Suddenly, all was clear: Richard groaned, tripped on the last stair, and collapsed heavily to the floor. In a final, fatal flourish.

A Triology: III
GOLD RUSH

He felt a hand, gently caressing his back. There was a pause. Then, her fingers began stroking the cheeks of his buttocks, and the soft skin between his cheeks. He shuddered, involuntarily. Vanessa's fingers slipped across his body, and surrounded his taut manhood.

Vanessa smiled, and looked her husband full in the face. '*Monsieur, you like?*' Ryan nodded. 'Yes'.

'And what do you fancy, today?' Ryan rolled on to his back, and viewed his penis with some satisfaction. 'You know,' he added, tersely.

Vanessa bestrode her husband, pushing his penis inside her, and began to rise and fall – slowly, rhythmically. She took her husband's hands, and placed them on her breasts. 'Is that OK?' she asked, soothingly. 'It's just fine,' replied Ryan. 'Just get on with it!'

Vanessa brought all her experience to bear in pleasing and pleasuring her husband. Ryan looked at his wife with eyes that seemed to be searching her; boring into her. The husband had leisure and space to examine his wife's physiognomy in exacting detail. She was still young – 27 – and pretty, with regular features, pure porcelain skin, and a shock of auburn curls. Her figure remained taut, supple; and her ample breasts shapely and pert, noted Ryan, approvingly.

Vanessa's movements became more urgent, more frantic. This was the first love-making they had experienced in more than a month. Then, as now, the sex had been initiated by Vanessa. She wanted it to be good; perfect, in fact. Memorable – for both of them. After around ten minutes, she felt Ryan come in her. He emitted a barely perceptible groan.

Vanessa rolled away, and hugged her husband, before licking her fingers, appreciatively. 'You like, sir?' 'Yes, it was nice. What does that taste like?'

Vanessa shrugged. 'It tastes like cum. We really need to do this more often. It feels so good!'

The husband made no answer. 'I think I'll jump in the shower,' he said, absently. 'I'm a bit sweaty.'

Vanessa remained on the bed, flushed and perspiring. She took a long look at her husband's semen, stretching it between her supple fingers. There was, literally, loads – probably enough to fertilise a million women; it looked fresh, healthy; strangely luminous, in the early morning sunshine.

Suddenly, Vanessa began to sob; gently at first, and then more violently; she hid her contorted face beneath the sheets. *Nice. It was fucking nice!* Why was her husband of five years, her childhood sweetheart, so cold, so unconcerned, so disinterested in his young, willing wife? His still *very* attractive wife? This behaviour – this lack of engagement, this *absence* – had been going on for a year or so, now. It was all such an effort for Vanessa; she was so willing to please, but felt unappreciated, un-valued; unloved.

Why? For God's sake, *why?* Ryan had pursued Vanessa eagerly, relentlessly, when they had first met at college, at the age of 16 – Ryan was 17. When they started dating, he quickly began to pressure Vanessa for sex. But Vanessa resisted – she wanted to be sure – sure that Ryan – her first boyfriend – was 'the one.' But Ryan was handsome, funny, clever. And fastidiously well-dressed, and immaculately groomed. What was not to like – or love? The couple became engaged when Vanessa was 18, Ryan 19, and Vanessa 'lost' her virginity that very day. She loved it; nothing was 'lost' – everything felt gained; a shared, orgasmic experience. They were naturals; it was like fish returning to the sea – their true element.

They had lain on their backs, afterwards, admiring their taut young bodies. 'Are you sure you've never done this before?' asked Ryan, rhetorically. 'Oh, quite sure!' replied Vanessa, kissing him. 'My darling, it's all for you!' There was a pause, then Vanessa reflected: 'And you?' Ryan hesitated. 'I'm not sure it really counts – you were my first real girlfriend – but, on my 16th birthday – before we'd met – my father paid for me to see a woman…' 'You mean a *prostitute*?' Ryan shifted uneasily: 'Well, a girl from an escort agency. She was 22. It really didn't mean anything.' 'But Ryan, that's terrible! And you went through with it!' 'As I said, it was before we met.' Vanessa was shocked; in fact, horrified. She said nothing more. There may not have been anything to forgive; but she would not forget.

Vanessa's mother – Sheila – had impressed upon her daughter – well, from the age of 14 – that the ways to a man's heart were merely two-fold: cunt and cooking. Vanessa seemed a natural at the sex route to Ryan's heart and, in their early married life, Ryan just couldn't get enough. Vanessa also became an accomplished cook. As newly-weds, the couple would sit down each evening, to culinary delights from all over the world – a feast of Bolognese, or risotto, or a roast, or casserole, or curry, or coq au vin. The coq would be followed, naturally enough, with lots of…

The couple were married when Ryan was 23, and Vanessa, 22; the wedding was all fanfare, trumpets and general approbation, from parents, family and friends. It was a splendid, blissful beginning. Ryan had recently qualified as a solicitor, having passed his final law exams; while Vanessa had started work in a car showroom. And the couple had their first house – a modern, if modest, semi, in a suburban setting – number 25, Richmond Avenue, Newbury. All seemed set fair – for a happy, fulsome, blossoming, married life.

While Ryan settled into the steady, if unexciting, world of selling houses – he was a conveyancing solicitor – and fulfilling people's dreams – Vanessa immersed herself in the exciting world of shiny new cars – and fulfilling people's dreams. Vanessa excelled in her work. And she dressed to impress. She was eye-catchingly pretty and immaculately presented; a picture of sophisticated beauty. While wives drooled over design, colour-schemes, interiors and dashboards – and fretted 'can we really afford this?' their menfolk drooled over Vanessa's own suave smile and shapely lines. And Vanessa's product knowledge – her in-depth intelligence on every model, every marque, every individual vehicle – was unsurpassed. She was, indeed, the complete package, subduing every concern, every caveat, in a welter of smiles, facts and re-assurance. Husbands were seduced, and wives subdued. Everyone was happy. Vanessa sold dreams – and made them reality.

Last year she had been 'Salesman of the Year' – the irony was not lost on her – and had been rewarded with an all-expenses holiday for two to Tenerife. Vanessa had felt free and uninhibited, and delightfully sexy: she would cavort topless – crying and whooping – in the surf on Playa Blanca beach every afternoon. Vanessa was deliciously aware that a hundred hungry eyes – and a few surreptitious long lenses – were trained on her shapely figure. A few years before, she would have been too embarrassed to have braced her naked body – in public – against the tingling spray. Now, she didn't give a damn. Ryan observed the scene with smug satisfaction. Their apartment was a mere 200 metres from the beach. Ryan knew that, in an hour's time, he would be licking that salt spray from his wife's all too-tempting flesh.

Vanessa would cavort, too, in the night-time – enjoying wild, frenzied sex with her equally uninhibited young husband. Sadly, surprisingly, that holiday's rampant sex was the last she could remember with real nostalgia, real regret. There had been very little genuinely spontaneous, genuinely pleasurable coupling, since then. Just *why* was a complete mystery.

Just what was going on in Ryan's life? There were no obvious clues. Another woman was the obvious candidate, but her husband had hardly mentioned anyone by name, even in passing; even inadvertently. Well, maybe he wouldn't, would he? Ryan was a careful, meticulous person. There would be no lipstick on *his* collar, or steamy texts on his mobile phone. And there were no obvious changes in her husband's behaviour: no spring in his step, no careful – or more careful – dressing; no changes in his habits, or in his conversation; no new hobbies or interests, that might disguise an illicit affair.

Even so, Vanessa was determined to leave no stone unturned. *Something* was amiss, surely? Unless it was her? Unless Ryan had fallen out of love with her – or her body? Vanessa undressed, and looked at herself in the full-length bedroom mirror. She saw nothing to displease her. A rather strikingly pretty young woman stared back at her, with those large, grey-blue eyes. Vanessa lifted her breasts, then let them fall. The action made her laugh. Still bouncy; still a massive turn-on for any man who was even vaguely alive. She began to feel aroused, and put a hand casually between her legs. Fuck it! Why ever not?

The experience re-inforced Vanessa's view that she was still desirable. In addition, two or three guys at work – was it so obvious that she was unhappy? – had recently made passes at her. She had brushed them off with a laugh. Chris was good looking, but young – and brash. No doubt she would be another notch on his bed-post. Mark – maybe 35 – was steady, and earnest; and separated. It might quickly become serious – from his point of view. Too complicated. Then there was young Ryan – another Ryan. Could she stand that after-shave and that mop of dyed blonde hair bobbing up and down on her, in that secret corner in the Parts Department? She was a married woman, she had told them all; Vanessa's tone, if a little patronising, also carried a hint of sympathy. She was not above being admired, in these circumstances; and the time may come when she might not laugh away a genuinely attractive man. A girl needed to feel loved; to feel *wanted*. But that time could be held in abeyance: Vanessa's priority must be to get to the root of her and her husband's problem.

When Ryan was away – and, frustratingly, he was not away from the house, apart from work, at all frequently – Vanessa would examine his 'gadgets'. Ryan's iPhone; his tablet; his two laptops – one personal, the other his mobile office computer. Vanessa conducted a thorough and forensic search: contact numbers, phone calls, texts, e-mails, Internet history, social media activity – she explored every possibility. But she found nothing suspicious – except, that is, to frequent visits to porn sites. What was the bloody point, she thought, when he had a real, living, willing wife, waiting upstairs? Whilst Vanessa viewed this discovery with irritation, at least this porn fixation proved that her husband had not entirely given up on sex – and was still in possession of his libido and sex drive.

There was one final possibility. Ryan always went out with friends – Dick and Lance – on Friday evenings; they had remained firm friends from College days. The friends frequented a few favourite pubs in the vicinity. These weekly sessions had become a ritual over the years, observed with almost religious intensity; the get-togethers rarely ever missed. It happened to be a Friday, today. 'So where is it tonight, Ryan? What's the lucky pub?' Vanessa asked, over their steak and chips dinner. '*The Swan*' replied her husband, without hesitation. 'We haven't been there for a while. Good pint of beer.' 'What time will you be back? I was just thinking about an early night?' 'Oh, don't stay up for me. I should be back before 12.' So, thought Vanessa, no chance of sex there, then. Maybe he's turned gay, she laughed to herself, and is screwing Dick, or Lance. Or maybe both!

Ryan bid his wife goodbye, and set off in his Audi Estate, at 7.30 precisely. Vanessa watched him leave, and checked her watch. She, too, would depart – for the same destination – in half an hour or so. She was not sure what story she would make up, on encountering her husband. But did she need a reason, still less an excuse? The couple lived on a quite recent housing development a few miles outside Newbury; she knew *The Swan* – a snug little 18th Century hideaway, a mere five miles – maybe 20 minutes – away.

On the journey, a sense of nausea overcame Vanessa. What was she doing, and why? What was she hoping – or fearing – to discover? Her legs trembled as she parked her much-loved Audi tt, and walked towards the winking, welcoming inn. Inside, there were just a smattering of customers; it was, after all, not quite 8.00pm. But a few seconds anxiously scanning the softly lit rooms was enough to convince Vanessa that Ryan and his party were not present.

Vanessa smiled at the bored looking barmaid in her white t-shirt and jeans. Shoulder length blonde hair; slim, supple figure. She wondered if *she* was Ryan's type? Her husband was a regular here; they were bound to know him. 'Hi! I'm just looking for my husband, Ryan. Have you seen him tonight?' The barmaid smiled back uncertainly. 'Ryan? Oh, of course. No – haven't seen him tonight – not yet anyway.' Vanessa shrugged. 'Anywhere else he could be?' 'No – I'd have seen him if he was here. Always buys me a drink. Can I get you one – while you're waiting?' Vanessa absorbed the intelligence, and ordered a glass of chardonnay.

Vanessa retired to a dimly lit corner table, and sipped her

wine until around 9 o'clock. No sign of Ryan. She thought of briefing the barmaid – 'tell him I popped in' – but thought better of it. She wasn't sure she could trust the absent-looking Debbie; and had no wish to bring a smirk to her face. Maybe *she* was screwing her husband? Surely, somebody was?

Vanessa returned home – to a brightly lit, but empty house, and poured herself a stiff gin and tonic. The puzzle grew ever more puzzling. She decided to call her husband. His phone was switched off; answerphone, only. Nothing for it; she would watch TV, and await her husband's return.

At midnight, Vanessa heard a key turn in the lock. 'You still up, Ness?' said Ryan, with some surprise (he was the only person in the world who dared call her 'Ness'). 'Yes, I've been catching up on all those recorded programmes. Good night at '*The Swan*?' 'Oh, there was a change of plan. Lance fancied '*The Plough*', instead. Actually' – he laughed – 'I think he fancied the barmaid!' 'Really?' said Vanessa with a smile, 'I would have thought the girl in '*The Swan*' quite fanciable enough...' 'I suppose so,' replied Ryan, thoughtfully, 'but '*The Plough*' it was.' There seemed to be some tension in the air. 'Is everything OK, Ness? Can I get you a drink?'

'Yes, I'll have a glass of chardonnay, please. Then we'll go to bed.' She gave her husband a meaningful look. 'I'm feeling a bit bushed, love. A long night. Maybe wait til we're rested and fresh.' Vanessa made no reply. She wondered if his dick was already worn out. Let's just wait and see...

Such were the couple's frantic workday lives, the following Friday arrived with unerring speed. Ryan and his pals were destined for '*The Green Man*', located in nearby Greenham. Again, Ryan left at 7.30, bidding his wife a hasty 'bye – see you later!' Vanessa waited only twenty minutes before she was ready for her own expedition. She had put on her figure-hugging little black dress as somehow fitting for the occasion.

This time, she felt more confident, and more determined: she had spent time planning for the expedition. Vanessa's first stop was not 'The Green Man' but her familiar haunt – 'The Swan'. There was barmaid Debbie, looking for all the world exactly as she had last week. Debbie smiled: 'Ryan? Sorry; haven't seen him – not yet, anyhow.' 'That's OK.' Vanessa ordered a coke, and bought Debbie a drink. 'Here's my number. If you see Ryan tonight, give me a call.' She slipped a tenner on the bar, and exchanged a meaningful glance with Debbie. If she couldn't bed her man, she might do worse than the barmaid. Pretty, with attitude. We might see about that… 'Fine' replied Debbie, suddenly coming alive. 'I'll be sure to let you know.'

Vanessa's next port of call was 'The Plough'. The pub's labyrinthine spaces were already filling up, as Vanessa squeezed through every nook and cranny. No sign of Ryan. Through the meleè at the bar, she attracted a barmaid's attention. She was wearing a similar black dress to Vanessa – though more daringly cut, and sculpted around her firm boobs; mouth-watering, thought Vanessa, when she pulls a pint. Vanessa quickly introduced herself, and ordered another coke. The barmaid – Amy – knew Ryan, but hadn't seen him tonight. Last week? asked Vanessa. 'Couldn't say,' replied Amy. 'We were busy – I don't remember him, though.' She smiled: 'Good looking guy – I think I would have…' Vanessa dropped a tenner on the bar, and gave her instructions. Amy nodded, appreciatively.

Right. Finally, on to 'The Green Man'. Four miles, fifteen minutes later, the welcoming lights from the 18th century inn hove into sight. Ryan's stated port of call. Surely, Ryan at last? Vanessa scoured the three separate bar areas, attracting a few admiring glances from the clusters of young men clutching their pint glasses. The good old male gaze – alive and well. But no glance of surprise from the absent Ryan. She sought out a resident barmaid – bar*men* would never do. Wendy was modestly clad in jumper and jeans. The focus must be on her fresh face, framed by luxurious curls. Yes, she knew Ryan. And, no, she hadn't seen him this evening – or, for that matter, for quite a while. Vanessa confided in her, conspiratorially: 'I have a big surprise for him. Here's my number. Just give me a call if you see him!' She slipped a tenner to the delighted Wendy, who seemed eagerly on board with the secret plan. 'Will do! No problem!'

Time for home, Jeeves, thought Vanessa, as the Audi offered a reassuring purr. 'Where in Hell is the bastard!' Vanessa was home before ten, sipping a g&t, and waiting, wondering, pondering, reflecting. It was 10.45 – and Vanessa was towards the end of her third g&t – when her mobile rang. It was none other than Debbie – of *Swan* fame. 'He's here!' 'Great – thanks, Debbie. Is he with Lance and Dick?' 'No – he's with a woman!' 'I see. Do you know her? Seen her before?' 'No, babe. But I can tell you, she's a cracker! Looks like Katy Perry!' 'Phew. OK, Deb, see if you can get a quick picture, and send it to me straightaway… And thanks again! I owe you one!' And, at this rate, I might give you one…

Minutes later, Vanessa's phone pinged, and she opened the message. There, unmistakably, was Ryan, smiling at, and sitting almost indecently close to, an extraordinarily beautiful young woman. Another bloody black dress! The body language did not indicate a business meeting; their hands were intertwined; the couple were staring into each other's eyes. What to do? Confront him? Accuse him? Leave him? No: she needed more intelligence; more evidence, before deciding a way forward. Vanessa did not want to lose her husband; did not want to lose her marriage. She wanted Ryan back. She needed – *demanded* an explanation. Let's play this cool – and hope for an innocent, or at least not irreversible, explanation. Vanessa was in bed – but wide awake – when she heard a key in the lock. It was midnight. Goodnight, loving husband! Disturb me if you dare!

The week flew by. There had been no further headway, no clues or signs given away by Ryan. But it was Friday night again; and Ryan was leaving again – following a superb casserole. Well, it was still only March, and pretty bleak outside; but Ryan was dressed lightly, casually. He kissed his wife quickly, and impatiently announced '*Swan*' to her enquiries. Vanessa smiled vacantly, and bid him goodbye. She would not be following – no more wild goose chases – this evening. Let's just wait and see. Slowly, slowly catchee monkey...

Vanessa prepared for a long night in. She was still considering her options when her mobile buzzed. 'Hi – it's Amy here, at '*The Plough*'. Remember? Your husband is here – he has company. She's terrific! Reminds me of Margot Robbie. Good taste, your husband – after all, he married you!' Vanessa sighed. 'Just do me a favour – take a quick snap, and forward it to me.' 'Righto!' said Amy, excitedly. How could she look like Margot Robbie – slim and blonde – when last week she looked like Katy Perry?

The picture duly arrived. Margot Robbie it was. With Ryan's arm around her. What the fuck was going on? Vanessa reached for a bottle of wine, and Ryan's laptop. And spent the evening watching her husband's collection of porn. It would either provide some insights, or entertain her, or both. The images did neither: Vanessa quickly fell asleep; bored, irritated, and frustrated.

A week passed, without further enlightenment; Ryan's behaviour appeared steady, calm and beyond reproach. Vanessa remained uncomprehending and bemused. She focused madly on her job, and waited for further events to unfold. Almost inevitably, there were no sexual relations between the husband and wife. And, suddenly, it was Friday again. How quickly Fridays came around! It seemed it was '*The Green Man*' on this occasion. A likely story. But, as it turned out, '*The Green Man*' it was.

Having settled down for a long, lonely evening, Vanessa's

phone began vibrating at around 8.30pm. 'Debbie, here, Vanessa. Just thought I'd call you. Dick and Lance have just arrived…and have ordered a couple of beers.' 'But no Ryan?' 'No – I asked them – Dick just shrugged, shook his head, and muttered: 'bastard!' Looks like your boy is flying his kite…' 'Cheers, Debbie, I owe you!'

The phone vibrated again at 9.15. 'Hi – it's Wendy, here. Your husband is in tonight! He's with a gorgeous woman. Looks like Beyoncé! Or maybe Rhianna!' 'Are you telling me she's black? I mean, not like Katy Perry, or Margot Robbie? Take a fucking picture, Wendy, and get it to me asap!' And there it was – she was – a strikingly attractive, svelte black woman, smiling engagingly at her husband. Three women? In three weeks? What, will the line stretch on 'til the crack of doom? What *was* going on? No wonder their sex life was extinct! Tonight would be *the* night that she would confront Ryan. It was make or break time. Time for explanation – if there was one – time for honesty – time for grovelling apology – time, possibly – for a fresh start. Vanessa paced the room, increasingly wobbly, given her substantial consumption of wine and gin – alcohol that only fuelled further her rage and upset.

In their separate spheres, the three barmaids – Debbie, Amy and Wendy – reflected on their respective roles in this domestic saga. All three women knew Ryan. He was a regular customer, a self assured young man on the make. They knew his type. They all knew – or at least suspected – that the dude was married. But for many months, now, his regular group of mates had been supplanted by a succession of striking young women – a different woman on each occasion. The bar staff had followed Ryan's peccadilloes with a mixture of fascination, amusement and disdain. The entry of Vanessa on to the stage – a real, decent and beautiful young woman – had galvanised their sense that something serious was amiss. True, nothing to do with them, and they didn't know the background; maybe Vanessa was a freak, or an abuser, or an alcoholic, or a lesbian. No matter; girls must stick together in the face of injustice and mischief.

Midnight arrived; a key turned in the lock. 'Good God! Still up, Ness?' 'Yep, still up. I wondered: how are Lance and Dick, these days?'

'They're both fine. In fact, asking about you.'

'Well, that's odd. Because they've spent tonight in *'The Plough'*, while you've been in *'The Green Man'*!'

Ryan coloured. 'I don't get it. What are you talking about? Ah, you've been drinking!'

'Yes, I've been drinking! And you've been screwing!'

'Have you gone mad? Let's just go to bed!'

'Bed? Are you still up for it, then? Can you still perform? After you've screwed *her* (she threw down a photo), and *her* (another) and *her*! (another).

'Where? How? I don't understand. I can explain!'

'Good. Well? I'm waiting!'

Ryan paused, hesitated, and burst into tears. 'Stop blubbing, Ryan, and tell me who all these women are. This one, for starters.'

'That's Katy.'

'Katy? Katy Perry?'

'Course not. Just Katy!'

'And her?'

'Mel.'

'And her?'

'Sinita.'

'OK, that's their *names*. But who the fuck are they? How did you meet them?'

'I *ordered* them!

Ordered? Where from? Fucking Tesco's!'

'Close – from an escort agency! It's called *Dream Girls*, if you must know.'

Vanessa slumped to the floor. 'You've been *paying* for sex? When you have *me*? How long has this been going on?'

'About a year.'

'A year…and how many of them, for God's sake?'

'23, I think.'

'23? You think? Are there one or two still hidden in your pants? 23 women, sucking my husband's cock, while his wife goes without! Just tell me *why*, you piece of shit, before I cut it off!'

Ryan paused. 'You remember, when I was sixteen, my father *bought* me a woman? A kind of initiation ceremony? She was Marie. That's how it started. I just couldn't get *her* – the idea, the *experience*, out of my mind. It was kind of obsessive, all-consuming. The way I'd felt just wouldn't leave me. The mystery, the anticipation. The feeling of power. It was just irresistible. Compulsive.' Ryan bowed his head. 'I call it my 'gold rush' – an illicit, humungous desire, and fulfilment. I just can't help it!'

'And did you think about *me*? Alone? Wanting, and needing, your love? Or me, sad and lonely at work, and surrounded by testosterone on all sides? Or me, at risk of catching the clap from one of your sluts?'

'They're all tested, regularly.'

'Well, that makes me feel a whole lot better!'

'Look, I know I've cheated on you. I know I don't deserve you. But I can't help it. God knows I've tried!'

'God knows you haven't tried hard enough,' replied Vanessa, bitterly.

'Ness, I'll change. Honestly I *will*. I just need help!'

'I'm sure you do. And so do I. Help to understand, for a start. What do they have that I don't? An extra pussy?'

'I just don't know. It's a kind of compulsion.'

'And I really don't know whether I can come to terms with all this cheating. It's just industrial. And this lying on a titanic scale.

But there are three conditions that you must agree to, if there's to be the remotest chance of getting through this.'

'Anything.'

'You must honour your wife, and your wife's body. Exclusively.' Vanessa smiled through her tears: 'at least we now know you've still got it in you!'

'Of course. And?'

'You must agree to psychotherapy, to sort out this appalling mental problem.'

'What a relief!'

'And, from now on, it's me who'll be going out on Friday nights. I'll be arranging quite a party for my new friends – Debbie, Amy and Wendy. It's going to be pretty orgasmic, I can tell you!'

'And what am I supposed to do?' bleated her husband.

'You can stay in, and consume a tidal wave of porn. If you dare!'

Ryan endured months of psychotherapy, and endured months of lonely Friday evenings. And he endured months of making love to his lovely wife. But it was all unendurable.

Six months later, a 'For Sale' board was erected outside 25, Richmond Avenue. Ryan, it seemed, could not change. But Vanessa could.

TO HULL AND BACK

For many years, John Hull had enjoyed a congenial, untroubled retirement. He had spent a great deal of time rambling with his dogs in far-flung corners of the UK, and photographing, and painting, dramatic landscapes.

John has also enjoyed the finer things in life, such as good food, good company (which included his wife, Hazel), and the end-of-day fortification provided by a g&t, and a couple of glasses of decent red wine.

After many years of unremarkable benign neglect from his local GP Surgery, John has – quite out of the blue – been contacted by his General Practitioner, mildly rebuked for not troubling her for so long, and asked to make an appointment. But, first, John was asked to undertake a blood test. The results of that test now available, one fine morning in April, John breezed in to the Surgery, not entirely without trepidation, to discuss his health with a doctor whom he had never met before.

'Dr Baig will see you now, Mr Hull,' said the Receptionist, breezily. 'Room 3.'

'So, how are you, Mr Hull?' said Dr Baig, more in tones of accusation than question, a thin smile playing on her lips.

'I feel fine, thank you Doctor,' John replied. 'Unless, of course, you know different…'

The smile briefly re-appeared. 'I'm afraid I have some quite bad news…'

A buzzing noise, not unlike an angry wasp, emerged from a handbag, lurking beneath the good Doctor's chair. 'I'm sorry, I must get this!'

Dr Baig wrestled among the bowels of her handbag, and wrenched out her smart phone. 'It's *most* important. I need the kitchen panels finished in marine blue. And the granite work surface must have a space for a microwave. Is that clear? Thank you.'

'Bloody workmen. Sorry, Mr Hull. As I was saying. Your blood analysis shows your blood sugar levels are quite high. The blood sugar count is 46. That's pre-diabetic. We need to take urgent action, before you develop the full blown condition. Let's just pop you on the scales, and take your blood pressure, to complete the picture. Well, I'd say you were around a stone and a quarter overweight, in old money, compared to your BMI. And your blood pressure's a little on the high side, too.'

'I'm not surprised', ventured John.

'No, neither am I', said Doctor Baig, curtly. 'The last time we saw you I was at medical school. Now my kids are at medical school!'

'Well, I've enjoyed pretty decent health. I didn't want to trouble you unnecessarily.'

'Well,' repeated the Doctor. 'We can't change the past. But let's start as we mean to go on. OK, start with diet. What kind of meals do you eat?'

'I generally enjoy three meals a day. With at least one of those being cooked. From scratch, as it were. I do have quite a lot of variety, though I really enjoy rice, and pasta. Or chips, as a treat.'

'Oh dear. Take me through a typical day.'

'OK, breakfast might be cereals, or toast. Or I might throw in a yoghurt if I'm feeling adventurous.'

'I see. Maybe with marmalade, or jam? Too much sugar! And lunch?'

'Maybe a sandwich, or soup.'
'On white bread?'
'Well, yes, sometimes.'
'Oh dear. Evening meal?'
'Usually meat or fish, with vegetables.'
'Anything else, Mr Hull?'
'Occasionally in the evening I might fancy a slice of pork pie, or scotch egg, with a few crisps. Or even a few chocolates.'

'I see,' said the Doctor, as though she had just unearthed a state secret. 'Well, there's far too much carbohydrate in your daily diet. I'll give you a diet sheet, but basically you'll need to cut out rice, pasta, white bread and potatoes. That includes chips. Modest amounts of lean meat, and boiled or oily fish is fine. But, mostly, you need to replace the foods you're cutting out with green vegetables and salad. Without dressing. And of course no – or extremely little – chocolate. High days and holidays, only. The bonus is that your new diet – your new *regime* – will help you to lose some weight, and lower your blood pressure. Now, what about drink?'

John felt his sense of humour returning. 'Mainly tea, coffee, and water,' he averred.

'And alcohol?' asked the Doctor, a little sharply.

'Well, a couple of glasses of red wine with my evening meal. And maybe a pint of beer while watching telly. Oh, and sometimes a pre-prandial gin and tonic. Maybe I could cut out a bit...'

'Frankly, I think you need to cut out a *lot* – if you're serious about reducing blood sugar. And of course your weight. Beer contains a lot of carbs. Though there's no sugar in gin,' said the Doctor, in a disappointed tone, 'provided the tonic is slimline.' She brightened. 'But gin *is* very high in alcohol – 40% proof, and your alcohol intake is well in excess of Government guidelines. The red wine is OK in itself – but maybe one glass, and not at every meal. So, Mr Hull. What about exercise?'

John beamed. 'I enjoy long rambles with my dog, *Mitch*. Sometimes, hiking in Cumbria, or north Wales.'

'That's fine,' said the Doctor, with apparent reluctance. 'Just take it easy – nothing too strenuous, or that risks damaging your joints. And if you lose your mobility, that can be extremely damaging for your long-term prospects…'

'OK, Mr Hull, we're nearly finished for today. Oh, yes. What about sex?' The Doctor gave what she imagined was an encouraging smile.

John thought: 'didn't know that was part of the service!' – then bit his tongue. Phew. 'Well, my wife and I have been married for a long time, now. And, of course, we're not as young as we were. So, sometimes. Is that OK? If not too strenuous?'

'Perfectly…' The Doctor's eyes narrowed. 'I was just trying to enquire whether you needed any help in that department?'

John laughed. 'No, thank you. I'll just let Nature take it's course…'

'Mr Hull. Excuse me, but I've just had another look at your medical records. I appear to have overlooked a key fact. The Records suggest that you're 86 years of age…Am I mistaken? Surely that's not right?'

'Well, much as I'd like to knock twenty – no, thirty – years off, I'm afraid, yes, it's correct!'

'I'm sorry to have wasted your time, Mr Hull. I mistakenly thought you were 66. Don't listen to a word I've said. Sometimes, a big change in your lifestyle can lead to unnecessary stress, which can adversely impact on blood sugar levels and blood pressure. Just keep on enjoying your life, as you are, for as long as you can. My compliments to Mrs Hull, and of course to *Mitch*. Only promise me – you won't change a thing…'

AN EMBARRASSMENT OF RICHES

Dominic Crawley had a massive headache. He was 79 years of age; and extremely rich. All from his company's fitting bathrooms and kitchens. And he had no idea what to do with his remaining time – or his wealth, amassed over fifty years.

Dominic's wife, Alice, had passed away four years ago, and he had few interests – other than carefully tending his money – and even fewer relatives. Nowadays, Dominic rattled around in his Neo-mansion in Charlton Park, Cheltenham, ruing his ill-fortune.

True: Dominic was in hearty good health. Maybe he'd been lucky, or maybe wise. He'd never smoked, drank moderately, and ate wholesome food, these days prepared by himself, and cooked 'from scratch.' But he knew that the good times wouldn't just continue to roll. Illness – followed by death – was a matter of 'when', not 'if'. And, he reasoned, he'd already enjoyed at least 79% of his potential life expectancy – and that was in the unlikely event of his living to 100 years of age. And, currently, there were only 14,000 people in the UK who had achieved that commendable feat of longevity. Even in the rarefied eventuality of his achieving such heady old age, Dominic reasoned that there would be pitfalls along the way – increasing feebleness, serious illness and disease, and possible dementia. In any event, he would hardly be dancing the Argentine tango with a smouldering young beauty in a Buenos Aires' bar.

So, sadly, despite his health and serious wealth – and those two Caribbean and Med cruises every year – Dominic often felt 'down' – even despondent. True, again, Dominic did have a daughter, Rachel, 55, and had planned to leave Rachel the lion's share of his ever-burgeoning Estate. But, sadly, Dominic and Paul, his brittle and fractious son-in-law, had fallen out over something trivial – what, ten years or so ago, now. It might have been over politics; or social trends; or immigration; or modern youth; or music. Or something else.

No-one could quite remember the cause, after so long. At the time, both father and husband had, quite unreasonably, expected Rachel's backing and support. But Rachel had been conflicted and stressed by the row, and attempted to smooth over the cracks – to neither man's satisfaction. Like a running sore, the rift had never quite healed, and Dominic rarely saw Rachel and Paul these days. Rachel would ring every week or two, to ensure her old dad was OK. And they might pop round at Christmas, for a quick drink; to check that the elderly, but irritatingly sprightly (for Paul) father-in-law was still *cognis mentis*. But that, really, was it.

Rachel was a veterinary nurse, and did what it said on the tin. All that was known about Paul was that he worked in a casino; he seemed to move in mysterious and possibly sinister circles, from what Dominic gathered from his golf buddies. Any questions Dominic had asked – in the early days – had been deflected with irritable, even angry, brevity. Strangely, there were no animals in the Anderson household. There was no space in Paul Anderson's life for children – let alone cats or dogs. There was already one animal too many, Dominic reflected, ruefully. He heartily wished for a more friendly and supportive son-in-law, given his age and circumstances. For, after all, when all was said and done, Rachel and Paul *were* his only family.

Lonely and increasingly dispirited, Dominic began to cast around for stimulation, for an answer to his problems. He tried music – learning to play the classical guitar. He tried social groups – bridge, bowls and chess. He tried therapy. He tried the Internet; trawled it, viewed it, explored it, researched it. My God, you could get anything on the Internet! Except, that is, for eternal life – or eternal friendship. No; golf and his golf 'buddies' must, it seemed, remain his chief salvation. But Dominic would reach the age of 80 in September; he was, at last, beginning to feel his age. The perimeters of his life were closing in. Despite every attempt to rally his failing morale, Dominic woke each morning – whether that day was bright, wet or overcast – to a feeling of *ennui* and increasing hopelessness.

Then, one fine day, Dominic received an e-mail, out of the blue, that he found intriguing. It was not from his regular network – not from his GP, or the golf club, or his electricity supplier; or even his favourite charity, asking for yet another donation. No: it was from a perfect stranger. A woman; introducing herself. In recent months, feeling depressed and lonely, Dominic had 'explored' a few dating web-sites, but had not had the courage – or conviction – to join any of the sites he 'chanced' upon. And he'd created a Facebook page. He could only assume that the e-mail had been spawned or seeded from one of these naive, exploratory forays.

Dominic was well aware of the plethora of scams and cons perpetrated on the Internet – many of them allegedly involving pretty young women – all plausibly, and inevitably, requiring an injection of ready cash. Many of these tempting offers originated from places such as Ghana and Nigeria, and involved unscrupulous young men – posing predictably, but convincingly, as attractive young women – needing friendship, and romance. And, of course, loads of money – often to rescue the alleged damsel in distress from a dastardly dilemma. Dominic was tempted to delete the e-mail. Just a click of a button, and gone forever into cyberspace. But as his finger hovered, Dominic thought: 'what the hell! No harm in opening the message!' So he did; and this is what he read:

> Hi! My name is Corinna. Sorry to bother you! I'm looking for someone kind and funny to share my life with. I'm 42 years of age, and a divorceè. No children. I own my own house, near Cheltenham. I'm a receptionist at a local car dealership.
> Please see picture, attached. I have only sent this message to you – you were mentioned by a mutual friend. This is not – repeat, not – any kind of scam, but a genuine opportunity. Please feel free to phone, e-mail, or text me. If I do not hear from you, I will not contact you again. However, if you do respond, I would be very happy to meet you. One step at a time, obviously. No obligation.
> Kind Regards, Corinna Westbrook.

Dominic scrutinised the attached photo; and enlarged it. The image showed a rather comely lady, with an arrestingly pretty face, framed by glossy dark hair. She looked about 35 years old. Must be an old photo, thought Dominic. Oldest trick in the book. What to do? What have we to lose? What have we to gain? Why write to *him* – whatever gloss he put on it, an old geezer? A gold digger, in all probability. And who could this 'mutual friend' be? Maybe sleep on it?

Dominic slept on the matter for 24 hours; and then responded to the e-mail:

> Hi Corinna –
> Thank you for the e-mail. Sounds most interesting. Although I'm a widower, and therefore unattached, you may

be aware that I'm a good deal older than you. However, if you are genuine, and you'd still like to meet, would you be available for lunch at The Red Lion on Saturday 13th? I'd be happy to 'pick you up', or we could meet there at, say, 12.30?

Please do let me know. I look forward to meeting you but, as you say, on a no-obligations basis.

Kind Regards, Dominic Crawley.

In the interests of transparency, Dominic attached a recent photo. At least he still had most of his hair, even if it was snowy-white. 'The Red Lion' was a modest little pub that served excellent food at affordable prices. He did not want to lavish loads of money on a stranger by taking her to an expensive restaurant, and creating reckless expectations. His guard was still well and truly up.

Within hours, Dominic received an affirmative reply. Corinna would be delighted to meet him at 'The Red Lion' – she knew the pub, on the environs of Cheltenham. Corinna wrote:

Dear Dominic –

Thank you so much for your reply. I would be happy to meet at 12.30pm, next Saturday, 13 May, at The Red Lion. I'll meet you there, if that's OK. I really look forward to meeting you, and hopefully getting to know you.

Kind Regards, Corinna.

Dominic was thoughtful. It was now Wednesday 3 May. He had just ten clear days to conduct some 'due diligence' on Mrs Westbrook. How to proceed? He didn't want to involve or alarm daughter Rachel – she'd think he was just a silly old fool. Likewise, his mates at the Golf Club – all sly nudges in the ribs, and knowing winks and smiles. And his expertise on the old Internet was pretty superficial. He'd leave great clod-hopping digital boot prints everywhere.

So – daringly, and quite expensively – Dominic sought an appointment with a private detective agency. But, he reasoned, better invest a grand or so now, than possibly lose a fortune later. Thus it was that, the following day, Thursday 4 May, Dominic found himself in a dingy, third floor office, seated in an ancient black leather armchair; and sitting across an equally ancient desk from Percival Peters. Better to be safe, than sorry. Was he, Dominic thought, acting responsibly? Or was he being deceitful and underhand? He did feel a frisson of guilt. But he also felt the need to protect himself. No-one was going to say to him, with a shake of the head: 'no fool like an old fool.'

Peters, a former policeman, and looking younger than his 40 years, with tousled, shoulder length hair, and a smooth, un-lined face, was re-assuring: 'It all sounds a bit dodgy, Mr Crawley. You are quite right to be careful, to do some digging. Remember the old adage: if it sounds too good to be true, it usually is. Youngish women, and – sorry – oldish men, aren't generally a marriage made in heaven. There can't be any guarantees, but we'll look into Mrs Westbrook – if she is Mrs Westbrook – and let you know our findings in the next few days. Don't worry – we're very discreet, very confidential. And very sensitive, where single women are concerned. She won't be aware of a thing.'

Within a week, a slim Report lay on Dominic's desk.

There were some pictures of Corinna, leaving her neat semi-detached home. There was a picture of her, at the reception desk, at the car dealership. The photos weren't great quality – they looked 'snatched', underhand – but revealed essentially the same youthful and attractive woman as shown in the photograph attached to Corinna's first e-mail.

The Report confirmed that Corinna Westbrook was the woman in the photos, and that that was her real name. There were no aliases, or identity subterfuge. No scammers lurking in plain sight. She was, indeed, 42 years of age. Corinna had divorced her husband, self-styled 'businessman' Mark Westbrook, three years ago, but retained her married name; her maiden name was James. One fly in the ointment: her former husband was described in the Report as 'a most unpleasant, unsavoury character, with possible criminal proclivities.' Though the next sentence read: 'We found no evidence that Mrs Westbrook was involved in any of her husband's nefarious business dealings.'

He was obliged to look up 'nefarious'. Still, thought Dominic – after dwelling on the word – they *are* divorced. And Corinna didn't appear to have a relationship with any man – or woman – at the present time.

Corinna owned her own house, and her own car, a VW Golf. She lived in the area of Hester's Way – not the most salubrious of neighbourhoods, (though Dominic reflected that Rachel herself lived nearby – only a few miles distant from her father). Corinna had a steady job, and there was no trace of any debts. There was no criminal record – for example, involving fraud, or drugs – and no County Court Judgements. Despite her former connections, Corinna Westbrook, it seemed, was a genuine, real deal.

For Dominic, this was a most satisfactory outcome. Indeed, almost unexpectedly good. But still he pondered. Something didn't add up. Why? Why him? What was this woman's motive? If there were plenty of fish in the sea, so there were plenty of guys – handsome young guys – in the Cheltenham area.

But, in the end, there was only one thing for it – to meet Corinna, as planned. Proof of the pudding, thought Dominic, before thinking the metaphor a little tasteless. Let's just frigging do it, he determined, suddenly anxious for the next few days to pass, as quickly as possible. If nothing else, it should be a fascinating experience. To underline his commitment, on the Friday preceding the er…'date', Dominic sent a short e-mail:

Hi Corinna –

I hope everything's still OK for tomorrow lunchtime. I look forward to meeting you.

Best Wishes, Dominic.

A few hours later, a reply duly arrived:

Hi Dominic –

Yes, all is fine. See you tomorrow! Kind Regards, Corinna.

Nevertheless, it was with some trepidation that Dominic drove to *The Red Lion* the following day, arriving a little early, at 12.20 precisely. He did not have to wait long – recognising, and greeting, Corinna as she stood on the threshold. Dominic grinned, then hesitated, before extending his hand. Corinna, in a mid-green summery dress, responded with a sunny smile, and a 'really good to meet you at last!' With a few encouraging words, Dominic ushered his elegant lady to their table in the pub's restaurant area.

The meal passed in a blur. Steak and chips, for him. Sole, and new potatoes, for her. Red wine for him. White, for her. But Dominic hardly tasted the food. His companion was hardly less attractive in the flesh than in her photographs. Fresh complexion. Dark, gleaming hair. Youthful looks. Laughing hazel eyes. A trim figure. Dominic could hardly lift his eyes from that smiling, animated face. And his conversation was small, laconic; in truth, he felt overwhelmed by Corinna's presence, her vivacity, her charm.

At last, he remembered his 'script'. 'Please tell me, Corinna, which mutual friend mentioned me to you? He must be a good friend indeed!'

'Why, it was my great uncle, Jimmy James!'

'Jimmy – my golf buddy – is your uncle! Goodness, wait til I see him next! Well, this is most interesting!'

After that, the 'date' went past as in a dream. They'd each

opted for a crème brulee for dessert, and then coffee. God, what now? thought Dominic. 'Corinna, I've enjoyed today immensely. I hesitate to ask – you've seen me now, in the flesh. But might we meet again? I mean, anywhere you like….' He laughed: 'No obligation, of course!'

Corinna put a hand on his, and smiled a sweet smile. 'I'd love to meet again! Either at a pub or restaurant, or maybe at your home, if you prefer.'

'That's really great!' Dominic looked around. 'This place is pretty low key, if pleasant enough. Maybe a little restaurant I know near here…Perhaps next week sometime?'

'That would be super! I really look forward to it!'

Despite Corinna's protests, Dominic paid the bill, and escorted Corinna to her car. She touched his shoulder, and kissed his cheek. 'Thank you…see you next week!' And, with a wave, she was gone.

*

In the days – six whole days! – before their next 'date', thoughts of Corinna dominated Dominic's every waking moment. She was so much prettier, so much more charming, so much more genuine than he could ever having imagined. Corinna seemed to be the real deal; the whole deal. Of course, these were still very early days, and many questions remained unanswered. Why was *he* the lucky bastard? Why hit on him, when the world was full of younger men, all looking for a good woman? Might – he reluctantly admitted to himself – his money be a real factor – even the *raison d'etre* – in this fast-developing situation? And, if his worst fears were confirmed, how awkward might it be to jettison this charming lady? But Dominic was beginning to be enamoured, to be entranced, and looked forward to revealing these answers like unwrapping the layers of an onion, to discover pure beauty, honesty, truth and nakedness. Nakedness? Ah, let's not go there; not yet. Let's just revel in the splendour of the moment, and enjoy the delicious company of this woman, who had so unexpectedly begun to turn around his life…

The venue for their next meeting – Friday, 19 May – was a classy little restaurant on the outskirts of Cheltenham – *La Petite Trianon*. Corinna arrived separately, looking a picture in a sculpted gold top, and knee-length black pencil skirt. She greeted her host, and kissed his cheek. The couple settled at a corner table, with a window looking out over the manicured gardens. The food was delicious, but almost irrelevant; the intimate setting was conducive to a deep, private, getting-to-know-you conversation.

'Corinna, you look ravishing!' Then Dominic added, a touch conspiratorially – and hiding his embarrassment – 'please tell me all about yourself. I'm dying to know.' Corinna took a deep breath. 'There's really not a great deal to tell. Mark and I divorced three years ago. We were married for 15 years, but he had some business-partner troubles, and started drinking heavily. In our final years together, his personality changed quite dramatically. I tried to help all I could. But then…then he…' Corinna began to sob, in big gulps. I'm sorry, I can't go on…'

Dom proffered a handkerchief. 'I'm really sorry, Corinna, I didn't mean to distress you, by stirring up unpleasant memories,' he added, gently.

Corinna collected herself. 'Anyway, then I found evidence of a string of affairs. I couldn't tolerate that – or, frankly, his vile treatment of me – and I sued for divorce. Luckily, I was able to keep the house – and my job. I gather there *was* a new Mrs Westbrook…but it didn't last long.' Corinna smiled weakly, and sipped her chardonnay.

'But an attractive woman like you…can't have been short of admirers?' Corinna paused for thought. 'Well, I suppose you're right. And your next question,' she smiled, 'will be, 'why have you sought out a mature gentleman like me?" Dominic laughed, a tad nervously.

'The two issues are linked, in a way. I have had dates, relationships, even – however briefly – with other men, since Mark's, er, departure. But they've been pretty disappointing. Sometimes their personalities have been superficial, or just darn unpleasant. Or their interests boring or banal. Or, frankly, they just want me for casual sex. Or they want rough sex, for goodness sake, on a first or second date. I'm not a piece of meat, Dominic. Or a porn actress. And I don't *need* just anybody. I really want someone to love me, and care for me. And I'll do the same for them. After that, age doesn't really matter. It's just a number.' Corinna laughed delightedly. 'Dominic, you came with some very strong recommendations – and you haven't disappointed!' Corinna took another sip of chardonnay, then leaned over impulsively, and kissed Dominic sweetly on the lips. He felt the scent of the wine on his mouth, and savoured the moment.

Corinna continued: 'But, Dominic, please tell me a little about *you*. I know the outlines, of course. But what about you, as a man? If you will, *my* man!'

Dominic beamed, and laughed. 'Well, call me Dom. As I think you know, I was married to my lovely wife, Alice, for more than 50 years. Alice sadly died four years ago. Since then, there have been no women in my life, except for my daughter, Rachel. She's married, of course. I enjoy golf, and I dabble on the guitar. Oh, I enjoy classical music, and a little theatre. And I love travel – trips to the countryside, in the old Mercedes, and maybe a couple of cruises a year. So, all in all, a pretty ordinary, unexciting life!' Dominic laughed at his own attempt at modesty.

Corinna laughed back. 'Sounds like the opposite of unexciting! And I hope I can contribute to that excitement, and bring some excitement of my own,' she added, quietly, her hand touching Dominic's. He smiled, in silent appreciation; and brushed away a sudden tear.

The rest of the afternoon seemed to pass in a reverie of smiles and flirtatious little asides, the couple's eyes locked on each other like lasers. 'Corinna, I wonder…would you like to come to my place for dinner in the next few days? I do a *mean* bolognese…' 'I'd be delighted!' she replied. 'Any particular day?' 'I'd like to see you everyday…so as soon as you can.' 'Well, I'm free tomorrow as it happens – Saturday. That OK? Or do you need more notice?' 'No, tomorrow will be just great! I can't wait!' It was 4.30 before they said their little goodbyes – sealed with a long kiss, instigated by Corinna. The pair were now, clearly, 'an item'.

Saturday arrived quickly but, from 4.00pm onwards, Dominic – let's call him 'Dom' – kept glancing at his watch. He had had the six-bedroom house cleaned from top to bottom, and re-arranged the dining room and drawing-room; and had himself fluffed the cushions, and placed candles in strategic places. Rachmaninov might sound 'over the top', but a little light Mozart might be just the ticket; a serenade or two – 'A Little Night Music'. Wine was chilled, and the bolognese sauce underway. Calm down, man. God, it was already 5.00 o'clock. Dom had a sudden panic attack: would she turn up? Or was it all too good to be true?

A gentle ring on the door-bell. There she was in the doorway. A blush-pink dress. A matching broad-brimmed hat, and high-heels; a burgundy-coloured handbag. What a picture! Dom kissed Corinna, and invited her into his spacious domain. 'What a lovely home, Dom! How beautiful you – and Alice – have made it! What a tribute to her memory!'

Dom kissed Corinna quickly, in appreciation of such tact, and asked whether she liked champagne. A bottle of Veuve Cliquot lay ready in an ice bucket. 'Why, my favourite!' averred Corinna. The delicious fizz did its job, and loosened slightly nervous tongues.

'I'm afraid I'll have to keep checking on the food, but it won't be too long,' apologised Dom. A bottle of chianti classico stood on the carefully dressed dining table. The champagne was quickly, but appreciatively, quaffed, and dinner served. 'Goodness, Dom, I think I'm a pretty good cook, but this excels anything I could rustle up. No-one told me you had *these* hidden depths!' 'You flatter me, Corinna; it's a tried and tested recipe with me. I love Italian food – and wine. I'm just delighted you're enjoying it…' Following the main course, Dom served timarasu with a flourish, and a smile. 'Dom, you surely didn't make this?' He smiled. 'It's fantastic!' Dom couldn't help but be entranced by Corinna's mouth and tongue, as she savoured every delicious spoonful of gooey dessert. 'It's so lovely…' she offered, flashing her fine eyes at her host.

At Dom's invitation, his guest repaired to the spacious drawing-room, to chat and relax. 'So, what shall we do?' Dom asked helpfully. 'Talk nonsense into the evening? Or view a bit of TV – we have Sky, or Netflix? Or a film, maybe?'

'Would you have *The Seven Year Itch*, with Marilyn Monroe? I love it!' 'Your wish is my command,' said Dom. 'For me, it could be the 57 year itch!' before reflecting that he had possibly clouded his wife's memory. 'Fab – it's my favourite film. I love Rachmaninov's Piano Concerto Number 2, that features so poignantly!' Damn, thought Dom, I could have put some Rachmaninov on the cd player, after all…

The couple settled on the sofa, absorbed by the shimmering images on the screen. A mesmerising Marilyn Monroe, as 'The Girl', playing opposite a plain, middle aged guy, Tom Ewell, as Richard Sherman – he of the 'seven year itch'. Corinna sought Dom's hand, and kissed it. 'Funny,' he said, in response. 'Beautiful young woman; older, ordinary guy. Sound familiar?'

'Well, you're not comparing *me* to that screen goddess! Besides, she likes him for what he is; age doesn't come into it…' 'But they never, er, get it on, if you see what I mean,' reflected

Dom. 'Just delightful flirtation, and inflated imagination.' 'True,' countered Corinna, 'but it *is* a comedy. And he *is* married. And this was 1955! Even then, that subway scene – with that dress – caused quite a stir...' Corinna paused, then added: 'an earlier Monroe film is called '*Gentlemen Prefer Blondes*'. She laughed. 'But the follow-up is called '*Gentlemen Marry Brunettes*'. She kissed her beau: 'That's me babe. That is, if you'll have me!'

Dom couldn't resist a final – if heart in mouth – protest. 'But my age, Corinna! I'm nearly twice as old as you! More to the point, I'll be 80 before I know it! Now, I'm not a great one for poetry – probably because it was beaten into us mercilessly at school – but I do remember the opening lines of a Shakespeare sonnet:

That time of year thou mayest in me behold
When yellow leaves, or none, or few, do hang...

That sums me up all right!'

'We were taught that poem as well,' replied Corinna, a touch archly. 'If I remember correctly, sonnet 73; it ends with the couplet:

This thou perceiv'st, which makes thy love more strong,
To love that well which thou must leave ere long.

'Dom, I just want to love, and be loved. If you'll have me, I'll try to make every day, every hour, special. Precious. Intense. Cherished. Lived, fervently. What more can either of us wish for?'

Dom embraced her tenderly, and kissed her gently. 'Thank you, Corinna! What wonderful words!'

Then, belatedly, Dom glanced at his watch. 'Corinna, it's getting rather late. Shall I call you a taxi...?'

'I'm going nowhere tonight, if that's OK with you!'

'That's fine. There's another bedroom that's made up, with *en suite*. But do you have a change of clothes with you?'

Corinna pointed to her handbag. 'Spare bra and pants, and toothbrush. All a girl needs. And, to avoid any confusion, tonight is for you, my love!'

Dom flushed with pleasure. 'Corinna, you're a constant surprise, a constant delight. But you'll find I'm a bit rusty in that department!'

His lover raised an eyebrow: 'Nothing that a bit of polishing won't put right…'

That very night, following passionate – polishing – lovemaking, Dom asked Corinna to marry him. He fancied that he'd benefit from a great deal more polishing…

Before her departure the following morning, Corinna prepared eggs Benedict for breakfast, washed down with orange juice and coffee. 'Your kitchen's very well organised, Dom. I'm impressed.' 'Well, I've just tried to maintain Alice's tidiness and sense of organisation…' He winced again at the mention of Alice, as though he was experiencing – enjoying – a guilty pleasure.

Over the many years of Dominic's marriage to Alice, the couple had settled into a kind of pattern; their relationship had been kind and caring, decent, dignified, and responsible. Life had been smooth, regular, predictable; comfortable. Dominic had to reach back into the dim and distant past – to the early days of his 'courting' Alice – since he had experienced such a wave of delicious emotions, such exhilaration as he felt now. Dominic had barely hoped, or expected, that his *being* would ever again be subject to such exquisite pleasures – and stresses. His mind was besotted with a single subject – Corinna. He could think of nothing else; nothing else mattered – not even his golf. If he was not *with* Corina, he was thinking *about* her. If he was in bed, he was dreaming of her. Corinna had taken over his life; commanded his very soul. She was his sole, his only delight.

*

But, even so, Dom had a stern duty to perform. Shortly after Corinna left that morning, he called Rachel, and arranged to visit.

'What the fuck does he want?' asked Paul, sulkily, on being told of the call. 'Doesn't he realise we've got lives to lead?'

'Look, Paul, I know you don't like my dad. I hear it every day. But please tone down your language, and at least *try* to be civil when he comes round. Remember that inheritance you keep talking about!'

'Why's he coming, anyway? It's either that he's dying – very unlikely, since he's determined to annoy me by living for ever – or he's found a floozy!'

'You mean woman? I very much doubt it. He's seen nobody since mum passed away. He's got too much respect for mum's memory. Anyway, he's far too old.'

'Well, let's see,' replied Paul, with feeling. 'I wouldn't put anything beyond the old sod. Anything to spite me!'

Dominic called round to his daughter's home at 10.30 on Monday morning. It was a sunny, warm morning, and ordinarily his spirits would have been lifted. But he felt a sense of unease, anticipating anger, and opposition, rather than love and best wishes. Oh, well, this had to be done. His very life depended on it…

'Rachel, Paul, I have an important announcement…' Dom's voice wobbled. 'I'm about to be married!' he declared, hoarsely, with emotion in his voice.

'What! Dad! My God, who is she? How long has this been going on? Why don't we know anything about it? We're your family!'

'That's a lot of questions, and I'll give you patient, considered answers. But, in the end, I hope you'll be happy for me…'

'Of course we want the best for you. But this is so sudden. So…so.. *unexpected!*'

'Sorry to spring it on you,' shrugged her father. 'I wasn't searching for romance. It just kind of found me...'

'Tell us everything..er..Dad,' Paul insisted. 'Sounds like some fuck...er, gold-digger!'

'Paul, you know, that's really quite offensive. Do you want me to tell you about Corinna, or not?'

'Corinna, is it? Corinna who? Who is she, dad?' urged Rachel.

'Corinna Westbrook. She's a lovely lady. A dream come true. What more do you need to know?'

'*Everything*! Who. What. How. When. *Why*! OK. One question at a time. How old is she?'

'She's forty two.'

'Dad! Your daughter's fifty-five! How's that going to look! I really thought you were past all that!'

'Past all what?'

'You know! And how long have you known this woman?'

'You mean Corinna? Just over a month...'

'A month! Christ, it gets better!'

'I really didn't expect this reception. I loved your mother, but it's been more than four years now. I have something of a life still left in me!'

'But, dad!' yelled Rachel, 'what about *us*! What about *our* future!'

'You have your present, and your future! You've made them what they are! Rachel, you're 55 years of age. You have a nice home; you both have decent incomes. You're surely not clinging to this inheritance thing?'

'*We* are your family. Not some bloody stranger you've just met on the Internet!'

'Hang on a bit!' interjected Paul. 'Was she married to Mark Westbrook? I had business dealings with that slime ball. The bastard did me over for at least £20k!'

'You do surprise me,' replied Dom, in a sarcastic tone. 'I can only hope that you reflect on things, and come to accept and *like* Corinna. I know she's eager to meet and get to know you…'

Dom spoke through gritted teeth. He left shortly after, angry and frustrated at his treatment, and the narrow prism of his daughter's perspective. As for his son-in-law…

Dom felt patronised like an old geezer who had lost control of his senses. Whereas, in reality, he had never felt more in control of his senses – or his life.

*

The very next evening, Corinna received a call from Paul (the number was stored on his phone).

'Hi, is that Mrs Westbrook? You don't know me, but I'm Paul Anderson, Dominic Crawley's son-in-law.'

'Oh, hello. Very nice to hear from you…How can I help you?'

'Thanks. I'm sure you *can* help. I understand that you and Dom have started some sort of relationship. I'm afraid that my wife Rachel and I have serious concerns about it. It's quite possible – maybe natural – that Dom is infatuated with you. But you must know that this situation is quite preposterous; quite impossible. So I'm calling to ask you to break it off, in your own interests, before things get worse…'

'Worse? But Dom loves me. And I love him. We're about to get married! What is the problem, exactly? Where are you coming from, Mr Anderson?'

'Just look at the age gap! In a year or two he may need long-term care!'

'Dom's the same age as Mick Jagger. I can assure you that all Dom's faculties are working just fine…'

'Good God! You're not referring to *sex?*'

'Of course not – I was talking about Dom's physical and

mental health. With my support, I'm confident his health can only get better.'

'But in the long term?'

'So you're concerned for *my* welfare, my well-being? Is that it?'

'And you know that Rachel's an only child?'

'Mr Anderson, Dom and I haven't even discussed money, or his future intentions. You may not know this, but I own my own property, and have a steady job. I'm not marrying Dom for his wealth. Your future's safe from me!'

'I'd really urge you to re-consider, Mrs Westbrook, before it's too late. By the way, were you married to Mark Westbrook? That bas…that guy did me over for at least £20k!'

'Mark is my former husband, Mr Anderson. With the emphasis on 'former'. His business affairs were always a mystery to me. Pursue *him*, if you can track him down. Anyway, I very much hope to meet you and Rachel soon.'

'Meet? Soon?'

'Yes. At our wedding. Goodbye, Mr Anderson.'

*

A week before the wedding ceremony, Dominic received a most unwelcome e-mail:

Hi Dominic Crawley – I want Corrie back. She's mine. I loved screwing her, and yes, slapping her around. She's probably told you. But if you really want her, it will cost you £1 million, in cash. Or I'll make your life hell. No negotiation. I know you can afford it! Let me know your decision asap.

Mark Westbrook.

Dom recoiled from the words, and from the luminous screen, with its toxic message. 'Corrie'! He hesitated, then forwarded the message to a gleeful son-in-law. Mr Westbrook had helpfully included a mobile number. To Dom's huge relief and satisfaction, Mark Westbrook was never heard from – or of – again.

Dom and Corinna were married on 19 July, at Cheltenham Register Office. There were sixteen guests at the Reception, at the 4-star Lyon Arms, in Broadway; all were friends of the bride and groom.

Rachel and Paul had, at an early stage, declined the warmest of invitations – entreaties – to attend the ceremony. But, without warning, a sea-change seemed to have taken place. Rachel and Paul parachuted in unexpectedly, and delightedly, to the wedding ceremony. 'Got my £20k back!' Paul whispered to Dom, happily. 'All's well with the world!'

Next day, the happy couple flew off for their honeymoon: a relaxing month in the Seychelles, at the exclusive Fisherman's Cove Resort, on the tip of Beau Vallon Bay. The hotel was white; the environment, blue, gold and green. An aquamarine, turquoise sea, with white-sand beaches. The couple spent long afternoons relaxing on the glowing, palm-fringed coast, beneath a broad parasol. At frequent intervals Corinna would walk lazily to the inviting waters, and wade up to her thighs in the limpid, translucent ocean.

It was during one of these magical afternoons that Dom told Corinna about the private eye investigation; he didn't want that information, unlikely as it might sound, to reach his wife's ears from any other source. Corinna smiled, and shook her head: 'Dom, I really don't blame you. It was the right thing to do. Especially with my past – married to that animal!' Corinna shuddered, as though a cold wind had swept across the beach, ruffling her hair along with the palm trees. Then she brightened: 'But without that investigation you wouldn't have had the confidence to meet me. And *now* I'm Corinna Crawley. How cool does that sound!' Corinna had just emerged from a 'dip' in the ocean but, damp though she was, she embraced her husband warmly.

Even so, Dom decided not to mention Westbrook's crude attempt at blackmail, to his beautiful new wife. A step too far; why create an angry cloud in that clear, cobalt sky? Anyway, Westbrook, he felt sure, was the past. While the future had never looked brighter.

Corinna gloried in this idyllic environment, and had brought seven bikinis with her – one for each day of the week – to celebrate her new freedom, and her body's kinship with the sea and sky. Dom would recollect what day it was from the shade of Corinna's apparel. Black was for Mondays; red for Tuesdays; gold for Wednesdays; pink for Thursdays; white for Fridays; green for Saturdays; tangerine for Sundays. White – Friday – was Dom's favourite. He watched the gradual deepening of his wife's golden tan, beautifully offset by that white bikini. 'His wife.' How blissful, how perfect that sounded!

The couple would return to their hotel suite around 6 o'clock for a pre-prandial drink, and insistent, delightful, love-making. Vigorous polishing, thought Dom, with silent satisfaction.

*

In *Ode on a Grecian Urn*, John Keats writes: 'Beauty is truth, truth, beauty...That is all ye know on Earth, and all ye need to know.' Corinna and Dom returned to Charlton Park, and began their new married life's journey – adventurous, happy, and fulfilled – replete with frequent trips to glorious, romantic destinations across the globe. Certainly, meeting Dom was Corinna's best decision – ever.

Although he could never forget his many contented years with Alice, Dom's cup, too, ranneth over; he was ecstatically happy; each day a revelation. He is now 89 years old, and more fragile than of yore. But, in Corinna's telling phrase, he still has full control of all his faculties. And still hale, happy, and hearty, and eternally grateful for his good fortune.

Son-in-law Paul died, aged 60, from bowel cancer. He did not survive to see whether he had inherited a thick slice of Dom's fortune, and died an angry, bitter man. Six months later, a relieved Rachel re-married – a retired solicitor, named Richard Bolton. At Rachel's bidding, Richard made earnest attempts to be-friend her father. He was pushing on an open door. The couple – and Corinna, who was simply longing for friendship – are now all bosom pals, and meet regularly for family get-togethers.

When he looks admiringly at his still lovely, loving, wife – which is many times a day – Dom sometimes thinks back, to Paul Anderson. And sometimes he thinks back to Mark Westbrook.

Sometimes. But not often.

A CURIOUS CANCELLATION

'Good morning. Mrs Hodgkiss? Nick Hodgkiss, here, from W. Hodgkiss & Sons, Funeral Directors. No relation, of course. How are you, these days, Mrs Hodgkiss?'

'Well, I've felt better, I must admit. It's only a month or so since David passed away.'

'Of course Mrs Hodgkiss. I quite understand. Time can be a great healer, though. Of course, it's still early days. Let's see, now, we lost Mr Hodgkiss on 25 December. It's still only 25 January. But, Mrs Hodgkiss, I'm calling with some good news. To be honest, it's been bedlam, here, for months, now. We've practically run out of space. The number of funerals has slowed to a snail's pace but, of course – very sadly – people keep on dying.'

'You said you were calling with some good news?'

'Oh, yes, thank you. I do go rambling on. As you know, Mr Hodgkiss passed away on 25 December – Christmas Day…'

'Thank you for reminding me.'

'As you also know, Mr Hodgkiss died quite naturally. There were no unusual circumstances. But we've struggled to find a date to lay him to rest. And here we are a full month later! But the good news is that we've now found a slot – on 25 February. The 'good news' is that there's been a cancellation…'

'A cancellation? I don't understand…'

'Well – Nick Hodgkiss sounded quite animated – it's a very

curious case. A Mr Jonathan Crichton – pronounced 'Criton', and known by his middle name of 'Henry' – appears to have suffered some kind of seizure. The circumstances are obscure, but it seems Mr Crichton was entertaining at home at the time. Although his companion was too panic-stricken to operate his defibrillator, she did have the good sense to 'phone for an ambulance. Unfortunately, Mr Crichton was pronounced dead at the scene by the paramedic team. The following day, Mr Crichton's daughter called us to arrange the funeral – which was to take place on 25 February. So far, so good, as it were,' continued Nick – with mounting excitement in his voice.

'So what happened?' asked Mrs Hodgkiss, with some incredulity.

'Well that's the *curious thing*, said Nick with emphasis. 'Some time later – somewhat to the horror of the hospital orderlies – Mr Crichton woke up – just as he was about to be placed in the mortuary! Apparently, he said: 'Ice! Is it time for a g&t?''

'Good gracious! You mean that he was alive – all the time?'

'Indeed, yes. Or else a miracle occurred. And he still is… alive, that is. So no funeral. His relatives – daughters, mainly – he's a widower himself – were appalled, as well as overjoyed. He's a wealthy man, I understand, so their feelings were understandably mixed. Even so, miracle or no, the nursing staff were quite cross – not just about a dead man talking – though it did give them quite a fright – but of the resulting paperwork. Took no *end* of sorting. After all, some poor blighter had signed a death certificate. And they had to find Mr Crichton a proper bed, so that he could be checked over, prior to his release. Well, discharge. Quite a kerfuffle, apparently. The glass is always half-empty, in this life, Mrs Hodgkiss. In fact, Mr Crichton was made to feel rather guilty for his inconsiderate and rather unreasonable behaviour!'

'But Mr Crichton must be most relieved. Surely, happy?'

'Yes. He is only 48 so, hopefully, a good few years in him yet. But, there was a degree of embarrassment. He has these two daughters, and his solicitor lost no time in acquainting them with the terms of his Will. It seems he left a far bigger share of his Estate to Emma than to Estelle – something about Estelle's husband's conduct. At the same time, Emma, too, was outraged – she thought she'd be left everything, in the circumstances. And now the poor man will have to face the consequences!'

'Really! I don't see why Mr Crichton has anything to reproach himself with! He could have left it all to a dogs' home! Instead, he was leaving everything to his family. But if you can't leave what you have to whoever you want, the world's gone mad!'

'Well, looking on the bright side, Mr Crichton's confided that he's going to live every day now as though it's his last. You may not know, Mrs Hodgkiss, but W. Hodgkiss & Sons also operates a dating – that is, relationship – website. It's called '*Henrys and Henriettas*'. It's most discrete, and most tactful. And tasteful. As well as conducted in the most dignified and professional manner. Not to mention providing excellent value for money. We very much regard the service as a 'bolt on' – adding value to our other activities. It's all about taking care of the living, you know, Mrs Hodgkiss. All about client satisfaction…'

'Strange, Mr Hodgkiss – that's my name – Henrietta.'

'Yes, life's full of these curious coincidences… Anyway, we feel strongly – on the basis of our long experience – that, at some stage, our clients will be looking to the future. Mr Crichton was quick to subscribe to our service, and has become an enthusiastic member.'

'But was Mr Crichton your client? After all, he was supposed to be dead!'

'A very good point, Mrs Hodgkiss. I'm afraid that, when he unexpectedly returned to life, and to his wealth, he was very much left to pick up the pieces. Including Hodgkiss's own costs, which were quite considerable. I would emphasise, Mrs Hodgkiss, that it is still very early days for you. But the future is a very long time. With the greatest respect, you're still quite young. Do feel free to take a look at *Henrys & Henriettas*, when you have a moment. After Mr Hodgkiss's funeral, of course. So that's 11.00am on 25th February? Shall we get on with it?'

'Oh, yes please! I don't think there's much chance of David's returning to life! Not after the lifestyle he led!'

David Hodgkiss Esq., 51 years, was buried on 25 February, with all due formality, tears and mournful ceremony. And finality. The Eulogy was described as most splendid, and entirely fitting. And the 'Wake', with its canapés, deep-filled sandwiches and fresh cream cakes, quite delicious and appropriate to Mr Hodgkiss's position as a restauranteur. Henrietta, 46, felt that a long chapter in her life – she had been married for 26 years – had closed. It was a chapter that provided her with a range of memories; happiness and pleasure – but also disappointment, sadness and pain. David was a *restaurateur*, a pillar of the community, and a *bon viveur*; with a wicked sense of humour. But he was also a philanderer, a drunk, and a depressive; with a wicked temper. David and Henrietta were childless, and Henrietta had always wanted a pet dog – but the long and irregular hours involved in running a restaurant had frustrated even this desire. But were not all long marriages a roller-coaster – of highs and lows, of frustration, of love and heartache?

And – this being the real world, in real time, that had no regard for personal tragedy – the business – the restaurant – *La Fourchette* – had been struggling, thanks to the horrible Pandemic. Henrietta felt that the worry had contributed to David's early and unexpected demise. But she now had the added burden of selling the business, and of making ends meet.

Henrietta had never been busier, and her time was stretched. She lost herself in a whirlwind of activity. But, eventually, she found herself a little space. With some reservations, but also some curiosity, and a little trepidation, Henrietta Hodgkiss 'surfed' *Henrys & Henriettas*. Her late husband had 'banned' mirrors from their home ten years ago, when he started losing his hair. But Henrietta had insisted on keeping the full-length mirror on the inside door of her wardrobe. She looked at herself, now; naked, for the first time in many a year. Not bad; not bad at all, she murmured. Life in the old girl, yet.

A month later – on 25 March – at a most discrete and private ceremony – Henrietta married the said Jonathan Henry Crichton. Neither Emma or Estelle attended the wedding service; they were both furious with their father – this time, for marrying a woman he barely knew. Meanwhile, the happy couple sold their respective homes – and sold *La Fourchette* as a going concern. They began a new life, far away from Croydon, and far, far away from Henry Crichton's daughters, and their husbands. Henry and Henrietta bought a substantial, 18th century stone mansion in Cornwall; where they run a dog's home. And have lived happily ever after.

Brief Encounter 4:
SUNSHINE'S SHORT STORY

This is a short story. Perhaps, a very short story, since the action it describes is contained within barely an hour. But what an hour! I awoke, on 20 May: a glorious slice of sunshine glinted through the bedroom curtains. I felt good; relaxed and refreshed. I threw on some clothes, bade my dog *Henry* a hearty good morning, slurped down a coffee, then closed the door firmly behind us. We were out, fresh and smiling, in the great outdoors; the big, bold, brilliant, wide world.

A brisk walk along deserted streets led us to the local park, a green sward bathed in early morning sunshine. There were a scattering of people about: dog-walkers, joggers, a personal trainer with her middle-aged and corpulent client. *Henry* led me on a tour of the park – a meander that was sure to introduce me to as many passing examples of diverse humanity as was physically possible. No matter: on such a gorgeous morning, full of hope and optimism, I was replete with irrepressible *bonhomie*. Could life get any better than this?

Henry sidled up to a youth slumped on a park bench. This was unusual at 7.15am on a Wednesday morning. The – I guess – 20-year old was clad in baggy, sporty black and, though he sported a hoodie, looked ashen-faced and unshaven. He was looking intently at his smart 'phone. Had he been here all night? Never mind; each to his own. 'Good morning to you! What a lovely morning it is!' 'What's lovely about it? My girl friend's been cheatin' on me, with me best mate. And I'm skint. If that's not enough, my Facebook account's been disabled. What a nightmare!' 'Well, I really hope things start looking up for you soon!' I warbled, apologetically, since *Henry* had already bidden *au revoir.*

Moments later, *Henry* drew alongside a youngish woman, perhaps aged thirty, and greeted her with a wag of his tail. 'Beautiful morning!' I announced with a confident finality. 'Is it?' she replied, distantly, absent-mindedly stroking *Henry's* head. 'I hadn't really noticed.' Her pink hair fluttered in the gentle breeze. 'Well, in England, even in May, this kind of weather is pretty unusual' I continued, in my best weather-man voice. 'I'm afraid when you've lost your job due to this bloody Pandemic, and had to move back in with your parents, the frigging weather's a bit beside the point.' 'Quite', I said, quietly. 'I'm so sorry. I'm sure things will look up soon – the Pandemic's nearly behind us, and the economy's sure to pick up in a while.' She looked at me doubtfully. 'It'll take me years to dig my way out of the debt I'm in. When you're down, no bugger wants to help.' *Henry* had heard enough, and was determinedly on his way. 'Well, good luck: hope to see you again soon!' I gasped, and sped gratefully on my way.

Henry, ever the curious one, had sidled up to a figure, draped in a greatcoat; a male figure, sat disconsolately on yet another park bench. I had, on a previous outing, counted 24 of these structures, thoughtfully provided by the local council for its fatigued and wayward residents. This guy looked about 40: his seating area was surrounded by empty beer bottles and grubby fish and chip papers. *Henry* gave the scene a hopeful sniff. 'Good morning, my good man! What a fantastic morning it is!' He looked back at me with bloodshot eyes. 'Not when your wife's kicked you out, and you're homeless!' he replied, in a leaden tone. 'I wouldn't notice if it was pissin' down!' I noticed an empty beer glass by his side, and his eyes met mine. His look warned: 'don't.' So I resisted the almost-irresistible pun. Not even half empty. Instead I mumbled 'I'm so sorry,' a little apologetically. I fumbled in my pocket, and offered the guy my business card. 'I manage residential property – I might be able to help you out,' I ventured, as an aside. 'Cheers. But with no job and no money, I'm not sure you'd want to take a punt on me!' he replied, with an air of finality. *Henry* had already made good his escape, and I looked upon his departure, enviously. 'Must go, I'm afraid! Good luck! *Henry*! Wait for me!'

The indefatigable *Henry* had found another be-seated curiosity: a lady of indeterminate age, and comfortable girth, seated, and immersed in a book. I glanced a greeting in her direction. She was around 50 years of age, and was well dressed in a middle-aged forgettable kind of way. A fawn-coloured pug lay patiently by her side. *Henry* was sizing up the creature, and deciding that it was of marginal interest. The book was *War and Peace*; she had got as far as page 1. 'Hi there! What a fabulous morning it is! Couldn't be better, could it?' The woman smiled a wan smile. 'I suppose it's passable. A bit of a cool breeze, mind. And my i-phone tells me there's a twenty percent chance of rain, later.' 'Well, fancy that!' I replied, relieved to enter into a more conventional conversation. 'Couldn't help noticing your book – it takes some stamina, but I can assure you it's well worth it!' I ventured.

'Thanks for that,' she replied, mildly. 'Thought it might take my mind off other things. Like my husband's having an affair. Or affairs. Have you heard of dogging? I hadn't – 'til now. And the bastard won't move out. And my son's just been busted as a drug dealer. I thought everything was just fine. Now my life's in ruins!'

'Goodness, I'm so sorry. All I can say is, get the best advice you can, whether from friends or a solicitor…' 'Of course I'll be sure to do that. But humpty can't be put together again. I've been married for thirty years. I'm too old to want to start again. It's more than enough with Steve – never mind bloody Jonathan.' 'Well, enjoy the sunshine, and all the best!' I added hopefully, but feeling vaguely stupid. 'I must get after that *Henry*!'

Henry, voting with his feet, had continued his circuit, in the hope of finding a more exciting arrangement. He duly found it – a guy engaged in press-ups, next to a park bench containing his 'equipment' – sports drinks, towels, dumb-bells and a rucksack. From a distance, dressed in t-shirt and shorts, he looked honed and taut. As indeed it turned out – but as I drew nearer, his etched face revealed he had enjoyed, or endured, at least 60 summers, and 60 winters. 'Good morning! What a super morning!' I began. 'Yep!' he replied, pausing his routine, and sitting on the grass. 'Not bad. I'm doing this while it's relatively cool. It'll be too hot later in the day.' This promising start encouraged me to go on, especially as *Henry* had clearly detected some pungent odours hereabouts. 'Yes, a great time of day for exercise – you certainly look very fit!' 'Well, I had a heart attack twelve months ago. Quite a shock, I can tell you. Since then, I've lost three stones, and I'm training for a marathon. Unfortunately, my wife has just been diagnosed with cancer – so I'll need to stay fit and focused to help her through her own challenges. You're not a doctor by any chance?' 'Sorry, no.' Meanwhile, *Henry* had exhausted the possibilities on offer, and was sidling off towards the horizon. 'Well, all the best – hope all goes well!' I waved, already speeding after the runaway hound.

I found *Henry* staring into space – that is, into the face of a woman of around 70 years of age. Dressed modestly in multi-layers of dark clothing, she looked anxious, staring at the ground as she walked, in an oddly concentrated way. 'Good morning! Hope you're enjoying the sunshine?' 'What? I'm still looking for my keys. I lost them ages ago, and they're still not here. Can you help me?' she pleaded. 'Oh, dear. Of course I'll help. When did you lose them? And what do they look like?' 'Oh, I lost them some time ago, now. Can't remember exactly. They're my house keys. On a fob that's shaped like a cat.' 'But are you OK to get back in your house – I could call a locksmith?' 'No, my husband's at home. At least, I think he's still there. I'm afraid I must get on. Those keys must be somewhere...' 'Well, I'll keep looking for you, and get *Henry* on the case...I do hope they turn up soon!'

Having exhausted his interest, *Henry* had travelled, leisurely but astutely, to yet another park bench – the very last on our circular walk – to find an old chap resting in the sun's warming glow. Although I could detect only a bit of face, and two fleshy hands, I guessed him to be around 80 years of age. A flat cap protected his head; a grey beard protected his cheeks and chin. As *Henry* sniffed his leg, contemplating mischief, the elderly gent stirred. 'Good morning!' I saluted. 'Enjoying the sunshine?' He opened one eye, and stared in my direction. 'This your dog? I used to have one like that. Great companion.' 'Yes. Golden Retriever born and bred. Answers to the name of *Henry*. He's most discriminating with people. He seems to have taken a shine to you!'

'Well, he knows I'm a dog-person,' he smiled. 'And yes, I am enjoying the sunshine. At my age, it's pretty well all you have left. Wife gone. Kids gone. Health gone. Dogs gone. And a world gone mad. You know, life keeps taking. And, the older you get, the more it takes. On the other hand, perversely, the longer you live, the more life keeps giving. Until it stops. So enjoy the sunshine, my son. I intend to squeeze every last drop out of it while I still can. My earnest advice is to savour each and every day – every minute – of your life. Because, to this pass each and every one of us must come. And, though I'm old, I still have the power of pleasure. To see, to hear, to enjoy, to take delight in. I sincerely hope to see you – and *Henry* – again tomorrow...'

Henry and I returned home, brooding in silence. Of course, we never came across any keys, never mind keys with a fob in the shape of a cat. But I had come down with a quite sickening headache. I gave *Henry* his doggy-treats; he then retreated to his bed, to dream about his unusual, possibly unique, catchment of new friends. I also retired to bed, enervated and exhausted. The sun invaded the chink between the bedroom curtains, accusingly.

COMING UP ROSES

Geoff and Sarah Graham had been married for 35 years; Geoff liked to joke that you didn't get that long a sentence even for murder. Sarah indulged his little joke; because they were happy. Indeed, they'd always been happy, even if not consciously, overtly so. But there had always been a deep, silent satisfaction to their marriage, that was based on a bond of friendship and trust. Looking outwards towards the world, the couple had always employed the maxim: '*be* good, *do* good'. On the whole, all things considered, kindness and compassion seemed to achieve a great deal more than anger and hatred. They knew it sounded naive: but confronting life's ups and downs with a positive approach, a smile on their faces and a determination to make good things happen had always worked for them.

Geoff was now 65 years old; Sarah, 64. Geoff had retired five years ago from a varied career in the Civil Service. Geoff had been the first of his family to progress to university, where he studied Modern European History, and French.

This latter demands a little explanation. From the age of 12 years, Geoff's class of boys had been confronted with the obligation to learn a bizarre, exotic subject – French. 'Exotic' because none of the boys had any idea how a smattering of fluency in a strange, foreign language might provide a scintilla of practical application in their adult life; unlike woodwork, metal work or even English. For not one of these boys had travelled beyond the confines of Wolverhampton; nearby Birmingham itself was regarded as a hostile, foreign land. France was a different entity entirely – far away across the sea, alien, and quite irrelevant to their present and future lives.

But Geoff had not only a lively imagination, but a natural facility for language, and he began augmenting his lessons with his own home-based studies. These were secret studies: his father would have been furious at such a frivolous waste of time and, as it happened, frequently turned off Geoff's bedroom light just as Geoff was in the midst of articulating verbs or tenses. 'You can burn the midnight oil when you pay for it!' his father hollered, before slamming the door.

But Geoff went on to study French at 'O' and then 'A' level, and decided to continue his studies at the University of East Anglia. Both Sarah and he were Francophiles, and they had visited that tantalisingly close, but mysterious and magnificent, country at least two or three times each year throughout their adult lives.

Following university – with few positions available where he might follow his chief passions – Geoff joined the 'Home' Civil Service, eventually attaining the rank of 'Senior Executive Officer.' Sarah had retired at the same time, from her own career as a social worker. She, too, had progressed to university, and had met Geoff after graduating, when they had both returned – as graduates then did – to their home territory, and family homes, in the West Midlands.

If Geoff and Sarah had been happy in negotiating their stressful, challenging career paths, they were blissfully happy in retirement. Geoff often jested – he did like his little jokes – that he had toiled ceaselessly in the Circumlocution Office; while Sarah had loved social work, despite its unrelenting challenges and stresses. In latter years, however, Sarah had become increasingly frustrated by seemingly endless layers of bureaucracy, and the failure to tackle the profound malaise corroding, enervating Britain's social fabric. So retirement was seen as a welcome release, after almost 40 years of supporting desperate families, struggling against (as Sarah saw it) a careless, uncaring – and under-funded – welfare juggernaut.

Geoff and Sarah still lived in the first home that they had purchased on marriage – on the strength of their 'permanent' jobs with secure establishments; a trim, prim, three-bed detached in a suburban setting, five miles from the nearest middling town. The couple had no children, but most of their family and friends lived fairly locally – including Geoff's brother and sister, Peter and Sue – and Sarah's sister, Sandra.

Geoff was a tall, spare man, good looking, but with a thin, pale, somewhat creased face – he did laugh a great deal – and a mop of silver hair. Geoff had lived a moderate, not to say ascetic, life-style; he was modest in his drinking, preferring red wine to beer, and modest, too, in his dietary 'regime'. For Geoff, the 'five a day' fruit and fibre maxim was regarded as a minimum, rather than a maximum; he loved broccoli, sprouts, spinach, and all kinds of blue and red berries. And he ate red meat sparingly, preferring fish and poultry. Sarah humoured – no, respected – Geoff's choices, while adjusting food preparation to cater for her own more free-wheeling palette. Although Geoff was friendly and gregarious – with a smallish clique of firm friends with whom he enjoyed golf and tennis – it was the bubbly, still blonde – and slightly, but carelessly, plumpish Sarah – who was the real party animal. Sarah's starry array of friends stretched almost to infinity, and retirement had given her lunch parties, dinner parties and evening socialising extra fizz and zest.

While the days of most people can be neatly sub-divided into three equal parts – working, sleeping and watching TV – the Graham family were made of different metal. The couple led useful, productive lives. Geoff and Sarah were energetic and vital: in addition to golf and tennis, Geoff played tenor sax in a jazz band, *The Blue Groove;* was an active rambler and naturalist with a local group, and had a passion for wildlife conservation. Geoff's and Sarah's busy, hard-working married life had been accompanied by – they worried – a frightening and unsustainable destruction of the natural world – in pursuit of 'progress' – that they regarded with increasing sadness, anger and horror. The couple felt keenly and deeply about the wholesale destruction of rainforests, pollution of the oceans, and the careless, man-driven extinction of natural species. From quite an early stage in their marriage, the couple had decided to dedicate 10% of their income to wildlife conservation; they only wished they could have afforded more; though that '10 per cent' had, in monetary terms, expanded ten fold as, over time, their income and wealth increased.

Geoff had also achieved some acclaim as a historian and authority on the Napoleonic period, with his book *The Peninsular War – Portraits*. Geoff's fluency in French was invaluable in his consulting primary and secondary historical sources. Sarah, meanwhile, organised monthly charity lunches, with guest speakers, and was a member of the local amateur dramatic society. *A Taste of Honey* was their latest production. Sarah was also a keen gardener, and wildlife gardener – witness their own colourful, scented, butterfly-bestrewn patch of heaven.

Retirement had brought a welcome release and new energy to leisure and social activity, together with a newly discovered passion for cruising. But cruising with a purpose: the couple's first cruise had been a long awaited and anticipated trip to Rio de Janeiro; and, from Rio, travelling to Manaus, capital of Amazonia. Several days of guided trekking in pristine Brazilian rainforest, where they saw – and heard – howler monkeys, macaws and even a jaguar – had made a profound impression on the couple. This first, revelatory trip, several months into retirement, had mushroomed into three-per-year over the preceding 12 months.

The Caribbean, the Med, and the Norwegian fjords had all featured on their helter-skelter new hobby-horse. Yet, there was always a conservationist, an environmental, a wildlife aspect and theme to their global wanderings that generated much soul-searching, and continued to give much food for thought.

Despite these deep, underlying concerns, all seemed set to continue seamlessly into a bright, smiling future. Then, apparently out of the blue, and without warning, Geoff struggled to eat on Christmas Day – of all days. For some reason he could not enjoy, could hardly eat, the traditional festive meal – which, in his own case, was quite modest in its proportions. And, having eaten as much as he physically could, Geoff struggled again to relieve himself of the waste in his system. This pattern – of poor appetite, with less and less of his favourite foods passing his lips – and of a congested, unresponsive digestive tract, continued for several weeks into the New Year. Geoff lost weight – weight he could hardly afford to lose – and appeared drawn and gaunt. He sought advice from his pharmacist, and obtained medication to relieve constipation. There was some relief; but not much, and not for long. Clearly, Geoff was in some discomfort, but remained reluctant to consult his doctor. Whatever the problem, it *must* clear up in time; things always had. He had a history of prolonged rude health. Sarah, understandably anxious, urged her husband to seek medical advice. Towards the end of January, there having been very little improvement in his condition, Geoff relented, and made an appointment to see his G.P.

'What's the matter with you?' barked the Receptionist, when Geoff 'phoned.

'I was hoping the doctor might be able to advise *me*,' responded Geoff. 'But, basically, I'm having trouble digesting my food.'

'Sounds like indigestion. Or maybe heartburn. Right, our first slot is 9.00am on 14 February.'

'But that's more than two weeks away,' replied Geoff, coolly. 'If you get any cancellations, could you please let me know?'

'OK, but unlikely,' the Receptionist blurted, replacing the receiver almost before her words were out.

In the two and a half weeks prior to the appointment, Geoff's condition deteriorated. He had now lost more than a stone in weight, and was listless and tired. And he was experiencing difficulty in sleeping soundly. Geoff's body, for the first time in his adult life, was struggling with an acute condition.

'Good morning, Mr Graham. You know, we haven't seen you in five years. You're one of our best patients,' the Doctor added, with a little chuckle at his own joke. 'So what can we do for you?' he asked, reverting to a business-like tone. The Doctor himself looked avuncular, but tired and stressed. Geoff thought he could do with seeing a doctor, himself.

Doctor Taylor listened to Geoff's description of symptoms, then examined his vital signs. 'Well, your blood pressure's OK, but you seem to have lost a lot of weight. And that's all happened in the last couple of months? Well, you're now significantly underweight. And you're suffering some discomfort in the bowel? I'm referring you for an endoscopy, and a CT scan, at Hurrell's Hall Hospital. I do wish you'd come to see me sooner. It can take some time to get to the bottom of these things. No pun intended,' the Doctor smiled.

'Well, I did try to make an appointment several weeks ago. But your Receptionist told me that nothing was available. How long for the endoscopy?'

'It's usually about three months. But I'll try to hurry it along.'

'Three months? Nothing serious, then?' Geoff attempted one of his customary laughs, but Doctor Taylor remained impassive.

Returning home, Geoff adopted a pleasant, re-assuring tone with his wife. But Sarah was not re-assured. 'Three months for a procedure? If it *is* anything serious, three months could make a big difference. It really isn't good enough. We've hardly ever needed the Health Service. Until now, that is. I just don't know why we pay taxes for services that barely exist. It's ridiculous!'

Over the next few days, the couple discussed the various options available to them. And, at Sarah's strong bidding, it was decided to seek an urgent private consultation. An endoscopy, and CT scan, were completed within two weeks, and the results made available two days later. Geoff had contracted bowel cancer. The cancer was advanced, and inoperable. A course of chemotherapy was advised as the only viable option. Suddenly, the future looked bleak, narrow and closed-in.

While Geoff's condition continued to deteriorate, and golf and tennis a distant memory, the couple remained determinedly optimistic. What was the alternative? They both loved life; and loved each other. It was far too soon to shuffle off this mortal coil. What had he done to deserve this? Geoff reflected bitterly, to himself. He'd lived a moderate, healthy life. And lived a *good* life. This was so unfair, and so undeserved. And Geoff began to worry about his legacy. What had he done with his life? What had he achieved? How might he be remembered? Would he even *be* remembered?

Sarah reminded him, and re-assured him. 'Just look how far we've come, Geoff! Just remember how far we've come! My mother was a hairdresser and cleaner, and my father a labourer; and your mother a school dinner lady, and your father a foundryman. Nothing wrong with all that, of course – all decent, honest, good hard work. But we've done well, Geoff. Very well. We gave ourselves a leg up, rather than just replicating the past. The ladder had – just – been put in place; but we still had to climb it!'

Geoff reflected, ruefully: 'I remember my father walking purposefully into our living room at home. I was reading a book on the Peninsular War, for my 'O' level studies. My father said:

'Can you put that book down for a minute and do something useful?'

'Like what?' I asked.

'The rose beds need weeding. They won't weed themselves.'

'But there's hundreds of bushes. That will take ages!' I replied, aghast.

'But, when it's done, at least you can see what you've achieved!' he said with finality. 'Anyway, what ya reading about now?'

'It's about The Peninsular War.'

'Penin…? When did that happen?'

'Between 1808 and 1814.'

'Good God! That's nearly 200 years ago! What's the bloody point!'

'I've always remembered that chat with dad,' reflected Geoff. 'What *was* the bloody point?'

'The bloody point' said Sarah, 'is that those studies informed your knowledge and world view, transported you to university, turned you into a decent, civilised human being, and helped provide you with opportunities, a life-style, prospects and a vision that were beyond your dear old Dad's dreams. And enabled you to write books that are admired for their depth and originality. If Dad had had *his* way, you'd still be weeding those bloody rose beds. For bloody eternity. Rather than writing books, playing jazz, and putting the world to rights!'

Geoff laughed. 'Yes. For Dad, history began in 1939. He didn't think through that history has made us *who* we are, and *what* we are. Arguably, the origins of World War 2 go back to at least the Napoleonic period, and early German nationalism and romanticism. Not to mention Prussian militarism. Even so, Dad did carry on carrying on what he did best – growing and showing roses. Right until the end – found, face down, in his rose garden, at the age of 93.'

Geoff pondered for a few seconds. 'But, seriously, Sarah,

apart from my marrying you – light of my life – what *have* I achieved? What have I got to *show* for my life, at journey's end?'

'You've got plenty to show for your life, Geoff. Plenty. Like the new manuscript you're writing, now. And the charity we're planning. And it's not over yet. Promise!'

Geoff endured three courses of chemotherapy that, with its severe toxic impact, eroded his energy and vitality, and subdued his once buoyant spirit. The cure was almost as unpleasant as the disease but, Geoff was assured, his illness had now been halted, and he was in remission. The cancer might return but, for the foreseeable future, he could breath – and live – again. There was much relief all round, and a few smiles. But, deep down, Geoff – and particularly Sarah – remained in a state of uncertainty and unease. Geoff had become a weakened, wizened, hollowed out, old man.

One glorious, mid-May morning, the sun coursing through the bedroom windows, Sarah awoke. It was 6.30am. She recollected that she was birthday girl: 14 May – 65 years young! Sarah felt under the covers for Geoff; she felt only a cold, empty space.

Hurrying downstairs with some trepidation, Sarah found the body of her husband, slumped in a chair beside the dining table. On the table, beside his trusty Parker fountain pen, was an open birthday card. It read: 'To my darling Sarah, on her special birthday. With all the love in the world, forever. Your dearest husband, Geoff xxx.'

Sarah called for an ambulance. But she knew it was a formality. Geoff's body was quite cold. Our little life is rounded with a sleep. Sarah accompanied her husband's body to the hospital, from profound love and respect. She was in a state of deep shock; shock accompanied by a strange sense of relief. There would be plenty of time for grief, anon. They had completed a long journey together, and she had supported Geoff every step of the way. Every journey must end like this. There was only pride; and no regrets.

Sarah reflected that there is only one shot at life, and theirs had been a long, looping, kindly shot towards the sun. They had created much joy, much good, much laughter, and barely any pain. With whatever time was left to Sarah, she would make that time count, and secure Geoff's – and their – legacy. A day or two following Geoff's passing, Sarah was ferreting out their Will to discuss with their solicitor when she discovered an A4 manilla envelope marked: 'To be opened upon my death.' The envelope was dated a mere week before Geoff's demise. Geoff had left helpful and detailed instructions for a modest, humanist funeral, with a wicker coffin, and poetry from Clare and Keats. And confirmation – though hardly necessary – of his eternal love for Sarah. Geoff also asked that his ashes should be scattered in their proposed new venture's first realised project.

Sarah lost no time in carrying out Geoff's wishes. Within weeks, a new edition of Geoff's *The Peninsular War* was issued. And Geoff's new book – that he had struggled to complete, with Sarah's secretarial help – was published. *Napoleon's Talisman: Joachim Murat* received critical and public acclaim. *The Blue Groove* issued a CD of covers, with Geoff's sax prominent on *Baker Street*. And *The Graham Foundation* was launched – a charity dedicated to establishing new wildlife habitats – its core funding provided by the inheritance left by Geoff's father, Eric. A key condition of funding was that wild roses were planted in the hedgerows of new nature reserves. Geoff's and Sarah's own resources would be exclusively directed to these charitable activities – augmented by Sarah's energetic and inspirational fund-raising lunches. Sarah's own grief was channelled into her own memoir, *Deep Waters*, an account of her and Geoff's life together. Sarah was even interviewed on *Woman's Hour*.

Geoff may no longer be physically present, Sarah thought

daily, but his influence, and his beneficial power, would be around for as long as the planet itself: for as long as the Earth spun in space. As John Keats wrote: 'Beauty is truth, truth, beauty. That is all ye know on Earth, And all ye need to know.'

THROUGH ETTA'S EYES

Hi. I think. My name is *Henrietta*. I'm black, and bold, and beautiful. Very classy, *I* think. My rich, glossy coat – as black as jet – gleams in the sunshine. And my emerald necklace – well, Charlie calls it a collar – complements my gorgeous eyes. My boyfriend – he lives next door – is called *Amadeus*. Also classy.

I'm lying on my *chaise longue,* in the studio, where I luxuriate all day; watching the world go by. The studio is spacious, but full of screens, photo-lights and props; mirrors and sky-lights flood the space with a luminous intensity. Yet the studio retains a bohemian feel – with scattered oriental furniture, sheepskin rugs and exotic drapes. A bit decadent, in fact. But always warm. A constant 25°. That suits me – and suits the furless, two-legged creatures who populate the studio – and perform each day. Charlie – my two-legged friend – runs the place. He sometimes refers to me as '*Etta*'. I don't like it. Most disrespectful. I'll forgive him – but only if he gives me fresh chicken tonight.

I enjoy watching the two-legged performers. Their behaviour is quite fascinating. Well, in small doses. The one type is nearly always clothed – but in the worst possible taste – and bald, fat and quite old. The other type is young, slim and fur-less. The first type seems to be male – though I can't actually see any sexual organs, I can smell that pungent, testosterone male thing. The other type – I'm pretty sure – is female. They don't have male members – but they do have teats. A dead giveaway.

There are three performers in the studio today. My friend Charlie introduced them to the photographic equipment – 'kit' – lights, screens, props – and to me. The three bi-peds introduced themselves to Charlie as Henry (plausible), Emilia (I wish), and the blonde – Donatella (as if). Emilia and Donatella? Well, I ask you. With those accents? Charlie seemed in a good mood. He charges £50 an hour for studio hire. He's so easily bought. I can twist him round my paw. Even so, throughout this 'induction', Charlie stroked my head in a familiar way that I have always found rather irritating.

Anyway, the two females smiled at me, and stroked me gently. The male – (that Henry) pulled a face. Bastard. The male was – as usual – fully clothed. Badly – in hoops and stripes, and baggy shorts. As usual, too, he was also bald, overweight, and very sweaty. The females were tall, slim and furless. Except, in the one case, for close-cropped dark fur on her head – and a strange, neat triangle of fur on her lower body. The other female had long, blonde fur on her head, that reached down to her shoulders. The colour reminded me of my beau – *Amadeus*. Her fur was luxurious – and her shape, for a two-legged animal, very pleasing. Both females had large teats. They smiled a lot. And they also smelled nice.

The two females began to perform. The bald performer raised a black box to his sweaty face, and said things like: 'look into the camera, babe! Give me that come hither look! Drop that chin! Blow me a kiss, babe! Square on, hon! Give it me full on! The camera loves you, hon!' Each time he clicked his small black box, there was a blaze of light that, for an instant, engulfed one performer or other, as if freezing them in the moment.

The dark-fur headed performer – very lithe – a little like a coat-less cat – was apparently called 'babe', as far as Henry was concerned. I prefer Emilia. Even better, Henrietta. The blonde performer he called 'hon'. I suppose it saved time: if he'd had to say 'Emilia' and 'Donatella' each time, before clicking his machine, he wouldn't have got much, as he put it, 'in the can.' But, for the next two hours, it was certainly all 'babe' and 'hon', as an excited – er, Henry – poured out his unctuous orders to his submissive, giggling performers. 'Hon – go to profile – hands through your hair! Pout at me babe! Love that lens! Babe – raise your arms – give it to me, babe!'

The female performers made light of Henry's demands – commands: bending, twisting and gurning to his heart's desire. Every time Henry uttered an injunction – do this, do that – the sweat poured down his florid face. 'This is great, babe! Give it some more! Right, it's in the can!'

I thought I saw – through my sleepy eye – Henry's shorts tightening. What was all that about, I thought? But then – after nearly two hours of posing and prancing – Donatella – 'Hon' – approached him with a smile, and put her arm around his waist. Well, at least she tried. 'Time for a fag break, Henry. I'm bushed!'

Donatella reached inside her bag for some stuff, and then lit a small tube. Unlike me, she obviously couldn't read the large 'No Smoking' sign prominently sited on the wall. Then all hell broke loose. Donatella – mistaking me for a cushion – almost sat on me. As a large, round mound of solid flesh threatened to squash me, I lashed out, and she screamed. 'The bloody cat's scratched my arse! Christ, how's that going to look on the shots!'

While Emilia searched frantically for talcum powder, the smoke alarm went crazy. By now, I was hiding beneath one of the drapes – I'm a stickler for health and safety – but Charlie burst in, and demanded to know what the – I'm afraid I can't repeat his intemperate language – was going on. His accusing eyes met Donatella's guilty expression – and smoking gun, as it were – but his expression changed when he glanced – for a little longer than was actually necessary, or indeed polite, I thought – at Donatella's teats. 'Donatella? When Henry's finished, I'd like to have a session with you. Make up for the smoke alarm fiasco. OK?' Donatella nodded her assent, with a smile expressing her relief. 'But first I need to get first aid on my ass! Your bloody cat's attacked me!'

I bridled at the description, as well as the attempt to shift blame. I had acted only in self-defence. 'OK', smiled Charlie. 'She's a bit feisty, that one. But I'll kiss it better, if that'll help.' Charlie gave her one of his 'I'm quite a lad' smiles. She smiled back; a touch patronising, but served him right. 'It wouldn't have happened if you hadn't sat on the poor thing,' sulked Emilia, who was suddenly feeling neglected. 'Don't worry, Emilia,' soothed Charlie. I'll need you as well...' Emilia gave him a winning smile. Henry looked hang-dog deflated. Strangely, perhaps coincidentally – I'm not an expert on this species – the bulge in his shorts had also mysteriously deflated.

Charlie seemed to notice – the hang-dog expression, that is. 'Henry, why don't you carry on for another half an hour? On me.' Henry's florid face brightened. 'After you've finished with hungry Henry, girls – he's never had enough – Emilia and Donatella, is it? – come round next door for a spot of lunch. Henry's hang-dog look re-appeared, as he realised he was excluded from the invitation. 'Then,' continued Charlie, brightly, 'this afternoon, we'll put you through your paces. We'll have a bit of fun! But do throw on a few clothes before coming round!' he laughed. 'It's chilly out there; don't want you catching cold!'

Charlie paused. 'She may have caused mayhem, but has anyone seen my cat – *Henrietta?*' 'That's more like it!' I thought. I emerged cautiously from beneath a purple drape, emerald eyes glowing. I must have looked fabulous. 'Ah, there you are! *Amadeus* is looking everywhere for you, you sly hussy!'

Is he, now? Well, I've had quite enough of these weird human bi-peds. Too predictable. Too boring. Too banal. And too – bald. With one bound, I was free.

ART FOR ART'S SAKE

For 'Giovanni', God smote, and soared; and shined;
While, in his Lodge, young Mozart gaily dined.
For 'Figaro', God sweated, swore, and sighed;
While Mozart kissed his sweet and scented bride.

Ralph – called 'Rall' – for reasons lost to obscurity – and pronounced as in 'tall' – and Kelly Withers, both 51, live in a suburban village near Winchester. They are also both secondary school teachers – though at different schools.

The couple have been married – to each other – for 28 years. Though they would have bridled at the suggestion that their relationship was 'in a rut,' 'humdrum' or that they were 'treading water,' Rall and Kelly are convinced – a touch complacently, perhaps – that the marriage is smooth, stable, and secure. Unexciting, OK. But, come on: 28 years! Boredom is kept at bay, quite unconsciously, by frenetic activity, professional and private, that leaves little space or time for thought. 'Come on,' Kelly might have said: 'this is modern life! Get used to it!'

The couple's evenings are generally spent on small talk – 'shop': the new generation of pupils' increasingly erratic behaviour; the challenges of banging a smidgen of knowledge into little shits obsessed with selfies and social media; the suffocating tsunami of demands generated by endless government bureaucracy.

In his 'spare' time – when there is any – Rall loves listening to classical music: mainly the marvellous Mozart; while Kelly gorges herself on the world's cuisines. Her holy trinity consists of Delia, Mary and Nigella – washed down with a soupcon of Gordon.

Rall and Kelly have invested time and energy in their – distracting – respective hobbies. Writing fiction, for him; playing an electronic piano keyboard, for her. But finding time for these pursuits is becoming increasingly frustrating…Here is Rall's day…

6.50am. Thank God – Saturday! Awake! But, God: everything to do! *'Art for Art's Sake'*! The title of my new piece; recounted in my dreams. Now I just need the time – *create* the time – to set it down, using the choicest words, in the most impactful order.

But wait. First I need a piss. Get the butter out for breakfast. Change my sweaty underpants. Fuss our Labrador dog, *Harvey*. Unlock the door. Let the cat – *Otto* – into the garden. Put the kettle on. Get the milk from the doorstep. Wash and shave. Comb hair. Get dressed. Switch on news. Christ! (*Only* bad news!). Get the toaster out. Oh; bid Kelly good morning.

7.00am. Slurp tea. Now then: *'Art for Art's Sake'*. Where was I? A short story; a conflicted couple. Unhappy; at a crossroads. Belinda and Saul. A French teacher; and an English teacher. They don't speak the same language. There is no distance – no dimensional shift – between work – school – and home. It's a kind of continuum of monotony. Neither understands how they've come to this. Married for merely five years, Saul could never have imagined that his feelings for his beguiling young wife could have become blunted, so quickly. Or Belinda believe that married life with a vital young husband become tarnished by the demands of work, and her husband's frustration and bitterness.

In her leisure time, Belinda is passionate about art – painting. While Saul is passionate about writing. Bel thinks in images; Saul thinks in words. She sells her paintings. He's trying to get published – poetry. Fat chance. They're both expert communicators. But not with each other. No longer connect. Artistically, or personally. Respectively, 26 and 27. Hardly tasted life! God, where *is* the plot going? Where is it meandering? And towards what conclusion?

7.10am. Chew toast. Slurp tea. First look at weather: mid-July. Shaping up for a broiler. Stay hydrated. Already getting on for 7.30! *Harvey,* where are you? Walkies time! Three laps round the Park! See you soon, Kelly, love!

'Morning, morning, morning' – to the bizarre, frazzled, community of dog walkers. Moan, moan, moan. Weather – yes, there's always weather! Yes, too bloody hot! Politics? Yes, and always politics! Crime! Yes, where are *your* little darlings? 'How is *Harvey,* today?' One walker: 'Bastard husband's done a runner!' Another: 'Our Sam's moved back in, with his girlfriend and sprog.' Another: 'Lost me mother yesterday…?' 'Lost? Have you called the police? Oh, I see; so sorry.' *Harvey* spots a bitch, and prepares himself for serious fun. The – lady – owner cackles. Cackles soon replaced by hysteria. 'Relax, lady, it's only nature…'

Thinks – while watching *Harvey* run after a ball: Art – a painting – is an artefact, each work created, unique. Because it's a physical object – as well as being 'art' – each piece is vulnerable: maybe destroyed by fire or flood, degraded or faded by the sun; cracked and damaged by the inexorable process of time. Yet, for decades – even hundreds of years – it can be treasured; valued; even lusted after. And, if the artist has a 'reputation', highly prized, highly valuable – to be admired in private or corporate spaces, or museums, or galleries.

But poetry can be immortal. Universal. Great poetry, once writ, once forged in the mind's white heat, cannot be un-writ. It enters the consciousness; enters the culture; enters the curriculum. We learn from it; we study it; we love it. But it rarely earns anyone a bean; once freed from the spirit, like air, or water, poetry is *free*.

This is the nub of the problem, between Saul and Bel: not merely boredom. Jealousy. Jealousy feeding on bitterness. Or bitterness feeding on jealousy. Same difference. Bel is naturally talented, and her paintings – portraits, seascapes, landscapes – are selling well, to private buyers, and commercial galleries. And she's accepting private commissions – for hundreds of pounds each.

Though Saul is working equally hard, and employing tremendous mental energy in the creative process, he's finding little interest in his work. Poetry – about love, about heartache, about betrayal – *should* have a value. But it doesn't. Like a note of music played, it just disappears. Read; heard. Gone. If Keats couldn't make any money…But it's making Saul feel somehow isolated, and under-appreciated…

8.10am. Arrive back home, breathless and knackered. *Harvey* in mock disgrace. Atterboy! Rewarded with *bonios*. See a bare thigh at top of the stairs. 'Kell, have we time for a quick, you know…?'

'Rall, you must be kidding. I know you can be *indecently* quick, but we're *Tesco* bound in five minutes. Anyway, I thought you were writing a story?'

'Fat chance!' Quick – *very* quick – shit and shower.

8.20am. Ensconced in the Volvo, with Kelly and the panting *Harvey*. How *does* the story continue?

Belinda is opulent: full, fresh and flowing, like a Renoir woman. Saul is taut, angular, sharp – like a Braque cubist painting: his sharpness enhanced by frequent visits to the gym. Saul is becoming fearful for their future; Belinda, self-contained, and confident in herself…but enervated by arguments, with peevish squabbling – alternating with sulkiness; with moodiness. Sex seems a distant memory.

8.40am. Tesco! Forty minutes foraging with shopping list,

and with trolley. Atomised couples, in their bubbles, meandering, or charging around. Check-out, pay, load car, stroke the ever-patient *Harvey*. Arrive home and unpack.

9.40am. Time for a coffee, and a chat. 'How's the story going, Rall…?'

'Well, it's *beginning* to take shape. But I don't seem to be able to find the time..' Kelly shrugs. 'Not to worry. There's no deadline, is there? But *please* don't forget the lawns this morning. And I think those window baskets need watering. Oh, and don't forget Melinda's popping round for a spot of lunch!'

'Melinda? Oh my God! *Why?*'

'Because she's upset, and needs some moral support. She's been traumatised – just about to announce to Paul, her husband of 25 years, that she was leaving him for a woman called Sonia – when *he* announces that he's leaving *her* – for a woman – his Secretary – called Sonia. The trouble is that it's the same bloody Sonia. But Sonia – no doubt pissed off with being a captive audience to their mutual sniping, not to mention their bedroom small talk – takes fright and buggars off to Spain with her fitness instructor, Wolfgang. But not before scamming her erstwhile lovers for 25 grand each – allegedly to put a deposit on a new apartment. So Melinda – and Paul – face a triple whammy: jilted by each other, jilted by their new partner – and robbed of their expected new life. A glass not just totally empty, but melted into a very rude finger. You really couldn't make it up!'

'I suppose not…'

10.10am. Begin mowing lawns. Come on, creative juices! Why do we *do* this creative shit? When we could be fishing, flying, fucking? Does anyone give a monkeys?

Mowing the lawns. Come on! I *know*: Saul has met a young woman at the gym, and begins an intense physical affair, following each workout. Two paradises in one. The affair with Skye – a married mother of two – goes on for three months, before Saul

– following a great deal of soul-searching, and worried by stray words – uttered in passion – such as 'love' and 'divorce' – brings it to a sudden close. He abruptly changes his gym membership, while dumping the nubile Skye. Saul feels guilty – not at the dumping – Skye was notorious in gym-circles – but at his betrayal of his beautiful – and innocent – young wife. But there is a sliver of a silver lining: Saul's sexual repertoire, under Skye's tutelage, has expanded exponentially.

10.40am, and lawns appear immaculately trimmed. Can we get creative?

'Rall, please don't forget that you'll need to pick up Melinda – and drop her off at home, later. Paul's taken their car, apparently. But, really, the Volvo needs a good clean first – inside and out – it's a bloody disgrace at the moment!'

'Christ! Thought I had five minutes! It'll take forever!'

11.00am. Begin cleaning car – inside and out. The buggar is large, and white, and filthy. I enter a kind of mental bubble...

Belinda is deeply saddened that relations – both emotionally and physically – between herself and Saul – have soured; it almost feels like an estrangement. But she is young and desirable. And pretty; and much admired. One of Belinda's patrons – a 35 year-old smoothie businessman called Tom Banks – clearly fancies his chances with the comely Belinda. Tom, a publisher, has convinced himself that, for £500, he's bought the portraitist as well as the picture. Mr Banks is lucky that he's found the young woman at such a low ebb in her life. One Saturday afternoon, visiting his home with the newly completed portrait – the crafty Banks has despatched his wife to *Waitrose* – the despondent Belinda allows herself to be seduced. Tom has gained, not only a glowing new – self-congratulatory – portrait, above his mantlepiece, but a glowing memory, in his bed. Tom's grin is now frozen in time, and he grins each time he looks up at his image. Ah, Tom Banks, you old rogue!

Belinda is shocked by Tom's ardour; his passion; his remorseless energy. God! Could it be like this!? But also shocked and ashamed that she has succumbed so readily; so easily has betrayed her (faithful) young husband. She tells herself that the episode is entirely her fault; a one-off that cannot be repeated. But yet – there is a new awareness; an opening to enticing possibilities, and inviting new vistas.

11.30am. Car now shining brightly, and worthy of receiving the tragic figure of Melinda. Drive the eight miles to her house, in the Hampshire sticks at Sutton Scotney. Put Mozart on the CD player: *The Marriage of Figaro*. A tale of a lecherous Count, and his ballsy servants. Ah, Mozart. The greatest operas. The greatest symphonies. Just how did he find the *time?*

11.55am. Arrive. Melinda sees me, and bounces down the four steps from her front door, in high heels. Remarkably well preserved, for 47. I recall I used to call her: 'Little Miss Dancing Tits.' 'Thank you, Rall.' Peck – over long – on cheek.

12.20pm. Arrive home. Over lunch, Melinda consumes *three* courses, and the best part of a bottle of chardonnay. Just where does she put it all? Melinda and Kelly very emotional, very empathetic, very close to tears… I maintain a respectful distance. Coca Cola, only.

2.00pm. Drive Melinda back to her house. Arrive. She leans over; I feel the warmth. Kisses me on the cheek. 'Do come in, Rall – I need your advice. *Desperately.*'

'Thanks, Melinda. But I need to be getting back. You know; stuff to do… And what about Paul? And Sonia?'

'They can go fuck themselves. You know, Rall, word has it you used to call me 'Little Miss Dancing Tits.' Do come in for a while…'

'You do know, Melinda, I'm a happily married man?' She smiles. And puts a hand on my knee. 'Then there really is no problem, is there?' 'OK', grudgingly. I'm longer than necessary;

longer than is acceptable, or explicable. *Now* I know where she puts it all…

While I'm – deeply, intensely – advising Melinda, words coagulate in an otherwise vacant mind. I commit urgent text to my head:

During coffee after lunch, Saul decides to confront Belinda with his fears: 'Bel, we must talk. We're young. We have so much to live for. We have decent jobs, decent incomes and a nice house. But we seem to be drifting apart. I just don't get it. I love you, Bel. I'll do anything in the world to make you happy!'

'Well, Saul, I don't *feel* happy. I haven't for some time. And I don't feel *loved,* anymore. You seem so distant and unapproachable. So *angry* all the time! So what are we going to do? How change?'

'Bel, I have a plan. But I can't do it all on my own. We need to work at it together!'

'A plan? Please go on. I'm intrigued. But I'm not being deliberately difficult. I just don't feel that we're a unit these days. But, I mean, there's no one else!'

Saul smiled. 'Well, that's a start. The first thing we need to do is to talk more. I mean, every day. About our feelings. Our needs. What we want from each other. Out of life.'

'OK. Second?'

'I'll learn how to cook; prepare our meals. Then I'll cook our evening meals every day – I know you've never enjoyed the whole thing.'

'Wow! What a relief!'

'Next, I think you need to go out more – with your friends. You're young; let your hair down – enjoy yourself, girl. Embrace some *freedom!*'

'That's great! I like the sound of that – consider it done!'

'Fourth, I'd like you to teach me to paint – a new skill, that will help bring us together. I'll never be in your league, but I'm sure I'll really enjoy the learning experience, and expressing myself creatively.'

'Really, not a problem. I am a teacher, after all – I can add art teaching to my repertoire!'

'In return, if you like, I'll guide you through the magic rites of poetry. So you can express yourself, in an almost infinite variety of styles…'

'Phew. Am I ready for this? But maybe in French? Possibly romantic verse? Well, so far, so good. I'm on board. Anything else in the plan?'

'Mmm…Maybe. Let's just stay intrigued, for now…'

I think – blimey, must do this more often! (Mental note: must learn some French phrases).

3.30pm. Start for home. Shaken and stirred. So what box does *that* fit into? Cheating? Exploiting a vulnerable woman – worse – friend? Providing moral support? Maybe all three. God, it's so hot! I'm sweating like a leaky bucket!

Put Mozart on the CD player: *Don Giovanni*. A tale of a lecherous Don, and his vengeful victims. Ah, Mozart! The greatest concertos; the greatest chamber music. Not to mention wife Constanze, and all those kids. Mate, how *did* you find the time?

3.50pm. Get home. *Harvey* is crossing his legs. As am I. 'You've been a while, Rall. Everything OK?'

'Yes, Kell. Only Melinda was anxious for my advice. So I gave her…My best…'

'Rall, while you were away, a strange thing happened – and this was a total surprise – Paul came round…'

'Paul? And? Everything OK?'

'Yep. He was very emotional. Very clingy. Always had a soft spot for me. Asked for my advice. I gave him. My best…'

'Phew. I say, Kell, think we could…'(No, I'm not Superman; just putting down a marker, for later).

'Rall, sorry. I'm completely knackered. Anyway, I need a shower. All these needy guys, hanging on my tits.' Fat chance. 'Anyway, *I* need some space. But listen: *Harvey* needs a good walk – or I think he'll sue us for neglect…'

4.10pm: walk the ecstatic *Harvey,* in local Park. Mercifully, no incidents. Too hot for hot dogs.

Think! Belinda and Saul have a lot of making up to do. Some extra-curriculum talking to do. An initial lesson in their respective area of expertise. Saul has never held a paintbrush – or pencil – before. He's a gadget guy. Or Belinda, a pen – though it feels natural. All, oddly, sensual. But the *thinking*, the *creative* process, is different in each case. They enjoy each other's tutorial. Facing each other. Observing the smiles. Watching the lips move. The little mannerisms: the way Belinda tosses her long, glossy hair. The way Saul's face twitches, occasionally, in a nervous but kind of attractive, familiar way. 'Bel, early days I know. But I'd like to draw *you*…' Bel smiles, showing her fine teeth. 'That's fine, I guess.' 'Topless,' he gestures. Without a further word, Belinda removes her blouse, and bra. 'Let's get to work…'

'I could look at you forever, Bel, but what am I trying to achieve? Your likeness? Your mood? Your personality? Your spirit?'

'Steady on, old boy! Early days. A likeness would be great, for starters. But this isn't photography: you have artistic freedom to achieve the results that you desire. So you may want to make me a little prettier; and my tits a little smaller. I'd suggest a 'B' pencil, that makes a softer, even blurry, impression, that you can shade and even smudge, for effect. Shall we begin?'

'But who owns the portrait, when it's finished? I mean, the copyright? And will it be sellable?'

'Shall we take it one step at a time? The artist owns the work. But this *might* be sellable only if I complete it, call it 'Self Portrait: Belinda', and sign it 'Belinda Hines'. Then it might fetch a hundred or so.' Belinda laughed. 'But you haven't factored in my modelling fees – that's £50 an hour. And just remember, in the next session I'll show *you* how *I* work – by drawing you – a la Michelangelo. That is, your torso, from neck to groin. With a sharp, pointed, 'H' pencil – Michelangelo would have loved those abs – and no doubt that cock! He wasn't the world's best draughtsman, when it came to women; but his male nudes are spectacular. So what are *you* doing in our next session?'

'That's easy – you. I'm sketching you, and painting you, 'til I'm satisfied.'

'Satisfied with what?'

'Satisfied that I've captured you as best as I possibly, lovingly can. In every medium.'

She smiled. 'I'm fine with that. But we can't flood the market with endless portraits of me. Scarcity is key to value in art. And don't forget that I'm a primary school teacher. Multiple naked images of me won't go down a ball with the School Governors!' Belinda tosses back her golden tresses, and adroitly replaces her blouse, while asking: 'So: what about the poetry?'

'Ah, yes. For now, don't worry about the form – the structure. Whether it rhymes; how it rhymes. Whether it's free verse, or blank verse. Think about what you want to *say* – what you want to *express*. What is the poem *about*? When you know what you want to say – though sometimes you will need to search for meaning, to explore what you're trying to express – the words will come. And don't wait for inspiration. Inspiration is great, but you can't beckon it at will. As with love-making, it's more perspiration than inspiration.' Belinda smiled, despite herself. 'Words are your friend. You will find the best words, the choicest words, to convey your meaning. And don't forget that, as poetry wishes to communicate, it often communicates through metaphor, through simile, and through *images* – imagery. So there's a connection with art – painting. Think of Keats' '*Ode* to Autumn' – full of concrete images that create a vivid, almost cinematic view of an unfolding autumnal scene. And to complete the circle, in *The Love Song of J Alfred Prufrock*, TS Eliot wrote about women – who come and go – 'talking of Michelangelo.' So what will be your theme, Bel?'

'Love. Love between two people. The joys and the heartache. The highs, and the lows. But I'll probably write in French – the language of love – the language *for* love. Amour…' 'That's fine,' enthused Saul. 'There's a rich tradition of French romantic, lyric poetry, from the Middle Ages onwards: *troubairitzes,* as well as *troubadours* – a tradition stretching from Ronsard, to Baudelaire. So, Bel, you're in good company! Only problem is, I don't speak French…' Bel smiled: 'Saul, you're married to a French teacher…'

Bel looked serious. 'You know, Saul, this publishing thing? All these rejections you've had. So unfair. Your stuff is *really* good. I'm sure I could help, but only if it's what you want: one of my new clients is a publisher…'

4.50pm. Return from Park. But a man's work is never done. 'What are your plans for the rest of the day, Rall…?'

'Well, I was hoping for a bit of space. To think, to write, maybe?'

'Mmm…well, of course. But we're way behind with the housework. All the muck from that bloody combine harvester, over the way. The whole place needs dusting, and the vacuum needs putting through its paces…'

'Jees…does it all need doing *now*? Oh, OK. But then I really need to find some me-time!'

5.20pm. Even men, it seems, are capable of doing two things at once. Dusting like fury, wiping surfaces, vacuuming the carpets, frees the mind for better things; at least, different things…

That evening, a smiling, carefree Saul – delighted that he might be published at last – is taught to prepare spag bol. 'Look at the recipe, Saul. You don't have to follow it slavishly; but only experience will teach you how to tweak the recipe, and improve things to cater for your own tastes. Then, gather your ingredients together, so they're all ready to go. What equipment do you need? – get *that* together. Look at the order in which you'll need the ingredients; and the timings. And don't forget to lay the table, with cutlery and so on. Preparation is all. Only then can you begin. So shall we make a start? Don't worry – I'll be there to hold your hand…Or maybe Nigella.'

Forty minutes later, Bel and Saul are sitting down to enjoy Saul's first 'scratch' meal, together with a bottle of Chianti. 'I really didn't realise it was all so complicated!' sighed Saul. 'Saul, this is delicious! You've been hiding your light under a bushel for far too long! Let's not stop here. Tomorrow, maybe try a nice casserole. Or steak and chips…I could get used to this…' 'OK. But I'm looking forward to my next art session!' Saul smiled. 'I'm told my model is a hot blonde…' 'Mmm. Let's not get carried away. In art circles, we must keep a sense of decorum, and professionalism. There must be complete trust between artist and model.' 'Point taken,' agreed Saul. 'You can keep your knickers on.'

5.50pm. Must walk *Harvey*, before we settle down for the evening. Kelly will be preparing spag bol – because it's Saturday. *Harvey* tugs me enthusiastically to the Park – his favourite – again. Gangs of teenagers – eager young guys, barely dressed young girls – messing around – waiting for dusk, and an emptying Park, before revelling in the reverie of booze and soft bodies.

6.30pm. Return home with *Harvey*. 'That you, Rall? You're missing 'Pointless'.' 'Really? How aptly named. I could kill for a g&t!'

7.20pm. Sit down with spag bol, and bottle of Chianti. Splendid. School small talk. Not to mention more Melinda and Paul. Apparently they've both decided to take multiple lovers, to exact some kind of revenge. I affect surprise. Gulp. Copious DNA – splashed all over Melinda's surfaces…

8.00pm. Washing up for me. Well, fill the dishwasher, while Kelly practices her organ. Sorry, keyboard. She's into the Lloyd Webber stuff. All screams and emotional extremes. So why is she all closed up, like a bud that cannot open? Bel would be into Beyoncé – rhythmic, sophisticated, sassy. Saul would be into edgy hard rock – *Sabbath, Zeppelin.* Yes – *Black Dog.* As for me, I can't stop thinking about the athletic Melinda. Or Bel and Saul – twenty years younger. White heat. Quite right what they say – youth's wasted on the young...

8.30pm. Kelly re-joins me, for a few chocolates, and some TV. Flick through the channels. Please: not news! So: Drama? Comedy? Sport? Occasionally memorable; mainly, forgettable. What will Bel and Saul be up to, after *their* spag bol? That's right: watching telly. But, in Saul's case, impatiently: waiting for the evening to unfold. For opportunity to present itself. As, indeed, am I. A beer or two, in the meantime. Kelly contents herself with white wine. Belinda and Saul, likewise.

10.30pm. Kelly, yawning: 'Well, it's bed time for me...You going to watch '*Match of the Day*'? Or there's a drama – '*Games People Play*' on the other side...'

Sigh. Serious gaze. 'There's only one game I want to play tonight!'

'OK, but I'll be asleep in ten...'

'I'll be just five...'

'Well, if you're sure...Been a long day.'

'Never been surer.'

10.32pm. Let *Harvey* in the garden for a final pee. *Otto* curled up on the hearth, after a day's serious snoozing. So where are we, with the story? It's harder – *harder?* – writing about sex than it is doing it! Maybe an advisory note to readers: only read this passage when you're about to have an orgasm. That should lift the words from the page – or your bloody gadget! Commit urgent text to my head:

'Bel: my plan. There's a final part, I'm afraid. Are we ready again for sex? I really want you so much…'

Belinda rolled her eyes. 'Why does it always come down to sex?'

'It never used to be a problem. You just need to tell me what you want. How to please you. How I can truly satisfy you. Honour you, with my whole self. Just trust me, OK? Hopefully, starting tonight…'

10.35pm. I glance at my watch. 'Mustn't miss my cue…' Kelly is reading; waiting. 'Kelly, you OK?'

'Fine. Can I read my book afterwards? Just coming to a climax. He's about to seduce her. Bodice ripper and all that. If I'm not too tired. And it's quick…'

'I can promise that it *won't* be quick. And that you will feel, er, satisfied; complete. And that I do aim to please. And that this will be different. No longer three minute man. Consider me a *new* man.'

'Some good lines, there,' I think, as I turn Kelly over, and encircle her ample *derriere*…Maybe use them, later. 'Kell, do you know the French for 'yes'?' 'Yes. *Oui.*'

'So, when we're, you know…can you say '*oui*'?' 'S'ppose so.'

'Rall! *What are you doing!*'

The strokes kept coming…and the lines kept coming. Inspiration, at last! Can't stop, can't climax, 'til the story is complete! Just be patient, my love! Just keep coming! The climax is in the climax!

'Oui. Oui. Oui. *Oui. Oui, oui, oui, oui*…oh Paul!!'

'Did you say 'Paul'?' 'No, no, I said fucking 'Rall'! Just get on with it!!'

'*Oui, oui, oui, oui, oui, oui*…Saul, oh Saul…this is fabulous…' 'No – Bel, *you're* fabulous, my darling!'

'Who the fuck's Bel?' 'Slip of the tongue, girl. Relax.'

'*Relax?!* Just fuck me, Rall!'

Later: 'Rall, Jesus, you're fucking killing me!! Ooohhhhh!!!'

Heavy breathing on both sides. I kiss my glowing wife. She returns my kisses.

'Thank you, my love...*Rall*. That was the best, ever... You know, you've just inspired my very first poem!'

'What's it called?' 'Oui!'

'Kell, that's a great line! Kell, my one and only...'

'Saul, oh Saul...*baise moi*, Saul! Ooohhh!!!' Saul kisses his glowing wife. 'Thank you, my lovely Bel. You are the best, ever!' 'Saul, my love, you've just inspired my first poem: 'Oui!'' Bel returns his kisses: 'Saul, oh Saul, *mon seul et unique!*'

Thank you Mozart! Thank you God! Does art imitate life? Or life imitate art? Hope you had some fun, some joy, along the way!